CW00972784

Street Cultivation

Version 1.2b

© 2019 Sarah Lin

Table of Contents

(NOTE: When writing Street Cultivation as a serial, I tried to introduce the elements of the cultivation system like I would a magic system in a novel. Readers were split about whether I gave enough information as elements became relevant or whether they would have preferred an infodump.

So you have two options! If you proceed forward, the story will explain what you need to know but may leave some open questions. If you don't like that method or prefer more context immediately, you can skip to the "Lucrim Mechanics" appendix and read that first. It will explain the majority of the magic in direct language. Read however works for you. ^-^)

Chapter 1: Dollar Store Power

Rick reached into his soul and brought forth the power within, in the hopes of convincing someone to beat the snot out of him.

There weren't too many likely customers at this time of day, since most had already gone home, but he hoped to catch someone else working late. Maybe some other poor schmuck who couldn't afford to go home at 5:00 PM would be interested in learning the mystic arts and getting a promotion.

The House of the Cosmic Fist sat in the middle of a run-down strip mall, stuck in between a ratty nail salon and a half-decent pizza place. It was far from the best lucrima training school, even just considering the cheap commercialized ones, but it was a job. Given the way his life had been going, Rick would take whatever he could get.

While Rick gathered his power into a blue aura around him, he glanced out over the parking lot for likely candidates. A few teenagers ambled past and briefly looked at him, impressed at his feeble aura only because they hadn't really begun to gather lucrim themselves. Only about five years younger than him, but they looked like kids - not a good choice. Likewise the woman going into the salon, the trucker smoking on the other side of the parking lot, or the man in the business suit flying past. Not likely customers.

Then he spotted her: a woman in her thirties pushing a stroller. Parents often needed more lucrim, and judging from her business casual attire, she had picked her kid up from daycare after work. Though she'd be haggard from her job, she was here at the mall instead of just going home to watch TV. Maybe she'd be receptive to his sales pitch.

"Awaken your inner strength today, at the House of the Cosmic Fist!" The cheesy line made Rick feel like an idiot, but he did whatever worked. "Whether you want to increase your lucrim generation rate or solidify your lucrima core, you can't beat our prices! And we're open sixteen hours a day, seven days a week, so we can fit in a training session whenever it fits your lifestyle!"

Though the woman looked a bit irritated by the sales pitch, she didn't ignore him or leave. Good enough. Rick turned off the cheese and gave her a normal smile.

"I can see that you're busy, ma'am, so just tell me if you're not interested. But I wouldn't have said anything if I didn't think we could help you."

"This isn't one of those shady schools, is it?" She stopped her stroller nearby and looked through the windows to the cheap mats and equipment inside. "You're not going to be recommending ether injections or special contracts?"

"Absolutely not, ma'am. We're certified by the Branton Chamber of Commerce." He tapped the sticker in the corner of the window, but didn't want the woman to be thinking about that. The House of the Cosmic Fist might be certified, but its owner wasn't exactly a model citizen. To distract from that, he bent down to the stroller and stuck out a finger for the baby to grab. "Wow, he's a strong little guy!"

The woman softened a bit as her son shook Rick's finger and gurgled happily. They made basic small talk for a bit, Rick saying all the usual things about her baby looking healthy and having a strong aura spark already. Polite nonsense. Since she freely offered up her name, which he dutifully memorized, she might be interested. But before too long, the woman folded her arms and regarded the door skeptically.

"I've never been to one of these gyms before. The idea of giving up lucrim in the hope of gaining more... I'd rather just train at home."

"And there's nothing wrong with that." Rick gave his best smile. "But the fact is, no matter how strong you are, there are limits to how much you can develop on your own. Even if you don't need instruction - though we have great instructors here - you'll improve your generation rate much faster sparring with a real partner."

"Hmm. How much do you charge for a month of membership?"

"We have a variety of different plans, and we're actually running a discount right now. Just 75 lucrim or $250 for your first month if you sign up for our most popular package. But I think for a driven mother like you, it can easily pay for itself in just a few months. Imagine if your ether score gets improved and that leads to a promotion at work. You're sitting at a generation rate of... maybe 35,000 lucrim?"

"It's rude to ask such things!" But from the way the woman looked away, Rick could tell that she was flattered.

In fact, he estimated her lucrim generation rate to be roughly 27,000 lucrim. Having worked in this job since he was in high school, he thought he was pretty good at analyzing even suppressed lucrima, at least for the lower ranks. It was usually a safe bet to flatter potential customers by overestimating their strength, though he held back on buttering her up since she seemed especially skeptical.

Eventually he got her inside and signing a contract. Rick kept his smile on his face the entire time, even when she ended up scheduling her lessons with Danny instead of him. He still got credit for bringing in a new customer, which had been the entire point.

Once she was gone, Jimmy sat back and grunted. Rick's boss was a middle-aged man, holding back his receding hairline with lucrim but unable to hide the fact that his warrior's body was getting flabbier. Not that it really mattered, given his lucrim generation rate was far above average. The older man scratched his stomach and scrabbled in the compartments beneath the counter.

"Suppose you'll be wanting your bonus right away?"

"If possible, sir." Rick stayed right next to the counter and stared at him to make sure he wouldn't "forget" this time. Eventually Jimmy straightened up and slapped some worn bills and a grimy marble down on the counter.

"You're not bad at bringing them in, Rick, I'll give you that." Jimmy stared at him a bit, then shook his head. "But you need to keep better clients. No more pissing off the whales."

"I'll keep that in mind, sir." But Rick was barely listening, instead focused on picking up his bonus.

He jammed the bills into one pocket, not bothering to count them. Though he needed money to support himself and his sister, no amount of money he'd likely see would make up for his low ether score. For that he needed lucrim, which is why he focused on the marble. It was an ugly little sphere, but it contained a small amount of raw lucrim.

Rick gripped the marble in his palm and breathed in, drawing the power into himself. He always imagined it as electrified water, pooling above his head and then trickling down over the systems of power he'd built within his body. They might not be as powerful or complex as those of most warriors, or even a career worker like the new client, but they were thirsty for power.

Since there were no new customers, Rick headed away from the entrance. He pulled out his cell phone and rubbed his finger over the built-in sensor, letting it analyze his aura. In the old days, warriors had given themselves mystical titles or measured their progress by colored belts, but the process had long ago been scientifically quantified.

Already familiar with him, the app quickly produced the result he'd hoped for.

[Name: Rick Hunter

Ether Tier: 19th

Ether Score: 189

Lucrim Generation: 15,000

Current Lucrim: 1037]

He winced at the total - his bonus had been 50 lucrim, so before it, he would have been below 1000. If he was rich, of course, his current numbers would have been near his generation rate. But given his life, that might as well be a dream.

Though he hadn't expected his ether score to change, since the ratings agencies reacted slowly, he was disappointed that his generation rate hadn't received a boost at all. The fact that the app displayed a round number suggested that it thought all of his efforts to work harder were nothing more than a rounding error.

Taking a deep breath, Rick tried not to feel sorry for himself. What mattered was that he kept moving forward. He wouldn't be working at the House of the Cosmic Fist forever, not if he worked hard enough. It might not be a true combat sect or a high-end job, but it let him train while supporting himself and his sister. That was more than many had.

Before he could spend too much time thinking, the bell on the door rang again. He glanced up and saw that it was Darin, one of their regulars. Actually, one of Henry's regulars, but Henry hadn't shown up when his shift was supposed to start.

It looked like Darin was realizing that as well. Though he was middle-aged, Darin didn't look it, with a tall and muscular body. As far as Rick knew his generation rate was around 55,000 lucrim, but he had been pooling it for years. Rick wasn't as good with judging lucrim portfolios, but he knew Darin had a lot. Potentially one of the richer men who still came to their little shop.

"Henry isn't here?" Darin looked around and scowled. "I'm paying for private training, so I expect private training."

Jimmy grunted. "He'll be in later. If you don't want to wait, Rick can take care of you."

"He'll have to do, I guess." Darin walked out toward the central mats, peeling off his shirt to reveal hulking muscles. "Get over here and show me what you got, kid."

Not how Rick would have wanted to end the day, but he didn't have a choice. He stepped out to the central mats and nodded politely to Darin. If they had done things traditionally they would have shaken hands, and some schools copied Asian bowing traditions, but the House of the Cosmic Fist didn't focus on ceremony. Besides, there was nothing ceremonial about what was coming.

Darin lunged forward and started with a sweeping haymaker that Rick only managed to duck because he expected it. Being the client, Darin could start however he wanted, but it wasn't exactly a fair move. Rick finished tugging on the thick mitts that would absorb some of the huge lucrim gap between them and raised his hands in defense.

Essentially his job was to serve as a living training dummy. What he'd said to the woman from earlier hadn't been just a sales pitch: many kinds of lucrim training really did require a living opponent. But as Rick warded off the aggressive punches, feeling numbness spread up his arms, he doubted that this was really about training.

No, a man like Darin wanted to feel strong. After a hard day of work, he went to a place like this to beat the crap out of someone. That explained why his lucrima felt so unsophisticated - his power reserves were huge, but they were just a blunt weapon, unlike the sophisticated portfolios of strength controlled by most true warriors. If Darin had obtained his full potential, Rick wouldn't have had a chance of sparring with him.

As it was, he was still left exhausted by the time they'd been sparring for a while. Darin finally got tired of striking at the mitts and pulled back. He took a swig from his water bottle, then glanced at Rick. "You're no Henry, but you'll do. Got any tips for me?"

"You have an impressive pool of lucrim," Rick said, "but you could do a lot more with it if you invested it into a Lucore or two. I could sugges-"

Pain shot through his jaw, then his back. It was only when Rick was falling to the ground that he realized that Darin had punched him in the face hard enough to send him crashing into the concrete wall of the gym. The raw power of that much lucrim was just overwhelming...

But it wasn't the first time. Before he fell, Rick managed to throw out a foot and catch himself, then straighten back to his feet. He raised the mitts defensively and faced Darin's stare.

"Don't lecture me, you little shit. If you're so smart, what are you doing working as a human practice dummy?"

He didn't want an answer to that question, so Rick said nothing. It was stupid of him to have tried to offer advice at all - he should have known Darin wouldn't want it. Yet Darin was a client and much higher tier, so there was nothing he could do.

When Darin attacked again, it was with new ferocity. Rick managed to hold his ground, but each time he blocked a punch, pain shot up his arm, even through the mitt. Even his defense seemed to antagonize Darin, who struck aggressively until Rick finally staggered backward and fell onto his side.

"That's what's wrong with kids these days. They think they can waste all their time in places like this, blow any lucrim they get. Get up, you bum."

Pushing through the ache in his bones, Rick pulled himself upright and prepared for the next attack. He tried to tell himself that it was good training, and it certainly wasn't the first time he'd endured a beating from a customer. But as much work as he'd put into the defensive Lucore within him, it was barely worth 5000 lucrim - nowhere near enough to endure such an assault.

The next time he fell back, he dropped, barely catching himself on the mat. Darin stomped closer but didn't attack, instead taunting him while he struggled back to his feet. "This is no fairy tale, kid. You're not going to just absorb lucrim out of the air, not anymore. If you want to become strong, you have to make something of yourself."

Hatred surged through Rick, driving him back to his feet. Darin had no right to say that when he knew nothing about Rick's life. Nothing about his sister, or their absent parents, or all the other factors that left him struggling just to make ends meet. How was he supposed to develop a large lucrima when the power was constantly bled from him?

When Darin began to punch again, Rick almost struck back. He might be completely overwhelmed when it came to power, but his opponent only had combat experience against weaker sparring partners. If Rick stepped aside from the next punch, used his opponent's momentum against him, struck the throat and then the eyes...

Across the room, his boss cleared his throat. Rick came back to himself, remembering why he was doing all this. His ego was irrelevant - he needed this job.

So all he did was endure the pummeling and try to ignore the lectures about how he should pull himself up by his own magical flying sword. Nothing Darin said really mattered, in the end. Since Rick failed to respond, eventually the older man got tired of berating him. After finishing his sparring session, Darin headed out, grumbling under his breath.

As soon as he was gone, Rick collapsed onto the bench beside the wall. He just lay there, not even removing the mitts - his fingers hurt too much for that. Jimmy looked up from the counter and seemed like he might be about to say something, but at that moment the bell rang again.

"What's up, Cosmic Fist?" Not a customer this time, but Henry. His coworker looked much too smug for someone coming in 45 minutes late. "How's it hanging?"

"You're late." Jimmy didn't even look up, just grunted in Rick's direction. "He covered for ya. I'll take that one out of your pay."

"That's fine, that's fine. Thanks for covering it, Rick." Henry at least had the decency to shoot him an apologetic smile, but he seemed excited despite their boss's disapproval. He pulled a six pack out of the bag he was holding and slapped it down on the table. "Serum is on me today, boys."

The possibility of free serum was enough to get Rick back on his feet. Though the cans in the pack only held a cheap version, and even the best serum didn't truly add to anyone's lucrim, it still helped with recovery from training. He'd discovered that he could do without, but it definitely helped with the aches and pains.

When he took a can, he quickly drank the entire thing and went for another. The power flowed through his aching body, both soothing his pains and stimulating the lucrim flowing within him.

Meanwhile, Henry still had a smug look on his face, and eventually Jimmy got tired enough of it that he glared at him. "Alright, what is it? Not like you to be generous."

"I can afford to be, because of this baby." Henry pulled up his left shirtsleeve, revealing not just muscular biceps but what appeared to be a tattoo of a crimson scarab. Though Henry had a couple other tattoos, this one was nothing of the sort. "I finally got approved for a demonic bond. I'm swimming in lucrim now."

"Huh. Congrats." Jimmy took one of the cans and walked off with it, unimpressed. Henry turned to Rick and grinned.

"Seriously, this thing is amazing."

Rick nodded along, not wanting to ruin Henry's mood. "How'd you get it? I thought your ether score was getting you rejected before. Did yours improve?"

"Nah, man. There's a new demon clan that wants to establish itself in Branton... or something like that, anyway. Point is, they don't just check ether score and reject you. They actually let me plead my case. I guess they liked what they saw, because they gave me one hell of a good bond."

"How much?"

"It maxes out at 5000 lucrim, but the maximum can go higher. But just the basic bond already bumped me up an entire tier. Seriously, man, you've gotta try them before they get all the people they need."

Though Rick nodded in general agreement, he didn't seriously consider it. Truthfully, he didn't know very much about demonic bonds. Plenty of people got them, even some people who didn't care about fighting and just needed more lucrim to make ends meet. Usually they had minimum standards, but they were one of the only ways for someone like him to gain considerable power in a short time.

Since the two already knew each other, Rick's app could bring up immediate data for Henry:

[Name: Hendog69 (pseudonym)

Ether Tier: 17th

Ether Score: 176

Lucrim Generation: 21,000

 - Demonic Bond: 5000

Current Lucrim: (private data)]

Just one demonic bond had taken Henry from around 16,000 up to 21,000 lucrim. In a matter of hours. It was enough to tempt him to do the same.

But according to Uncle Frank, relying on demonic bonds always turned out badly in the end. Considering that his uncle was the only person in their family to make something of himself, Rick generally took his advice when it came to... well, anything. He was certainly a better role model than Rick's parents.

"You look kind of messed up, man." Henry looked at him seriously. "Was Darin rough on you? I'm guessing you pissed him off somehow and he did his whole speech about kids these days?"

"Yeah." Rick finished off his second can and shamelessly took a third. "My fault for not realizing his type. You must have a rough time with him."

"Nah, you've just gotta know how to work him. But all that rags to riches stuff he says is definitely bullshit." Henry leaned back against the counter, looking out over the empty gym. "Nobody gets that strong on hard work alone. For people like us, pretty much our only chance of getting out of the lower tiers is something big. Getting a great Birthright Core, or getting picked by one of those independent mystics."

"Or getting demonic bonds?"

"Nah, that's just catching up." Henry frowned down at the scarab. "People with better ether scores just get handed bonds worth 10,000 lucrim or more. "

"Still, congrats, man."

"Not gonna lecture me?"

"Hey, it's your life and your lucrima." Rick did his best to shrug and not judge - he had enough to worry about taking care of himself.

"I'm hoping if I do well enough, they might offer me a second or third bond. But I gotta say, the rush of power is great. I'm on a hot streak, so I should donate a bunch to the independent mystics while my luck lasts."

That was definitely throwing his lucrim away, but Rick held his tongue. He didn't need advice from his uncle or anyone else to see that the independent mystics were running scams. Over the years he'd seen plenty of his friends donate thousands of lucrim and get excited over getting a few hundred back, when they would have been better off just focusing on their own development. Getting lucky and having a mystic choose you as a pupil could bring great power, sure, but everyone else was trying exactly the same thing.

Since no new customers came in, they sat and talked about nothing for a while longer. Eventually it was the end of his shift, so Rick got up to head home. Due to the serum, his body actually felt fully recovered from Darin's beating. It was a nice change of pace to head home without any aches and pains.

"Thanks for the serum, man." Rick nodded to his coworker, who just waved it off.

"No problem. Headed back home?"

"Yeah, I'll see if I can't get back before it gets too cold."

"See ya later, then."

But as Rick collected his things, the bell rang again and three young men pushed into the gym. The hair on the back of Rick's neck immediately stood up as their lucrima surged into the room. Henry felt it as well and stood up with his customer smile.

"Evening, gents. Welcome to the House of the Cosmic Fist. We're happy to help if we can, but I don't know if we have any staff here who can keep up with you."

"We're just curious." The man at the head of the group looked around the gym with undisguised disgust. "This is what the Cosmic Fist is, huh? Show us your best."

"Well, since it's late, most of our staff aren't here..."

Though Henry tried to reason with them, Rick had already decided that it was pointless. Even if he hadn't been able to feel their power, he could tell that the three weren't here for training. With clothes as nice as theirs, and one of them wearing an ether watch, they were coming to the slummier part of town to cause trouble and blow off steam.

Unless he missed his guess, all three were Birthrighters. They'd had expensive training from a young age, of course, but that paled in comparison to the Birthright Cores burning within them. Incredible amounts of power, just handed to them by their parents. Lucrima training was probably just a hobby to them, a way to round out their resumes, or something to do before they took over their parents' companies.

Not that it mattered. Each of the young men had a generation rate of at least 100,000, and they planned to use it. Rick set down his things and sighed, realizing that he wasn't going home uninjured after all.

Chapter 2: Birthrighters

The three Birthrighters swaggered into the center of the gym, clearly wanting a fight. Rick glanced toward his boss, but the older man simply sat back and pretended to be absorbed in the magazine he was reading. Unless the place got trashed, he didn't care. In fact, for a miserable little school like the House of the Cosmic Fist, any attention at all was good attention.

"It's time for my usual sparring match," the leader of the group said, "but we found ourselves too far from home. Somebody will have to step up, or it will harm my development."

A feeble reason to beat up someone, but when someone with a generation rate of over 100,000 lucrim spoke, logic tended not to matter so much. Beside him, Rick saw that Henry was moving forward, trying to do things the right way.

"We might be able to find someone to spar with you, but since you aren't members, it will b-" The head Birthrighter punched Henry in the stomach, instantly folding him in half, then dropped him like trash.

Though a real blow from someone with that much strength would have killed, even the light blow must have dealt terrible damage. Henry curled up around his stomach, gritting his teeth to avoid crying out in pain. His whimpering made the Birthrighters laugh and the leader tossed two pearl bars onto his body.

"That should cover the fee, shouldn't it?"

Rick did his best not to stare at the bars. They could hold far more lucrim than the cheap little marbles that most used to transfer lucrim, perhaps 1000 or more. Those two bars might be worth more than he was paid in a month. Part of him wanted to grab for them, but he knew that would just invite the Birthrighters to mock him. He might be poor, but he had his dignity.

Across the room, Jimmy glanced up from the counter. "Yeah, that'll do it. You spar with him, Rick."

One of the Birthrighters standing in back laughed. "Funny, that's almost like your nickna-" He hurriedly cut off as the leader glared at him. "Just saying."

"It doesn't matter." The leader turned to Rick and gestured for him to step out onto the mat. "To you, I'm Mike. You'd know my family if I mentioned them, but there's no point. I paid good lucrim for the chance to kick someone's ass, so I hope you don't fold right away."

"I'll do my best." Rick smiled politely and took his time getting into position, pretending that he needed to stretch.

Meanwhile, he actually worked on his lucrima. Though he set aside his phone to prevent it being broken, he knew exactly what it would say about him:

[Rick Hunter's Lucrima Portfolio

Foundation: 7000 (Lv II)

Offensive Lucore: 3000 (Lv II)

Defensive Lucore: 5000 (Lv III)

Total Lucrim: 15,000]

Normally, his current available power would be divided between the different Lucores in proportion to the investments he'd made during training. That wouldn't work now, not against an opponent with over 100,000 lucrim at his disposal. There was nothing he could do to avoid spending almost half of his strength on the foundation that allowed him to fight, but he poured the remaining 53% into his defensive core.

It might not be anything special to his opponents, but Rick was proud of his defense. The exact formation of the Lucore had been his sister's idea, actually, built to help him avoid serious internal injuries. Lots of people who worked at sparring gyms ended up broken by middle age, and he couldn't afford that. Fueled by all the strength he could muster, it offered Rick a defense much stronger than anyone would expect for someone like him.

As Mike pulled off his jacket and let his lucrima aura blaze up around him, Rick wondered if it would be enough. He'd never sparred with anyone who had a generation rate in six digits before...

"Come on, little man. Show me what you've got." Mike put up his fists and hopped back and forth a few times, inviting an attack.

So Rick punched at his face. Even if the blow had landed, it had nothing more than physical force behind it, so it wouldn't have done any good. But as he'd expected, Mike didn't give him a chance, slapping his arm aside and then slamming a fist into his ribs.

Even though the blow had been pulled, Rick felt pain rush through his entire left side. He wanted to lie down and groan, but forced himself to stay on his feet. The only way through was to endure it.

Mike looked surprised that he hadn't fallen down, but only let it stop him for a second. He attacked again, a wild swiping blow that Rick barely managed to dodge. His opponent kept lashing out, each blow fueled with more power than Rick could generate in an entire day. And that was just a fraction of the power being put out by his Birthright Core. Seeing one up close, Rick was infuriated by how unfair it was.

His fury made his focus waver and he lost his position. Mike closed on him, furious blows pushing him further and further back until his only choice was to take the next one. Instead of dodging until he failed, Rick chose a blow to endure, raised his arms in a cross before his chest, and let it strike him.

Immediately he slammed into the opposite wall, his arms aching as if they'd broken. The wall was reinforced by ether enchantments for the sort of fights that took place here, yet the force of the blow shook it and made a few cracks expand.

"You can take a punch, kid!" Mike grinned and slapped his fist into his palm a few times, even those gestures radiating out more force than Rick's actual attacks could. "But you're not gonna win unless you can hit me!"

Obviously, Mike wanted to goad him into a reckless attack, then counter hard enough to drop him. Judging from the way his two friends were snickering, he had done this before. Rick knew he would be seriously injured if he didn't focus on defense, but he also couldn't make it through unless he let Mike get what he wanted somehow.

So Rick moved back onto the mat, making a few weak attacks while working to defend against his opponent's brutal blows. What options did he have? Henry wasn't watching the fight, clutching where he had been struck. Jimmy had collected the money and likely wouldn't be any help - he might be able to stop these Birthrighters, probably even beat all three of them, but he wouldn't do a damn thing.

Another blow crunched into his shoulder and Rick couldn't hold back his grunt at the pain. When his opponent laughed and began a series of weak jabs, he decided to just take them. These blows didn't have the strength to break his arms, so better to let his opponent enjoy landing a lot of blows.

Each one of them sent pain shooting through his arms as he desperately tried to defend, but Rick wasn't paying attention to that. Instead he focused on the Defensive Lucore within him. Though it was failing to defend him from the overwhelming power, it was also growing.

Lucrima cores grew in strength either from individual training or from interacting with other lucrima. Faced with such staggering power, the core couldn't help but absorb some of the excess lucrim thrown against it, adapting to the new challenge. That was the real reason he'd been willing to stand up and get the crap beaten out of him: losing this fight might earn him more power than months of training.

So he endured the barrage of punches and tried to ignore the signs that his body was failing. He let himself forget about his core as well, needing all his attention to avoid taking a devastating blow. Even if it didn't cripple him for life, he might not be able to afford the treatment for a serious internal injury.

"It's over!" Mike let out a roar and charged at him, swinging in a wild haymaker with huge openings.

Before Rick could stop himself, his training took over. He grabbed his opponent's arm as it passed, endured the burning of the other man's aura, and used his own momentum against him. The technique should have slammed his opponent to the floor.

Yet as he tumbled, Mike let out a shout. His aura went from a glow surrounding his body to a raging fire, hitting the floor first and stopping his fall.

For a moment, he floated in midair, staring at the floor and realizing that he would have crashed into it. But a moment later he recovered from his surprise and let out a growl, propelling himself upright on aura alone. He might be a clumsy fighter, but he was no novice.

The next blow, fueled by anger, was going to be the worst one. Rick knew he couldn't dodge or his opponent would just get angrier. He needed to let it clip him and hope he could survive the impact, but-

A leg slammed into the back of his knee and Rick fell. Too late he realized that one of Mike's friends had gotten behind him. Though he managed to catch himself by landing on his knee, his body ached too much to dodge, much less retaliate.

"We paid you for a sparring match!" The last of the Birthrighters kicked him in the chest, flipping him heels over head. Rick hit the mat painfully and then the young man put a foot on his chest. "Where do you get off using tricks?"

"He threw me fair and square." Mike stomped over to them, his aura fading slightly but his eyes hateful. "Step back. We might as well continue this little match."

As soon as his friends retreated, Mike kicked him in the side. Rick couldn't hold back a cry of pain as he was flung across the room. Had one of his ribs cracked? His defensive core had been growing throughout the fight, but it couldn't keep up with this. His opponent lunged after him, raining down blows, and he felt his core beginning to give out entirely.

Without it, blows like these would destroy him. Defending effectively was impossible now, it was the most Rick could do to focus on his defenses and keep them intact. And hope he could recover from this... no, that was a distraction. All that mattered was lucrima defense.

"That's your time." Abruptly Jimmy was standing beside them, holding out a fresh towel. It didn't seem like a man of his bulk could move quickly or quietly, but somehow he had crossed the room. "You won. Congrats."

"Obviously I won." Mike glared at him, but after a tense pause, accepted the towel and began to wipe off the sweat. "You need better sparring staff, old man."

"I work with what I got. Thanks for not breaking him."

"Hmph. I was holding back too much for this to even be fun." Mike kicked at Rick again, exactly where his ribs were sorest, and Rick barely choked back another grunt of pain.

He knew that the smart thing to do was stay down. Tried to tell himself that he was the winner in realistic terms, because he had increased his defensive strength and his opponent had gained nothing. Yet when Mike kicked him, he found himself grabbing the other man's leg and beginning to pull himself up.

"Know when to stay down!" Mike punched him in the chest and Rick automatically reached up to grab at his wrist. He couldn't stop the blow, but he ended up striking the other man's watch. It was an expensive ether piece, radiating power out in all directions at the impact.

The blow knocked Mike back a step. He looked infuriated, but when he moved up for another kick, Jimmy subtly moved into his path. "You've had your fun, kid."

"He could have broken my watch! My father gave this to me!" Yet as Mike examined it, his face twisted into a sneer. "But no harm done. Apparently Rick here isn't even strong enough to damage a watch."

"Yeah, I'll think about replacing him." Jimmy slowly herded the group toward the door. The three Birthrighters hadn't gotten exactly the fight they wanted, but as they looked back at Rick lying on the floor, they seemed satisfied to have shown him his place.

Which is why he really should have stayed down. Yet Rick found himself struggling back to his feet. His entire body ached, he was pretty sure several of his ribs were broken, and blood from a cut on his forehead was running down into his eyes, but he forced himself up.

As he left, he caught a glimpse of Mike staring at him. For just a moment, the Birthrighter looked surprised. After that moment, he sneered again and left with his friends, laughing a little too loudly. But Rick had seen the uncertainty in his eyes in that moment.

Rick wavered on his feet, trying to feel inside himself to see how his Defensive Lucore felt. It felt like pain, but he thought it had improved. Possibly enough for it to be rated IV instead of III, which would be significant progress. Almost worth the serious injuries.

A moment later, Rick collapsed to the ground. Strangely, as he fell unconscious he heard a woman cry out in dismay, but he was out before he could recognize the voice.

Chapter 3: Combat Massage

Rick didn't feel any pain, and that bothered him.

He should have been happy to feel only warm and relaxed, yet his mind refused to accept it. Yes, that was right... he had taken a severe beating from that Birthrighter. It had broken several of his bones, left him with deep internal bruises, and possibly damaged his lucrima soul. After all of that, he shouldn't be feeling fine.

As he started to put things together, he began to come back to the world. He could feel that he was lying on the mat, though it seemed like someone had put a pillow under his head. Voices talking about what had happened... his boss Jimmy, his coworker Henry... and Lisa. That explained it.

Struggling to sit up, Rick finally managed to open his eyes and saw her. As usual, Lisa wore loose sweatpants and a t-shirt. She was still wearing her jacket, so he couldn't see the shirt, but there was a 99% chance it had an obscure band logo on it. At the moment she had her blond hair up in a ponytail, as if she'd come to spar.

Even though she'd obviously healed him and he should have been grateful, Rick found himself a bit irritated by her presence. He would have been gone if the schedule had progressed normally - was she wanting to spar with someone else? Of all the clients he had, Lisa was the only one he thought liked him more than superficially.

When she saw that he was awake, however, she rushed beside him with a look of concern. "Are you okay, Rick? I did what I could, but you took serious hits from a six digit fighter..."

"I feel fine, you did a good job." Rick shook his head and forced himself to look at her. "But I really can't afford your rates..."

"Oh, don't worry about that!" Lisa laughed away the awkwardness. "You've always done a good job and I've never tipped you or anything. Besides, I need you in decent shape if we're going to work out, so it's for my benefit too."

"Right, about that... if not for the incident, I would already have been gone."

Lisa sighed and stuck out her tongue. "Yeah, I messed up my schedule today and I was just hoping I might catch you working late. Good thing I did, huh? I'd completely understand if you weren't feeling well enough to spar today, though."

"I can, just give me a bit to get my bearings again."

"No problem! I need some time to warm up anyway."

Rick looked after her for a moment while she went out to the mats and began stretching, then very intentionally looked away. Not that it wasn't a nice sight, but he didn't want to be a creep and Henry would bug him about staring. Besides, he had other matters to take care of before he could go back to work.

Based on how he was leaning against the wall, Henry had also been healed of the blow to his stomach. Based on how he was flipping through his magazine again, Jimmy was not going to give any kind of bonus for enduring the beating. Rick might be lucky to get out of this without getting his pay docked for making Jimmy get off his seat and do something.

"Glad you're doing okay, man." Henry gave him a lazy smile. "I was seriously worried there for a bit, but Lisa showed up and helped out."

"I'm just glad things were resolved without anyone getting killed." Rick returned the smile briefly, but then focused on his boss and something much more important. "What happened to the lucrim they left as payment? Since we convinced new clients to come in, we should get part of it as a bonus."

Without looking up, Jimmy grunted sourly and nodded his head toward Henry. The other young man gave him a grin and then dropped the two pearl bars onto the counter. "Don't worry, I made sure he couldn't run off with them. I was thinking you could use them to pay for treatment, but even if you're okay now, I think you still deserve them."

"Oh... thanks." Though Rick was truly grateful, he hesitated to pick them up. "I was thinking that you should have one of them. You did convince them to pay, and you took a hit, too."

"Nah, man, I don't need it." Henry grinned and tapped the tattoo on his arm. "Demonic bond, remember? I have 5000 lucrim on call whenever I want. Might not have been enough against Birthrighter assholes, but I can afford to be generous."

"Then I appreciate it." Rick swept up both bars quickly, resisting the urge to draw the power into himself. They felt like they had 2000 lucrim or more within them - he didn't get a windfall like that very often, so he needed to invest them carefully.

As he put them with his backpack and the rest of his things, Rick took stock. He still felt a bit fatigued, and he knew his side would ache the next day, but Lisa had managed to heal all the serious damage. That left him in much better shape, so he decided to check his status in the app.

[Name: Rick Hunter

Ether Tier: 19th

Ether Score: 189

Lucrim Generation: 15,750

Current Lucrim: 3158]

[Rick Hunter's Lucrima Portfolio

Foundation: 7250 (Lv II)

Offensive Lucore: 3000 (Lv II)

Defensive Lucore: 5500 (Lv IV)

Golden Lucore: 10 (N/A)

Total Lucrim: 15,750]

The improvement in his Defensive Lucore was everything he had hoped for: not only had its value increased, it had advanced to the fourth rank as well. His defense had already been good, but once it recovered from its encounter with the Birthrighter, it would be a step better. If he could just improve his other cores and make his foundation a bit more efficient, he could punch above his weight.

But the "Golden Lucore" listed made no sense to him. He'd heard of a few famous schools or fighters that used "Golden" in technique names, but didn't know what this could be referring to. Even weirder, it wasn't included in his total. When he reached inside himself, he certainly didn't feel anything new. It might be a glitch, but he'd never seen one quite like that.

Baffled by the development, Rick pulled out his phone and searched a while for some answers. After filtering out irrelevant results, he had basically nothing, not even rumors. Though he wanted to keep searching further, he saw that Lisa had finished warming up and was bouncing on the balls of her feet, waiting for him, so he slid his phone into his backpack and went out to meet her.

"Let's do the basics today," Lisa said. "I just need to loosen up my lucrima after work."

"Frankly, I could use the same thing."

She winced. "Yeah, yours really got pounded. Dense power is good, but believe me, it's just going to cramp if you don't relax it afterwards."

Lisa was actually a massage therapist first and a warrior on the side. She'd realized that unless she could treat lucrima problems as well as muscular ones, she was going to be relegated to scrounging up minor jobs. That had brought her to the House of the Cosmic Fist, where she'd gotten an appetite for sparring...

and definitely enjoyed how much the increased power improved her work.

To be honest, it probably would have been smart for her to leave them and move elsewhere. He judged her to have a generation rate of around 52,000 lucrim - well above the average client. Yet she kept coming back, and she was a nice client, so he did his best to keep up.

Before they began sparring, Lisa suppressed her power down to his level to make things fairer. That didn't reduce the efficiency of the Lucores she'd built within herself, though. Even if she didn't hit like a truck, she was incredibly fast, and there was a sharpness to her blows that he couldn't quite match.

They traded moves, adopting a grappling style instead of focusing on striking. That made things a bit easier on him, but Rick still found himself struggling to keep up. Unlike clients who just focused on raw power, Lisa had picked up decent skills. Combined with the Lucores she continually polished via her work, she was formidable.

Normally he would have forced himself to go longer, but when his side started to ache, he raised a hand to call a halt. Lisa immediately moved closer, examining him in concern. "You alright? Does it feel like you're bleeding internally again?"

"No, I'm okay." Rick leaned against the wall and took a few painful breaths. He should have just toughed it out and kept sparring, but getting the crap kicked out of him had soured his mood. "Lisa... why do you keep coming back here? You could get into a better gym."

"I tried, actually."

That surprised him enough that he looked up sharply, but Lisa had turned away, redoing her ponytail. "Which ones?" he asked.

"Nowhere too fancy. I actually got in without any trouble, but... I don't know, I didn't feel like I fit in there. Most of their clients have huge lucrima portfolios and can just throw lucrim at any problem. The people here know how to focus on skill and train efficiently, and that's what I really need for my work."

"Huh, really? I'd assumed healing would be helped along by bigger lucrim numbers..."

"It's not like that." Lisa turned back, making vague gestures with her hands that didn't clarify anything to him. "Think about it: my top clients already have a ton of lucrim, usually way more than me. If their stress or injuries could be fixed by flooding lucrim, they'd have already done it. There are therapists who train to flood even more, but I can't compete with them. My calling card is finesse, and here is still the best place for me to train that."

Rick wasn't good with taking compliments, particularly ones as unusual as that, so he just gestured for them to start sparring again. While they did so, he found himself thinking about what she said. He could feel a tiny bit of pride at his skill, and he was glad she kept coming to the gym, but beyond that he felt like his skill just didn't matter.

Not only could a strong enough opponent just smash through all his skill with raw power, Rick knew that he wasn't truly exceptional when it came to his strengths. His technical skills were decent, but a lot of real warriors were better. Having an offensive and a defensive core in his portfolio put him above amateurs, but others had huge portfolios of more advanced cores. And his foundation was sadly inefficient, absorbing just under half of his lucrim generation.

He managed to avoid feeling sorry for himself by focusing on the sparring until he was exhausted. Lisa wasn't sweating that much, but it looked like she'd gotten a decent workout. After getting a drink of water, she pulled her jacket back on and examined the dark sky outside.

"Getting pretty late," she said, glancing over at him. "Sorry for keeping you."

"It's okay, I'll get overtime."

"You live in south Branton, right? I can fly you most of the way there, if you want."

Rick shook his head much too quickly. "Thanks, but I'll pass."

"You sure? It's on my way."

"I appreciate it, but it's good for me to get in a run before the end of the day." Normally he wouldn't exercise any more, given how much his body had endured that day, but that wasn't the real reason. Lisa was skilled enough to fly, but she didn't have any lucrim vehicles or skills that carried others or anything of the sort.

He was *not* going to go back home dangling in the air. He had his dignity.

Lisa respected that he wasn't going to take the offer and didn't press on it. Instead she flashed him a smile, headed out, and vanished into the night sky.

Though he needed to get home soon, Rick found himself leaning against the window and staring out into the sky. As usual when he had made significant lucrima progress, he was exhausted. Maybe he could afford to hire a taxi back home instead of running? If he was a few tiers higher, he could have used the bus system, but at the moment public transport was forbidden to him.

"Don't moon over her." Henry came up beside him, grinning. "I'm not saying she isn't hot, and she might like you, but it's bad form, man."

"I wasn't-"

"Deny it if you want." Henry leaned back against the window and folded his arms. "I guess that's another option for those of us who want to get out of the trash tiers: marry into wealth. I hear there are some great training options for couples that will really increase your growth in a short time."

Though Rick wasn't sure how to respond to that, they were interrupted by a grunt from Jimmy. He didn't look up from his magazine, but he did address them. "Not worth it, kid. Seems hot when you're young, but you'll regret it in the end."

Henry rolled his eyes. "That sounds like sour grapes. Unless there's a Mrs. Jimmy you've been hiding from us?"

Jimmy grunted as if considering what to say next, but at that moment Rick's phone rang. He saw that the caller was his sister and answered it quickly.

"Hey, sis. You doing okay?"

"Rick..." Her voice was difficult to hear and he automatically began grabbing his things while he strained to hear her words. "Are... are you getting back soon? I was feeling okay this afternoon, but..."

He was already out the door, sprinting into the night.

Chapter 4: Ether Void

After staying on the line with his sister long enough to confirm that she was stable, Rick jammed his phone into his pocket and put everything he had into sprinting. He was nowhere near as fast as the lucrima masters who blurred through their own lanes, but he was a good bit faster than the average runner just due to his physical condition.

It would have been very dramatic to run all the way back home, but pointless. His goal was just to get away from the suburb his lousy strip mall was in to a busier street, where he could find a taxi. He kept his eyes open, but hadn't spotted any yet.

Usually he didn't even notice the people moving overhead, but now he found himself noticing when one passed by. Not so many in a small city like Branton, but he saw a red streak of aura pass him by overhead, and five minutes later a woman passed by in a lucrima manifestation. It was shaped like one of the early World

War III era planes, which was just pretentious, and he found himself glowering up at it.

But he didn't let himself get so distracted that he didn't notice the taxi. Rick hailed it wildly and fortunately the driver pulled over for him. He jumped into the back, scrambling for his ID and swiping it through the reader.

The driver was an old man who stared at the screen until the information came up. Only once his account and rating information appeared did he look back. "Where to?"

"1867 Fifth. Hurry, if you can."

"Hmph. It'll be quite a day when a customer tells me to take my time." But the old man pulled away and into traffic without any delays, leaving Rick to catch his breath.

Usually he didn't pay much attention to politics, but he was glad that a bill had changed the national ID laws during his last year of high school. It used to be that everyone's tier was printed on their card, which might have prevented him from using some taxis. Now government IDs didn't discriminate by lucrima, though your rating was still relevant for everything else.

Sometimes he wondered if it wouldn't have been easier to take a different path. Just take however much lucrim his employer gave him and not worry about fighting, like most people did. If he'd done that, he could have gotten a ride with someone doing ride-sharing, but for someone like him, who had some power but not enough strength to defend it, the risk was too high.

But he'd fallen into this path because he was good at sparring in school. His test scores were good but nothing exceptional, and Uncle Frank had advised him against going into business young. If his parents hadn't been such deadbeats, he might have gotten into a combat sect or a university, but even combining his scholarships with government loans, it just wasn't enough to afford it.

Which left him working as a human practice dummy in a cheap little strip mall.

As they passed the Branton Arena, his eyes couldn't help but wander over it. There had been a time when he'd thought about being a professional fighter, though the truth was that less than 1% of all fighters had a shot at going pro. Once he'd enjoyed watching the matches and picking up what he could, but now it was too depressing.

Sure, the fighters in the professional leagues were all brilliant and dedicated to their craft. But they also had truckloads of potions, steroids, and alchemy to boost their lucrima portfolios. Competing on that level wasn't even a dream at this point.

When the taxi began slowing down, Rick immediately jerked from his distracted thoughts. He peered forward and saw that they were entering heavier traffic... and it looked like everything had jammed at the intersection ahead. If they had turned sharply they might have avoided it, but the driver was already getting locked into traffic.

"This is close enough." Rick glanced at the meter and hastily tugged several bills from his pocket. He wasn't rich enough to just throw them and tell the driver to keep the change, but he rounded to the nearest dollar and handed over the wad. "Thanks."

With that, he hopped out of the taxi and darted ahead of the slowing cars to the sidewalk. It was only a few streets now, so he sprinted the rest of the way to Fifth. Of course, their house was quite a few more blocks down from the main streets, but the taxi ride had let him rest, so he took them at top speed.

Rick and his sister lived on the third floor of an apartment complex that made the strip mall where he worked look positively upscale. No ambulance in the parking lot, which was a good sign. No police cars either, which meant the meth dealers and the power junkies were still doing good business from the other side.

He took the stairs three at a time and practically tore open the door to their apartment. "Sis? You doing okay?"

When he didn't get a response, Rick rushed inside, barely remembering to lock the door. No one in the living room, television off. He checked the bathroom was empty before opening the only other door, to his sister's room. For a moment he thought she was missing entirely, then he saw her.

Melissa lay on the floor off the side of the bed, eyes closed but shivering intensely. It looked as though she had reached for something on the nightstand and fallen. Her long hair, a shade lighter brown than his, fanned out over the carpet. She'd changed out of her school clothes to more comfortable ones, but her glasses lay several feet from her.

"You okay, sis?" Rick bent down and lifted her in his arms, placing her more comfortably on the bed. She didn't answer, though she shivered less intensely at his touch.

This one was serious. Rick got out his phone and flipped to check on her - not with the cheap combat app he used for himself, but a medical app with a lucrim subscription. He gently settled the sensor against her forehead, letting it take a reading and then checking the results.

[Melissa Hunter

Lucrim Generation: 3114

Current Lucrim: 19

Ether Void: -2487]

He winced at the numbers - things hadn't been this bad in months. Rick stroked the hair out of her face while he grabbed the bottle of pills she had been reaching for. The normal dosage was one, but the instructions said that she could take two in an emergency. Even if she'd already taken one that day, this qualified as an emergency.

Thankfully, she didn't struggle when he fed her the pills, swallowing them easily. He felt one of her hands grip his arm, and a moment later her eyes fluttered open.

"Rick..." She gave him a weak smile. "Sorry to... worry you..."

"You're going to be fine, Melissa. Did anything bring on this attack?"

"No... normal day..." Her eyes were already beginning to fall closed again, so Rick decided that he didn't have a choice.

He carefully removed the two pearl bars from his backpack and drained the lucrim from them. In an ideal world, he would have absorbed the energy himself and used it to increase his strength. But compared to his sister's life, that didn't seem so important. Rick set up a stream of power into her body, where it gently washed through her before it disappeared.

It wasn't absorbed into her body, the power simply disappeared into a void. Melissa had a rare condition that left her lucrima foundation with a hole that constantly drained her. Though her generation rate was above average for a girl her age, in practice she never had that much strength. With medication she could live a normal life, but occasionally the ether void would grow more intense and drain all her strength. If the ether void number ever rose above her generation rate, death was certain.

Not if she had been in a proper medical facility, of course. If they had been part of a major sect or been wealthy enough, there were a variety of effective treatments. From what Rick had read online, rich people with the same condition could lead normal lives, and some of them even fought competitively. Those weren't options for them.

When he had drained away enough of his new lucrim, Melissa finally stabilized. That left him with only about 500 lucrim from his unexpected windfall, but he just felt lucky that he'd had it. Without that, he would have needed to drain his own lucrim into her, which wouldn't have completely reversed the fit and would have left him too exhausted to care for her.

Instead, he could see a bit of strength returning to her. His sister had always been ghostly pale, and her body was much too thin, but she stopped shivering. When she next opened her eyes, there was a bit of a spark in them again.

"Hey, Rick." She smiled up at him gently. "Sorry to worry you again."

"No, I should have been home earlier. I ran into some problems."

"Really? A bad client?"

"Not exactly... believe it or not, a group of three Birthrighters came into the gym to pick a fight."

"Haha, oh my gosh, really?" Melissa sat up, a big silly grin on her face. Seeing her expression was a huge relief and the tension finally drained out of him. "Like in an 80s movie or something?"

"A bit, though they didn't challenge us or threaten to close down the local martial arts school unless we could raise a specific amount of money." No, those were problems that had easy solutions, whereas this was just mundane cruelty. He kept all of that off his face. "Anyway, one of them beat me pretty good, but Lisa showed up and healed me. So I actually came out of it 500 lucrim richer, plus it helped my defensive core."

"Wow, your day was a lot more eventful than mine. I had a normal day at school and I was just going to veg out for the rest of the night. And before you ask, I already finished my homework."

Melissa hopped up to go to the living room, and though his instincts wanted her to stay in bed, he suppressed them. Now that the incident had passed and her lucrima had stabilized, she was essentially healthy. Forcing her to stay in bed would only push her toward depressing thoughts, so he just followed her out.

They sat on the couch and watched bad television, cracking old jokes that weren't funny to anyone else. For the first time in almost the entire day, Rick was truly able to relax. Given how rough things had been, he really needed it.

But as soon as he felt his lucrima regain a placid calm, he began his usual training exercises. They were nothing elaborate, just simple meditations he could repeat while watching TV, but he practiced them religiously. In fact, he couldn't remember the last time he had missed them, if he didn't count the one time he'd fallen unconscious at work and lost an entire day.

Such work wouldn't revolutionize his life, but he was slowly and surely increasing his lucrim generation rate. He didn't have a choice, not if he wanted to support his sister, much less ever make anything of himself. For the thousandth time he considered applying for a demonic bond, or taking bigger risks for greater profits. But the truth was, given his life, a single major failure could ruin him, and that would ruin his sister's life as well.

"God, that guy is such a... such a mallard head." Melissa's joke was interrupted by a loud yawn. "Wow, I am way sleepier than I thought. Will you be okay without me if I turn in early?"

"I don't know, sis. Without your guidance I might end up jamming meth into my eyeballs."

"Don't do that, ya dummy." She hit him in the shoulder playfully. "You have to *smoke* the meth."

"Wow, really? You're such a good role model."

"And don't forget it!" Melissa wandered into the bathroom to brush her teeth and get ready for bed, leaving him alone on the couch.

Watching TV was boring without her and he'd already finished his exercises, so Rick instead began doing some more research on what this "Golden Core" in his profile might be. But despite his best efforts, he didn't end up learning anything useful. He might need to ask someone about it, and the problem there was always finding someone he could actually trust. If only his uncle was taking calls at the moment...

"Oh, by the way." Melissa poked her head out the bathroom door. "I grabbed the mail on my way home and it's all on the little table. I threw out the junk, but I wasn't sure about those ether course flyers. Anything that might be useful to you?"

"Nah, those are almost all scams."

"I figured, but I kept them just in case. Anyway, other than the bill, the only other letter is a big sealed one. It had your name on it, so I left it alone."

"Thanks, sis."

Rick forced himself to get off the couch and walked over to the "little table", which was also the *only* table. Another running joke that wasn't really funny, just a comfortable habit. There he brushed aside the useless flyers promising instant power, glanced at the bill, and then examined the big sealed envelope.

Immediately his relaxed mood evaporated and he tore it open. The return address was for the legal agency that handled everything related to their parents. There'd been a time when he'd hoped their parents would come back, but ever since his mother had abandoned Melissa, he'd given up on that. He'd expected that he wouldn't hear from them again until they died, unless they ended up calling to try to make bail.

So he wasn't sure how to feel when he learned that his parents were dead.

Rick read the simple sentences several times, trying to glean more significant information from them. It sounded like it had been illegal fighting, no doubt undertaken for more drug money. The letter danced around the subject, but that kind of thing happened often enough that he could read between the lines.

It had actually happened several days ago, it had just taken until now for the authorities to take care of the details. Now Rick needed to go take care of his parents' effects. The letter claimed they left him a Birthright Core, but he doubted it could be much of anything - more likely there was a small amount of compensation based on how they'd died. He'd take it.

Still, he found himself wondering. The meeting wasn't for three days, yet he couldn't put it out of his mind as he wished Melissa goodnight, brushed his teeth, and lay down on the couch to sleep.

Had his parents left him some sort of core? He told himself that it was probably nothing, and he'd find out soon enough, but it was still difficult to get to sleep.

Chapter 5: Liquor Store Powerup

The meeting with the attorneys was on Friday, so Rick spent all his time before then training. In theory, whatever his parents had left him would probably dwarf the small gains he could make in that time, but he felt that he needed to be prepared. Even when it came to inheritance, dealing with lawyers always made him nervous. That was what came from growing up having to pick up his parents from the local jail.

They were dead now, though.

Even two days later, that thought still stopped him. It wasn't like they had been close, or ever been real parents to him. Melissa hadn't even cried when he'd told her, just sat quietly for a while. But even absent, they had still been a part of his life that was now entirely gone.

Rick pushed such thoughts aside and focused on training. On Wednesday he threw himself into sparring with all his clients, dusting off his own skills. He'd had Thursday off anyway, so he asked his boss for Friday off as well. There was a lot of grumbling, and he had to reschedule with Lisa, but in the end he was allowed to use one of his vacation days. That meant he could attend the official meeting and see what his parents had left him.

Before that, he needed to use the last days before the meeting to finish preparing. Since Melissa had been in good health since then, as she usually was for a while after an incident, he decided that he could afford to invest his lucrim.

Which meant he was going to the liquor store.

As he walked down the weed-covered sidewalk, Rick checked his status again:

[Name: Rick Hunter

Ether Tier: 19th

Ether Score: 196

Lucrim Generation: 15,950

Current Lucrim: 12,378]

[Rick Hunter's Lucrima Portfolio

Foundation: 7300 (Lv II)

Offensive Lucore: 3100 (Lv II)

Defensive Lucore: 5550 (Lv IV)

Golden Lucore: 10 (N/A)

Total Lucrim: 15,950]

Not a bad improvement, mostly working through the aftermath of the big fight. That amount would be overwhelmed by what he could purchase that day, though. Maybe in the old days it was possible for lone warriors to become powerful by meditating alone, but today you needed money and lucrim, no matter what you did. Most likely even the old days had been similar, though, and the easy routes to power were just fairy tales.

He had gotten his paycheck on Wednesday and spent a good chunk of it absorbing lucrim, which had raised him near his generation limit. It wasn't often that he was close, usually needing to spend lucrim on other things, so he enjoyed overflowing with power for once. But if all went well, he'd be in much better shape for the meeting with the lawyers.

Finally Rick arrived at the liquor store, stepping over a man lying in a training stupor. A bottle that had once held something potent lay beside him, and his body glowed with power, but he was out cold with a pool of vomit spreading beneath his face. Probably a power addict.

Inside there were mostly regular drinkers who stuck to themselves. The inside of the liquor store was normal enough, mostly just shelves filled with bottles. But one corner of it by the door was a massively reinforced cube of glass. Travis the owner sat inside it, capable of both dropping a metal door over the entrance if anyone tried to run or projecting power outside the glass if necessary. He was a large, greasy man, but he made enough money from owning the store to gather some real power.

Rick didn't come there often, so he needed to take some time to find what he wanted. He kept his head down and avoided a loud group of students from one of the combat sects. Too much of a chance they might be looking for a fight, which he couldn't afford right now.

After scanning the walls and finding only normal alcohol, Rick gave up and approached the glass cube. "Do you still sell philosopher's elixir here?"

"Ah, yeah." Travis scratched at his stomach where it protruded from his shirt. "Had to put it behind the glass due to new regulations from the local board. Apparently some idiots couldn't handle the lucrim surge and smashed up some things downtown. Now I'm only allowed to sell what people can handle."

"That's understandable. I'm looking for some, so if-"

"Gotta test you first." A glass plate opened, revealing a small machine with a needle at one end and a collection disc beneath. Rick sighed and looked up at the owner.

"Travis, you've sold elixir to me multiple times, you shouldn't need to test me." Plus, it was well known that he sold both alcohol and stronger substances to whoever could pay.

But it seemed like Travis was going to force him to jump through the hoops, possibly just as a power trip. Rick reached forward and pricked his finger on the needle, letting a drop of blood fall onto the disc. The blood was instantly whisked away and the machine rumbled for a moment before it gave a readout on the other end. Whatever it said, it made Travis grunt affirmatively.

"Alright, I can sell to you. All the philosopher's elixir is in the top row behind me, but I'd recommend a 10k if you're looking for an edge, a 25k if you want to boost your training." Travis stared at him for a moment, judging his build with an undercurrent of scorn. "You're a gym rat, right? Maybe try a 20k mix instead, unless you want to get roided up."

"No, I'd like to try the 100k." Rick was confident that he knew his limits better than Travis did, and he wasn't going to let the man's scorn slow his development.

"That's gonna knock you right out, kid. You have any idea how strong six figures is?"

"I had one of them as a client the other day." He left out the details, of course, just stared back at Travis and refused to budge. "But if you don't want my business, I can go somewhere else."

"Eh, it's your funeral. How much do you want?"

In the end, Rick bought only a single bottle of 100k philosopher's elixir. If he'd spent all his money, he could have purchased three. That would have been enough to invest a huge amount of lucrim into himself, which would have been a substantial boost to his strength.

It would also have been stupid. Something in the apartment could break, or Melissa might need money for something at school, or they might have to pay for a medical emergency. Only someone with no responsibilities and no sense of long term planning could blow all their money on training supplies. Just buying this bottle was already extravagant for him, but he justified it because he'd soon have his parents' inheritance. Even if it was meager, what they left him could pay for one bottle.

Once he received the bottle, he hefted it with one hand, feeling the tingle of power even through the glass. Just to make sure he wasn't making a mistake, he opened it and took a sip. He was pretty sure just a sip wouldn't knock him out cold, but if so, better to do it here, where someone would call for help. At least, they probably would.

To his surprise, though it tingled as it went down his throat, he handled it easily. Had fighting against the Birthrighter improved his tolerance that much? If so, he was actually getting much stronger...

No. Abruptly Rick realized that answer might massage his ego, but there was a much simpler explanation. He checked the label again, frowned, and turned back to Travis.

"Are you sure this is right? It doesn't taste like 100k to me."

Travis grunted and didn't look up. "Don't go complaining just because it's more than you can handle. No returns after you open the bottle."

"No, I'm saying it tastes like less than 100k. And I'm wondering just how that could have happened."

That got Travis to look up, beady eyes glaring. "Are you accusing me of something, kid?"

"No, of course not." Rick gave him a flat smile and tapped the bottle against the glass idly. "I just assume that you would be concerned if your supplier gave you an inferior product. Seems like something everyone would be concerned about. Maybe we could ask all those students to weigh in and give their impressions?"

"You little shit." Travis glared at him a while longer, but his eyes flickered toward the sect students milling in the aisles. "Look, most training addicts can't tell the difference, they just want something to burn through their system. I didn't mean anything by it."

"No harm in an honest mistake. But I really did need 100k for my training..."

Though he cursed under his breath, Travis gave in. He reached beneath the counter and pulled out a different bottle: it looked identical to the first on the outside, but the clear liquid inside burned a little brighter. When it moved through the security door, Rick compared it to the first and then took a sip. Yes, that was definitely stronger.

Travis leaned forward, one hand pushing against the glass. His hand was fat enough that his flesh flattened against the surface, but it also burned with power. "That makes us even, kid. Unless anyone hears about this, in which case we will *never* be even. You understand me?"

"Perfectly. Thanks for the elixir." Rick gave him a smile and headed out the door, though he took care to secure both bottles in his backpack first.

The entire way home he found himself tense. Part of it was just carrying something so valuable, but another part of it was the confrontation. Liquor stores needed to care about security, particularly if they also dealt in lucrim-related drinks. He didn't think Travis had directly threatened him, or that there would be any consequences, but the possibility left him uneasy. If mobsters broke his legs, he wouldn't be able to take care of his sister and his training would be set back years, putting them in a hole they'd never escape.

Though he wasn't a power addict, he couldn't forget about the 100k elixir he carried. As soon as Rick got back to the apartment, he double-checked that everything was locked and then brought the bottle out. Getting two bottles changed his plans a little, but only a little.

To make sure that Melissa wouldn't find him in a pool of his own vomit, Rick poured a small glass of elixir first. It burned going down and he sensed the strength kindling within him like hot coals, but he only felt a little dizzy. So he sat down on the couch and gathered his nerve, preparing himself fully.

100k philosopher's elixir didn't contain 100,000 lucrim - that was only a marker of the quality. What the elixir *could* do was restore his strength up to his maximum generation rate. It was a better way to restore one's strength than serum, though the cost started high and only went higher as one's lucrima soul required higher quality elixir.

But his goal wasn't to restore himself to average, it was to push himself further. If he drank the entire elixir, for a short time his body would be burning with far more power than he could normally handle. Power addicts just enjoyed the rush and got a small boost from it, but the real gains came from trying to absorb the flood. If all went well, the elixir would expand the pool of strength he could control and boost his generation rate.

Before he could talk himself out of it, Rick tilted back his head and drank the entire bottle.

For several seconds he felt like living fire, his body shuddering involuntarily against the couch. He managed to get it under control, though the strength still raged inside him. Gritting his teeth, Rick demanded that the power obey him. All the strength he had, even the lucrim he had collected before, all went into smashing through his current limits.

Several hours later, his mind came out of the rigid training exercises and began thinking normally again. At some point he'd slumped over on the couch, though he hadn't vomited or drooled. Actually, his jaw was sore as if he'd been clenching it the entire time.

He didn't remember dropping the bottle, but saw it lying on the carpet, fortunately unbroken. They didn't have a vacuum, so broken glass was a real pain to clean up.

That simple thought brought him fully back. His efforts had been successful, though he wouldn't know how much progress he'd made until his lucrima soul recovered. Right now he felt completely drained, but that wasn't a problem thanks to the other bottle.

Rick drank that one slowly, not trying to blast open his power, just letting the tingling restore him. He guessed that this bottle was in the 70k-80k range, though he didn't have as much experience with high end elixir. Though it might help him a bit, the main benefit he hoped to gain was just restoring himself to full strength.

Before he finished the bottle, he became ravenously hungry. He got up and began to eat through what they had - a lot of it was junk, but it wouldn't do him any harm because right now his body was a calorie furnace. Only after swallowing several snack cakes whole and finishing the bottle on the couch did Rick realize how much of a trashy fighter stereotype it was.

Not that it really mattered. When it came time to meet the lawyers, he'd be ready.

For the rest of Thursday Rick did more recovery exercises, testing his new strength. By the end of the day after spending some time relaxing with Melissa, he felt stable enough to check his strength again.

[Name: Rick Hunter

Ether Tier: 19th

Ether Score: 196

Lucrim Generation: 17,400

Current Lucrim: 17,400]

[Rick Hunter's Lucrima Portfolio

Foundation: 8100 (Lv II)

Offensive Lucore: 3500 (Lv II)

Defensive Lucore: 6000 (Lv IV)

Golden Lucore: 10 (N/A)

Total Lucrim: 17,600]

He was in the best shape of his life and he felt great. True, the boost had cost him a huge percentage of his paycheck, and he wouldn't be able to get another boost like that without going to even more expensive elixirs. Still, after so long stagnating, it felt good to have broken through.

His ether tier and score remained unchanged, but that was only a matter of time. Just his progress from the elixir might be enough to raise his score above 200, which would mean fewer institutions would reject him. Combined with whatever he inherited from his parents, he'd likely see his tier increase as well. Perhaps enough that their lives would begin to turn around.

On Friday morning he helped Melissa get off to school, then spent an hour pacing around the apartment before he realized that he should just go. He might arrive at the offices early, but that was better than wallowing in anxiety. After spending so much on the philosopher's elixir, he decided to run the whole way, using the time to clear his head.

Most importantly, he let his pessimism reassert itself. Maybe this would change his life, but probably not. His parents had probably been close to penniless when they died, so whatever they left him would be minimal. He shouldn't get his hopes up, just invest whatever they left as best he could.

When he reached the address, he discovered that the law firm's office was an impressive building, but Rick barely had time to look at it. Instead, his attention was entirely absorbed by the parking lot. Amid the luxury cars and lucrim hybrids, there was a beaten red pickup truck with a nearly naked woman painted across the front.

That was his uncle's truck, and not the good uncle. Uncle Alan. Why would the lawyers have called him here too? Rick put aside all optimistic thoughts and rushed inside to find out.

Chapter 6: Inheritance Dispute

Though Rick's mind was mostly preoccupied with why Uncle Alan would be coming to a meeting about his parents' estate, he couldn't help but be taken aback as he entered the building. This was no small legal office, but the headquarters of one of the largest local firms.

He didn't know much about legal firms, but everything about the offices of Pine, Jade, and Swift Associates projected power. Lush but tasteful carpet, furniture that looked like it cost more than his apartment, lucrim crystals glittering in the windows... it all demonstrated that they had money to burn, and money meant power.

Trying to ignore all of it, Rick headed directly to the front desk, avoiding thoughts about how shabby he looked in a room like this. A woman sat behind a computer there and she smiled at him with no trace of scorn, however. "Can I help you?"

"Uh, I hope so. I'm Richard Hunter, and I received a letter from you guys." He held it out to demonstrate, feeling incredibly awkward. "There's supposed to be a meeting?"

"Of course, Mr. Hunter. You're a bit early, so would you mind waiting in the lobby?"

"No, but my unc - another family member appears to be already here. I'm not sure why."

The woman frowned and glanced at her screen briefly, then returned the same polite smile to him. "I'm afraid I don't know anything about your specific case, but I can assure you, things will begin at the appointed time. Please take a seat."

He was too nervous to sit down, but he did wander into the lushly-appointed lobby. This area was clearly for clients and visitors, so it included a wall with a number of ornate carvings chronicling the history of the firm. According to the official story, the Highest Pine, Jade Hand, and Swift Elegance had been combat sects without peer in the Midwest before they joined forces to create the modern firm.

Most likely the official story involved some exaggeration. Whenever any place talked about its history, somehow there were unrivaled schools and legendary martial artists everywhere. But that didn't mean that they weren't significant.

For one, everyone who worked there was stronger than him. Even the woman at the desk had a generation rate in excess of 50,000 lucrim. And when a well-dressed man who looked like he might be a lawyer walked through, Rick actually had to take a step back. His rate was 200,000 or more, so high that Rick couldn't even properly evaluate his strength.

To top it off, that power wasn't just granted in a lump sum like the Birthrighters. Oh, the lawyer probably got a significant Birthright Core from his parents, but it was dwarfed by the many polished cores within his lucrima. In his current state, Rick struggled to even aspire to such power.

Before he could get too uncomfortable in the lobby, the woman called his name and gestured him toward one of the doors in back. A young man guided him through the wood-paneled corridors, apparently not wanting to chat, and soon left him in front of a door marked with nothing but a number.

Swallowing, Rick pushed inside. On the other side he found yet another tastefully expensive room, though this one was rather spare. Plain carpet, and aside from the table and chairs, there was no furniture at all.

But there was no time to think about that. What mattered was that a lawyer sat on the other side of the desk, while Uncle Alan slouched on the closer side. He'd gotten heavier now, but the signs of the fighter he'd once been were obvious in his body. He wore blue jeans and a shirt with the arms torn off, showing both muscular arms and many scars from days pit fighting.

Only one chair remained, obviously for Rick. He walked inside slowly, eyeing his uncle, and paused long enough by the chair that the lawyer had to gesture for him to sit.

"Please, make yourself comfortable."

While Rick slipped into the seat, his uncle frowned at him. "Thought you wouldn't show up, boy."

"Why wouldn't I?" He swallowed the acidic words on his tongue, not wanting to seem childish in front of the lawyer in case that ended up affecting the results.

"Because you were always playing your little games," Uncle Alan said. "Never showed up when the family needed you."

It was more that he refused to allow the rest of the family to drag him down, separated himself because he didn't want Melissa to end up in a dead end life like so many of them. Rick knew that he should shrug off the insult, but found himself smiling bitterly instead. "When was the last time you visited my parents, Uncle? I assume you're just here to give your condolences, right? What they left behind has nothing to do with it?"

"Looks like you've turned into a smug bastard." His uncle's fingers gripped tightly into the armrests of his chair and he started levering himself up. But at that moment the lawyer raised a hand. Just a slight gesture, but he also flexed his aura as he did so. Unlike a visibly manifested aura, it simply rippled through the room, but the raw power of it was a wave of pressure keeping both of them in their seats.

Rick sat without moving and waited for Uncle Alan to calm down. When they both sat silently, the lawyer gave a flat smile and positioned a piece of paper in front of him before speaking.

"Since the two of you obviously have business of your own to consider, I'll be brief. Our meeting today is to distribute the belongings of the deceased. They were in some debt, so the majority of their belongings were claimed toward repayment of some of that debt. By law, however, surviving Lucores must be distributed to next of kin."

The lawyer lifted a briefcase onto the table and opened it toward himself. Still speaking, he removed two devices and placed them beside the briefcase. "Due to the unfortunate circumstances, there was significant deterioration and so we are left with only two viable Lucores. To wit, these."

Each device was a black square with four steel tines rising from the corners, arching together to meet in the center. The air quivered with the field they produced, and in the exact center of the space pulsed a nearly invisible speck of power. Though there was no difference between the two, they retained just enough familiar essence that he knew they came from his parents.

Those two cores were all that remained of his parents. Rick stared at them for a while, not sure what to feel, but then he needed to focus, as the lawyer swiped his hand through the air and created a lucrim display.

[Birthright Core

Family Designation: Hunter193

1108 lucrim]

[Birthright Core

Family Designation: Hunter193

1944 lucrim]

The larger one had been from his mother, the smaller from his father. He looked over the numbers, having long ago comprehended them, just trying to decide how to react. Though he should have felt more emotion, at the very least curiosity about how they had died, the information in the letter had told him what he basically expected.

His parents had lived lives that were simultaneously reckless and unremarkable. Now, they left him two unremarkable cores. True, they were significant compared to his current abilities, but they were nothing much for a pair of adults. Mike the Birthrighter's 100,000 lucrim core had probably been only a tiny fraction of his family's accumulated power.

"Not bad, bro." Uncle Alan reached out toward the cores, surprisingly eager. If he needed lucrim cores worth just 3000 that badly, then his situation really must be difficult. No wonder he was trying to steal what never should have been his.

Rick reached out and grabbed his wrist. "Why should they go to you? They were my parents."

"You're a damn boy! Would you even know what to do with that much power?" Though he scowled at him, Uncle Alan did pull his hand away. He sat back in his chair and stared at the cores, while Rick looked past them.

"The law on this matter is frustratingly vague," the lawyer said. "Though it surprises many clients, the law does not actually enshrine inheritance rights for children. Under most circumstances this is handled via a last will and testament, but our searches have presented reasonable doubt that any were ever created. As such, there is actually some uncertainty as to the distribution of the Birthright Cores."

Frowning, Rick did his best to stay calm. "I don't think I've ever heard of Birthright Cores not going to the children. Why wouldn't they?"

"While that is unquestionably the modern custom, there are also legal precedents that favor senior family members."

Uncle Alan grunted. "Yeah, what he said." He turned in his seat, staring Rick straight in the eyes. "Here's the deal kid: I'll let you have the smaller core and you can just walk away. I think I'm being pretty damn generous, considering how much you've brushed off this family."

Rick considered it for only a moment before he thought about what those cores could mean for Melissa. "No. You have no right to take them."

"Don't say I didn't warn you." The older man growled and pushed himself out of his chair, reminding Rick just how tall he was. "Then we do this the hard way. You're a junior member of the Hunter family and you're owed *nothing*. If you have a problem with that, you can take it up with me."

The lawyer sighed. "A ritual challenge, then. While this is not unexpected... please make it quick. We have more business to attend to today."

"Oh, it'll be quick." Uncle Alan cracked his knuckles and let his aura rise from his body. It flowed a muddy red and moved roughly, but it was as large as Rick remembered it.

With an odd movement, the lawyer made his chair and the table slide across the floor, soundlessly gliding to the corner and leaving the center of the floor empty. Fighting on carpet in a wood-paneled room felt wrong, but Rick didn't have a choice. There was no way he was backing down from this one.

Rick stood to his feet and took a deep breath. If there had ever been a time to spend all the strength he had been gathering, this was it.

Chapter 7: Family Conflict

Rick carefully pushed his chair out of his way, trying to maintain his focus. That was difficult when his uncle was blasting aura in all directions and snarling at him. Uncle Alan grabbed his own chair and hurled it single-handed, effortlessly sending it against the opposite wall. It bounced off the paneling without leaving a dent and tumbled to the ground.

Despite how nice it was, this room was clearly built to accommodate fights like this. But they hadn't been given any specific rules to this challenge... would the lawyer step in before anyone was seriously injured? The man was sitting back and watching them with a flat gaze as if he just wanted it to be over.

At that moment, Rick had his attention pulled back to the fight. His uncle began moving forward, striking one fist into his palm. "You're going to regret this, Dick."

"That's Richard to you, Uncle."

"It doesn't matter. I'm going to beat you so badly you won't even remember your own name!"

With that, his uncle lunged at him, crossing the room far faster than someone of his bulk should have been able to move. It was an impressive attack, fueled by lucrim with little wasted movement. His uncle wanted to take him off guard with a deciding blow right at the beginning, and it might have worked.

Except his uncle looked slow.

Rick ducked away, easily evading his wild swipes. He remembered that his uncle had always seemed like a monster, unstoppable in the cage fights where he made his money. Yet now he could see that though his uncle was strong, he wasn't the fighter Rick had believed as a child.

Every day at work, Rick had been training against people who outclassed him. Mike and the other Birthrighters had struck much heavier blows. Darin had attacked more aggressively. Lisa was far faster and more dangerous.

Though part of him began to believe that this might be easy, he didn't let himself get overconfident. Instead of trying to throw his uncle to the ground, he instead dodged to the side and then delivered several quick jabs to his uncle's stomach.

All he got was a grunt of pain, then his uncle let out a roar and charged at him. The blow looked clumsy and Rick started to automatically switch to a soft style and use his opponent's force against him.

Yet when he reached to grab his uncle's wrist, his instincts screamed that he was in danger. Rick leapt straight back, narrowly avoiding the sweeping claw that tried to grab him. He ended up skidding back across the carpet all the way until his shoes hit the other wall. His jump had taken him further than he expected - he wasn't entirely used to having this much strength.

Instead of trying to take him out, Uncle Alan stalked sideways, glowering. Rick moved to the side as well, keeping distance between them and considering his options.

He had been right not to try to throw his uncle. Most people viewed western-style pit fighters as brutes who could only punch, but he'd grown up seeing the matches, so he knew the truth: they were very good at grappling. Such a contest would pit his strength directly against his uncle's, which would be the one way he would certainly lose the match. Better to keep him at a distance, where his footwork and skill could bridge the gap.

That gap wasn't as large as he'd expected, though. He estimated that his uncle only had a generation rate of about 31,000 lucrim. Most of it seemed to be invested in an offensive core, so he was definitely dangerous, but he had plenty of openings.

To his surprise, his uncle raised a hand and his aura focused into a ball. It gathered slowly enough that Rick was able to leap aside, and a moment later the sphere of aura flashed out, exploding against the opposite wall. His uncle had been hiding something like that?

Rick was too poor to afford any special techniques or trump cards. But that didn't mean he had no advantages. Now that he had a feel for his uncle's strength, he began advancing more aggressively.

Ducking underneath another aura sphere, he moved in and struck several times at his uncle's face. Light blows, just testing him, and they all bounced harmlessly off his defensive block. That was just bait, since his opponent soon saw his chance and punched at his side.

Uncle Alan's fist connected and Rick winced at the pain... but he only winced. It didn't hurt as badly as the blow from the Birthrighter, and his defenses had grown stronger since then. For just a moment, his uncle looked astonished, never having expected that someone much weaker than him could have such a strong defensive core.

Then Rick's elbow collided with his nose. This time, he didn't hold anything back.

The blow broke his uncle's nose and snapped his neck back, knocking him off his feet. As his uncle hit the ground, Rick didn't let up, kicking at his side again. This blow dealt more damage than his light jabs as he felt his uncle's defensive aura give way. That one would hurt the next morning.

His uncle writhed and clutched his side... but he was faking it. Rick backed off and kept his guard up, preparing for the next round.

"You little shit..." Uncle Alan crawled to his feet, roughly swiping at the blood pouring from his nose. It ran into his teeth, making them a gruesome sight as he clenched his jaw. "You're gonna regret this. I'll beat the shit out of you until you're begging me not to do anything worse than breaking your nose."

"You talk a good talk, Uncle." Rick faked a smile at him and saw the other man's rage.

It wasn't enough to prompt him into another wild charge, though. Instead his uncle raised a hand and gathered another sphere of his aura, except this one didn't fire at him, just spun in place above his hand. A moment later it burst into flames, the power within it increasing substantially.

"It's too late to surrender, boy. You're going to burn."

But as dangerous as the attack was, Rick just kept smiling. When the sphere flew out at him, he leapt away from it, easily avoiding the attack as well as the small explosion that followed.

Of course, that had always been a feint. As soon as he landed near the wall, he saw that his uncle had already released another flaming sphere. There was no way he could dodge this one, but that had never been the plan.

Instead Rick grabbed his chair off the floor and swung it directly at the approaching sphere.

A few flames licked his hands as the two collided, but the chair deflected the explosion away from him. Good, that part had been a risk. But he'd noticed that the room had taken absolutely no damage from their fight, so he'd been willing to bet that the firm reinforced the furniture as well. He risked a glance at the lawyer and saw that the man was perusing papers, apparently entirely ignoring their battle.

"That's a cheap trick." Uncle Alan created a sphere on either side of him, the flames growing more intense. "But it's not going to work again. You can't dodge forever, and then I'm going to burn all that attitude out of you."

"You're wrong." As dangerous as the spheres looked, Rick saw them for what they really were: desperation. His uncle might be strong, but he was usually desperate for money and running low on lucrim. Normally Rick was in equally dire straits, but at the moment he actually had more stamina than his uncle. Everything so far had been an effort to beat him quickly or intimidate him into surrendering.

"Wrong? You think I'm going to take that from a little shit who can't even make it in real fights?"

His uncle hurled both spheres in quick succession and Rick avoided them as best he could. Though he felt a bit scorched, he was still uninjured. More importantly, when his uncle created two more spheres, his control faltered a bit. He was sweating and gasping for breath now, but his eyes still raged.

"You won't win, Uncle." Rick tried not to look smug, since he was sincere: better to end this without injuring anyone and leaving vendettas behind. "You think you can wear me out first, but that isn't going to happen. You should admit you've lost."

"Never!" His uncle hurled the spheres, but his movements had slowed down even more.

Instead of dodging to the side, Rick leapt toward the spheres, passing between them before they could explode.

Suddenly he was within his opponent's guard and his uncle was too tired to counter-attack. Rick staggered him with a punch to the injured spot on his side. Dodged to the side of the predictable haymaker. Dealt a kick to the back of his uncle's leg, making him drop, then lunged straight in with an elbow to the side of his head.

Rick jumped back as his uncle fell, expecting the large man to explode with force and burst from the floor. Yet to his surprise, Uncle Alan lay where he fell. His face was bloody and his eyes were unfocused. Beyond the damage he had suffered, it looked as though he couldn't believe that he had been defeated.

For a while, Rick couldn't believe it either. The adults in his life who were fighters had always seemed unstoppable to him when he was young. And though his uncle had been stronger than him... a generation rate of just 31,000 lucrim was nothing special.

For the first time, when Rick looked at his uncle he felt only disgust and a bit of pity.

"If you're all quite done, may we continue?" The lawyer looked up from his papers as if the fight had been nothing more than a bathroom break. "Bring a chair over here and do try not to break it when you do."

The chair didn't seem to have taken any damage from its use in the fight, but Rick still seethed at the insult as he set it up in front of the desk. To the lawyer, both of them probably looked like impoverished brutes squabbling over loose change. Refusing to care about the other man's judgment, Rick just sat down and waited to receive what he was owed.

"This concludes the ritual challenge, and clearly you are the victor. Therefore you will take possession of both Birthright Cores. We would recommend you absorb them immediately and we can help facilitate that process if you like."

Rick stared at the two cores, but they had never been for him. The offer was tempting for Melissa, however, because he wasn't sure if she had the strength to absorb them unaided. "How much would that cost?"

"Oh, it's part of the overall fee. Which your relative will be paying, by the way. When the one who issues the challenge is also the loser, they're required to pay all legal costs for both parties. Provides a disincentive for spurious challenges, you see."

"Right, I understand. But what I'm wondering is if you could implant the cores in someone else?"

"Our gratis service only covers services for you today, but the cores are yours to do with as you wish. You can give them to anyone you want, or use them as paperweights for all I care."

"The person I have in mind is also a-"

Sighing, the lawyer waved his words aside. "We can figure out the details later. First we need to finish bestowing your parents' assets."

Rick stared at the lawyer. "They have more? But you said their property was taken... and surely they didn't have more cores."

"No, they did not. Before they died, your parents took on a number of significant debts, primarily in lucrim." Still with the same flat smile on his face, the lawyer reached down into his briefcase. "Those debts are not discharged by their deaths. As the inheritor of their estate, their debts are yours as well."

"But... you said their belongings were sold to cover them..."

"Some of them."

His hands rose and Rick was already jumping to his feet even before he saw it. The lawyer held a ghostly blue lump in his hands that began to writhe from his fingers. An aura leech. Though Rick had never seen one in person, he'd seen enough of them in cheap crime dramas to know what it could do, and that he needed to get away as soon as possible.

Yet he barely made it two steps to the door before he suddenly found himself slammed back against the wall. The lawyer calmly held him there with one hand, not displaying any visible aura, but radiating overwhelming strength.

If Rick had been fully charged and fresh, he might have been able to strike back or struggle away. But having exhausted so much of his strength against his uncle, and still feeling his burns, it was simply impossible. This opponent was stronger than anyone he'd ever faced, without any obvious weaknesses. To make matters worse, he had the law on his side.

"This isn't fair," Rick said, glaring at the lawyer. "If you had told me their assets included lucrim debts..."

"Yes, we've had difficulty getting anyone to accept estates under such conditions, and one of our core duties is to ensure the repayment of such debts." The lawyer shrugged and raised the leech. "This will only hurt at first."

With that, the lawyer set the leech on his chest over his heart.

It bit down and cold pain lanced through Rick's chest. He managed to choke back his scream, his body thrashing uselessly against the wall. Worse than the pain was that he could immediately feel the leech draining his strength.

Even as he watched in horror, it sank down into his chest, merging with his lucrima. He knew that it would stay there, draining his power until the debt was repaid, but at that moment all he could feel was terror. Not just that an alien being was burrowing into his soul, but that it would stay there, robbing him of the strength he desperately needed to survive and help provide for his sister.

Yet just when he started to think that he had come to grips with his new reality, he saw that the briefcase was floating into the air. The lawyer gave him a false apologetic smile and reached into it again, pulling out another ghostly leech.

"Apologies for the discomfort, but your parents acquired several different debts before they passed..."

Rick struggled with all the strength he had left, but it was too late. When the creature latched onto him, the world slipped away and he fell into the darkness. With his last thoughts he cursed his parents, then there was nothing left.

Chapter 8: Aura Leeches

Pain reminded Rick that he was still alive. For a while he just lay there, not sure how he felt about that.

But no, he had too many obligations to give up. Struggling to open his eyes, Rick found himself staring at a sterile white ceiling. He sat up and discovered that he lay in a room that reminded him of a hospital, but without most of the equipment. Just two beds.

Uncle Alan lay in the other bed. It seemed that he'd been given minimal medical treatment, but he still looked pretty rough. Rick stared at him, unsure how to feel. He might have experienced a bit of lingering pride if not for the ache in his chest.

He felt absolutely terrible. Though he couldn't sense the leeches squirming around inside his soul, he knew they were there, and he definitely felt them draining away his strength. How bad was it? He realized that since all of this was perfectly legal, it would probably be listed in the usual app. Finding his phone lying beside him, he brought up his profile:

[Name: Rick Hunter

Ether Tier: 18th

Ether Score: 152

Lucrim Generation: 20,602

Effective Rate: 11,102

Current Lucrim: 2071]

He groaned when he saw his basic profile. Though he'd finally passed 20,000 lucrim for his generation rate, the "effective rate" represented his strength minus the leeches' draining effect. All told, he was even weaker than before. Worse, his ether score had been downgraded, placing any advantages from reaching 200 firmly out of reach.

Except that the numbers didn't add up properly. The fight against Uncle Alan had probably strengthened him a little, but not that much. Rick pulled up his portfolio, afraid that he already knew what he was going to see...

[Rick Hunter's Lucrima Portfolio

Foundation: 8150 (Lv II)

Offensive Lucore: 3550 (Lv II)

Defensive Lucore: 6050 (Lv IV)

Birthright Core: 1944 (Lv I)

Birthright Core: 1108 (Lv I)

Aura Leech: -5000 (Stage II)

Aura Leech: -3000 (Stage I)

Aura Leech: -1500 (Stage III)

Golden Lucore: 10 (N/A)

Gross Lucrim: 20,602

Net Lucrim: 11,102]

His portfolio had reorganized itself to measure his weakened state, and the aura leeches were a horrible mark against him, but the worst part was confirming his suspicions: he'd already been implanted with both Birthright cores.

For a long time Rick just stared at the screen. Where did he go from here? Giving up wasn't an option, but having his hopes be crushed so thoroughly left him floundering. He wasn't even sure how they could make ends meet, with such a large drop in his generation rate. *This* was all he'd bought with his limited strength?

Before he could find any answers, the door opened and a young man in hospital scrubs stepped in. He gave a quick smile that Rick couldn't return.

"You're awake, huh? We completely finished the process and you took it well, so you're free to go whenever you like."

"I didn't want the cores implanted."

The man's smile wavered and he shrugged. "I'm sorry about that, but I can only do what the sheet tells me."

"Those were for my sister. She's sick."

"That's tragic, but..." The man picked up a clipboard from beside his bed and ran his eyes over it, wincing. "Bluntly, man, you need it more than she does. Without the increase in generation rate, those leeches would be doing a serious number on you."

Rick felt a surge of anger and rose to his feet, only to halt at a twinge of pain. He clutched his chest, breathing heavily. "This... is just how it is now, huh?"

"Well, at least for a while. I know it's not much comfort, but you can work those off. Once they've absorbed enough, they'll automatically detach and then you can get rid of them."

Right, once he just paid off a debt of almost 10,000 lucrim. Except the debt was actually much more than 10,000 lucrim as a currency - Rick tried to ransack his memory for information on how exactly such debts worked and couldn't remember. Uncle Frank had always told him to avoid demonic bonds and leech debts, so he hadn't thought it mattered. Yet now he didn't have a choice.

At that moment, his other uncle let out a curse. Uncle Alan lurched up to a sitting position, muttering more curses under his breath.

When he saw Rick, however, he let out a malicious chuckle. "Didn't go as well as you thought, did it, boy? Guess I should be thanking you for putting in so much work to beat me. I really dodged a punch there."

"Alan..." Rick wanted to hit him again, but outside of a formal challenge, that would be assault. He could have mocked his uncle for losing or rubbed it in, except that he felt only bitterness. "Do you know how sick Melissa is? You talk about family, but she's the one who will suffer from this."

"You're not family. You're going to end up just like Frank, thinking you're too good for us. Getting involved with even worse shit." Alan stood up and glared at him, but when Rick didn't back down, he hesitated.

"Umm..." The nurse glanced between the two of them awkwardly. "Listen, can you deal with this stuff somewhere else? Since we finished everything, Mr. Hunter, you're free to go."

Uncle Alan scoffed, though he couldn't entirely hide the fact that he was the one to back down first. "Fine. Enjoy your leeches, boy."

"Ah, I didn't mean you." The young man stepped into his path. "There's still the matter of paying for the legal fees, the formal challenge, and the medical treatment. As the firm would have disclosed to you, we do need you to balance those accounts before you go - the total comes to just under 13,000 lucrim, how would you like to pay?"

"I..." Uncle Alan looked extremely nervous for a moment, then tried to push through. But the nurse simply struck him on the chest with an open palm and he immediately crumpled to the ground.

"Then I'm afraid you have a debt as well. Hold still while I set everything up." With that, the man looked up at Rick and gave him the same smile - it still seemed honestly friendly, but Rick's blood ran cold. "You can go, Mr. Hunter. Have a nice day."

Rick left the building as quickly as possible. On his way out, he heard his uncle cry out in pain and guessed that an aura leech was being applied to him as well. If his uncle was so desperate to drive all the way from the trailer park to steal a few small cores, then he was likely in poor shape. Having another drain on his lucrima... well, he wasn't likely to be a problem for a long time.

Though seeing his uncle get what was coming to him could have been satisfying, Rick was just reminded of what the lawyer had said. The law firms didn't care about fairness, they just wanted to keep everyone in the lower tiers of society constantly paying off debts so they could never rise up. His uncle might have gotten the slightly worse end of the stick, but...

Yes, that was cold comfort compared to the new reality Rick had inherited. Such large negative numbers... he needed to read up on how exactly aura leeches worked, but he just felt exhausted. Far too tired to run, but now he definitely couldn't afford a cab.

But his uncle's words reminded him of his other uncle. While he headed down the sidewalk, Rick dialed Uncle Frank's number. As usual he only went to voicemail, and even though he should have expected it, he still found himself not sure what to say.

"Uncle Frank, my parents... well, you probably already heard. They left me a lot of debt. I assumed that would go away when they... is it possible that this isn't legal?" Still on the line, Rick rubbed his eyes roughly. No, a large firm probably wasn't going to do something explicitly illegal. He was rambling and needed to pull himself together. "I'm not sure what I'm going to do and I could really use some advice. Call me back when you can."

As he put his phone away, he noticed that it was already 4:30, which meant he'd been unconscious for some time. Perversely, despite the fact that there were much more serious problems in his life, he found himself frustrated that he'd lost his vacation day. He usually worked Saturday, and there was no way his boss was giving him a day off.

Plus, he'd need the money and training more than ever, to cope with the aura leeches. Yet where could he go from here? How was he going to help Melissa? For a moment he considered just sacrificing everything and converting all he had into a core for her. That might slow down her condition enough for her to live a long life. Yet he knew that too much would be lost in the transfer, especially since his lucrima soul had just been manipulated so much.

In fact, he had to consider that the debts might go to her next. He didn't think debts could be inherited, but apparently this was one of those things they never told poor people. No, the best way he could help her was to stay alive and work his way out of this. Besides, it wasn't like him to give up. Though he couldn't see the path through, he'd find a way.

While he walked home, his eyes wandered to the signs above the Branton Arena. Perhaps he could use his combat skills to earn more lucrim on the side. Obviously he couldn't compete in the Arena itself, and he knew that underground fights could be extremely dangerous, but he might be able to find something. His coworker Henry had mentioned participating in a few street fights, so maybe he would know.

The risk of injury, though... Rick went back and forth over the subject until he finally reached their apartment complex. Going up the stairs to the third floor, his entire body felt too heavy to move, but he forced himself to keep going. Just unlocking the door took a significant effort.

"Whoohoo, weekend!" Melissa grinned at him as soon as he entered. "I'm gonna get drunk and make poor life decisions!"

Normally he would have chuckled, but he was just too tired. Melissa immediately realized that something was wrong and her smile faded. She leapt up and helped him down onto the couch.

"You look pretty bad, Rick... what happened at the meeting?"

He told her the events without trying to hide how bad things were. There was no point keeping the truth from her or treating her like she was fragile just because of her condition. But when he finished, he saw the pain in his sister's eyes and realized that he'd made a mistake.

"I'm sorry... if it wasn't for me, you..."

"Don't say that." He put an arm around her shoulders and pulled her firmly to sit beside him. "Blaming each other... that's what our parents would do. And they're the reason we're in this mess, not you. We need to be better than them."

She stared at him sorrowfully for a time, then one corner of her lips twitched. "Good motivational speech, bro."

"I do what I can." He sighed and let himself relax fully back into the couch. "I'm gonna need to go to work early tomorrow, so we might as well talk now. Did you have a good week?"

"Mostly. There's this one girl at school... ugh, it feels petty compared to everything else."

"I've had a heavy day. I could use petty."

Rick sat back and talked with his sister, putting aside all thoughts of lucrim and fighting aside for a while. Just talking at home, he felt okay. There were plenty of people who lived their lives with less power or even greater debts, after all. If they could make it through, he could too.

Eventually he found himself getting rather sleepy. Melissa brought a blanket and tucked him in, but he couldn't go to sleep yet. Instead he forced himself through his normal exercises. It hurt, but it was even more necessary than usual after everything his lucrima had been through that day.

How many days of exercises would it take to build up enough to get rid of the aura leeches? He couldn't do the math in his head, but it would be a lot. But avoiding them would just make him fall further behind, and he couldn't allow that.

Before he finished his work, his phone rang. He considered ignoring it, then saw who it was and immediately picked up. "Uncle Frank?"

"Richard!" His uncle's voice was warm and resonant. "Sorry I haven't called lately, work has been busy. And I'm sorry to hear that you're going through such a rough time."

"Yeah, it's... things aren't great." He told the story again, almost the same as he had with Melissa. It felt somewhat humiliating to repeat it all, even though it wasn't his fault. But his uncle just listened thoughtfully and didn't cast any judgments. When Rick finished, Uncle Frank paused for only a moment before responding.

"I'm afraid they're right: all of that is completely legal. Some debts are discharged at death, but lobbyists have been pushing to restrict lucrim forgiveness for years. The good news is that you can definitely take care of these aura leeches. I'm not promising it will be easy, but you'll come out of it leaner and meaner."

"Thanks, Uncle Frank."

"I'd offer to come down and check on you, but I'm afraid work is going to make that hard. Though... would you consider taking a job here? You'd have to move across the world, but you and Melissa could move here and I could do better for you than that little gym. It wouldn't be charity, either - we need the help."

"That sounds tempting, but... it's the middle of a school year. I want to let Melissa graduate here."

"No, that makes sense. And I have to admit, it's hard to find good schools here." Uncle Frank was quiet for a while, then sighed. "Will you let me give you some advice? I think I have to insist on it, because I'll feel bad if I can't at least do that for you."

"Please, go ahead."

"If you just train normally, those leeches will be on you most of your life. There are people who get used to them, actually, but that's no way to live. What you want to do is invest all your lucrim directly into the leeches. You'll get rid of them much faster that way and you'll be able to restructure effectively once they're gone.

"Another thing: don't take any demonic bonds. I know they're usually harder to get, but the demons like exploiting weakness. I guarantee once your data gets sold, demon sects will come around offering you deals. Maybe even enough to to wipe out the debt entirely, but trust me, transferring it to a demonic bond is worse. Just refuse all offers."

The idea that they would prey on those who had little strength to give surprised him, but Rick realized that he shouldn't be surprised. They were demons, after all. Worse, they were demons organized into corporations. Expecting anything like mercy was foolish.

"Beyond that, just stay focused. You're a hard worker and a smart kid, so you'll dig yourself out of this."

"Thanks, Uncle Frank." He considered letting the conversation end there, but abruptly realized that he had another question to ask while he had his uncle on the line. "Oh, I had one more question. Have you ever heard of something called a 'Golden Core'? That's all it says in the app."

In response there was a long pause, so long he wondered if they had disconnected. When his uncle spoke again, his voice was a bit flatter. "It appeared after the other cores were implanted?"

"No, before that. I'm not sure exactly when."

"Richard... I can't tell you for sure what it is. Usually lucrima programs give color or metal names to cores that are unregistered. And it might not seem like it, but unregistered cores are bad news."

"Then it could be a problem? Should I get a specialist to check it?"

"No, don't do that. Just..." Another long pause. "Are you sure you don't know how it showed up?"

"Well, I can guess." Rick told the story about Mike and the other Birthrighters. Unlike usual, his uncle didn't ask any questions or make affirmative noises, just listened in silence. When it was finished, he sighed.

"Best case scenario, it's just a minor accident. Worst case scenario, you could get arrested for theft. Unless I'm entirely wrong, the 'Mike' you fought was Michael Maguire. His father is CEO of Maguire Incorporated, and it wouldn't be out of the question to think that he gave something experimental to his son."

"And it just... broke off in the fight somehow?"

"It's possible, not even that uncommon. A lot of Birthrighters often don't have great control, so these things happen." Uncle Frank sighed heavily. "I'm going to look into this further as soon as I can. Right now I recommend just not touching it."

Great, one more thing going wrong in his life. After what had happened that day, Rick wasn't even surprised. He and his uncle chatted for a while longer about less serious matters, but it was obvious they were both distracted.

As soon as the call ended, Rick lay down on the couch. Even tired as he was, it took him a long time to go to sleep.

Chapter 9: Picking Up the Pieces

When he woke up the next morning, Rick felt surprisingly refreshed. Oh, there were still three aura leeches inside his soul and his strength was still diminished, but he felt ready to take on this new challenge. Of course, it was his life, not just a challenge, but he wasn't going to back down.

It helped that Melissa was already awake, munching on a bowl of cereal in her room. When she heard he was awake she came out into the main room and they had a normal breakfast, not talking about anything serious and just joking with each other. Almost like it had been years ago, when they had been children with no other concerns.

Though Rick still resented his parents for leaving him with such a debt, he'd come to terms with it. He hadn't been born with a silver spoon in his mouth and he'd never been a Birthrighter, handed everything for free. It would have felt wrong to just be granted a powerful core in return for nothing - if he gained power, it would be power he earned himself.

Eventually, though, he saw the time and realized that he had to go. Melissa groaned and grabbed his arm ineffectually. "Are you *sure* you have to go? You can't get another day off?"

"Fat chance of that. If World War V happened tomorrow, Jimmy would still want me to come in the next day."

"And if the whole strip mall got nuked?"

"I'd have to put in overtime to rebuild it."

"Haha, I'm not looking forward to getting a job after I graduate." Melissa let go of his arm and just patted it. "Have a good time at work, then. But eventually we've gotta spend a whole weekend just lazing around like we used to, okay?"

"Yeah, sure." Rick smiled at her one more time, then grabbed his keys and headed out the door.

On his way to work he thought over the coming day. It was likely to be a fairly boring one, since he only had a few scheduled clients, not including Lisa. That meant a lot of time with walk-ins or trying to persuade new people to sign up. But it also meant he had plenty of time to work on his own issues.

It took him longer than normal to run to the strip mall, since he'd grown used to a bit of extra speed from his lucrima. The difference between 15,000 and 11,000 wasn't much - pocket change to many warriors - but it meant every part of his body was working just a little bit less efficiently. His foundation especially was struggling to maintain itself.

That was his answer, he realized abruptly. What he needed most of all was free lucrim to destroy the aura leeches, which meant he needed the fastest possible profit. Though it might not be easy to improve his foundation, it was definitely the least efficient part of his lucrima soul, hence the most room for improvement.

Rick cut off all extra strength to his body and forced himself to run the rest of the way on purely human stamina. He was already pretty frugal with his energy expenditure, using practically nothing compared to the people sprinting through special lanes or flying overhead, but he could improve. Every drop of extra power he could squeeze out of himself would go into improving his foundation and giving him an edge.

When he arrived at work, he found that Henry was sparring with Darin. Rick kept his eyes down and tried not to look at the difficult client, just checking in with Jimmy and changing into workout clothes. But he wasn't able to avoid attention entirely, as Darin noticed him on his way out.

"So, it's the little genius." Darin cast him a scornful look. "Did you get *weaker*? What could you possibly blow so much lucrim on so quickly?"

"Family emergency." Rick kept a polite smile on his face, though it was a struggle.

"Right, always a 'family emergency' with your type. Does that mean you knocked up some poor girl?"

Before Rick could answer, Henry hopped up beside them, grinning like he didn't notice any tension at all. "Great progress today, Darin! Look forward to seeing you next week!"

Darin grunted. "Sure, next week." He gave Rick one more look and then stomped out of the gym. That left it entirely empty, though the lull wouldn't last for long.

As soon as his client was out of sight, Henry glanced over with an apologetic shrug. "Just don't let him get to you. But are you doing okay, man?"

"Had some rough times." Rick did *not* want to explain what happened again, especially to coworkers. "I'm going to need to play catch up. Hey... I'm not sure how to ask this, but you do some fights on the side, right?"

"No need to whisper like it's something super illegal." Henry did glance toward their boss and lower his voice, though. "The cops look the other way when it comes to the underground fights, since we're sort of under the umbrella of legit organizations. It's a hobby, anyway - why?"

"I need extra lucrim right now."

"I get that, but... I don't know if I'd recommend it." After an awkward pause, Henry dropped his gaze. "Look, man, I won't lie: the lowest tier of fights is brutal. People aren't there to see skill, they want to see people kick the shit out of each other. And the way you are right now, you'd go in the lowest tier. I didn't get out until I managed that demonic bond."

Rick sighed and nodded. That was the answer he had more or less expected.

"And if you didn't guess it, you don't get any health care. Hell, Jimmy doesn't give us any health care." Henry said that part louder in the direction of their boss, who flipped them off without looking up from his magazine. "Now me, I'm on my parents' healthcare plan until I'm 25, so I just have to keep myself alive. But if I'm not pretty strong by the time I'm on my own... I think I'd probably quit. Just not worth it."

"Yeah, I can see that. Thanks, I was just asking." He had far too much to lose, so the risk didn't seem worth it. Instead, he'd just have to see how far he could get on his own.

Most of the rest of the day blurred past. In between sparring, or while outside trying to attract new clients, Rick did his best to search for new foundation techniques.

True, looking for lucrima techniques on the internet was not exactly glamorous. But his family had no secret arts, he couldn't afford access to the big skill databases, and he had no way of entering one of the hidden sects. The internet was the best he could do. Besides, everything was fiercely debated on the lucrim forums, so even if it was a bit difficult to sort through it all, he did get quite a bit information about many of the basic options.

By the end of his shift, he thought he'd made a good choice. He was usually experienced enough to have good instincts about these things, but just in case, he went over to his boss's counter and displayed the Wikipedia article about the technique on his phone.

"Have you heard about this one, boss?"

"Buffet's Buffer?" Jimmy glanced at the phone briefly and shrugged. "You could do worse. The problem is, everyone thinks they can do the technique, but most actually can't. Most people online who say they're doing the Buffer technique are just aura masturbating, basically. If it was that easy to make your foundation more efficient, everyone would do it."

"I get that, but most people online said that it's more likely to work if you've been exposed to heavy lucrim fluctuation."

His boss actually looked up at him for a moment, then grunted affirmatively. "Give it a try, kid. You'll probably hit the limit of what you can do with it for now pretty soon, but you won't waste your time until then."

Having his plan confirmed, Rick walked back across the gym to one of the meditation machines. They were nothing fancy, just metal contraptions with comfortable seats that allowed for either straight meditation or combined muscular exercise. Rick placed his hands lightly on the bars and pushed them just enough to feel tension through his body, then focused on the technique.

In the past when he'd tried to improve his foundation, he'd quickly realized that he was accomplishing nothing. It was just too central to the same power he was using to try to make the changes. Yet he was surprised to find that he almost immediately made progress, summoning his aura and then folding it on itself.

Getting beaten by arrogant Birthrighters... draining all his lucrim into his sister... fighting his uncle... enduring the aura leeches... Rick took all of those violent fluctuations in his power and converted them into fuel.

When he completed the exercise, he had partially condensed his foundation. His aura was just as strong as before, but it now required a smaller investment of lucrim to maintain that strength. Almost 200 less, according to his phone. That meant he could reinvest those lucrim into his cores, though instead he sent them toward the aura leeches.

They thrashed within him and then went quiet, sated by the surge of power. For a time he felt rather light and he knew that he was going to be glad he took his uncle's advice. According to the internet, the leeches partially fed themselves and partially absorbed power to pay off the debt. Just letting them drink normally, they'd barely pay off one lucrim a day, which meant it would take an absurd 26 years to pay it all off.

He wasn't letting those things stay inside his soul for that long. Lucrim he pushed into them were lost to him, but they got him far closer to being free of them entirely. In the long run, it would pay off.

Over the next several days, Rick focused on repeating the Buffer technique. Unfortunately, the value of it decreased each time. Still worth repeating, and he enjoyed the improvements in efficiency, but it was obvious that he needed more experience to get more out of it.

Next Thursday, it was finally time for another session with Lisa. She came in just a bit late this time, apologizing and quickly tugging off her jacket to spar. When she really looked at him, though, she hesitated. "Wow, Rick... are you okay?"

"I'm fine." He moved out onto the mats, but even as she followed she kept staring at him.

"Are you sure? I can't feel the source of the leak, but it feels serious... if someone did that to you, you should really press charges."

"No, it was completely legal. This is the Birthright Core my parents left me." He sounded incredibly bitter and regretted it, but Lisa only nodded in sad understanding.

"That's absolutely awful. My parents are far from rich, but they've always tried to take care of themselves so they'll never be a burden on their kids."

"Let's just spar, okay?"

He managed to work off some of his frustrations sparring with her, though Lisa struggled to suppress herself down to his new level. After knocking him to the ground for the third time, she pretended to be tired and headed to the side. Needing some time to recover, he went with her.

"Is there anything I can do, Rick?" She handed him a water bottle, at least not pitying him. "I don't like seeing you like this."

"Actually, I wanted to ask about that. My parents' debt is being taken via aura leeches... I know you can't just remove them but is there anything you can do to make them drain less or something like that?"

"Afraid not. There *are* some lucrima massages that will ease the pain, or make them sleep temporarily, but those aren't real solutions. They just loosen up your body so you can use your lucrim more effectively, so they don't do much to help the underlying problem."

"That's fine. You actually knew more than I expected - have you worked with aura leeches before?"

"More than you'd think." Lisa sighed and leaned back against the wall. "There are some clients - mostly fighters or businessmen who have gone into debt - who decide to accept that they'll never pay them off. Instead they just find ways to deal with the drain. If they can increase their overall lucrim generation rate more than the drain, they figure they can mostly ignore it."

Rick blinked, not having even considered that option. It definitely wasn't a choice for him, not when the leeches took such a large percentage of his strength. "That sounds like a rough way to live. Though I guess it's good that you get regular work."

Lisa laughed. "Oh, I wouldn't say so. Aura leeches make people feel a bit creepy, so I'd rather never work with them again."

He wasn't sure if she was intentionally cutting off any possibility of him asking for direct help. Not that he would have asked. Back when she'd become a client, he'd figured out that there was no way he could afford her massages, at least not the ones that had an impact on lucrima.

In any case, Lisa didn't treat him any differently and they kept up their normal schedule. Rick threw himself into his work and his exercises, making as much progress as he could. As his uncle had suggested, he started receiving offers for demonic bonds, but he turned them all down. Practically aura leeches by another name, that much was becoming clear to him.

Days later, he found himself walking to work on another Saturday. He had to resist checking his progress too often, but since it had been two weeks since the disastrous meeting with the lawyers, he decided it was worth it. Rick pulled out his phone, scanned his aura, and looked over the results thoughtfully.

[Name: Rick Hunter

Ether Tier: 18th

Ether Score: 153

Lucrim Generation: 20,650

Effective Rate: 11,500

Current Lucrim: 1541]

[Rick Hunter's Lucrima Portfolio

Foundation: 7750 (Lv II)

Offensive Lucore: 3575 (Lv II)

Defensive Lucore: 6100 (Lv IV)

Birthright Core: 1944 (Lv I)

Birthright Core: 1108 (Lv I)

Aura Leech: -4860 (Stage II)

Aura Leech: -2857 (Stage I)

Aura Leech: -1368 (Stage III)

Golden Lucore: 10 (N/A)

Gross Lucrim: 20,650

Net Lucrim: 11,500]

It was decent progress, much better than average for a period of two weeks. But it wasn't enough. Melissa had been completely healthy during that span, but it was only a matter of time before she had another fit. In an emergency he could buy more medicine for her, but he was usually too lucrim-starved to be able to help her if there wasn't time for that.

Though he didn't like the idea, as he walked to work he convinced himself of it. When he entered, he was glad to see that Jimmy was gone, leaving Henry at the counter. He glanced up and smiled.

"Hey, man, what's up?"

Rick took a deep breath. "Can you get me into the underground fights?"

Chapter 10: The Underground

Rick lived in a bad part of town, but as they headed away from the suburbs of Branton, he realized that there were very different kinds of bad. In his neighborhood everyone knew the meth dealers and cops always traveled with lucrim weapons. But the one he was entering was where he suspected the meth came from, and he doubted the police came by very often.

As he got further in, he regularly saw demolished houses. A few of them might have been formally taken down, but more looked as though they had been burned or smashed apart. Arson, fights, accidents? There was no way to tell, though he suspected some of all three.

Beyond that, the people were different. There was some violence in his part of town, but everyone generally kept to themselves, casting suspicious looks at most. If people had looked at him with the sort of predatory cruelty he saw now, he would never have let Melissa live there.

"Don't look nervous. If you look nervous, they'll target you," Henry said. This was not helpful.

"You think that's going to make me *less* nervous?"

"You shouldn't be, man. We might not be hotshot fighters carrying a lot of lucrim, but that actually works in our favor. We're dangerous enough that nobody is going to bother us, not for what we'd be worth to them. I mean, don't carry anything too valuable through here, but you'll be fine."

Trying to settle into that mindset, Rick pretended to ignore the others as they walked through the dingy streets. "Nobody recognizes you from the fights?"

"Nah, man, I haven't been fighting long enough for anyone to have a clue I exist. You've gotta understand, way more people try out the fights than stick around. Either they survive and get the money they need, or they get seriously injured, or they just realize they aren't as strong as they thought they were and run off."

"Huh. Does that mean that most of the people in the lowest tiers aren't very experienced?"

"You got it. Seriously, man, you'll be fine."

They finally left the street, entering what appeared to be an abandoned warehouse. There were several men and women loitering around the entrance who looked dangerous, but when Henry nodded to them, they just nodded back. Inside... it turned out to be an abandoned warehouse.

Henry chuckled at his expression. "The arena is underneath. This way."

Several more guards emerged from the shadows, this time getting in their way. Henry nudged Rick to step forward, so he cleared his throat and didn't back down. "I'm... here to sign up for the fights."

"Fine." A huge man in a biker's jacket gestured for them to follow. "We'll take you to Alger."

They headed to what appeared to be a random dusty spot in the warehouse, but their guide stepped onto a piece of metal and passed lucrim to it. The floor began to move, the apparent dust remaining fixed in place. Fake dust. They were a bit too serious about security, given that these fights were supposed to be quasi-legal.

The secret entrance led to a narrow set of stairs lit by only a single flickering light bulb. As they left the sky entirely behind Rick felt tenser, but he saw that Henry was still taking everything in stride and told himself that this was what he needed to do.

Once they left the stairs, they entered a surprisingly nice room. Despite being in a hidden underground location, it had a carpet and several old but comfortable-looking couches. Unlike the flickering light bulb from before, the entire room was lit with soft lights that gave the place a pleasant look. Though the biker nodded for them to sit, they didn't get a chance before a man walked in through another door.

"Do we have another volunteer? Just in time!" The new arrival wore a dark purple suit and a red hat, just on the line between stylish and absurd. He entered smiling, but when he saw them his expression flattened. "Hmm, this one looks a bit desperate. Too many like that these days."

Apparently this was the "Alger" he was supposed to meet? Henry had mentioned that the owner handled a surprising amount of business personally, so this must be him. Wanting to make a good impression, Rick nodded politely. "Good evening, sir. I was hoping to-"

"Get him signed up." Alger ignored him entirely and waved at the biker. "Hurry with it. I want to get two melees in early."

As the man left, Rick watched him carefully. The most troubling thing was that he seemed to have no lucrima at all, which would have meant he was dead. Eventually he realized that Alger simply had the ability to suppress his aura beyond anyone he'd ever met before. A strange man and a strange meeting. Rick looked to Henry, who shrugged.

"Alger is the owner, and he's weird. He forms opinions about people really quickly. Didn't seem to like you, but that's just as well."

"Enough talking." The biker gestured for them to follow through another door. "Let's get you signed up."

They entered another comfortable room, this one with a desk and several sheets of paper. The form was extremely simple, however, just giving his name, lucrim generation rate, and desired types of matches. Except the bottom section for matches was already filled in.

"New scrubs have to start with the general melees," the biker explained. "That's even below the bottom tier. To get into fights proper, you've gotta buy in."

"Buy in?" Rick stopped signing his name and looked up skeptically. Risking a few injuries was one thing, but if he needed to bet money, or worse, lucrim...

"Nah, not like that. With points." The biker didn't seem inclined to say more, so Henry sat down on the desk beside him and explained.

"The Underground has a points system to group fighters into different brackets. You'll still usually be against people with similar lucrim generation, it's just a question of if you're important. You can't get into any of the more lucrative matches until you've earned points in the general melees."

That wasn't so different than he'd been expecting, then. Rick finished filling out the form, which the biker only glanced at briefly before nodding. "Alright, let's go. You fighting too?"

Henry shook his head. "Nah, I don't have a brawl tonight and I wouldn't be fighting against you anyway. Knock em dead, Rick."

"It's just a phrase, but..." The biker gave Rick a hard look, then turned to go. "Don't actually knock anyone dead. Accidents happen, but they cause problems. You hurt anybody too bad in a normal match, you'll be docked points. Just focus on keeping yourself standing for the first few matches."

With that, he was shuffled out through another door. Rick had expected some more time to talk to Henry, find out what he could expect for his first fight, but he was already out of time. As he was pushed onward into a less pleasant room with chain link fences on either side, he hoped he wouldn't regret this decision.

After the surprisingly pleasant back rooms, the main arena was more like what he expected. It was a massive room lit only by harsh white lights suspended overhead. A large part of the filthy floor was fenced off entirely, with barbed wire overhead. Outside the fences there were cheap bleachers on all sides except for the entrance paths.

His eyes were first drawn to all the people already in the ring. Plenty of suspicious-looking types and several who were clearly suffering from withdrawal. Rick winced as he saw how many of them had generation rates of 20,000 lucrim or more. If this turned into a brawl, it could be ugly.

But since the match hadn't started yet, he made sure to check the stands as well. Right now there were only a few people watching, including Henry. He assumed that other matches would be better attended. Just before he looked back down, he saw that Alger was present as well, though he sat with a bored expression, barely seeming to look at the arena at all.

They all waited in the center awkwardly, not talking to one another. Rick just focused on breathing evenly, gathering his strength internally. He could do this, though it would be wise to immediately get his back to one of the fences and avoid getting involved in the main melee.

"Is that everyone?" Alger finally looked up, though his expression suggested that he didn't hope for much. "Alright, then... fight!"

He snapped his fingers, somehow producing a ringing sound. A few of the tougher-looking fighters immediately launched themselves at the people nearest them and suddenly the arena became an ugly brawl.

Rick started to back up, only to have an old man throw himself at him with a knife. They were allowed weapons in this match? Desperately reacting on instinct, he dodged the knife, grabbed the man's arm, and threw him to the floor.

Considering the man's age and feeble frame, he crashed down and didn't rise. Rick felt a bit guilty even though he'd been attacked with a knife, but he didn't have time for guilt, because a much more muscular man was charging at his back. He whirled, starting with a testing jab to the face.

His blow connected. Rick was almost as surprised as the other fighter, but recovered faster and hit him with an elbow to the side of the head, knocking him to the floor.

What startled him so much was that his opponent had nearly 20,000 lucrim. Yet it was completely disorganized, even before taking the blow to the head. Rick realized that his opponent was just some young gangster looking for a fight, not someone who had trained properly. He'd probably just earned his lucrim at work, not solidified it via training.

Though he tried not to get overconfident, Rick couldn't help but begin to move more surely. Opponents came at him from different angles, never in an organized formation, and so he took them down one at a time. They weren't warriors, just desperate for money or too naive to know their own limits.

One man in a cut-off leather jacket obviously knew what he was doing, but Rick had no intention of playing fairly. He slammed an elbow into the back of the man's head, knocking him forward. Since his lucrima was actually organized, the man only stumbled a bit before whirling on him, fists flying.

Rick backed away, deflecting or dodging the blows. This opponent obviously had experience and he was no slouch, so it took him a while to find an opening. Eventually his opponent overextended his leg, so Rick lashed out, kicking him in the shin, then slammed an elbow into his chest.

Except the man caught the blow. Though Rick was surprised, he didn't hesitate for a moment and headbutted the other man directly in the face.

That finally dropped him. Rick took a step back, breathing heavily and looking for more contestants. Too late he felt someone jump onto his back, trying to stab with a rusty knife, but Rick elbowed him in the throat before he could connect. The man dropped and Rick automatically turned to kick him in the side and make sure he stayed down.

Now he was the only one left standing. Though Rick should have been happy, he found himself considering his own performance. He'd been sparring for a long time, but he hadn't expected it would translate into a brawl like this. Since all his martial arts focused on discipline, he had expected it to be difficult to harm other human beings, but it had come surprisingly easily to him. Was that normal, or did it say something about him?

"Oh, bravo! Bravo!" Alger stood up, clapping. His face had completely transformed from the boredom earlier, instead overflowing with cheerfulness. "Well done, lad! I didn't think you had the spirit of a fighter, but I see I was wrong! One point for participating, one for making it through, and one for being the last person standing!"

"Uh..." Rick looked around for other officials, but there was no one. "Do I need to record my points somewhere?"

"Never fear, that's all handled by computers these days. Someone really must have you download the program for it. You can't get it in the app store, you'll understand." Alger flowed down the bleachers to the edge of the fence, watching him with bright eyes. "I must say, lad, I think I like you. In return for showing me such spirit, how about I give you a little gift, hmm?"

Rick had no idea how to take that, so his gaze wandered to Henry. To his surprise, his coworker made a hasty cutting sign across his neck, but when Rick turned back, it was already too late. Alger fixed him with a beaming smile, a perfect picture of contentment and satisfaction.

"Normally you would have to wait until the next introductory melee, but I'll waive the rules in your case. Oh, this is exciting... you get a chance to earn more points right now! Send everybody in!"

He opened his mouth to object, but it didn't matter. Staff rushed into the arena, dragging out the fallen fighters. More importantly, they brought with them new fighters, and these were not desperate novices off the streets.

All of them had lucrim generation rates between 15,000 and 30,000, but that wasn't the worst of it. Every single one of them had hardened their lucrim into combat cores and they clearly had experience fighting. There was another biker, a young woman carrying a spiked club, an old man in combat leathers, a man who had to be over seven feet tall and 300 pounds of muscle... there was a lot of diversity, but they all looked like they had been through multiple melees.

"I do hope you enjoy the match!" Alger gave him another bright smile, then sat down, crossed one leg over the other, and laced his fingers over his knee. "Oh, this will be such fun. Fight!"

He snapped his fingers, the room rang with another clear tone, and then everyone attacked at once.

Chapter 11: Bonus Melee

With powerful warriors charging from every side, Rick did the smart thing and leapt for cover.

There was no actual cover to be found in the arena, of course, but he managed to jump beside one of the fences before he was attacked. He noted with some discomfort that the entrance paths had all been closed off, trapping them all inside until the melee was done.

He realized he should have asked more about the rules and cursed himself under his breath. But during the previous round, he'd been given points separately for making it through and for being the last person standing. Though he didn't see a timer anywhere, the distinction implied it might be possible for more than one person to get through a melee still conscious.

Though as he watched the brawl spread out, he wasn't sure that he'd be one of them.

The huge man who looked like he should be brawling was throwing freaking lightning from his hands. Not just a flashy trick, either, but bolts that moved faster than anyone could possibly dodge. They didn't appear strong enough to take someone down, and there was some inaccuracy, yet they were sending people flying in all directions.

Others had pulled out their own tricks. More than a few threw aura spheres. Someone had lit up in green flame. Another had summoned a shield and sword that glowed a brilliant white. He didn't know who was doing it, but he heard the sound of aura gunshots. There was just too much going on at once...

So he focused on the woman swinging a spiked club directly at his head.

Rick dodged backward, but she came after him just as quickly. When he tried to dodge again he ended up stumbling, somehow turning it into a roll. By the time he got back to his feet she was right on top of him again, swinging her spiked club overhead, but he managed to grab her arms before she could properly build up momentum.

Not wanting to test her in direct combat, Rick instead redirected her momentum, sending her stumbling into others. One of the aura shooters caught sight of her and released a sphere. It was batted out of the air with the club and then the two of them were engaged, but Rick had no time to notice because he had to dodge away from bursts of flame coming in his direction.

It was just too much. Too many opponents, too many variables - the exact opposite of the tactical one-on-one matches he'd trained in. He didn't even know how *many* opponents he was facing and briefly wished that he'd counted, but now it was too late.

Then he felt a pain in his chest, followed by the sound of a gunshot.

He looked down numbly and saw a hole in his shirt, with a spot of blood behind it. For a moment he thought that he was dying, but realized that it had only been a low caliber aura pistol. If it had been firing lucrim bullets, he would be dead.

But there was no time to think about that, because a bolt of lightning shot through him the next moment. His defensive core couldn't begin to defend against it and he shook violently, overwhelmed by the pain. Before he could recover, someone hit him in the face and he slammed back into the filthy floor.

Lying there, Rick stared at the barbed wire spinning overhead. The smart thing to do was just stay down. While he wasn't outclassed in this fight, he had no superiority over any of his opponents, so he didn't have much of a chance in a chaotic melee like this.

However... his biggest problem was lack of experience, and he wasn't going to gain any experience lying on the floor. So Rick slowly managed to pull himself back to his feet.

As soon as he was up, someone targeted him again, but he managed to slump out of the way of the aura spheres. He devoted all his attention to trying to stay upright, tracking all his opponents and make sure that none of them could take him down.

The first thing he needed to do was categorize all of them, get an exact sense for all the threats he faced. That was easier now, as several others had gone down and not risen. Four physical brawlers, two aura shooters, the man with the lightning, the woman with the club, the flame guy...

Before he could focus too much, the melee enveloped him again and he was forced to defend himself. Yet it was getting a little easier. He didn't have eyes in the back of his head, but he was getting a sense for avoiding obvious openings. There was a rhythm even in the chaotic melee, so if he could just master it... yes, just a little more, then he could begin fighting back...

A bell rang and the remaining fighters slowed to a halt.

Though his body wanted to collapse on the ground, he ended up just standing there. Not to prove his endurance, but because he was stunned. The entire match had finished without him properly attacking anyone. That wasn't awful for his first battle, and it was probably a valid tactic, yet he found that he was disappointed in himself. Not good enough.

"Hey, not bad, man." Henry came up beside him, grinning. "I got my face bashed in during my first match and had to take like three days off. I think you should sit down, though."

"Yes... maybe sit down..." Rick numbly went with him, moving through one of the open doors to the bleachers.

He realized that the stands had partially filled during the match. Given how noisy the crowd was when no one was fighting, he was surprised that he hadn't noticed them. His focus had been entirely on the battle, though if he'd known he had such an audience, he might not have been able to ignore them and ended up choking.

"They had..." Rick shook his head sharply, trying to banish his confusion. "Everybody seemed to have invested heavily in an ability core. Is that standard here?"

"Oh, definitely. Makes you stand out from the crowd."

"Does that matter?"

"If you want to get picked out for the important matches, it definitely does." Henry pointed his chin toward the opposite side of the stands and Rick realized that there were seats beyond the bleachers. They were cloaked in shadows beyond the main lights, but enclosed viewing areas wrapped around half the arena. "Nobody important will be watching a random melee like this, but there's more than just fighting in the Underground. Lots of people bet on the matches, or even sponsor fighters. If you get lucky enough, you might get a patron."

"Huh. Does that happen often?"

"Most of us are grubbing along, just hoping for that." Henry sat back and sighed. "Honestly, I think I have a better shot of getting picked by one of those independent mystics. No, for me the Underground is just about earning a bit extra on the side."

"Fair enough." Rick mentally set such subjects aside and focused on what mattered. "How did I do? Do I get any kind of reward for participating?"

"Ah, yeah, let me get that set up for you."

Henry pulled out his own phone and showed him how to get the official app for the Underground. It was unsigned, and Rick was a bit nervous about putting it on his phone, but he figured that he didn't keep anything important on there anyway. Eventually it was all set up and he connected his account, soon being given a clear screen:

[Melee Performance:

Participation +3

Endured Match +7

Fall (x1) -1

Passive -1

Total Reward: 8

Cumulative Points: 11]

The system was easy to understand, at least. He assumed the "Passive" modifier was a penalty for not getting involved with the fight, but since it only cost him one point, that meant that just dodging was an entirely valid strategy. Not a satisfying one, and he resolved to do better, but this was about being successful, not about his pride.

"Ah, yeah, lost a point for not attacking." Henry read over his shoulder and nodded knowingly. "You can get -2 or -3 for that, though, so it's not as bad as it could be. Anyway, what you want to do is get 100 points as quickly as possible, so you're not thrown into the worst matches. Believe me, these melees are chaotic, but they're gentle compared to the other options."

"That's nice, but you never answered my more important question. Do I get paid for this? You can't exactly buy food with 'points'."

"For that, you'll need to talk to Alger. I mean, usually someone else handles it, but-"

At that moment Alger appeared beside them, grinning down. "I usually try to greet the new arrivals! Come right this way, into my office... these stands can be so noisy, can't they?"

The crowds parted when he strode away, so Rick and Henry followed after him. They left the main arena and returned to the office-like area. It was surprisingly quiet in comparison, enough that he realized that his ears were still ringing from the fight. He'd need to be careful not to end up with long term damage from all this.

"That wasn't bad!" Alger sat down on the edge of his desk and pulled his legs up into crossed position. "A bit cowardly, but I liked that you were trying to get a read on your opponents. I think I do like you a bit after all. Would you like another little gift?"

"Uh... no thank you." Rick didn't need to see Henry's nervous expression to know that he did not want to see what Alger would force him into next. The owner of the Underground sighed in disappointment, but nodded as if he'd been expecting it.

"You already got the program on your phone, yes? And you'll get your money from one of my associates. I just wanted to welcome you." Alger hopped to his feet with one hand sweeping to his chest. "There's so little space left for a noble warrior in our society! Oh, there's lucrim left and right, but where's the *soul* of it all?

"There was a time when combat schools ruled the world, and powerful individuals could change the course of history! We were better men and women then, seeking power and respect above all else, living for the thrill of combat! Now... now the bureaucrats rule the world and control the lucrim. Fights like these are the last refuge of the true warrior!"

Rick just stared at him, unsure how to take such a speech. He decided that nodding would be a good idea.

"So glad you agree! I really do think you have the spark of a warrior in you... try not to get killed, will you? That would be inconvenient for all of us." With that, Alger hopped up and sped out of the office, leaving both of them sitting uncertainly.

After a pause, Rick cleared his throat. "Is he always like that?"

"Yeah." Henry sighed and slumped back into his chair. "From what I've seen, anyway. He liked my first melee too, but I don't know how often he-"

"A lot." The gruff voice interrupted them and they turned to see the biker from before entering the room. "He gets depressed if he goes more than a day without finding someone to get excited about. You did okay, kid, but trust me: you want to get to 100 points as soon as possible so Alger can't throw you into the meat grinder."

Though Rick wanted to ask about that, he wasn't sure where to start. Before he could, the biker opened a lucrim-reinforced and ether-enchanted safe on the wall and pulled out several wrapped bundles of cash. Rick felt a moment of pleased surprise before the biker tugged out only a few bills and handed them to him.

"There's your money. Aside from that..." He flicked a crimson marble into the air and Rick barely managed to make his body move in time to catch it. "That's all you get. See you next time, kid."

It was enough. Rick rolled the marble slowly between his hands, feeling the lucrim within. Roughly 250, which was small change to most true warriors, but significant for him. The money might help, but the raw lucrim was what would let him get rid of the aura leeches. He was tempted to try to apply it to them immediately, but realized that this might not be the best place for that.

"Come on." Henry tugged his arm to pull him up. "They're pretty casual about things around here, but if we lurk around the offices they'll get mad. But good job today."

"Thanks, Henry. And thanks for bringing me here."

"Not a problem, man. You want to stick around and see all the other fights? I wasn't going to fight because I have to work tomorrow, but this is what I do a lot of nights."

It would be good preparation for potential future matches, but Rick found that he was too tired. Even if he hadn't taken a debilitating injury, he'd taken a serious beating. "Maybe another time. I'm wiped out for today."

"Yeah, that makes sense. Come on, let's go get something to drink. I'll buy for you this time, but after this, we're competitors. No friends in the Underground, huh?"

Rick wasn't sure how to respond to that. He gripped the marble tightly in his hand and hoped that he hadn't made a mistake.

Chapter 12: Special Event

Participating in an underground fighting tournament seemed like it should be the sort of thing that would revolutionize someone's life, but in the end not much changed.

Rick worked the fights into his schedule as if they were just an extracurricular activity. He developed a three day cycle: fight on the first day, training exercises to solidify his gains on the second, recovery on the third. Occasionally he extended the latter two steps as necessary, since he absolutely needed to avoid taking a permanent injury.

So far he hadn't been in serious danger. It seemed that many of the main melee contestants were just looking for a friendly fight. That wouldn't stop them from smashing you in the face or shooting you, but they weren't out to kill. A few times they'd ganged up on him and he'd gone down, but he'd only needed to use some of his winnings for healing with no long term harm done.

Of course, he kept hearing hints of much bloodier matches. There had definitely been blood left in the arena sometimes when he arrived, and based on the crowds, he could easily imagine more dangerous events. But so far, he'd played it safe, content with the smaller rewards available.

After the first, he'd competed in six general melees. That had earned him 1500 lucrim, a decent amount of extra cash, and 51 points. He'd intended to put all the lucrim toward getting rid of the leeches, but instead invested much of it into his combat cores, using the justification that he needed to get stronger if he wanted to keep earning. It might just be an excuse because he was getting more of a taste for combat, though.

In any case, he didn't regret another use of his winnings: doing a little better for himself and Melissa. When she aced a set of tests, he decided to splurge and they ordered out from a decent Chinese place. Both of them sat on the floor of their living room eating out of their to-go boxes when Melissa abruptly looked up at him seriously.

"Where'd you get the money for this, Rick?"

He didn't hesitate a second. "Selling meth."

"Be serious."

"Fine, I got it by *taking* meth. It's a very complex scheme."

That got a bit of a smile from her, but she didn't joke back, so he knew she was serious. Rick examined his sister for a moment, realizing that there was really no question as to what he should do. Obviously it was best to be honest with his own family. That didn't mean he couldn't stretch it out more, though.

"In all seriousness, I've been selling my body. A randy old rich woman-"

"Richard Hunter!" Melissa folded her arms and pretended to scowl. "If you don't stop messing around, I shall be *very* cross!"

He paused for a moment, finishing his current mouthful, then set down his box. "I'm fighting in a place called the Underground. So far it's been mostly safe, but I'm not sure that will last. I didn't want to worry you unnecessarily, but I get that it was a bit of a dick move to keep it secret. Sorry."

"Oh, is that all?" Melissa sat back and began chopsticking more food into her mouth. "I saw that you were in bad shape some days after you came back, so I was worried that you were getting into something drug-related."

"Seriously?"

"Not, like, dealing heroin or something. But I figure people who sell lucrim-related drugs probably need muscle to do things, and my imagination got away from me thinking about how you might have convinced yourself you had to get involved. But underground fights? That's not such a big deal."

"I'm glad you're taking it well."

"I mean, now I do kind of want to go with you and see you fight, but I'm guessing there's no way that you'd let me do that, huh?"

"Absolutely not." Rick spoke more sharply than he'd intended, but didn't apologize. He tried to never pull rank with his sister or act like a parent, but he didn't want that idea going anywhere. "It's been safe so far, but I'm honestly in over my head, Melissa. I need to get stronger and learn a lot more about how the Underground works before I feel remotely safe there."

"That's fine, I get it. I wish you didn't have to do this, but..." Melissa drifted off and he stayed silent to give her time to think.

But some time later, when she set down her box, he saw her hands trembling violently. Rick immediately pushed his food aside and moved closer to her, checking her forehead. No fever, but she was trembling all over and he could feel her body's lucrima destabilizing.

"I-I'm okay." Her words were barely a whisper. "This is... a m-m-minor one..."

"We should still take it seriously." Rick leapt up to fetch her medication and brought her a pill with a glass of water. Her hands shook when she took the pill, but she managed it without spilling much water. He considered taking her to rest, but she resisted when he started to pick her up.

"No... I was having fun..."

His instincts told him to carry her anyway, but she did know her own body better than he did. Besides, the shivering seemed to be subsiding, even before the medicine would have taken effect. Just to be sure, he passed some of his lucrim into her body. It disappeared into a void, as usual, but the emptiness seemed weaker than before.

There'd been a time when he'd hoped that small incidents like this meant that she was getting better. Rick no longer held much hope of that, he was just glad that the danger had passed. Melissa scooted a bit so that she could lean back against the couch, then reached for her food.

"Gimme." He passed it to her as he sat down beside her, their backs against the couch as they faced the dark television. Melissa shoveled food into her face for a bit before speaking up again. "Have you learned big fancy techniques like they always have in the movies?"

Rick chuckled. "You're joking, but there's actually more of that than I thought. The fights ultimately make money by attracting an audience, so I guess it makes sense."

"Huh. So are you seriously gonna get something flashy?"

"Not for now. I've done a little research on it, and it requires a substantial investment in a new core. I don't think it makes any sense to do that until I've improved my foundation and gotten rid of the aura leeches."

"So you're just going to run around punching people, huh?" Melissa smiled over at him. "You're not dressed for it. Doesn't this underground fighting ring have some sort of dress code? Bunch of S&M-looking gear or something?"

"There's no dress code, but I might have to expand my wardrobe."

"Or you could go the other way and kick ass in a frilly pink tutu. That'd definitely give you a psychological edge in a fight, wouldn't it?"

"I think they'd get over it way before we started fighting."

"Nope, that's why you'd wear one of those big flasher coats. You'd really freak them out thinking you were some kind of pervert, then you'd throw it off to reveal the tutu and they'd *know* you were a huge pervert. That'd probably be enough to take them out on its own, no punching needed."

Though he stayed alert for any further complication from her condition, the night passed without incident. Despite the brief scare, it was actually quite relaxing, and he felt better now that he'd told Melissa about the fights. A cynical part of him said that it was necessary, since there might come a day when he couldn't come home, but all he could do was keep working as carefully as possible.

On his next fight day, he headed out earlier than usual in order to catch Henry's fight. His coworker had been skipping more days at the House of the Cosmic Fist lately - Jimmy wasn't happy, but apparently Henry was starting to make enough money from some of his fights that he could afford fewer hours. It might be interesting to check on his progress.

By now the route to the Underground was familiar. Nobody really recognized him, but he had the confidence to walk through the neighborhood with no more than normal caution. Ever since the first time, he'd entered via a different secret entrance that led directly to the main arena, though the procedure was basically the same.

Inside, he discovered that he was a bit late. Pushing through the crowds, Rick searched through the melee for Henry. Odd that there were so many people for a simple brawl like this. Though Henry wasn't on the trash tier like he was, the melees generally didn't get a huge audience. Perhaps there was someone popular taking part.

At that moment a yellow light pulsed through the underground complex, briefly illuminating even the upper boxes. Rick tracked the source and finally found Henry, his eyes glowing yellow and his body encased in phantasmal yellow armor. He struck out and sent one of his opponents flying, then tore into the others.

Huh, maybe Henry was the one people had come to see.

Though the armor was definitely powerful, it wasn't enough to completely dominate the match. Henry seemed to know that, choosing his opponents intentionally and avoiding getting mobbed. As he watched the fight, Rick realized that it wasn't exactly armor: instead, it was more like a ghostly shell in the shape of a rather stereotypical demon.

That might explain how he'd gained so much strength so quickly. The bell rang to end the match and the remaining fighters all cooled down, giving Rick a chance to check Henry's profile:

[Name: Hendog69 (pseudonym)

Ether Tier: 16th

Ether Score: 216

Lucrim Generation: 27,500

- Demonic Bond: 10,000

Current Lucrim: (private data)]

The demonic bond seemed to be working quite well for him. Though his encounter with the aura leeches left Rick unwilling to even consider anything of the sort, he had to admit that his friend had made far faster progress than he had. No doubt the power available through the bond made it even easier for him to expand his natural generation rate as well.

With the match ending, Henry caught sight of him and loped up to the stands. "You finally caught one of my matches, huh? What did you think?"

"That's a strong technique. You manage that yourself, or did you get it through your bond?"

"A bit of both - they upgraded my bond, by the way, which is nice." Henry flexed his fingers, eyes unfocusing as he looked within himself. "I figured I've always trained with martial arts, so there's no point trying to gain an entirely new skill. But the shell basically just enhances all my physical abilities, so I don't need to relearn anything."

"Smart. I'll consider that, once I actually get some lucrim to spare."

"You'll get there, man. Especially if you keep doing well." Henry sat down beside him, staring out as the arena was cleaned. "You fighting yet tonight? I'll stick around if you are."

"Yeah, I'm fighting. But it will be a bit, yet, so I'm guessing there will be other matches first."

They stuck around to watch, since there was no point trying to go somewhere else. The melee was followed by two one-on-one matches, but they proved disappointing. One was ended almost at the beginning by a powerful technique, while the other dragged on with two durable warriors pounding on each other.

The audience was getting restless... troublingly so, Rick thought. He'd grown used to the types of crowds at the Underground, and they were usually only as raucous as the audiences at normal sporting events. But the crowd tonight seemed bloodthirsty in a way he couldn't interpret.

Following the two quick matches there was a brief pause, two staff members talking to Alger. He was looking glum after the disappointing matches, but perked up and suggested something. After some time reorganizing, he clapped his hands to signal the start of something different.

Instead of either a duel or a melee, the next match appeared to be a battle between four different warriors, all of them rather strong. Rick hadn't seen any of them before, so he eagerly watched their skills as the match started.

In the beginning they watched each other cautiously, but the crowd began to jeer and scream. The noise pushed one of the men to lunge at the others, his aura expanding into a spiky shape that threatened anyone who came near. It seemed to be a strong technique, because it pushed back the first man who tried to strike him.

Without warning, the spiky aura split in half. For a second Rick didn't even know how it had happened, then he caught sight of one of the women in the match. She stood nearby, one of her arms encased in a purple aura that extended beyond her hand in a long blade. Not only had she crossed the distance immediately, she'd cut through the man's aura in a single blow.

The crowds roared in approval and the other fighters immediately converged on her, but she had clearly been expecting that. With her aura blade slicing around her, she could threaten a huge area, effectively preventing them from using their numbers against her and even turning the momentum back on them.

Rick gave her a closer look. She wore shapeless gray slacks and a dark hoodie, like someone going out of their way to look unremarkable. But she had a lean, pretty face, and her dark hair had a streak of blue in it. He had to wonder just who she was.

More importantly, how she was fighting so effectively. He judged her lucrim generation rate to be around 85,000, which was nothing to sneeze at, but all four fighters had at least that much and one of the men had 125,000 or more. Were her cores that efficient? If so, the fact that she could ward off multiple opponents meant that she was even better at punching above her weight than he was. There weren't any major flaws in her movements, though she wasn't too much better than him. Yet he couldn't help but feel that it was something else he was missing...

"Noticed her, huh?" Henry elbowed him hard in the ribs. "I'm shocked that you would cheat on poor Lisa."

"I thought you were done with that joke." He took his eyes away from the woman to stare at Henry. "She's strong. Do you know who she is?"

"Her name is Emily and she's one of the mid-tier fighters. Not so famous because she only participates in matches occasionally, but I noticed her because she's smoking hot. But before you ask, I'm pretty sure she's a lesbian or something, so don't even try."

"Lesbians can't discuss lucrima techniques?"

"Oh, haha. Don't pretend you aren't interested."

Rick didn't bother, instead focusing on the match. Emily fought to a draw with one of the others before the time ran out. The crowd cheered when they left the arena, but there were a few yelling angrily as well. He was starting to get uncomfortable with the whole thing, yet at that moment it was announced that the next match would be his melee.

Since he was in good shape and his schedule called for another fight, Rick headed out to the arena with the others. It looked like a mix of people he'd seen before, along with some new candidates, only a few of whom looked dangerous. His mind was running hot with ideas to improve himself, but he resolved to play it safe and stick to battle-tested strategies. There would be time enough to take risks later.

Once everyone was in the arena, Alger rose to his feet. It was rare that he announced the matches, but now he spoke loudly, audible even without a mic. "Ladies and gentlemen, it's time for a very special event! All of our noble fighters enjoy these melees, but their warrior's spirits call for more. Can they be satisfied with these simple matches? I tell you, no! True warriors must be forged by true challenges! They must be forged in blood!"

At that moment, one of the new arrivals threw off his cloak, revealing that he had jagged metal claws attached to both hands. But far more dangerous than his weapons, the man's aura intensified rapidly, taking him from an average 25,000 fighter to a generation rate of over 150,000. Rick's first instinct was that this must be a mistake, but even as he thought it, Rick knew that wasn't true.

The crowd sat forward, fixated on the arena, hungry for spectacle. Henry was on his feet, eyes wide, but there was nothing they could do. As the man with the claws began hunting, the chain link barriers around the arena solidified with lucrim and all of them were locked inside.

Chapter 13: The Slayer

"Slayer! Slayer! Slayer!"

The crowd was chanting the name over and over again as the man with the jagged metal claws raised his hands to either side. Most of the other fighters in the arena looked confused, but they were rapidly understanding that this was not another simple melee.

Rick tested the chain link fence, found that the reinforcement made it much too strong to break, and cursed under his breath.

He glanced toward Henry, but his friend could only shrug helplessly. This was going to be ugly. It probably wouldn't end with dead bodies, but that didn't mean he could survive the injuries from the match.

Would it be best to play dead? Yet judging from the crowds, he had a feeling that might backfire on him. This match had been sprung on them, so he had no idea what the conditions were to end it. Plus, this might be a rare opportunity to face a trained warrior more powerful than him. If he could avoid permanent injuries, then this could work in his favor.

Then there was really only one good option: he had to fight. As Rick turned back around, he saw that it had already begun.

One of the fighters let out a scream and tried to sprint for one of the locked exits. In a flash the Slayer was behind him, jabbing him in the back with one claw. He stabbed his other claw in as well, then tore them in opposite directions. Not a killing blow, but it opened a large gash in the fighter's back and flung strings of blood in both directions.

Around them, the crowds went berserk, pulsing with a bloodlust that had been held back until now. Rick swallowed, wished one last time that he hadn't taken this risk, and then focused wholly on how he was going to make it through.

Realizing that running wasn't an option, several of the long range fighters began to hurl aura spheres at the Slayer. But he had clearly expected this, ducking the first set and then sprinting directly toward one of the ranged fighters.

She only had time to release a single sphere, which the Slayer dodged, before he was on her. One claw caught beneath her armpit and the Slayer jerked up, sending her flipping into the air. After colliding with the barbed wire above, she dropped heavily, screaming in pain and clutching her arm. It was intact, but it wouldn't be functional soon, or maybe ever.

After raising his arms to the roaring crowds again, the Slayer lunged for the next ranged fighter. Before he arrived, a bolt of lightning shot through his chest, knocking him back. He landed lightly on his feet, mostly uninjured, and rushed toward his newest attacker.

It was the huge man who usually wielded lightning. Rick had seen him several times since his first match and he was a formidable opponent. But he wasn't equal to the Slayer, who sprinted at him with a loud laugh.

The next bolt of lightning shot out, and though it should have been impossible to react, the Slayer somehow intercepted it with one claw. He stopped for a moment, grinning to let everyone see the electricity dissipate harmlessly, then lunged for the kill.

Rick rushed in low and kicked him in the knee.

Though it felt like kicking solid steel, the Slayer did wince in pain and slow down. Then he turned on Rick, eyes blazing. Rick tried to leap back, but his opponent was simply too fast, following him quickly and raising a claw to strike into his chest.

Before it landed, two other fighters tackled him from the side. They actually drove the Slayer to the ground and one of them began stabbing with a shiv, but Rick saw that the point was failing to penetrate the man's defensive aura. With no way to help while they attacked wildly on top of their opponent, all he could do was retreat before the inevitable happened.

One of the Slayer's claws snapped up, going through the neck of one of his attackers. The Slayer burst to his feet, throwing the body into the others attacking him and sending all of them tumbling into the ground. As soon as he was back on his feet, another bolt of lightning shot at him, but he absorbed it into one claw and then roared for the crowds again.

They erupted in response, chanting "Slayer" over and over. Only a few looked at the man lying on the floor, blood bubbling from the holes in his throat.

Forcing down panic by sheer willpower, Rick considered his options. Strangely, the most recent bolt of lightning had come from beside him, which meant its user had changed location. He saw the huge man from the corner of his eyes, but the man wasn't attacking.

"My bolt hurt him," the man said, "but now that he's wise to them, they're not going to hit."

Rick nodded grimly. "Could you land another one if he's distracted?"

"I doubt it. My control isn't good enough to avoid collateral damage or target shots well enough to take advantage of it."

"Could you hit him if you ignored collateral damage?"

That got a dark chuckle from the man. "The bolts aren't strong enough to go through someone, not and pierce his aura. But... I could transfer the power. It'd hurt, but you might be able t-" At that moment they were interrupted as a body flew toward both of them, hitting the chain link fence and scattering blood in all directions.

Before they could return to finish their conversation, the Slayer rushed in their direction. They had no choice but to split up and sprint in opposite directions. Though the Slayer went after the larger man, by this point the others had begun working together, hurling ranged attacks to slow him down.

Several teamed up to rush him at once, giving Rick a chance to analyze their opponent as he tore through them. This "Slayer" was definitely strong and experienced, with most of his strength in offense. His defenses were average and if he had any weakness it was speed - he was faster than most of the fighters in the arena, but given how much he outclassed them, he should have been much faster.

His style was a bit hard to pin down. Though he played up the brutality for the audience, Rick thought that he was well-trained. The technique actually reminded him of a perverse form of aikido, throwing his opponents via injuries instead of normal throws. That was going to be difficult to deal with.

The huge man was across the arena, waiting for a chance to strike. Actually, he was trying to get Rick's attention. Presumably he wanted to continue the plan from earlier, but what had he been trying to say? Then there was no more time to think, because the Slayer threw aside his nearest opponents and rushed at Rick.

That claw lashed out at his face with terrible speed, but Rick desperately swept aside his opponent's arm. Just deflecting the attack made his forearm ache, but he'd managed to hold off the Slayer for one second. Unfortunately, no one else came to help. The claw lashed out again and he managed to deflect it with his other arm, but now both of his arms felt heavy and he knew he couldn't raise them in time to block the next attack.

Then the lightning bolt hit Rick in the back.

For an instant everyone was shocked. Rick trembled in pain as the lightning coursed through him, wondering if his ally had misfired. Yet the large man was now firing a second bolt, distracting the Slayer, and instead of passing through, the lightning continued crackling in Rick's body.

Rick struck the Slayer in the chest with his palm and all the lightning exited his body, blowing straight through his opponent.

The Slayer staggered backward and then fell to one knee, taken completely off guard. For a moment the crowd was quiet, then they let out another huge roar. Screaming back at them, the Slayer leapt to his feet, but at that moment several other fighters attacked him from all sides.

Which was good, because all Rick could do was collapse.

Redirecting the lightning had been a smart move, but it had taken more out of him than the Slayer. Even just holding the power in his body for a moment seemed to leave every part of him singed. Having felt it directly, he realized that the technique wasn't actually lightning, but lucrim charged to follow similar patterns. Rick considered that with mild curiosity until his brain snapped back into gear and he realized he was still in the middle of a potentially deadly fight.

Barely managing to crawl back to his feet, he discovered that the fight was going poorly. There were only three or four of them left standing. At some point while he had been down, the Slayer had struck the lightning user to the ground, though he seemed to be getting back to his feet while the Slayer was distracted.

Realizing that he would only be able to fight a short while longer, Rick tried to consider his best options. His aura was burned by the lightning, but his defensive core was still in good shape. Unless he could team up with someone else, the only way he could land another hit was to leverage his defense.

Rushing in knowing he would take a hit was madness, yet if he allowed the Slayer to control the momentum, he might not even get that chance...

While Rick stared, another one of the remaining fighters swept a hand against the Slayer's back. His hand was clenched like a claw, and he had some sort of technique that cut lines through the Slayer's clothing. Immediately the stronger man whirled, but the fighter tightened both hands into claws and attacked with surprising ferocity.

It was like he poured everything he had into a few seconds of combat, clawing out at his opponent's chest repeatedly, slicing through his clothes and cutting ribbons of blood across the Slayer's chest. In response the Slayer roared and stabbed out, but the man slammed both of his hands together, fingers interlocking just in front of the jagged blade.

The man's aura snapped down like an enormous pair of jaws, closing over the Slayer's wrist. There was a loud snap of bone breaking and the jagged claws crumpled.

In response the Slayer let out a roar of pain and stabbed his other claw directly into his opponent's chest. He began to attack with even more ferocity, wildly slashing at the remaining fighters with his remaining claw. It was only a matter of time.

Rick's heartbeat pounded in his ears, seeming to merge with the mad roar of the crowds. Intellectually he knew that the Slayer was slowing down and getting sloppier in his rage, yet the idea of rushing in seemed downright suicidal. With only a few more seconds to plan his attack, Rick risked closing his eyes for a moment, regaining his focus.

When the Slayer came for him, he rushed straight at the man. His opponent was too experienced to be taken off guard, slashing at his arm.

Instead of trying to dodge, Rick just took the attack. He felt the claws tear deep into his arm, saw a glimpse of flesh and even bone, but couldn't let himself focus on the injury. What mattered was that he was still alive and his right arm was working.

His elbow slammed directly into the Slayer's throat.

The blow managed to get through his weakened aura and the Slayer went down, clutching at his throat and struggling to breathe. When he fell away, his claws tore out of Rick's arm. Suddenly the pain was rushing through him like wildfire and Rick collapsed to the ground.

Had he won? Did it matter, if his arm was useless? It lay beside him, an ugly mess of torn flesh that refused to respond. Rick stared at it, wondering if he had made the wrong decision...

And then he saw that the Slayer was staggering back to his feet.

Just as he started to feel despair, the huge man appeared again, firing a bolt of lightning at point blank range. It would have been suicide at the start of the fight, but battered by injuries and with only one functional hand, the Slayer was staggered. The huge man gathered lightning in both hands and slammed them into his opponent's chest.

The Slayer hurtled across the arena, smashing loudly against the chains and then falling to the ground. This time, he did not rise.

After a moment of silence, the crowd roared out their approval. The last standing fighter raised his arms in triumph, crackling with more lightning. They had won against an opponent who had been meant to tear them apart for the crowd's entertainment.

Rick lay on the bloody floor, struggling to move his arm and then just to stay conscious. As the darkness claimed him, it didn't feel like victory.

Chapter 14: Granny Whitney

When Rick awoke, he discovered that he was lying on a stiff bed in a dingy room. It was terribly lit, but he was glad he couldn't see more, because it seemed like the room was filthy, two cockroaches visible on the walls. Perhaps it was easier not to see how bad it was.

Slowly he gathered himself, remembering how the battle had ended. He must have been moved to this facility after the fight. It seemed his injuries had been roughly bandaged and it felt as though he'd received minimal treatment.

His arm refused to respond when he tried to move it. Beneath the bandages, it felt like his flesh had been torn apart.

Rick stared down at the injury, wondering if he had the nerve to look under the bandages. He realized grimly that he wouldn't recover from this. Fighters who were strong or rich enough could afford elaborate lucrim healing that could even regrow an arm entirely, but those cost more than everything he owned combined.

What would life be like without his left arm? He might be able to work some jobs, but would anyone want to spar with a one-armed man? Rick swallowed, blinking away tears and bitterly regretting his decision to join the Underground. Even though he'd known something like this would happen eventually, he'd let himself be drawn in by the benefits and ignored the risks...

"Oh, you're up already! What a durable young man."

He looked up and saw just about the last thing he expected: a small old woman walked into the room. She wore an old-fashioned floral print dress and a knitted shawl around her shoulders. When she gave him a kind smile, the wrinkles on her face shifted as if she smiled often. She looked like she was a grandmother who doted on a dozen grandchildren.

As she came to sit down beside him, however, he noticed other facts. Her back was very straight, and despite her age, she radiated vitality. Definitely an advanced lucrima user, though he couldn't judge her strength. She put a hand on his forehead and he felt a wave of soothing energy pass through him. Despite how depressing his situation was, for a moment he felt at peace.

"There you go! Alger only asked me to help out with the basics, but that one is just a little favor from me." She beamed and patted his cheek. "I liked you better than that lad with the lightning."

"I..." Rick's voice caught in his throat and he had to swallow before trying again. "You're the Underground's healer?"

"Not exactly, dearie, but I get involved from time to time. Social security isn't what it once was, oh my lord no. It might pay for cat food, but Granny's tastes are a bit more expensive than that."

"Thank you."

"Oh, it's my job, dearie." She smiled at him again. "Please, call me Granny Whitney. If you keep fighting in the Underground, you'll probably be seeing me again."

"I don't know that I will." Rick sat up painfully, hating how his arm hung from his shoulder. "This injury... is there any way you can heal me? I don't have much lucrim or money, but..."

The old woman shook her head sadly. "You seem like a diligent young man, but I'm afraid there's no way you can afford such a healing. As much as Granny Whitney would like to heal everyone, you have to understand that such things are expensive for me as well. It costs a great deal of lucrim to restore an arm in such bad condition."

"I see." He leaned back against the wall and closed his eyes, trying to resist the bitterness.

"Might we be able to come to some sort of other arrangement? I'd hate to see a young man with real potential lose an arm like this. Perhaps you could find a way to pay for the operation bit by bit...?"

"No... I think I'm done here. I've learned my lesson."

"That's a crying shame, but it's your life, dearie." Granny Whitney rose to her feet and patted him on the cheek again. "If you change your mind, you just come talk to Granny Whitney, alright? I've finished all my work for the day, so I'll be having a restorative little tea out on the balcony."

He just nodded silently, his remaining hand going subconsciously to his arm. If someone like her said that it cost too much to restore his arm, then there was no chance that he could afford the operation at a real hospital. Rick started to pick at the bandage to see how bad it was, but at that moment the door swung open again.

"Rick!" Henry pushed into the room, saw his arm, and winced. "Shit, man, I'm sorry. If I had any idea they were going to do something this bad..."

"Do they do this often?" Rick should have felt angry, but his body was just numb. Henry shifted nervously, not meeting his eyes, but eventually he answered the question.

"Slayer rounds are so rare I'd only heard rumors of them. Usually the worst is blood matches, or the tight cage fights... shit... is that arm as bad as it looks?"

"Yeah. I guess this is it for me."

"No way, man. You can't give up on the fights now or you'll never get that arm healed." Henry bent down beside him, lowering his voice. "Your best bet is to get a patron who will pay for the healing. You might not be the hero of the match, but you did a good job. There's a chance someone important saw the match and might be willing to invest in you."

After a flicker of hope, Rick shook his head. "If I did, they'd own me, wouldn't they? Something like they'd take all my future earnings until I paid back the debt?"

Henry shifted uncomfortably. "Well, yeah. But it isn't all bad. If you're somebody's chosen fighter, they'd help you with all kinds of things because they'd want you to keep winning. The top fighters are showered with all kinds of-"

"No. They'd be able to tell me when and how to fight and I'd just get further caught up in all this." As he said the words, Rick realized that he was content with that decision. He couldn't lose sight of the point of it all, which was to earn a living for himself and Melissa. Getting ensnared deeper in this system would just be digging a deeper hole.

"Fuck man... I don't know what else to tell you. Think about it, alright?"

"Yeah, I should take some time to think." Rick slowly got to his feet and brushed past Henry into the hallway.

As he walked, his body felt surprisingly okay, but that was nothing compared to the weight of his arm hanging from his shoulder. He tried to ignore it and instead observed the building, looking for the easiest way out.

They seemed to be in another partially abandoned building in the seediest part of town. Presumably injured fighters were taken here for treatment, though he wondered if they were taken by secret tunnel or something. The hallway was mostly doors into other dirty rooms with injured fighters. When Rick passed a large window, he was surprised to find they were pretty high up: 20th floor or more. There weren't that many buildings that tall in Branton.

Just as he thought he was about to find the entrance, he spotted the huge man. He towered over the crowd of people around him, which included Alger and several rich-looking men. Clearly they were all fawning over him, the hero who had defeated the Slayer. But just when Rick started feeling bitter, the other combatant saw him and immediately pushed through the crowd to approach him.

"Everybody is focused on me, but you played just as big a part." The man extended a large hand. "I'm Tom."

"Rick." He shook the other man's hand, glad that he had extended the right hand, or things would have become awkward. It seemed as though Tom's injuries had been entirely healed already, though Rick tried not to feel bitter about that.

"Listen, I was here because I needed money, so there's not much I can do for you now. But I promise that I won't forget. If I do well enough, I'll find a way to get someone to take care of your arm. That's just fair."

Though part of Rick bridled at the idea of accepting such pity, he didn't have many choices. He found a smile somewhere and nodded to Tom. "That's kind of you. I don't know if I'll keep fighting with this injury, but maybe we can exchange information."

They did so quickly and Tom even gave him access to his lucrim profile. But after that, the crowd was starting to pull him back and he needed to go. Alger especially was beaming, and though he shot a smile at Rick as well, it was obvious who he was focusing on. Soon the crowd was gone, leaving him alone in the corridor.

He knew it would just make him unhappier, but Rick still pulled his phone back out to check Tom's profile. He struggled a bit with the phone, surprised to find that he sometimes used his left hand as well, but eventually pulled it up:

[Name: Tom Jackson

Ether Tier: 15th

Ether Score: 273

Lucrim Generation: 33,500

Current Lucrim: (private data)]

While he had the app open, Rick considered checking himself as well, but it didn't feel worth it. There were stories of one-armed fighters who attained great fame, but they usually already had immense strength or got incredibly lucky. Enough lucrim could make up for the loss of a limb, even without regeneration, but how would he earn that much without a functional left arm?

No, his only real hope was to trust Tom's charity. He didn't like it, but it was better than nothing. Rick put his phone away, resolving to find a way to make ends meet until he could get his arm back. Heading down the corridor, he-

He saw the Slayer walking up the stairs.

The man looked to have been healed, but he was still in terrible shape. For a moment Rick actually considered him as a fellow human being, realized that this man had his own reasons for fighting in the Underground. It looked like he'd had the money to restore his mangled hand, but not to fully heal him overall and certainly not to restore his spent lucrim.

"Hey, sorry about the match." The Slayer gave him a smile as he spoke, closing the distance between them smoothly.

Rick turned around and left. Yes, the "Slayer" might be just another person, but Rick knew very well what people could do to their fellow human beings. It was just an instinct, but the Slayer's smile struck him as false and he didn't like something in his eyes.

He'd barely gotten around a corner when he heard feet slamming into the floor. Rick started to run, but the very first time he looked over his shoulder he saw that the Slayer was already coming after him, his smile morphing into something predatory.

"Too smart to fall for it, huh?" The Slayer kept after him and Rick barely stayed ahead, clutching his injured arm so it wouldn't bounce painfully. "But that's just going to make this worse for you."

"You... can't do this..." Rick managed to get out the words between breaths, hoping that his opponent was just raging after the match. But when he caught another glimpse, he saw nothing but cold fury in the Slayer's eyes.

"Oh, we're not supposed to kill anyone. I'd never break that rule. But the kid with the claw tech already died of his wounds, and you will too..."

Given how easily the Slayer was speaking while running, it was only a matter of time before he caught up. But as Rick turned another corner, he saw his chance: a woman in a doctor's coat was pushing a man on a gurney in front of them.

Not hesitating, Rick dropped to the ground and slid underneath the gurney as the woman gave a cry of surprise. He managed to pull back to his feet after the slide and looked back, hoping that the Slayer wouldn't just attack the woman and keep coming after him.

But the Slayer was gone.

Rick stared for a long moment, his first thought the absurd idea that the Slayer had somehow gone invisible. But no, more likely he just couldn't afford any witnesses. That meant he was held off for now, but there was no chance that he was going to give up. The doctor was giving him a strange look, so he gave her an apologetic look.

"I'm sorry, but I'm being chased. There's som-"

Immediately she raised her hands. "I don't get involved with your vendettas. This is just a job to me."

"But he's seriously going to kill me!"

"I don't get involved."

Gritting his teeth, Rick accepted that and desperately considered other options. "Do you know someone who calls herself Granny Whitney? She said she would be at a balcony nearby..."

"Right, Whitney." The doctor gave him a strange look, but nodded. "She *does* get involved, so I suppose it's worth trying. Her balcony is down that hall and to the right."

"Thanks." Rick immediately turned away and sprinted in the direction she'd indicated.

As he ran he expected to hear footsteps pounding after him at any moment, or worse, have the Slayer emerge completely silently from one of the corridors ahead. Yet no attack came and he was too tired to sprint forever. He slowed down to a jog as he spotted a sliding door that led to the outside.

It was less a balcony than a small area of the roof with a guardrail, but he knew it was the right place. Granny Whitney sat at a small metal table, a blue china tea set beside her. The delicate china looked absurdly out of place on the grimy roof.

The old woman turned to smile at him. "My, you're in a hurry. Come and sit down, dearie."

"Someone..." Rick looked backward nervously, but saw no one. "The Slayer is coming after me. He threatened to kill me. Can you help?"

"Ah yes. The poor lad was expecting a night of beating up people weaker than him, but he ended up humiliated in front of such a crowd. No wonder he's furious." Granny Whitney stared at Rick thoughtfully. "A nice boy like you shouldn't be killed here. Of course I'll help you. But I wonder if you might not give a thought to my offer?"

"What... what do you mean?"

"I think you're a nice young lad, so I'll be generous. I'll have your arm healed for free, give you some nice medicine to help along your development, and invest 50,000 lucrim in your success. Up front, without any immediate compensation."

Rick stared at her, hoping that this couldn't possibly be what it looked like. "Are you saying... that you'll let him kill me unless I agree to your offer?"

Granny Whitney clucked her tongue sharply, then stood up, gave him a warm smile, and patted his cheek. "Dear boy, what kind of person do you think I am? But I do hope you'll consider my offer."

"You haven't said what I'd give you in return."

"Well, I hope you would take some advice from dear old Granny Whitney about how to proceed, but you wouldn't be obligated to. What I really need from you is to participate in a special event a little over five months from now. There's something at stake that's important to me, and there would be a considerable reward as well. If you gave me your share of the reward, I'd consider us square. What do you say?"

On the surface, that appeared to be essentially an interest-free loan. Considering that it would restore his arm immediately and get him away from the Slayer, it was a tempting offer. But there were too many unknown terms and he felt uncomfortable about the whole thing. No, his earlier thought that he needed to get away from the Underground had been the right one.

"I'm sorry," he said slowly, "but I can't accept. I don't think this life is for me."

"Oh dear. That'd be such a shame - a boy with your talent leaving so soon."

Before she could say anything more, Rick heard footsteps in the hall. He looked desperately to Granny Whitney, but she didn't seem to have heard them. Before he could warn her, the Slayer charged onto the balcony after them.

He ignored Rick entirely at first, instead thrusting his claws to the old woman's neck. "You stay out of this, Whitney. I just want the boy." The Slayer kept his claw by her throat and turned back to Rick, that savage grin returning. "Just let it happen. No matter what, I'm going to find and kill you. You can either die now, or you can cower in fear until the day I find you and kill you much, much slower..."

Granny Whitney was utterly still, staring at the claw by her throat, so she wouldn't be much help. Rick swallowed and decided his only option was reason, as poor a choice as that seemed. "All we did was fight for our lives."

"No, you *humiliated* me! You have to pay for that!"

"But why me? Tom was the one who finished you."

The Slayer grimaced. "But everyone is looking at him, and he's Alger's favorite for now. No, my only chance to get revenge on him is in the arena itself. But you... there's nothing stopping me from taking you out and reminding everyone that I am *not* to be trifled with."

"You don't need to - I'm going to quit. I promise, you'll never see me in the Underground again."

"Not good enough. If you thought your arm was bad, you should see what I'll do to the rest of your b-"

He cut off as Granny Whitney stepped past his knife and poked his neck with two fingers.

Feeling the pulse of lucrim too late, Rick took an involuntary step backward. The Slayer went slack and began to crumple, overcome by some sort of disabling technique too subtle for Rick to understand. But before he fell to the ground, Whitney grabbed him around the side of the neck.

Having no trouble with his weight, she dragged him to the side of the roof, then dumped him over the railing. Rick stared in horror as she looked over the edge, then clucked her tongue and shook her head.

"Oh dear, that's a messy landing. The boy should have kept his head." Granny Whitney turned back to him, unnaturally calm, and Rick realized that he was right to feel fear. "It's a shame that the two of you couldn't put aside your differences. But really, dear boy, it was a mistake for you to track him down and kill him while he was so injured. Children these days."

Rick took a step backward, but there was nowhere to run. "This... are you blackmailing me?"

"I just want what's best for you, dearie." Granny Whitney sat down in her chair, took a sip of her tea, and then gave him a warm smile. "Now, have you given another thought to my offer?"

Chapter 15: Core Obligations

It still didn't feel quite real, but it was done. Rick sat on a clean bed, feeling his arm recovering, and just stared at the ceiling.

He'd done what Granny Whitney had suggested, telling the security forces who appeared that the Slayer had attacked him. They'd believed his story surprisingly easily, leaving him uncertain if that was because Whitney sat beside him, or if she had tricked him into accepting her agreement. Of course, given her obvious willingness to murder, he hadn't really had much of a choice.

At that moment she sat back, humming a little tune to herself as the doctor from earlier worked on his arm. The old woman actually hadn't done anything else to heal him, making him wonder if that was really her job. Subtle layers of lucrim cascaded from the doctor's fingers as they worked over his arm, which was no longer shredded. In fact, it felt back to normal, though Granny Whitney had done something to make his arm go limp so the doctor could keep working.

That was a reminder of just how easily the old woman could turn on him. Since he was stuck in this situation, his only chance was to find out precisely what she wanted. She must have had an ulterior motive for pressuring him into the deal and he needed to play into that to stay alive.

"It's obvious you're going to get what you want." Rick stared at the old woman as the doctor continued working on his arm. "Unless what you want is to torment me, please make it clear what exactly that is."

"So much cynicism for one so young..." Granny Whitney clucked her tongue and shook her head. "If I wanted to hurt you, I wouldn't go to all this trouble. No, I want you at your best, which means I can actually be a great friend to you."

Skeptical as he was about that, Rick would take what he could get out of his arrangement. "Fine. But I have obligations beyond the Underground, so I don't know how much I can do for you."

"Hmm. And what obligations would those be?"

"My parents left me with a lot of debt. I'll never be able to make anything of my life unless I can get rid of that debt entirely, which means cutting a lot of corners." He'd planned that lie to avoid mentioning Melissa, since he'd never forgive himself if she got wrapped up in this. It wasn't much of a deception, but he suspected that Whitney already knew about the aura leeches and an extravagant lie would be too easy to detect.

"Ah, that does explain why such a dedicated young man has gathered so few lucrim." Her eyes flickered over his face with a bit of hard skepticism. "I'm not sure that's the whole story, though. Keeping something from Granny Whitney, are you?"

He stared back at her, refusing to give anything else. To his surprise, she simply smiled.

"I'm not going to use it as leverage against you, dear boy... I already have enough of that. But if I'm going to be helpful to you, I need to know more about your life. Keep what secrets you want, so long as they don't interfere with our arrangement."

"How often do you need me to fight?"

"Perhaps every week or so? Those will honestly be just simple bets to bide our time and earn a bit of extra profit on the side."

"Right, this event in five months." Rick closed his eyes and leaned back, accepting that he'd need to take her objectives as his. "What is it, that you need to recruit random new fighters? Even with help, there's a limit to how much I can grow in only five months."

"This is not public knowledge, but Alger will be running a rather curious tournament at that time. Teams of five against five, but to keep things interesting, you aren't allowed to stack your team with your five strongest. No, you need people in five different power classes." Granny Whitney smiled up at him and sat back in satisfaction. "I'm afraid my old featherweight candidate got herself killed, so I'm looking for someone new."

Rick sighed. "So I'm classed as a featherweight? You're going to tell me that's the lowest, isn't it?"

"That's not so bad, dearie." She reached past the doctor to pat his hand. "There's a class below that called bantamweight, though they aren't included in the tournament. You're quite good, for a featherweight, and that defensive core of yours is solid. I don't make these decisions randomly."

"Alright, but that's far in the future. What do you need from me in the short term?"

"Oh, in the short term I'm going to be the one helping you. Those things I suggested weren't just enticements; I do intend to help you succeed."

Though she might have said more, the doctor finally pulled back. "I'm finished. Give me what we agreed, then you can scheme as much as you want once I'm gone."

Before answering, Granny Whitney reached out and tapped Rick's shoulder. "How does that feel, dearie?"

Since his arm suddenly worked again, Rick tested stretching it, then made a fist. It felt fine. Better than fine. Instead of being torn apart, his arm looked strong and it felt fresh. He'd been slightly muscular before, but now all the muscles in his arm stood out rigidly.

"Run along, dearie." Granny Whitney pressed something into the doctor's hand and waved her away, then sat down next to his bed in the same chair. "Now, young Richard... the arm was a start, but I have several more conditions. We might as well start with the simplest: a bit of an incentive for joining me."

She reached into her handbag and pulled out a pearl sphere. Unlike the cheap marbles that most used, this one appeared to be made of solid pearl. After siphoning out some of it, the old woman set it down beside him. When Rick hesitantly took it, he immediately felt the density of the lucrim within.

"That's 50,000 lucrim exactly. I hope you'll invest some of that in yourself, but it's up to you what you do with it. Oh, and do you need any spending money? I might as well give you some." She fished out a stack of bills and set it down as well, but Rick was still focused on the sphere.

"This is a lot..." If only the aura leeches could be bought off directly with this, but their values were more akin to generation rate, not generated lucrim. Still, this would be a significant advance.

"Just the start, dearie. But I'm afraid I can't give you complete freedom, since your development is now my concern. Can you bring up your lucrima portfolio for me, dear?"

There was no real choice, so he did so:

[Name: Rick Hunter

Ether Tier: 18th

Ether Score: 156

Lucrim Generation: 21,200

Effective Rate: 11,900

Current Lucrim: 578]

[Rick Hunter's Lucrima Portfolio

Foundation: 7700 (Lv II)

Offensive Lucore: 3700 (Lv II)

Defensive Lucore: 6400 (Lv IV)

Birthright Core: 1944 (Lv I)

Birthright Core: 1108 (Lv I)

Aura Leech: -4755 (Stage II)

Aura Leech: -2723 (Stage I)

Aura Leech: -1262 (Stage III)

Golden Lucore: 10 (N/A)

Gross Lucrim: 21,200

Net Lucrim: 11,900]

"These little devices are so handy. Checking portfolios was far more work back in my day." Granny Whitney looked over the screen, humming to herself. "Well! It's clear the first thing we need to do is get rid of that third aura leech."

Rick blinked. "The third one specifically? It's the smallest, so it's hindering me the least."

"Oh, but it's Stage III, which means it's draining you faster than the others. You can wait to get rid of the others if you like, but that one... that one needs to go. It looks like you've been feeding all the leeches equally. Stop doing that and focus all your effort on the third."

"Okay, I understand." He didn't like taking orders from her, but he had to admit her suggestion was logical. The lucrim that she'd given him would definitely help with that.

"We need to do something about your foundation, but you're not really in a position to redo it entirely. You'll have to stick with an R-type for now."

"An R-type?"

"Just jargon, dearie." Granny Whitney set down the phone beside him and patted his knee. "There are several different fundamental ways to structure your foundation, plus more complex techniques on top of that. Most people start with an R-type and it's hard to switch to an M-type, so that's not really a problem. But you should look into changing it eventually."

He could only nod, making a mental note to do more research about it eventually. The terms sounded vaguely familiar, now that he thought about them, but he'd never gotten deep into the forums where they were used.

"Anyway, your biggest weaknesses are lack of a speed core and lack of a Generation Core. You can't make those overnight, especially with those leeches, but you *can* use those Birthright Cores toward them. You notice how they're just sitting there, unchanging?"

"Yeah. I tried focusing on them during my training, but it didn't have any effect."

"Because those are essentially inert cores. The Birthright Cores given to most rich folks actually grow in strength over time, beyond just providing you with energy. But you're tired after today and I can see that you don't want a lecture. Let me just give you a few things for you to work on until we meet again."

"Actually, I had a question." Since she'd already looked through his portfolio, he didn't see any reason not to just ask her directly. "Do you know what this 'Golden Core' is?"

Granny Whitney blinked at him. "You mean you don't know? I assumed that you'd participated in a clinical trial for money or something of that sort. How did you get an unregistered core, then?"

"I'm honestly not completely sure."

"Well, what I *can* tell you is what function it's supposed to serve. What you have is just... a prototype, you could say. It doesn't actually function. But what it's intended to do is fundamentally alter lucrim flow. Instead of your body going through a natural cycle, this core would let you draw all lucrim at all stages, developed or incipient or recycling. Like borrowing power against the future, you could say."

"Is that... healthy?"

"Goodness no! That lucrim would be going to heal small injuries, increase your strength, and many other things. This core would burn all of that in an instant for a burst of power." Granny Whitney gave him a rather unpleasant smile. "Had you used it, you'd have thought that you obtained some grand ability and marveled at the new power you received, but it would have cost you in the end."

Though a bit disappointed, Rick nodded in understanding. "I see."

The old woman pulled her handbag into her lap and began looking through it. "Such things have long existed, of course, but they're usually for strong warriors who can afford to take such risks. The notable thing about yours is that it seems like it was designed for the weak."

Rick had no idea what to make of that. Part of him had still been hoping, despite everything, that the mysterious core was something that could grant him great power. Apparently this one was not only non-functional, but its function was something he wouldn't want in any case.

"Anyway, dearie, I have some medicine and exercises you can do to prepare to improve your portfolio a bit. All quite harmless stuff, so do as much as you can."

"Thank you."

"Oh, not a problem, dearie." Granny Whitney set down an old book, a small bag, and a bottle of pills on the bed. "There you go. Now, there's just one more thing before I go, and I'm afraid it's going to hurt a great deal."

He started to move away on instinct, but he was much too slow. The old woman grabbed his newly restored arm by the wrist and pinched down. Her lucrim speared into his body, creating a moment of blinding pain.

Then it was over and he was gasping for breath, staring at his wrist. It didn't look any different, but he could feel that there was something inside it. He wanted to check to learn more, but he was distracted by Granny Whitney rising to her feet.

"Just a little insurance for old Granny Whitney, okay? I can't have you running off on me. But if all goes well in five months, then I'll take that back out and you'll be as good as new. Take care, dearie!" With that, she bustled out of the room, a pleasant smile on her face.

Groaning, Rick massaged his wrist for a while before pulling up his profile again. He soon discovered that what she had done was clearly listed:

[Tracking Bond: 100 (Lv XIII)]

He stared for a moment before realizing why it seemed familiar. One of his cousins who was often in and out of jail had a similar bond placed on him, alerting the authorities if he left his house. This one couldn't have the same restrictions, but he was willing to bet that it would let Granny Whitney find him anywhere. Just what he needed.

Though his body felt good overall, his mind needed some more time, so Rick stayed in the hospital bed and looked over what he'd been given. The book seemed to teach lucrim techniques, while the pills were an expensive medicine and the bag contained something that looked like sand. Hopefully the book would explain what he was supposed to do with those.

Eventually he made his way out of the hospital. Guards took him down what appeared to be a hidden elevator, which opened up in what looked like a normal parking garage. They nodded to him as he went out, then the doors closed and he was free. Except he wasn't free at all.

Rick walked home slowly, taking time to digest everything that had happened to him. It felt like ages ago that he'd headed to the Underground to watch Henry's fight and have a simple match of his own. According to his phone not much time had passed, but his mind was swimming with thoughts of the brutal fight against the Slayer, working together with Tom, the attempted murder, and Granny Whitney.

Just Granny Whitney would have been too much.

By the time he got back to the apartment, he had no solutions but his mind felt a bit clearer. He found Melissa still awake, struggling to keep her eyes open while she watched television. As soon as he came in, she hopped up.

"Rick, are you okay?"

He stared at her a moment, then shrugged. "I got in a really nasty fight at the Underground and then somebody tried to kill me and it's fine now but I have to work for someone and I am *very* tired."

"Haha, I'll bet." Melissa moved to put a shoulder under one of his arms, helping him to the couch. "You can tell me all about it tomorrow, okay? Right now you really look like you could use the sleep."

"Yeah... you too, though... school tomorrow..."

"It's Saturday, silly." She helped him lie down and pulled his blanket over him. Rick tossed his phone and his keys onto the floor and decided to just sleep like that. After smoothing his hair a bit, Melissa turned to go.

At that moment his phone rang. Rick groaned and pulled the sheet over his head. He heard Melissa walk over and pick it up. "Uh... it's your boss. Should I tell him you're sick?"

"He wouldn't care." Rick forced himself back up and reached for the phone. "I should talk to him."

As far as he remembered, he didn't have to work that Saturday, though there was no guarantee that wouldn't change abruptly. It felt petty to be forced to go to work after everything he'd survived - he was holding the phone with the arm that had been destroyed not long ago - but that was his life.

"What's up, boss?"

"I should be asking you that." Jimmy sounded slightly more irritated than average, which for him was absolutely furious. "Just what are you getting yourself into?"

"Uh... I mean, I've been fighting in the Underground, but Henry does that too and it's not-"

"I don't meant that. I mean that fucking Birthrighter."

Rick sat up straight, all chance of sleep falling away. "What? You mean Mike?"

"The one that kicked the shit out of you, yeah. He came by today, without his friends, and asked about you. I told him to fuck off, and off he fucked. But then I get home tonight and I have a letter from his dad's company? The letter doesn't explain shit, but they sound pissed."

Falling back against the couch, Rick groaned. "I have a vague idea what this might be about. I'll take care of it."

"You'd better, or you can kiss your job goodbye. We do *not* need prying eyes around here." With that, Jimmy hung up without saying goodbye. Rick's hand fell down to his lap, his phone dropping onto the couch. He stared forward for a while longer. Out of the corner of his eye he could see that Melissa was waiting in concern, but he didn't have the strength to explain it to her.

Life couldn't ever give him a break, could it?

Chapter 16: The Obvious Choice

The last time Rick had been unprepared, he had ended up in a death match against someone who was literally called "the Slayer." This time he planned to do everything he could before things got ugly.

He began by leaving a message with his uncle, since Uncle Frank had seemed to know something about this "Golden Core." When he didn't get an immediate call back, he began doing research of his own. For a start, he confirmed what Granny Whitney had said about special cores. Though all the details seemed to be confidential, there was definitely information that abilities like that existed, at least if you were rich enough.

While he didn't know anything for sure, he could piece together an approximation of what might have happened. Maguire Incorporated must be testing a new form of core that could operate at lower levels of lucrim generation. Either as an experiment or just as a perk of being the founder's son, Mike Maguire must have held one of those cores. During their fight, his inexperience might have fractured it into core fragments, one of which Rick absorbed.

That last part was the weakest link. While something like that must have happened, his knowledge of Lucores was too basic to be sure about any details. Whatever exactly had happened, Mike and then his father's corporation had figured it out and now they were after him.

Research into Maguire Incorporated had quickly proved daunting. It was like a lot of conglomerates, in that it contained a private combat sect and owned a variety of conventional manufacturing companies. Once they had power of one kind, they tended to seek any power they could seize for themselves. That often included cutting-edge research into lucrima and related phenomena.

Faced with an aggressive multinational corporation threatening legal action, his best choice was obvious: give them what they wanted.

There had been a few movies about plucky heroes taking on multinational corporations, and of course the lone warrior challenging the dominant combat sect was an old cliché. But those were stories, and this was reality. Maguire Incorporated had thousands of ordinary employees who were stronger than him, much less their elite combat groups. He had people he needed to protect and few resources, so his best bet was to cooperate and hope it went well.

However, that didn't mean going unprepared. All during his shift on Sunday, he trained as intensely as he could, trying to solidify his recent combat experiences into real gains. Though he wanted to read Granny Whitney's book, he decided it was safer to leave it at home.

When he finally got back, however, he found Melissa desperately trying to save a scorching pot roast and realized that he couldn't dive into training just yet. She winced when she saw him come in.

"Aww... I was hoping I'd have everything ready before you got home, but I kinda screwed it up..."

"It smells okay." He stepped in and helped her with the heavy pot. "Bit burned, but okay. What's the occasion?"

"I just wanted us to eat a bit better for once. We've been so busy we've just been eating whatever was around, and that can't be good for us." She gave a sheepish shrug. "But it turns out cooking is not really my strong suit."

They salvaged what they could and sat down on the floor to eat. Aside from the burned smell, it was actually quite good, heavy but with more subtle seasonings. Certainly better than the cheap crap they'd been eating lately, so he took the time to enjoy it.

Before too long, however, his sister stopped eating and instead glanced at him. "So... while you were gone, I shamelessly snooped through your things."

"Hey."

"Kidding - I saw it when I put your stuff away, after you passed out. Anyway, it looks like you got some valuable stuff. I'm not good at estimating lucrim, but I haven't seen a container that fancy before. Not to mention the old book and the weird medicine."

"Yeah. I'm going to have to work them off eventually, but these will be a real step forward." He was silent for a while, chewing another bite of potato. "Some of it will take a while, but I intend to take all of the lucrim and see how far it will get me."

"Couldn't you just use it to pay off the leech things directly? Or is that not how it works?"

"Not how it works." Rick ate in silence for a while, trying to think about how to explain it. Some things had been so obvious to him for such a long time that it was easy to forget that it was all obscure to some people, and others he had only recently started to understand himself. "Normal people dealing in lucrim are talking about increments of energy, which is what I received. But when lucrima users talk, they're almost always referring to their lucrim generation rate. Another way to put it might be lucrim capacity."

Melissa cocked her head at him. "Those don't seem like the same thing."

"It makes sense if you think about the old days. Back before we mined the atmosphere so effectively, trained warriors could gather lucrim to themselves just by focusing. But there's a limit to how much people can gather and hold at one time, which is your generation rate. The general rule, which is where the official numbers come from, is that your maximum capacity is the amount you can generate in one year."

"Oh, so the name is kinda outdated? That makes sense. It didn't seem like everybody could actually be generating that much all the time."

"Right. So the 50,000 lucrim I received... I could use it to buy things, or I could use it to recharge myself several times. But you can recharge with cheap serum, or even just resting enough, though the rate is extremely slow thanks to the lucrim mining. A much better use of excessive lucrim is to absorb it all, then try to crunch it down into your lucrima soul. You burn through it, but in the end, your capacity increases. That lets you hold more power at once and invest it into useful applications, hence that's why everybody is most concerned about generation rate."

"Got it." Melissa nodded thoughtfully and chewed for a while. "So you're going to do all your main preparations, then head to this corporate place?"

"Just the branch office in Branton, but yeah. That's the plan."

"Then... good luck, Rick. I hope that ends it and I don't get something else to worry about."

She didn't mean to make him feel guilty, but that was definitely his main reaction. The extra stress couldn't be good for her, and based on how things were going with the Underground, he was likely to just add more to it. He was nervous about how things might go with Maguire Incorporated, but better to address the issue directly than to let it sneak up on him and make things even worse.

After the meal he felt satisfied and a bit sleepy, but there were too many hours left in the day to rest. Instead Rick cracked open the book he'd been given and looked through it carefully. It seemed that it was a collection of technique descriptions. Like most books of its kind, it was easy to skim, but more difficult to fully comprehend and far harder to put into practice.

What Granny Whitney wanted him to do was fairly clear, at least. One of the first major exercises taught was called Graham's Focus. It promised to improve cohesion of one's lucrima portfolio - done consistently, he would be able to absorb the two Birthright Cores fully.

That step would have to wait, but he could start with the initial exercises. The book also explained the purpose of the sand-like substance: apparently it was used as part of a purification ritual. It sounded like it was rough on the body and it required mastery of a few basics, so he would have to leave that behind.

Figuring out the pills was as easy as reading the label on the bottle. They helped restore one's lucrim reserves, but also helped purge damage done to a lucrima soul. The leeches were definitely leaving behind a lot of issues, so he could use the pills to help recover as he got rid of them. For now, he resolved to finish doing all his training before he took any, since they looked expensive.

It took him two days to work through the basics and feel stable enough to risk a visit to Maguire Incorporated. Plus, he couldn't get a day off work until then.

He'd looked up the location of the branch office, but he felt a little uncomfortable about just showing up there. Of course, it was even more uncomfortable trying to go to work with his boss constantly breathing down his neck about the pressure.

He had an unusual shift that day and went home early, so Melissa was still at school. Rick repeated his new exercises a few times, wondering if he was just wasting time instead of acting. Just as he was beginning to work himself up to the point of leaving for the headquarters, he got a text message.

It was a short message from Uncle Frank, indicating that he should set up video chat. They only had a creaky old laptop, but Rick fired it up and opened the program.

Soon his uncle appeared on screen, smiling. It was night on his side of the world, but it appeared that he was calling from some sort of ancient ruin. That wasn't surprising, but Rick was pretty unclear where he was getting electricity or internet. Perhaps it was a satellite connection, though he didn't bother asking because they had much more important issues.

"Richard!" His uncle smiled broadly. "Sorry, but I only just got your message. I can't talk long, but I wanted to check in with you."

"Thanks, Uncle. Do you think I'd be making a huge mistake with this?"

"Well, to be honest, the problem is that all your other options would be much bigger mistakes. You don't want to get on the wrong side of Maguire Incorporated." Uncle Frank took off his broad hat and balanced it on one finger idly. "The real question is how exactly it happened and who they believe. Based on the fact that this Mike fellow was looking for the core himself, it's possible that they're viewing this as his fault."

Rick breathed a sigh of relief. "I was thinking that, but I didn't want to assume anything might go my way."

"It's still good to be cautious, but I think you should go visit them. However, there's one thing you definitely need to do first: go to an independent professional and get the core properly extracted and stored. You do *not* want to let them do it themselves or they'll be able to take you for even more."

Now that it was said, it seemed obvious, but he had been planning to head in without it. Another dirty trick they pulled against people like him, but at least he was prepared this time. "Do you have anyone you can recommend?"

"Honestly... it's been so many years since I've been to Branton, I'm not sure. Heck, just look up ratings online and pick someone who looks half-way decent. The main thing is to have their core extracted in a form that you can just hand them when you walk in."

"I definitely will. Anything else?"

"I've been looking deeper into this Maguire Incorporated and I can't say I like the look of what I've found. Not that they're involved with anything illegal - if anything, they seem overly concerned with the rule of law. But they like using the law against people and they've done a lot of lobbying. Better to wash your hands of them as soon as possible."

"Thanks, Uncle. I definitely will if I can."

They talked about Melissa's condition and a few other topics, but then his uncle said he had to go. As the call ended, Rick felt lighter than he expected. Though his uncle might not be able to help him very much directly, it was good to have someone whose advice he could trust. With his uncle's blessing on the plan, he decided that he might as well get started that day.

After leaving a note for his sister, Rick headed out into the city. Searching through lucrim-based businesses on his phone, he quickly found one that looked like it could extract the core properly. He started to psych himself out reading one star reviews that talked about horrible side effects, but those seemed to be present for every single store in existence. Eventually he made his choice and headed down.

The location was a simple building, a clinic with a pharmacy attached. He'd seen the picture online, but it was much smaller than he'd anticipated. Rick headed in and discovered a small, clean lobby. A middle-aged woman looked up from the front desk and smiled at him.

"How can I help you?"

"I have a core fragment that I need extracted and preserved."

"Hmm." She frowned a little, examining something on her screen. "We can definitely help you, but the price will vary depending on how much it's meshed with the rest of your lucrima portfolio. Some Lucores aren't very discrete, you see, and it can be a long operation."

"This one was just an accident, so I doubt it merged with anything."

"Our expert will decide that, but hopefully so!" The woman gave him another sunny smile and took him to one of the back rooms.

Their expert turned out to be an old man in a traditional combat robe and a cowboy hat, as if he was going to challenge someone to a lucrim pistol duel at any moment. Rick tried not to let it bias him - it might be out of fashion today, but that outfit had once been widely respected.

In any case, the man certainly knew what he was doing, quickly isolating the Golden Core. As Rick had hoped, it would be an easy operation. The cost was just over 500 lucrim... there was a time when that amount would have made him hesitate, but now it was a cost he could absorb. If it let him finally be finished with Mike and his family's company, it was more than worth it.

"Sit down and relax, sonny," the old man said. "This isn't going to work unless you've completely suppressed your aura and put your whole portfolio in proper order."

Since he'd been training at that for some time, that part was easy too. The old man raised a hand in his direction, muttering to himself for a while, then lowered his hand. Rick frowned and glanced at him. "Is something wrong?"

"No, I'm done." The old man shifted his hand palm up, a tiny golden fleck floating within. As he transferred it to a small containment device, he cast Rick a disapproving glance from beneath his bushy eyebrows. "You're better off without this, sonny. Getting a bunch of power early might seem nice at first, but you'll pay for it in the end. If you ask me, they shouldn't even be allowed to sell these."

Rick had a feeling that this man gave a lot of opinions regardless of if anyone asked him or not, but he had no reason to argue. He carefully took the containment device and stood up. As he turned to go, the old man called after him.

"Just a minute, sonny. You bought the device, so you want the core... you're not keeping it as a souvenir or anything, are you?"

"What? No, why do you ask?"

"Because it's not going to last long. A core that small can't survive, not unless you've got some serious containment equipment. So if you want to do anything with it, you've got... oh, about twelve hours or so before it starts deteriorating."

"Ah. Thanks for telling me." Rick managed to keep a neutral expression on his way out, but as soon as he left the clinic, he scowled.

Showing up without no core and a suspicious story about losing it would be insane. He'd been hoping to take another few days to choose the right time, but instead Rick found himself hailing a taxi for the ride across town. It seemed he was going to Maguire Incorporated that day.

Chapter 17: Maguire Incorporated

The corporation's offices were all the way across Branton, so Rick waited nervously throughout the ride. Eventually he got out at his destination and spent a moment staring over the complex. This was just a branch office?

Maguire Incorporated's local headquarters spread out over ten acres, several buildings sprawling over a park-like space. The largest of them loomed over the others - not as tall as the buildings in the center of town, but far taller than anything out here. He stared up at the shimmering windows and looked over the name, letters higher than he was tall.

If this was a mistake, it was one he was committed to. Rick sighed and headed in.

Though not as intensely extravagant or powerful as the lawyer's offices, the corporate complex definitely spoke of wealth. He passed numerous people with lucrim generation rates of 50,000 or more, just normal employees. The outer part of the park area was open to the public, but when he approached the central building several private security guards emerged, all in six digits.

"You're free to enjoy the park," one of them said, "but to head further in, you need a badge. Got an appointment?"

"No, but you told me to come here." Rick had hoped he'd be allowed to talk to a secretary or someone instead of getting confronted. If it came to this, he decided to lead with his best card, so he pulled the core out of his pocket. "I don't know what this is, but I suspect it's way above your pay grade. I suggest you ask someone if they're missing an experimental core."

The security guards glanced at each other nervously, not having expected that. One of them started to reach for the containment device, but another slapped his hand away. "Don't touch it. And you... just stay there."

One of the guards, presumably the leader, moved away and spoke into a walkie-talkie. Rick couldn't quite hear the conversation, but it went back and forth for some time and included several awkward pauses. Eventually the leader came back wearing a grim expression.

"Okay, we're supposed to escort him in. Someone will come to pick it up."

Having armed security guards form ranks around him and force him to walk wasn't exactly comfortable, but Rick went quietly. That was better than it could have been, unless they were planning to take him somewhere private before attacking him. But they only escorted him to the main lobby of the building before drawing back to their places.

The central lobby was mostly white and silver with dark gray highlights, a massive room that spanned three floors. He could see people moving industriously on the upper levels, smartly dressed and packing a significant amount of lucrim. As many businesses as Maguire Incorporated was involved in, it was clear that this was their lucrim-focused branch.

Before he waited long, he spotted someone who stood out like a sore thumb. It was a man only a few years older than him, with a scruffy goatee and a shirt with stylized blood spatters. He slouched into the lobby, looked around, then headed in his direction.

"Oh, hey, are you the guy with the core?" He sounded much too casual for a place of business like this, grinning unevenly. Rick wasn't sure what to make of him, so he just pulled out the core again.

"If you mean this one, yes."

"Wow, great." With troubling speed the casually-dressed man slipped forward and took it from him. He drew it close and peered at it, then glanced toward him eagerly. "You're not part of the test group, but I gotta ask, did you feel anything? It's supposed to be a future lucrim burn, but if the core wasn't working right maybe it would have just felt like a drain?"

"Sorry, but that one is only 10 lucrim. Maybe a fragment. I have no idea what it is or what it's supposed to do, but I didn't feel anything strange." He decided to stick with that, hoping that they would brush him off as simply ignorant. The other man seemed disappointed.

"That sucks, man, but I guess that's how it goes. Though... how exactly did you get this thing? Weird that it got out, but the higher ups don't always tell me things."

Rick hesitated, completely unsure how to answer that question. He'd assumed that they knew exactly how he got it, so he hadn't prepared any lies on the subject. Before he could think of anything, they were interrupted by a man wearing a black suit, sunglasses, and a wire. His lucrima was tightly suppressed, but he immediately set Rick's teeth on edge.

He stopped nearby and swiveled his head toward the unkempt man. "You've confirmed recovery of the core?"

"Yeah, this is it. Looks like he had it removed by some competent rando. But no sign of damage or anything."

"Then you can go back to your work. I'll take it from here." With that, the man in the suit pivoted to look at Rick. "Come with me."

Saying no didn't really seem like an option, so Rick followed him. They left the main area and entered a hallway as lightly colored as the rest of the building. If not for the signs on the walls, Rick would have quickly become lost. They didn't go far, soon pulling into a small office. The man in the suit sat down and gestured for him to sit. It was not an offer.

As soon as Rick sat, bracing his strength despite himself, the man pulled out a sheaf of paper. Rick actually didn't see where he had been holding it, but there was no time for that because it was already being placed into his hands and the man was speaking.

"Maguire Incorporated appreciates you coming forward and returning our intellectual property voluntarily. However, we need you to sign this nondisclosure and anti-indemnification agreement immediately. If you do, our corporation will be able to appropriately compensate you for your assistance."

Rick shrugged off the play to his greed. He might be poor, but he couldn't be bought that easily. "Okay, just give me time to read all of this."

"That is not necessary."

"You want me to follow the entire agreement, don't you?" Though the suited man stared at him so intensely the entire room felt oppressive, Rick forced himself to read every single line carefully. It said that he couldn't sue for anything related to the core, couldn't hold them responsible for any losses, couldn't talk about the core's existence to anyone else, and more.

Seemed mostly like the company covering its ass, nothing too scary. Though he was surprised to note that a later clause directly said he couldn't sue or bring charges for any injuries taken during the acquisition of the core. The language of that clause wasn't in the same legalese as the rest. He wondered if it had been put in later, specifically regarding how Mike had attacked him.

"That is sufficient time. We need you to sign the agreement."

"Can I get a pen?" Since the suited man was putting off ever more dangerous vibes, Rick decided that he didn't have a real choice. The man handed him a pen, again slipping it out of his hand like some sort of magic trick, and Rick signed at the bottom of all the pages.

"Very good. Maguire Incorporated thanks you for your cooperation."

"You said you'd compensate me for my assistance?"

The man stood up, no longer looking at him. "Your reward is that Maguire Incorporated will not bring charges against you for theft of our intellectual property."

Typical. Rick frowned at the man, but internally he breathed a sigh of relief. Though it might have been from watching too many conspiracy movies, he'd halfway expected them to try to eliminate him after they got the core. In real life corporations didn't kill needlessly, though, just did whatever was necessary to get what they wanted. Which meant the core and his silence, in this case.

Since it seemed like their business had concluded, Rick stood up along with the suited man. Before they could go anywhere, the suited man cocked his head at an angle, listened for a moment, then turned back to him. "Stay where you are for several more minutes. Then you may go."

Those seemed like nonsense instructions, but Rick played along. He hadn't sat in the office very long before the door opened again and a wall of solid lucrim washed over him.

The man who walked in was middle-aged, with a full head of gray hair and an expensive suit. But all of that paled in comparison to the power within him. Rick thought that he had a decent amount of personal lucrim, but it was difficult to see through the radius of the Security Lucore.

Such cores were unbelievably expensive, used by politicians, celebrities, and other powerful figures in order to prevent assassination by lone warriors. The aura it put off was invisible, though obvious to anyone with the ability to sense lucrim, but it would stop most ordinary attacks cold. Whoever this man was, he was serious business. Several aides came along with him, bearing tablets, but he waved them back as he stepped in.

"I understand you had a little scuffle with Mike." The man had a soft, smooth voice. Somehow Rick felt that it would be a very bad idea to lie to him.

"He came into our gym and asked for a match. It was my shift, so I did my best to keep up with him. That's part of the job, sir."

To his surprise, the man chuckled. "Yes, I'm sure that it was all that polite. In any case, my people tell me that you managed to tear part of an experimental core from him."

"Uh..." Rick felt like the question was dangerous, but couldn't look away. "That might be how it happened, sir. I'm not sure."

"Relax, Richard. This turned into enough of an issue that I wanted to stop by myself, but the company isn't going to hold a grudge. This isn't the first time I've had to clean up after my son."

Rick kept a smile on his face while doing the exact opposite of relaxing. He'd just learned three things that made him far more nervous.

First, this man was Mike's father, the CEO of Maguire Incorporated. Second, he bothered to take a few minutes out of his schedule to visit personally, which couldn't be a good sign. Third, the man had just casually used his first name. While it was possible that he'd gotten it from the legal forms, Rick had a feeling that he'd just been threatened.

In any case, the CEO gave him a thin smile and turned away. "I approve of your initiative, young man. Be on your way and stay out of trouble."

With that, he left the room, already speaking with his assistants again. The oppressive aura went with him and Rick breathed a sigh of relief to be only under the scrutiny of the suited agent. When the man gestured for them to go, Rick went willingly.

He braced himself for things to go wrong at the last second, for guards to ambush him or a bullet to go through him. But instead he was escorted to the door and allowed to go. Once he was out in the park, walking away from the company headquarters, he finally stopped holding his breath.

Dealing with the matter directly had definitely been the right decision. Perhaps there was some way he could have profited off the Golden Core, but trying to mess with a company this big was insane. He didn't need any corporate intrigue in his life - dealing with all his other problems was more than enough trouble for him. As he headed out, Rick finally let himself smile.

A moment later, he felt a burst of power beside him. Honed by his time in the Underground, he moved to dodge immediately, but wasn't fast enough to stop a blurring fighter from rushing up to him and grabbing the front of his shirt.

"You bastard!" It was Mike. His blond hair flew wildly and fury burned in his eyes as he tightened his fist in Rick's shirt. "My own father... I'll never forgive you for this."

They were still in sight of multiple people in the garden, so Rick focused his lucrim defensively and made no move to attack, just raising his hands to either side. "I didn't mean to do anything. Whatever happened, it was an accident."

"Bullshit! I'd beaten you and you grabbed at my watch like a little thief! I'd been entrusted with that for testing purposes and you... you..."

It looked like Mike wanted to punch him in the face, so Rick braced for it. Yet he found his eyes wandering to the other man's wrist, which now wore a much less expensive-looking watch. So the experimental Lucore had been stored within it? That was odd, but not shocking. In any case, what had happened was finally known - not that it did him a lot of good.

"Listen up, you little shit." Mike had obviously noticed that people were watching, so he slowly unclenched his fist, but the hatred in his eyes grew. "I will *never* forget this. You are nothing to me, do you understand? However miserable your life is, I will find some way to make it worse. I'll grind you under my heel until you regret *ever* standing up to me."

The best choice would have been to end things peacefully, but when Rick looked into Mike's eyes, he knew that was an impossibility. So he couldn't stop himself from replying. "Come by any time for a rematch. I think I'll need to raise my rates next time, though."

Mike let out a growl and struck at him, but Rick managed to step back from the wild blow. For a moment the other man stared at him, seething, then he turned away and stormed off. Rick stood there for a little longer, then headed away, his smile disappearing.

So this wasn't over after all. To make matters worse, he saw that his phone had collected several messages, the timestamps suggesting that messages had been suppressed while he was in the building.

One from Melissa saying he needed to pick up more of her medication. Another from Jimmy telling him he needed to cover an extra shift tomorrow. And finally one from Granny Whitney listing a time he needed to arrive at the Underground for a match.

It never ended. Rick sighed and started walking back.

Chapter 18: Tea Training

For a couple of weeks, Rick managed to juggle everything without any of it going horribly wrong. At first he was constantly alert for Mike to attack him, but it seemed that his threats weren't going to be carried out immediately. Given that, Rick was able to slowly dig his way out of the holes fate had forced on him.

He'd expected Granny Whitney to throw him into horrible fights with life-threatening conditions, but her requests were nothing special. Just more general melee events, except she requested that he target certain candidates and make sure they went down.

So far he hadn't found any pattern to them, so he decided there was no reason not to cooperate.

More importantly, he earned 10-14 points for each of those events. That finally put him over 100 - specifically 112 - which meant that he had more control over the types of events he took part in. That included not getting thrown into Slayer matches according to rumors, though based on how much Alger had enjoyed it, Rick wouldn't put anything past the Underground's owner.

Granny Whitney had implied that something more important than average would occur when he passed 100, but had been busy with her own issues when it happened. Now he received a message indicating that he should meet her at a different address, which turned out to be a small building next to the Underground's makeshift hospital.

When he entered, he found her seated at the center of a couch with embroidered cushions piled to either side. She was currently working on knitting something, her knitting needles clicking back and forth with a practiced air.

"Hello there, dearie!" She smiled at him and gestured toward the seat opposite her with the back end of one knitting needle, not missing a stitch. "I do hope you have been keeping up all your training, because today we might be able to make some significant progress."

"I've been doing my best. I've advanced to the second stage of Graham's Focus, as described by the book. The restoration pills helped, and I think I did the sand ritual properly. Plus I've been trying Buffet's Buffer on my own, improving my foundation and putting all the extra toward removing the worst of the aura leeches."

"Well, look at you! How much progress have you made?"

"It's been reduced to..." He had to check his phone, since he found it easier to avoid focusing on the exact number. Better than he'd expected. "462 lucrim remaining. That's less than a third of the original debt."

"Wonderful, wonderful!" Granny Whitney beamed at him, as if proud of a favored grandson. It gave him a warm feeling for a split second before he became deeply suspicious. "I think I'll help you a little with that, dearie. You deserve a bit of a reward for all your hard work, plus you'll need to face more difficult challenges than simple melees from now on."

She set down her knitting needles for a moment, reaching into the handbag beside her... and pulled out a bottle of 100k philosopher's elixir in a liquor bottle. Then a china teacup. Then another liquor bottle. While Rick stared, she arranged everything on the coffee table in front of her.

"Would you be a dear and get the tea for me? It should be done by now."

He looked around the room and spotted an electric teakettle on a table in the corner. When he went to pick it up, he found it surprisingly heavy, much more so than he would have expected, to be filled with just hot water. When he carried it back to the table, Granny Whitney beamed at him again.

"Thank you, dearie! Now, sit back for a moment while I whip up a little something special."

When she began pouring the elixir into the teapot, he had to say something. "Is it really safe to mix philosopher's elixir and... whatever kind of tea that is?"

"Not only is it safe, it's delicious!" She filled the teacup and then pushed it across the table toward him. "The tea is a special recipe of mine, and adding the elixir gives it a bit of a kick. But what matters is that the two balance each other out. While the elixir spikes your current lucrim, the tea soothes your lucrima soul. Not ideal for growth, but excellent if you want to remove something holding you back, like an aura leech."

"Then I suppose I'll give it a try." He hesitantly took a sip and found it... strange. The mix was thick and sweet, not really like either component. Instead of a rush of power, it was more like a strong current, pushing his aura upward. "It's not bad."

"That entire pot is for you, but don't drink it all at once. It'll be most effective if you savor it."

He nodded and kept drinking, watching her over his cup. "Thank you for the gift, then. What else did you want to do?"

"You mean you don't want to sit and chat with your dear old Granny Whitney?" She clucked her tongue and began knitting again. "Show me your Graham's Focus."

Rick obeyed, going through the exercise several times while he continued to drink the tea. It was a bit more difficult with the liquid flowing through him, but he kept it up. All the Lucores within him seemed to melt a little into the current of his power, and after a time the old woman nodded.

"You've done well. We can move on to the real purpose of all this: reinvesting your Birthright Cores. They're not doing you very much good as they are now, so you might as well use them for something else, hmm?"

"No need to convince me, I completely understand." Plus, he would feel better not being regularly reminded of the mess his parents had left him, though he kept that to himself. "Could I apply those to the aura leeches and wipe out the debts entirely?"

"While you could, I don't think that would be a very good use of your strength. No, I had you do Graham's Focus in particular so that you could move on to something better than that: Graham's Stake."

He frowned, trying to remember all the details of it from the book. "I read that part, but the book was pretty obscure. I don't know if I can do the exercise, and even if I did, the book doesn't say a thing about what it actually does."

Granny Whitney shook her head. "The exercise is just a step toward developing a Lucore - a special sort of Lucore. Most types, you need to work terribly hard to improve them, but this one will naturally gather lucrim on its own and provide you with some of it. Slowly at first, yes, but it adds up over time. Graham's Stake is a simple form of this type, but there's nothing wrong with it. You won't regret having it in your lucrima portfolio even if you become a Perpetual Soul."

"But this new Lucore wouldn't grant me a direct capacity, would it? I understand the value, especially long term, but in the short term don't I need speed or an ability more?"

"Tut tut, young man. Believe me, one day you'll thank me for this. You might be able to progress quickly by just pouring everything into strength at first, but slow and steady wins the race."

"Then I'll bow to your superior wisdom." Also, he didn't have any choice in the matter. Granny Whitney beamed at him, knitting needles clicking even faster.

Following her instructions, Rick advanced forward with the exercise. Normally it would have been difficult to dissolve the Birthright Cores inside him and create something new, but the tea helped lubricate the whole process. Plus, the constant flow of new power made everything easier. He understood how rich people could become powerful, if they could develop themselves like this.

But apparently this "Graham's Stake" also helped them become more powerful, so he devoted himself wholly to mastering the technique. It involved drawing all of his aura up into a sphere, but unlike a normal core, this one had raw, mostly unrefined lucrim packed within. That was what produced the growth, or so he thought.

Bit by bit, he forced his spirit to conform to the shape he wanted. In the end, he felt utterly exhausted and every lucrim in his body was spent, but he'd dissolved the old cores into a new one. He fell back in his chair, taking a moment to breathe.

Granny Whitney smiled and filled his teacup. "Well done, dearie. Have another drink and pep yourself up. We'll be rid of that aura leech before too long as well."

"Really? But it..." Rick trailed off as he felt inside himself and realized how much the aura leech had grown. It was still draining his strength the same as before, and the creature itself was actually stronger than it had been, but it was nearly sated. He would finally be free.

"You've made more progress than you know. This path can seem like hard work and no play at times, but occasionally it pays off." She took the teapot, chopping up some sort of root into fine pieces, and then poured the entire second bottle of philosopher's elixir into the pot. "Now, are you familiar with drinking games?"

"What?" Rick stared at her and she smiled back.

"They can be great fun, you know. In any case, this next part... there's no way to do it in a civilized fashion, so you will just have to push through. What do children say these days? 'Chug'? Or am I behind the times?"

"Are you saying I'm supposed to drink all of it at once?"

"As much of it as you can, anyway."

Shaking his head, Rick eyed the teapot. Was he really going to just drink the whole thing? "Should I put it in something else, or just... directly out of the spout?"

"Stop being a pussy and drink it, dearie." Granny Whitney shook her head. "Oh, forgive my language. It's a rather silly phrase, isn't it? But seriously, drink it."

Driven by the desire not to have an old woman using language like that at him, Rick picked up the entire pot and began drinking from the spout. It burned more than the mix of tea before, but unlike drinking elixir directly, it wasn't like fire through his body. Instead it was like molten lava pushing through his veins.

He wanted to stop, but he felt like if he did, he couldn't convince himself to start again, so he drank the entire thing.

Somehow he set the empty teapot back down, then he slumped back in his chair. For a while he just did his best to stay conscious.

Eventually he came to, still in the chair and without having vomited or anything else embarrassing. Granny Whitney seemed to be brewing a new pot of tea, hopefully a normal one this time. When she saw he was up, she turned back to him and smiled.

"Very good, dearie. Now, let's get rid of that leech, shall we?"

He couldn't quite believe it, but he realized that it was true: the third leech was no longer draining his strength. When he focused inside himself, it didn't burrow into his lucrima, instead rising to the surface. Going on instinct, Rick reached inside himself and tried to push the aura leech out.

To his surprise, it worked almost immediately. The creature emerged from his chest, flopped around on the floor a while, and then suddenly curled up into itself and vanished. It was gone. One of the three was entirely gone. He felt stronger already, though it was just a single step in the right direction.

Both procedures had left him weak and drained, but that was apparently why Granny Whitney was making tea. She finished and brought it back to the table. Once he had a cup of it, he felt much more himself, and ready to make use of all the new strength he'd been given.

"Go on," she said, "I can see you're itching to get out that phone of yours. See what you've made of yourself."

Rick didn't need to be told twice.

[Name: Rick Hunter

Ether Tier: 18th

Ether Score: 161

Lucrim Generation: 22,800

Effective Rate: 15,547

Current Lucrim: 16,426]

[Rick Hunter's Lucrima Portfolio

Foundation: 7400 (Lv II)

Offensive Lucore: 3850 (Lv III)

Defensive Lucore: 6550 (Lv V)

Graham's Stake: 3100 (Lv II)

Aura Leech: -4641 (Stage II)

Aura Leech: -2612 (Stage I)

Tracking Bond: 100 (Lv XIII)

Gross Lucrim: 22,800

Net Lucrim: 15,547]

For a moment, he was satisfied with all the progress he'd made. He had a new high quality core and one of the leeches was gone - he'd been working toward those things for a long time. But the next moment, he felt a bit of disappointment: all of that work just to get back to almost where he had been before his parents had left him the terrible debts.

After that, however, Rick forced himself to be more positive. It wasn't true that he was back in the same position: his lucrim generation rate might be about the same, but his use of it was far more effective. He'd made significant progress, and he'd make even more as he kept moving forward.

"I think I've hit my limit for the day," he said, "but what do we aim for next? Can we take out another one of the leeches?"

"You'll certainly want to do that in time, but perhaps not right away." Granny Whitney didn't sit down again, instead coming over to put a hand on his shoulder. "You've done well today, but I'm afraid we're running out of time. Let's get down to the Underground so that you can have your match, hmm?"

After so much time spent working on himself, a fight sounded good. Plus, it was going to be a new type, which might be interesting. Rick followed Granny Whitney out of the building and over to the Underground, his steps surprisingly light.

When they reached the chain link fences leading into the arena itself, she stopped him. He was focused forward, noting the large crowd and lack of other fighters, but she pulled his attention back to her. After looking through her handbag for a time, she pulled out a large blue pill and handed it to him.

"Take this pill, dearie. This is going to be a difficult fight."

"Alright." He swallowed it without any water, hoping that it would give him the edge he needed. Yet as he felt it dissolve into him, his head spun. All the strength seemed to be draining out of his body and he found himself clutching the fence just to stand up. "I don't feel... should I have taken that...? So soon after the rest...?"

"Oh dear, it seems you've misunderstood me. This battle is going to be difficult *because* of that pill I just gave you." Granny Whitney patted his cheek. "Now get out there and try your best, dearie."

Chapter 19: Handicap

"Another three way match!" Alger sat forward in his seat, watching gleefully. "Three more contestants who have begun to prove themselves... fight!"

Rick's vision was blurring horribly and his body felt like it would shrivel up at any moment. The announcement was actually his first indication that he was only fighting two other people, since it was hard to focus on those in the arena versus those watching.

Then one of them burst into flame. Okay, he was easy to see. Rick slumped backwards as fireballs started flying, managing to avoid the initial burst.

It would have made sense to close the distance and attack the burning opponent, but the dizziness made even walking difficult. His hope of the other two fighting each other was dashed as well when he felt someone else rushing at him. Focusing, he could barely see that it was a middle-aged woman in a track suit, moving pretty fast directly for him.

If he was going to make it through, he needed to finish the match quickly. She opened with a kick that had a fair amount of lucrim behind it, but he managed to dodge aside. Another kick came immediately after, but he pulled himself together, deflected it, and then slammed an elbow into her face.

Except she caught the blow.

Normally he would have reacted in time to evade, but disoriented as he was, he ended up taking a kick to the chest. Rick staggered back, his defensive core preventing serious injury but not blocking the pain as it normally should. Worse, she lifted her leg, aiming to bring it down on his head.

Fighting through his symptoms, Rick dodged the downwards kick and struck back. She deflected his next blow and returned it with one of her own. As they traded blows, Rick realized that she was not only stronger than him, she was probably more skilled. Some type of kickboxing style reserving her hands for defense.

Direct physical contact was a mistake, then, but he didn't have the time or mental capacity to come up with a better plan. The ring just kept spinning around him and the strength he should have had simply refused to come. He mentally cursed Granny Whitney for putting him in this situation, then realized that he was overreaching and was going to take a vicious kick.

He was saved by an onslaught of flames from the third fighter. They definitely hurt, but he was able to tank them, while the woman had evaded backward. That gave him a few moments of freedom, which he used to stagger clear. Given how his condition was worsening, if anything, this might be his only chance to turn the tide of the fight.

Forcing himself to focus through the haze, Rick ducked beneath another burst of flame and sprinted toward the burning opponent. Another bolt shot directly at his face and he had no time to think, just smashed his hand at it. Though it singed painfully, he managed to deflect it and came into range.

Punching the flaming aura hurt like hell, but he felt his opponent stagger backward. Rick knew he should take advantage of that and follow up, yet he felt as though he'd used up everything in that charge.

When his opponent restored his flames, Rick realized that he needed to return to defense. The flaming man spun in a low kick that released a swath of flame across the ground. All Rick could manage to do was jump straight up, avoiding the flames but leaving himself vulnerable to a direct strike.

Or the woman grabbing his ankle while he was still in midair.

She swung his body directly into the flaming man, sending both of them smashing over the ground and into the chain link fence. It was the most Rick could do to hold back the flames threatening to scorch him, then slowly push himself back to his feet.

After that, it was only a matter of time. He refused to give up or fall easily, but he didn't have the strength to land any attacks, so he quickly wore himself down. Over time he managed to regain some focus despite the dizzying haze around him and his overall weakness, but it wasn't enough.

Blow by blow, flame by flame, he eventually dropped. Rick was lying on the ground wishing he was dead when he finally heard the bell marking the end of the match.

Someone pulled him from the arena and gave him basic medical treatment. He drifted in and out of consciousness for a while, then gradually returned. Strangely, though his bruises and burns ached when he sat up, he felt less horrible than he should have. The strength that had been taken from him was flowing again, leaving him in decent condition.

With no other options, Rick pulled out his phone to check the results.

[Match Performance:

Participation +5

Fall (x3) -3

Endurance +1

Total Reward: 3

Cumulative Points: 115]

That was his worst match so far, entirely because Granny Whitney had handicapped him from the start. He should have felt anger, but when he was honest with himself, he knew that he should have expected such a thing. When he saw her enter the room, he just gave her a flat stare.

"Are you going to tell me what that was about?"

"Collecting points is a fine hobby, dearie, but it won't matter in the end." She walked in and handed him something that looked like... like a mint, actually, though he could feel lucrim within it. "Right now, winning is less important for you than training."

"And getting the shit kicked out of me is training?"

"Actually, the point was to kick the shit out of your foundation. Test yourself, see how it feels."

He closed his eyes and tried to do so, and to his surprise, he found that his foundation had changed. It felt denser, but not the way it did after normal condensation. Instead, it was as if parts of it had been burned and hammered into a different shape.

"That pill I gave you exists for foundation improvement, but there's only so much you can put yourself through during the critical period. No matter how much willpower you have, you won't be able to be as hard on yourself alone as you would be trying to fight two opponents who aren't holding back."

Rick nodded slowly, accepting that she had a rationale other than cruelty. Didn't make too much of a difference to what he was facing, though. "I'm guessing this isn't the last time?"

"Goodness, no. Get used to the side effects, dearie, because you'll be feeling them every match from now on."

"Are you sure this isn't bad for me? My foundation might be denser, but it feels... damaged."

"Don't worry your pretty little head about that. You'll be fine if you take your medicine and keep going." Granny Whitney pointed to the pill she'd handed him and then turned. "Having said that, I need to be going now. Lots to do, lots to do. Have fun until your next match, okay, dearie?"

All he could do was nod. Rick swallowed the pill she'd given him and did feel a little better. Though it tasted and dissolved *exactly* like a mint, so part of him had to wonder if it wasn't just a piece of candy and the placebo effect. It was hard to put anything past the old woman.

After taking a moment to collect himself, he left the room and almost immediately ran into Henry. His friend had a bandaged cut along his forearm but otherwise looked fine. "Hey, man, looks like we had matches at almost the same time. Are you alright? That was a pretty weak showing out there."

"I don't want to talk about it."

"That's cool, man, just saying. Try to get as many points as you can - there's a rumor that there will be a big event in a couple months or so, but not everyone will be able to participate."

Most likely that was referring to the multi-tier tournament that Granny Whitney wanted to use him for. It felt odd knowing more about the Underground than Henry, though Rick wasn't sure it was worth the price. Besides, it felt like his friend had improved again. "That demonic bond seems to be working out for you."

"Kind of." Henry headed out and Rick kept pace with him as they headed back to the surface. "I got it upgraded to 12,000 lucrim, but I don't think it's going to improve much more than that. I could take a second bond, but the terms would be worse. Basically, I'm starting to see the limits of trying to gain power this way."

"Well, it definitely helped you this far." Rick didn't say anything about the real limitation: the consequences of overusing a demonic bond. Especially not since Henry would just needle him about his recent poor performance.

"It's like I said earlier, man - nothing's set up to help out the little guy. We're doing a lot better than some and we're still not able to get ahead." Henry shook his head as if to shed those thoughts and then smiled at him. "You want to do something, man? Since I haven't been working as much lately, I feel like we haven't hung out in forever."

"Why not? I'm not doing much right now and I could use some recovery time."

"If that's what you want, there's a place not far away that makes lucrim shakes. They're not gonna change your life, but they're cheap and they should help you recover a bit. I could go for one myself."

After the recent challenges, that sounded good to him. "Sure, let's go."

"Alright, just let me stop by the shrine on our way."

Rick held his tongue and didn't complain. Soon enough they arrived at the shrine, a gaudy little place next to a gas station. The upper tiers were plastered with posters that declared the incredible power of Malcor the Magnificent - another independent mystic with a gimmick, basically. Trying not to judge, Rick just stayed back and watched.

Bending down in front of the lucrim collector, Henry focused and extracted some of his aura. He created a large drop in his palm that must have cost him 100 lucrim or so, then dropped it into the collection bowl.

Mystic lights flashed overhead, power flowed around the bowl to consume the aura, and then the collector spat out a ticket.

Henry grabbed it, then repeated the process several more times. Once he'd collected five tickets he stood up, pocketing them with a pleased expression on his face, as if he hadn't just blown 500 lucrim on nothing at all.

"Really, man?" Rick knew that he shouldn't, but found himself unable to help it. "You know the chances of the mystic picking you are like a million to one. It's throwing lucrim away."

"Nah, man, I have a system." Henry flashed his tickets with a grin. "The mystic doesn't like to pick students from the same location too many times in a row, so I change up which shrine I use based on the past winners. Plus, your odds go way up if you donate five times or more."

"Sure, five in a million. Have you ever even met the mystic? Gotten anything?"

"I mean, I haven't gotten lucky yet, but he sent me a pretty nice scroll once. Learning the tech on that thing raised my generation rate by over 150 lucrim!"

And most likely he'd spent far more than that acquiring it, but Rick got himself under control because he didn't want an argument. Uncle Frank had always said that the independent mystics were basically just increasing their power by parting fools from their lucrim, and it seemed that was true. In the old days, they had to sit on their mountaintops and rely on intrepid fighters to offer donations. These days, they could automate the whole system and gain far more power.

They started to walk away from the shrine and Rick tried to think of an easy way to change the topic. Before he could, the door to the gas station opened and two people walked out - two people he wouldn't have expected to see at all, much less together.

The first was Emily, the fighter from the Underground. And the second was one of the two Birthrighters who had beaten him with Mike. Rick stared in shock, wondering what to do, and then they made eye contact and he didn't have a choice anymore.

Chapter 20: Emily

For a moment no one said a word. Rick turned away, almost hoping that it would pass without any comment, but then the Birthrighter took a step forward.

"Holy shit, it's that guy Mike was looking for! You have any idea how pissed he is?"

Rick sighed. "He mentioned it to me."

"He said we should take a swing at you if we got the chance. Maybe I will..."

Though Rick didn't want to get into a fight outside a random gas station, he realized that he might not have a choice. Just one more twist of fate for life to throw at him.

The guy looked a couple years older than Mike and had his dark hair cut unfashionably short. He wore jeans and a polo shirt that looked normal but that Rick suspected cost an absurd amount of money. For a Birthrighter he was pretty built and he still had a strong aura. Now that Rick was more accustomed to powerful lucrima, he suspected that this one had a core that produced a generation rate of around 110,000 lucrim.

"Cool it, Glenn." The woman had a stern normal expression, but now proved that was nowhere near a frown as she fixed the Birthrighter with a vicious gaze. He turned to her and scowled back.

"Why are you getting involved? You know these losers?"

"They're just random people from the Underground, but I've had enough pointless fights for the day. Back off."

For a moment they stared at each other, auras seething. As far as Rick could tell, Emily had a generation rate of roughly 85,000 lucrim and should have been at a disadvantage, yet that didn't seem to be the dynamic between them. She was entirely calm, while Glenn was the one putting up a front and eventually backing down.

After taking several steps back, he turned back to jab a finger in Rick's direction. "Alright, you get off today. But it's only a matter of time..." He ran a finger across his throat, smiled unpleasantly, and then turned and stalked away.

Emily watched him go, then turned to them with an irritated expression. "I don't like that I got involved in this, but since you made him go away... I'll call us even."

"What exactly was this?" Henry glanced at Glenn's retreating back, then smirked. "Fight with your boyfriend?"

"Hardly." Emily cast both of them a look of pure scorn and Rick winced to be included in it. "We used to work together and he wanted me to bail him out again."

Henry started to say something else that probably wouldn't help, so Rick stepped between them and cut him off. "I know you said you didn't want to get involved, but even a little information from you could help me a lot. Mike and Glenn have it out for me, as you probably heard. Do you know anything about them?"

"Not very much. I just used to work for Mike's dad." Emily gave a shrug. "It was a decent job and their tech staff are good, but too many of the executives are douchebags with Birthright Cores and trust funds. I saw Mike a few times but I never met him."

"And Glenn?"

"He was over our department - his dad went to school with Mike's dad or something, so he got him a job. Something something nepotism. I wasn't paying attention at that point - I was on my way out because I was tired of cleaning up Glenn's messes. But because he's an incompetent tool, he came to ask me for more help."

Rick nodded thoughtfully, absorbing the new information. Not exactly actionable, but it gave him a better idea what he was dealing with. Based on how they'd worked together, and what Glenn had said earlier, Rick was afraid that Mike had both of his friends looking for him. Even if this was a solely personal vendetta and Maguire Incorporated didn't get involved, he had three threats to worry about.

While Rick was thinking, Henry spoke up again. "So, where do you work now?"

"Not that it's any of your business, but EthCom."

"Seriously? A cute girl like you shouldn't be a slave to a corporation like that."

There might have been worse things to say, but Rick wasn't sure what they could have been. Emily's eyes went extremely cold. "Excuse me?"

"What, don't tell me you're going to defend your corporate masters? They don't care about you, you're just a cog in their machine, a-"

To Rick's surprise, Emily laughed, though not pleasantly. "Unless you're secretly a terrorist, you're a lot more enmeshed in the 'machine' than I am. I'm an engineer with a valuable specialty - I could leave EthCom any time I wanted. I'm guessing the two of you don't have that option, whatever form of 'wage slavery' you take part in."

"Hey, I was playing nice, but-"

"Henry." Rick put a hand in front of him to shut him up and focused on Emily. "We don't want to pick a fight here. If Glenn visited here, does that mean he knows about the Underground? Do you think it's likely that he'd tell Mike and they might try something?"

"Probably." Emily folded her arms and regarded him coolly. "Glenn and his buddies are more bark than bite, so it's not like they'd put a hit out on you. But there's a good chance they'll show up. Honestly, if I was in your shoes, I'd just make myself scarce. It's not like you have much of a chance against them... especially not if you're blowing all your lucrim on independent mystics."

Rick bristled and tried not to overreact. "I don't play those games, Henry was the one who-"

"Hey!" Henry grabbed his shoulder. "Don't try to lie to impress her, man! You're always going on about winning big and becoming a student to some mystic!"

Completely stunned for a moment, Rick stared at Henry, who gave him a smug grin. Okay, maybe it had been a dick move to throw Henry under the bus, but he hadn't wanted Emily to get the wrong impression. He really wanted to get to know her better, for multiple reasons, but right now that seemed very unlikely.

She regarded both of them and he could tell she was analyzing them as fighters. Unfortunately, with his lucrima portfolio hampered by life circumstances and bearing the two remaining leeches, he must have looked pathetic. Though there wasn't quite scorn in her eyes, he didn't like what he saw there.

"What does Whitney see in you?" She spoke almost underneath her breath and he wanted to inquire further, but after that Emily turned away. "I'll leave you two to your fun." Before he could object, she lifted into the air and disappeared in a streak of purple aura.

Not the introduction he would have wanted. So she was an engineer of some kind... that explained her high lucrim generation rate, though not what she was doing fighting in the Underground. Her reference to Granny Whitney was strange as well, since it might have been a simple observation that she assisted him, but it also could imply that he was missing information.

"What a bitch." Henry glared after her sourly. "Okay, maybe I came on too strong, but seriously. She was looking down on us from the start."

"Why are you acting like a dick, man?" Rick turned on him, but his coworker just chuckled.

"Come on, man, you know you don't have a chance with her."

"I don't care about that, I care that she might have information about the guy who promised violent vengeance on me!" He didn't raise his voice often, but realized that it had gotten out of control. Henry's eyes widened as he realized that they weren't just messing around and he raised his hands.

"Sorry, man. Honestly."

"Does she come to the Underground on any sort of schedule?"

"Not that I can tell. It's pretty random."

"Fine." Rick turned away, considering his options. Based on what Emily had said, it wasn't likely that she had any terribly sensitive information about Mike and his cronies. But he wanted to ask her about her aura and the methods she used to fight more powerful opponents. There was something more solid about her lucrima that he thought might hold some secret he was lacking...

"You wanna just go get those lucrim shakes?"

Though Rick wanted to snap back, he realized that he was acting childishly. Henry was just being his usual self and he shouldn't have expected anything different. He wouldn't gain anything by lashing out or making a big deal of it. "Alright, man. Let's see if they're as good as you say."

As it turned out, they weren't bad. Not the best thing he'd ever tasted, but really cheap for a lucrim-based drink. Things were only awkward for a little while before they got back to normal and left the matter behind them.

At least out loud. Internally, Rick found himself wondering about his decisions. Honestly, Henry was probably the sort of person his Uncle Frank would disapprove of, participating in illegal fights and taking on heavier and heavier demonic bonds. Though Rick thought of himself as independent, he couldn't deny that he might be influenced subconsciously. Emily had glanced over both of them like they were exactly the same, beneath her attention...

Several days passed without anything significant coming of the encounter, though Rick kept watching his back. The way Emily had talked about Mike and Glenn made him slightly less worried, but he still didn't want to be on the receiving end of their wrath.

Now that he knew that Granny Whitney was going to be handicapping him in every match, he was able to prepare differently. He tried to keep himself at full strength, which was easier now that he had more money and lucrim to work with. Some days he even considered if he could quit working at the House of the Cosmic Fist, though the rational side of his brain told him that would be far too risky.

For now, anyway. Rick wasn't sure what had caused it, but something had changed within him. He didn't want to be working at a crappy little gym his entire life, to be someone people like Emily looked down on, to get kicked around by the powerful.

Of course, neither did anyone else. But he found himself driven to change it in a way he never had been before.

When Melissa had another severe incident, he didn't let it slow him down. Instead of panicking, he made sure she had her normal medication, let lucrim flow to ease the ether void, and even purchased another item from the pharmacy that was supposed to lessen her symptoms.

But this time, she didn't get better.

Chapter 21: Worth Any Price

Rick sat on the couch, staring at the carpet as if it would give him answers. Currently Melissa lay in her room, sleeping soundly after her condition had flared up again. The life-threatening emergencies seemed to come and go, but the ether void within her soul refused to go away. He kept feeding her lucrim in order to keep her at 1000 or more, but it was no true solution.

The bitter part was that he kept getting distracted by trivial details. She had missed school the previous day and the school had called, and to add insult to injury, they refused to believe anything without a doctor's note. Of course, if they could afford a doctor, they wouldn't have this problem. Now his sister's life was at stake and he was being pestered by administrators about school absences.

It was obvious that he couldn't resolve this alone, it was just a question of what he could actually do. After considering all his options and trying to call Uncle Frank, he decided that he had no choice but to beg.

One more time he glanced at her profile:

[Melissa Hunter

Lucrim Generation: 3249

Current Lucrim: 1000

Ether Void: -3]

The void had already gone to -3, even though she'd taken medication so recently. Though it wasn't worsening faster as far as he could tell, the fact that it never subsided completely made this into a nightmare that would eventually take her life.

Padding into the bedroom, Rick checked that his sister had everything she needed. He bent down to lightly touch her hair and her eyes opened immediately. Right now she was doing okay, with no obvious pain or shivering, but he thought she was hiding her discomfort from him.

"I'm going out for a bit, Melissa. I need to talk to a few people about what we might do."

"I'm really sorry about this." She hadn't apologized since the beginning, but now there were tears in her eyes. Rick hastily shook his head and sat down beside her.

"Don't even start. This isn't your fault, and we'll get through this together."

"But you have so many other things you need to worry about..."

"I'd give even more to help you. We're the only family we have, sis. We stick together."

She smiled and nodded. "Then go. I won't push myself, but I'm really feeling pretty good right now. Don't fret about me, just do what you can."

Managing to find a smile for her, Rick headed out. After getting his keys and locking the door behind him, he leapt from the third floor of their apartment and began running.

Though he didn't expect her to collapse the instant he left, he didn't want to be away from her for long and he had a great deal he needed to do. If he could, he would have spent everything he had on a lucrim vehicle to fly him to his destinations, but that required a higher ether score than he possessed to do legally, and he couldn't afford the risk of any of the unofficial options.

In between caring for his sister, Rick had done his best to research more, even though it was mostly going over the same sources they'd read long ago. Researching about her new condition did turn up a few new sites, but they were mostly filled with the desperate and grieving.

Of course there were a few who declared all of modern medicine to be a hoax and that natural medicines could keep the condition at bay. The frustrating thing was that the world was filled with special herbs and ancient remedies, so they could always find a way to justify their position and avoid being seen as complete quacks. But based on how his sister's condition had come and gone, he doubted there was anything more to their remedies than confirmation bias.

His first stop was Granny Whitney's house near the Underground. He didn't want to take that step, but with his sister's life on the line, he couldn't afford to ignore it. Since he had already called ahead to say that he would miss his previous match, she was waiting for him.

"This isn't how this relationship is supposed to work, dearie." Her smile was as grandmotherly as always, yet somehow discomforting. "But since you've been a good lad so far, I decided to hear you out. What's troubling you these days?"

"I haven't mentioned her, but I have a sister with a serious medical condition..." He described the situation briefly, ending with the recent difficulties. Granny Whitney listened quietly and nodded once he was done.

"Yes, ether voids can be very troublesome unless they're taken care of early."

"I know that there are cures for those with enough money," Rick said, "but I haven't been able to find out what that cure actually entails."

"The details are always hidden, and many corporations or sects claim to have special cures, but they all come down to the same thing: removing the core of the patient's lucrima and entirely rebuilding it."

Rick blinked. "That's possible? I mean, you can survive that?"

"Not without assistance." Granny Whitney shook her head. "You see, most of us have a tiny seed of ourselves at the core of our soul. The lucrim equivalent of an aura spark. Lucrim from the natural world stick to that seed, and over the years the lucrim grow by accretion until you have a proper lucrima soul. But not everyone is the same. For example, some seeds are naturally 'sticky', making a person develop sooner, and some are so 'slippery' that the person never develops any strength and dies not long after birth."

"And my sister's seed is wrong somehow? It can't maintain its grip on lucrim?"

"She doesn't have one at all. At the core of her being there isn't the seed of a soul, but... a flame, you might say. It might be able to gather lucrim around it, but the flame eats it away from within. Given extremely expensive surgery, it might have been possible to snuff out that flame and transplant a synthetic seed... when she was younger. Now, the flame has likely grown too intense."

All he could do was stare at her, wishing that someone had told him this earlier, that things could have been different. But what could he have done, other than be born into a wealthy family? "Are you saying there's no hope? No other way to help her?"

"In theory, it might be possible to build a shell of lucrim around the flame, one durable enough that it isn't drawn in. If she trained enough, she could maintain that shell herself." Granny Whitney shrugged. "But the arts for that are rare and the process would be expensive. There's likely nothing that can be done."

"Please..." He would have gotten down on his knees if he thought it would help, but looking in her eyes, he didn't see any mercy there. "You've helped me get this far... can we take everything you were going to give me and give it to my sister instead?"

Granny Whitney shook her head slowly. "Dear boy, think this through. I'm willing to help you because it benefits my interests in the end. Your sister isn't a part of my plans."

Rick stared at her numbly. He had suspected that she would turn him down, but he still wasn't sure how to deal with her looking him in the eye with that kind smile and telling him that she didn't care about his sister's life. Yet as they maintained eye contact, he knew that it was true.

"I'm sorry that it has to be this way, dearie, I truly am. Ether voids are an awful shame, but since the condition is rather rare, there's been no real need to move beyond the established solutions."

"You aren't sorry." Rick took a deep breath and stood up. "But you've already invested time and money in me for your little contest. You don't want to throw that away."

Her eyes glittered sharply. "Just what are you saying?"

"That if you do nothing and let my sister die, my life won't be worth enough to me for you to blackmail me. I might not be able to threaten you with any real harm, but you can bet that I'll do everything in my power to make your investment worthless."

To his surprise, Granny Whitney chuckled. "You have a strong spine, lad. But as I told you, your sister is likely too old for the replacement operation, and in any case that would require far more wealth than I ever intended to spend on you. I might be willing to cooperate a little... but you'll need to make me a better offer."

"What about the other option, the shell? I imagine you wouldn't simply give us a technique that rare or pay for someone to implement it, but does the process have to be done all at once? Surely even a semi-permanent shell would be an improvement over the current situation."

"It would prolong her life, yes. Perhaps buy enough time for a better solution."

"Then we'll do that. I won't ask you for a single lucrim - but you have to give me the basic knowledge of how the technique can be performed, or we have no hope at all."

"Unfortunately, such techniques are closely guarded secrets that even I haven't uncovered." Just when he was about to object, Granny Whitney leaned forward, a spark in her eyes. "But I have given this problem a little thought myself, and I can show you an alternative. Perhaps one that would even be more suited to your situation..."

She outlined the basics and he committed it all to memory. When she dismissed him, Rick was tempted to thank her, but realized that she probably wouldn't care. So instead he just nodded to her and left, rushing back home on a route that would take him past the liquor store.

The basic concept involved several steps. First, overload Melissa with new lucrim - easy to do with philosopher's elixir. Second, have her solidify that into a core with no other purpose - she'd gotten good marks in Lucrim Education in school, so she should be able to do it. Third, find some way to push her lucrim away from the core flame - that one would be the problem.

If they succeeded in all of those, then Melissa's condition should stabilize for the short term. More importantly, if she could find a way to maintain the sphere of lucrim and turn it into a proper shell, it could become a long term solution. Perhaps not a cure, and maintaining it sounded ludicrously expensive, but it was worth trying.

Inside the liquor store, Travis sat in his glass box, drinking from a plastic cup. The store was empty and the owner seemed vaguely irritated to see a customer, illogical as that seemed. But Rick had no time for such concerns today.

"I need philosopher's elixir, as high quality as you have."

"You can't afford the highest, kid." Travis stared at him for a bit, then grunted and pointed to a grimy sheet of paper with prices listed. "That's what we have. Money on the counter first."

Looking over the list, Rick saw that he was right: there was no way that he could afford the highest quality elixir the store sold. Above 250k, it actually required payments of lucrim in addition to money. But with all the money he had been earning from fights in the Underground, he could just barely afford the 250k option.

"A bottle of 250k, then." He set his money down on the transaction counter, but to his surprise Travis didn't grab it immediately.

"That's strong stuff, kid. I'm not supposed to sell it to somebody like you."

"Are you really going to turn down my money?"

"Ain't that simple. For one, if you get yourself killed or do something stupid, it could come back to me." Travis watched him with a smug look. "And based on your behavior last time, I'm starting to think that you might be prone to irrational behavior."

Gritting his teeth, Rick began to consider his other options. The glass cube was built to withstand people stronger than him, but it wasn't invincible. He knew intellectually that robbing a store would never lead him to a real solution, but he was running out of options...

Something in his eyes must have changed, because Travis switched to a frown. "Tell you what... if you pay me for that bottle you cheated from me last time, and you get down on your knees and beg, maybe I'll sell it to you."

Rick slapped the money down on the counter and dropped to the floor. "Please... I beg you. Someone I love is very sick, and without-"

"Alright, already." Travis shifted back in his seat, staring at him. He tried to laugh mockingly, but it just sounded uncomfortable. "Didn't realize you'd be that shameless. If you're willing to go that far, it's yours. And don't think about testing this one... believe me, it's 250k."

The money had already been collected, so Rick stood up and accepted the bottle. This one glowed brilliantly in his hands, though he still checked as best he could. It definitely felt far more intense than any philosopher's elixir he'd ever handled before, intense enough that he didn't dare try it personally. But hopefully, that meant it would be enough for Melissa.

Travis started to say something else to mock him, but Rick turned around and walked out without listening to a word. He had almost no money left, so if this didn't work...

Better not to think about that. Securing the bottle in his jacket, he headed back as fast as he dared.

Chapter 22: Flame in the Void

When Rick returned home, he found Melissa in the middle of another fit, one that would have been a crisis until recently but now happened regularly. Despite her shuddering, it looked as though she'd taken one of her pills and was clutching several of the lucrim-filled marbles he'd left with her. She was getting better at resisting the symptoms, so if only they could find a solution...

"Melissa, can you hear me?" He touched her shoulder gently, afraid that she might break. Her eyes fluttered open.

"Rick? Do you... have something?"

"I found a temporary solution that might make you feel better. But it's going to require a lot of work on your part..." He explained the basic theory of the consuming flame where her soul should have had a lucrim seed. To his surprise, Melissa sat up and became much more alert, then actually smiled as he finished explaining.

"Is that really it? It's funny, but hearing an explanation like that makes it seems so much more manageable... I thought there was just a hole in me, but..." She cut off, wincing and grabbing her heart. "Gh... it's not... not a real fit... just hurts a bit..."

"We should start early. You're going to need to create a sphere of lucrim within yourself. Similar to what they taught in L.E. about building cores, but it's going to be much more difficult."

"Show me."

Since she seemed determined, Rick launched straight into the explanation. Melissa had always been sharp, so she picked it up quickly. Though she didn't have much experience working with lucrim and her body shivered involuntarily at times, she threw herself into the task. Soon she actually had the basics right, though after that she slumped back against the baseboard of her bed.

"I think... I got it a little... but I'm just so tired..."

"That's what this is for." Rick pulled the bottle of philosopher's elixir out of his backpack and held it just out of her reach. "Now, this part is going to be a little dangerous. In theory, because you don't have a core, the elixir can't latch on and burn you. But you do have lucrim inside you and it will react to that, so it will hurt a lot, and you'll need to be careful."

"Rick... what type is that? How expensive was it?"

"Don't worry about that - you need to focus 100% on getting ready to use it."

Though Melissa gave him another nervous glance, eventually she nodded determinedly. When he handed her the bottle she took a whiff and looked queasy, but kept exposing herself to the intensity of it. As she did so, she began repeating the core exercise as well. Seeing her try so hard made something in him ache, but he didn't know what to say and so he just helped guide her a little.

Eventually there was no sense in trying to prepare more, especially because another fit was likely before too long. Melissa gave him a weak smile and lifted the bottle without saying anything. Normally she would have made some quip, or at least referenced an old joke, but she was silent. She really was quite worn down... but if she thought she was ready, he wouldn't stop her.

She took a sip of the elixir and a violent shudder went through her entire body. Rick automatically reached out and caught the bottle before any of it could spill, and got ready to catch her as well. But instead of collapsing, Melissa straightened her back and closed her eyes, repeating what she'd practiced.

After several minutes, the rush of power from the sip became a glow within her. Rick knew they weren't out of the woods yet, but his tension eased a little. If they had been entirely wrong, that sip of philosopher's elixir could have killed her. This might work.

"Haha, so weird..." Melissa opened her eyes in his direction, but didn't seem able to focus. "It's burning... I feel drunk... I mean, I've never been drunk, but I think this is how it would feel..."

"Was that a weak cover for your underage drinking?" He tried for a joke since she seemed a little better, but instead of responding, Melissa just gave another giggle and reached for the bottle. Something about her behavior bothered him a bit, but he handed it to her.

Her second sip went more smoothly, not dropping the bottle this time. She took a third, then a fourth, repeating the core exercise with greater fervor. When she tried to take a fifth drink from the bottle, Rick held it gently.

"Don't go too fast, sis. Give yourself time."

"I feel... I don't know... I've always felt broken, but now..." She shook her head, eyes still unfocused. "I need more."

"Your core work feels good as far as I can tell, but a core isn't enough - your flame will just eat through it. Somehow you need to push the inner lucrim of the sphere outward so it forms a hollow shell. Honestly... I've never done something quite like that before, so I don't know what to tell you."

"I'll figure it out, Rick. Don't worry." Melissa gave him a sharp smile and pulled the bottle back. "Trust me, I'll be okay. Just keep me from hitting my head on anything."

Though he wanted to hover around her, Rick decided that he could trust her to continue on her own. Melissa kept drinking from the bottle, larger doses each time. After several drinks she set the bottle aside and slept for a few hours, but when she woke she went back to work almost immediately.

Rick sat at a distance, technically working on his own training but struggling to focus on it. He'd never seen Melissa quite like this. She could be determined and hard-working, even stubborn, yet there was something else. The singular intensity with which she threw herself into the task before her was slightly manic in a way that troubled him, but he had to trust that she knew herself best.

When only a quarter of the bottle was left, Melissa finally set it aside. Her fingers trembled in a way that they hadn't since she'd started the exercise, but not quite the same as a shivering fit. Once the bottle was in place on the nightstand, her arm fell back to her side as if it had no strength.

She opened her mouth and might have tried to say his name, but no sound came out. Rick rushed to her side.

"Are you okay?"

"Tired..." Melissa struggled to keep her eyes open, but she was failing. "It kind of worked... but kind of not..."

"What do you mean?"

"I feel better, but only because I have a lot of power in me." As she explained, Rick helped her lie down in a more comfortable position and tucked her in. "I kind of have a sphere, but... I'm wound up really tight. It needs to be harder, but I'm afraid it's gonna break... maybe try again... in the morning..."

Considering how hard she'd been working, it was more than time for her to take a break. Once he confirmed she was well on her way to sleeping peacefully, Rick headed out and closed the door behind him.

Then he just sat on the couch for a while, recovering. His emotions had been through such a wringer, it was difficult to even feel relief. That emotion would be premature, anyway, not when the solution was incomplete. Such expensive philosopher's elixir would have delayed the side effects of her condition anyway, so this proved nothing. Not until they settled things.

There was nothing he could do to help her with the core of her task, because ultimately everyone's lucrima was their own. You could only do so much to help fellow fighters get the feel for it, much less someone with a rare condition like his sister.

What she'd said at the end, however, was something he could work with. Repeating exercises designed to modify cores often left people with tension they described as their soul wound up like a spring. Pressing too hard was actually bad for long term development, since a tense lucrima would develop more slowly. In his sister's case, it could prove to be the flaw that made the entire plan come crumbling down. He might be able to find a solution to that, but not that night.

Rick slept for a while but was woken in the middle of a chilling dream of Melissa dying and coming back as some sort of zombie. He left the nightmare behind, yet his mind filled up with endless thoughts of things he should be doing. She needed more philosopher's elixir, and more pills, and likely some new medications. Even if certain elements of her situation were unique, he could assist with other elements.

Overflowing with such thoughts, there was no way he was getting back to sleep. Instead he stayed up and trained feverishly, watching his phone's clock. For once, he was awaiting the time he needed to go to work. Earlier he had been planning to skip it, but now he had a reason to go.

Before he left, he woke Melissa up, just to be sure she was okay. Though a bit sleepy, she seemed determined to go back to her exercises, so he managed to convince himself it was okay to leave her. He rushed to work as quickly as he could.

One of his clients was already waiting and Rick did his best to actually focus, though he wasn't successful. As soon as his client was gone, Rick headed over to where Jimmy sat at his counter.

"Boss, can I ask for a favor?"

Jimmy grunted without looking up. "Wish I could stop you."

"I need my paycheck a few days early."

"What?" That got his boss to look up, staring at him with death in his eyes. "Why the fuck would I do that?"

"There's a family emergency and I can't afford everything I need. Come on, boss, I've been working here for years and I've always been a good employee."

"Feh. Not so much recently, getting into fights and bringing trouble back here."

"Do you honestly think I'd run off with the money or something? You know I'll still work here, I just need an advance."

Jimmy stared at him for a long time as if the very idea disgusted him and eventually Rick had to give in. Fine, he wasn't going to get his paycheck early.

While he worked with his next client, he considered his other options. There was no way he could get a conventional loan quickly enough, but if he paid in lucrima he had options. The most obvious would be to get a demonic bond. It would probably be a low quality bond given the circumstances, but if that was his only option, he would do it.

"Uh, Rick. You okay?"

He looked up and discovered that Lisa was already in the gym, watching him with a worried expression. Most likely he'd been sitting there and muttering to himself like a madman, so he understood her concern. All he could do was smile weakly. "Sorry, I'm just thinking about my sister. She's... well, she has a condition. Things have been bad lately."

"Oh, I didn't know!" Lisa put her hands to her mouth, eyes filling with concern. "You always said such nice things about your sister and how she was doing, I never thought she might... well..."

"Because she wouldn't want it to define her. But now..." Rick took a deep breath and tried to put away any sense of shame. "Lisa, I can't afford to pay you right away, but could I convince you to help my sister? She's working on a lucrim technique that will improve her condition, but it's tightening her lucrima. You have something that can help with that, right?"

Lisa nodded seriously. "Most likely. Plenty of my clients over-train themselves and need to have ether tension worked out. Some even plan for it and just consider it part of the job, though I think that's probably unhealthy. And you don't need to worry about paying, I-"

"No, we're not asking you for charity. We just-"

"Don't be stubborn! If you really want to pay me, do a good job sparring today!" Lisa smiled at him and he couldn't keep arguing... though he did plan to pay her for the treatment at some point.

Now that he had her cooperation assured, he was able to relax a little more. He did the best he could to spar with her. She'd improved her lucrima since the last time, and even though his portfolio was in worse shape, he was much more experienced fighting against stronger opponents than before. Somehow he managed to barely keep up with her, forcing her to work hard to land any blows.

Until his phone rang, his concentration vanished, and her next punch sent him flying into the wall.

"Oh, I'm so sorry!" Lisa rushed after him, shocked at her blow, but Rick didn't even feel the pain. He just crawled over to where he'd set his phone and accepted the call from his sister.

"...made a breakthrough... but..." Her voice faded in and out, extremely faint even at the best of times. Rick leapt to his feet, holding it tighter to his ear to try to listen. "...draining too much... I need... have to..."

"Melissa? Melissa, stay awake, I'm coming!"

Rick kept the phone by his ear in case she said anything else, but there was only silence from the other end. He turned to find some way to apologize to Lisa, only to find her standing nearby with a serious look on her face.

"It's your sister, isn't it? Is she in trouble?"

"I think so." Rick pushed past Lisa toward the door. "I'm sorry, I have to go. She probably needs someone to stabilize her..."

"Or you could let me help." Lisa moved alongside him, her aura flaring up around her. She opened the door with a wave of her hand and gestured for him to go, smiling grimly. "Don't even try to convince me otherwise. Come on, let's go."

Given the circumstances, he couldn't argue with her. They needed to get home as soon as possible and hope it wasn't too late.

Chapter 23: Brotherhood

Letting someone carry him while flying didn't sit well with him, but it didn't matter compared to his sister's life. Lisa lifted into the air and hooked her arms under his shoulders, which pressed her against his back, but it barely occurred to him to be uncomfortable. All that mattered was that this would be a much faster way of getting home.

Lisa's aura expanded around him and they lifted into the air. It had been a very long time since he'd flown with anyone, probably when he had been little and Uncle Frank had taken them on rides. This one was less smooth, but he was glad to see the city flashing underneath them. He directed Lisa to the apartment complex and they were soon touching down in the parking lot.

As they headed up he felt a twinge of embarrassment that Lisa would see his neighborhood and crappy apartment. Judging from how surprised she looked at some of the usual characters nearby, she was obviously used to nicer suburbs. But she was still going to help Melissa, so he would suffer much worse than that.

When he got the door open he forgot about Lisa entirely, rushing in to find his sister. Instead of shivering, she lay in bed with her back arched and her fingers clawing at the sheets.

She wasn't fading, she was on fire. Rick wasn't sure what to do, so he just sat down beside her and felt her lucrima. The sphere hadn't been consumed, but he felt an enormous ether void - that must be the flame burning hotter than usual. Since she didn't even seem to notice his presence, he tried to take her hand, slowly peeling her clenched fingers away.

Abruptly they snapped to grab his hand, gripping tightly. Melissa closed her eyes and made a soft painful sound, but he wasn't sure what to do. When he extended a stream of lucrim like usual, her spirit sucked it in like water on parched ground, so he extended more to her.

By the time it was over he felt exhausted and drained, but the fire seemed to be quenched. Melissa finally turned her head to focus on him, her entire body relaxing gradually. She let go of his hand and instead reached up to touch the side of his face.

"Thank you... I knew you'd... come for me..."

He held her hand in both of his own and maintained eye contact, keeping her from drifting away. "I'm glad you're alright now, but what's your condition?"

"It hurt a bit, but I actually made a shell... just a weirdly stiff one..." Melissa started to gesture to herself, then jumped a bit. Rick tracked her gaze and saw that she'd noticed Lisa standing in the doorway. The older woman was watching them with a smile on her face. "Oh... hi..."

"Hello, Melissa," Lisa said. "I've heard good things about you from your wonderful brother."

"Yup... really wonderful..."

Rick nodded between them. "Melissa, this is Lisa, the massage therapist I help train. She has lucrima techniques that should be helpful to you, if you still feel like you're carrying too much tension."

"Yeah, I am. That's just what I needed." Apparently feeling better with each passing moment, Melissa sat up and gave him a hug. "I can't believe you actually brought someone here. You're the best brother ever."

Smiling broadly, Lisa stepped backward from the room. "I'll give you two some time alone, okay? Melissa, I can give you a massage that should help loosen your lucrima and heal soul scarring, but it's not something to get into while you're feeling uneasy. It would probably be best after another round of exercising when everything is stiffest, if you're up to that."

"I'm feeling a lot better now thanks to my big brother! Just give me a few minutes to get back on my feet."

"Of course." Lisa backed out and closed the door.

Though for a moment Rick wondered what Lisa would think of their apartment, he soon turned back to Melissa and raised an eyebrow. "Okay, I get that you'd be grateful, but you are *really* playing this up. Are you sure you're okay?"

To his surprise, his sister giggled. "Oh, I was absolutely playing it up. Did you see how Lisa was looking at you?"

"What?" He just stared at her, prompting her to stifle another giggle and pat his shoulder.

"Big bro, guys who can be nurturing are really hot. Lisa's heart was just melting over there."

Though he felt immense relief to see his sister teasing him again, Rick just scowled and swatted her hand away. "Okay, I think you've had enough to drink."

"No, no!" She laughed and leapt to grab the bottle before he could take it. "I'm going to do just what she said and do the exercise again. In fact, I think with everything I've learned I can handle all the rest of this at once. If her massages can really do what she claims, then that should be perfect. It won't be exactly a permanent shell, but I'll be in better condition than I've ever been."

"Lisa is a professional with clients who have hundreds of thousands of lucrim. I'm sure she'll be able to help you, so if you're feeling up for it, we can try now."

Melissa's smile faded and she looked at him in concern. "That means she's really expensive, right? Can we afford this?"

"No, ah... she was insisting that we don't have to pay. I still want to, but..." He trailed off as Melissa smirked at him. "What is it now?"

"So she's offering to help you for free, huh? Yeah, I'm sure she's just an especially kindhearted individual with *no* interest in you whatsoever. Yup, that's definitely it..."

Rick rolled his eyes and stood up. "Okay, if you're healthy enough to mess with me, you're healthy enough to give this a try. Let me know if you need anything, otherwise I'll leave it to you."

As he walked out, he saw Melissa drinking everything remaining in the bottle of philosopher's elixir in one breath. That much high intensity elixir would have knocked him out, yet his sister was fine. When he felt her lucrima it didn't feel large or healthy, still a burning void within a shell, yet he had to admit that from the outside, she certainly seemed to be doing much better.

He and Lisa chatted for a bit, but soon Melissa called her in. They closed the door for the massage, leaving him abruptly alone.

When he started to sit down on the couch he practically fell into it, his body heavy. Perhaps it was the lucrim he'd poured into his sister, or perhaps his body was just exhausted from the stress. Though he couldn't entirely relax, he at least felt as though the worst was past.

With no current crisis looming, he was able to focus on his exercises again. They felt a bit like familiar friends now and it was good to focus on his own lucrima. His new core had grown, just as it was meant to, which was encouraging. When he began repeating Buffet's Buffer, he was surprised how much good he got out of it again. Apparently all his recent work had produced new gains to harvest.

Had the massage only lasted a short time, he would have been completely content. But as time extended on, less pleasant emotions began to creep in. He found himself thinking about how much he had spent recently and how much of his own lucrim he had drained. If he had invested those back into himself, how far could he have come?

Immediately Rick felt intense guilt and he tried to shove the thoughts from his mind, but he couldn't deny that he'd felt them. Maybe that made him a bad brother, but he was only human. Still, he was a human being who loved the only family he had left. It had been worth the sacrifice.

When the door opened he leapt to his feet, but Lisa raised a finger to her lips as she exited. He looked past her and saw Melissa curled up in bed, apparently sleeping peacefully. There was no shivering or draining and when he checked the medical app, it still displayed an ether void value, but also complete stability. That was probably their goal for now.

"Well, that was intense." Lisa spoke quietly and padded closer to him, having taken off her shoes at some point. "I feel incredibly drained, but it was worth it, just to experience a client like that. I had to stretch myself a bit, but I gave her what she needed to finish her work."

He wanted to reassure her again that they'd pay, but other issues came first. "So she's formed a stable shell?"

"It feels that way to me. The first one was dangerously brittle, but when I helped her relax she caught on quickly. I'm no expert on her medical condition, so I can't make any real promises, but I feel like she's in excellent shape."

"That's a huge relief. Thank you, Lisa."

"Oh, no problem." She dropped down heavily onto the couch and sighed heavily. "If you want to thank me, let me stay here tonight."

"Uh..."

Lisa went from tired and relaxed to flushing and waving her hands abruptly. "I didn't mean like that! I'm just really drained, and even if I restored my lucrim, I don't think I'm safe to fly. So let me crash at your place and in the morning I can check on your sister again. That's all I meant."

"Right." Rick nodded slowly. "Of course you can stay. We owe you a lot."

"It feels weird to be sitting while you're looming around. Sit down."

Since she seemed insistent, Rick sat down beside her. Lisa sat back against the couch, not quite touching him. She seemed far more relaxed than he would have been in a stranger's home. He wasn't sure what to say, so found himself drifting back to the subject of payment. "While I won't be able to pay your fee right away, I'm earning enough that I-"

"Oh, stop it." Lisa looked at him with a frown that slowly became a smile. "I'll be offended if you keep talking about payment like that. We've been sparring together long enough that we're friends, aren't we? Friends should be able to help each other."

"I... thank you, Lisa." He smiled back at her.

It was a warm, comfortable moment. But it was less warm because over Lisa's head, he could see into his sister's bedroom. No longer asleep, she had sat up to listen. When he met her gaze she wiggled her eyebrows at him. He wanted to groan, but that would just have led to uncomfortable questions with Lisa, so he kept his expression neutral.

"I admire you," Lisa said quietly. "I had two little brothers growing up and I don't think I could ever have taken care of them the way you take care of Melissa. Honestly, I'm not that close with my family at all. It's nice to see an older brother who cares so much..."

As she spoke, she leaned against him a little more, pushing against his arm. Rick resisted the urge to react at first, not sure if it would be the wrong move, but eventually decided he was being stubborn. He put an arm around her shoulders in a merely friendly way, supporting her while she rested. It was just companionable silence, that was all.

Over Lisa's head, Melissa made a circle with her thumb and index finger and then poked one finger from her other hand through it vigorously, grinning all the while.

Despite the circumstances, Rick grinned back and rolled his eyes at her. He wasn't sure if his sister was right or what he thought of such a development, but it didn't really matter. The fact that his sister was joking with him again was a significant sign that things were actually okay.

He felt certain that meant something new would go wrong shortly. But for a time, at least, he was at peace.

Chapter 24: Past the Storm

Rick woke up, groggy and disoriented, and for a moment was convinced that he'd been kidnapped and taken to some remote location. That would fit with how his life usually went.

Then his mind reengaged and he remembered that after some arguing, he'd slept on the floor the previous night. There were rumpled blankets on the couch from where Lisa had slept, though it seemed that she was already awake. Not in the living room with him, which meant that there weren't really very many options for where the other two could be.

When he got up, however, he found that neither of them were in the bedroom. Just when he started to worry, the two of them emerged from the bathroom.

Rick blinked at them a few times. "Did the two of you go to the bathroom together *in the same house*?"

"There's only one and we both had to get ready." Melissa stuck her tongue out at him, then turned to Lisa. "You wanna stay for breakfast? I'm pretty sure your only options are expired cereal and also expired cereal, but you can mix the two if you want a really crazy time."

Lisa smiled but shook her head. "Sorry, but I need to run to work."

"Oh, sorry, did we mess up your schedule?"

"No worries, I'm actually closer than I would be normally. I just had a lot of appointments scheduled for today." Lisa stepped up to Rick and stood awkwardly - for a moment it looked like she might shake his hand, which would have been incredibly uncomfortable, but she settled for just smiling at him. "I'm glad I could help the two of you, Rick... I really am. I'll see you at the gym, alright?"

He nodded. "Sure, see you next time."

With that she headed out of the apartment. After lingering on the walkway for a moment, glancing back, she stepped over the railing and lifted into the air. Instead of watching her go, Rick walked back inside and locked the door slowly, knowing what he was going to face when he turned around but delaying it while he could.

"I like her a lot." When he turned, Melissa snapped her fingers into double finger guns. "If you know what I mean."

"Oh, I wouldn't dream of standing between the two of you."

"Haha, you'd *better* not be dreaming of it, ya perv." Abruptly his sister's smirk dissolved into a softer smile. "Rick, for the first time in so long... I feel like I can beat this. I always thought I'd just need to take what I could from life before... well, the inevitable. But now..."

Melissa shook her head slowly and moved forward to embrace him. Rick wrapped his arms around her and held her for a while, like they hadn't since they'd been much younger. They'd spent a lot of time sitting side by side, but after making it through such an experience, they needed the connection.

When the moment had passed and she started to pull away, though, he couldn't resist. "It's still inevitable, you know. We're never going to be rich enough to become immortal, so medical condition or not, we're gonna die."

She grinned and punched him in the stomach ineffectually. "Way to ruin the moment, bro."

"Sorry, I guess that's your job."

"Seriously not messing around for a second, I do think Lisa is into you. She doesn't have as many social circles as she used to and her clients tend to view her as just a contractor. Plus she has creepy types, given her job. I'm not going to push, since it's your life, but I'm sure she thinks of you as a friend instead of just somebody she pays to beat up."

"Wait... did you get all of that from the very first time the two of you met? I guess that's the connection between women..."

Melissa rolled her eyes. "Or, you know, she spent several hours helping to save my life - that tends to break the ice a bit. I was nervous and so she started talking to calm me down, and we had a lot of time to talk."

"You don't have a lot of time right now, though - you need to go to school." When Melissa groaned he just kept talking over it. "I know that it seems ridiculous, but they were already pretty upset about yesterday. But it's just half a year now, then you'll graduate."

"Yeah, I know. Just a huge letdown after everything else." She went to get her things, but kept glancing back at him as she got ready. "There's something I wanted to ask you about before I go, just something odd with the solution we found. I considered asking Lisa, but I *did* just meet her. Besides, this feels..."

He stepped closer, concern on his face. "Are you alright?"

"I think I am, but that's why I wanted to check. See, you suggested that I was supposed to push the lucrim away from the fire where my soul should be."

"It's not that you don't have a soul, it's that the form isn't what you'd commonly expect. The exact terminology of 'soul' is a bit of a misnomer bec-"

"Aw, shut up, let me pretend to be a soulless abomination." Her smile faded quickly and she stopped gathering her books, focused on him. "The problem was that I couldn't push the lucrim. I saw what you wanted me to do, but it was just too difficult."

"Creating a lucrim shell with an empty space inside it is both complex and counter-intuitive, so I'm not surprised. But when I sense you... it feels like you created a shell anyway. What happened?"

"Well... I kept trying, which made me think a lot about the flame. I'd always held back since it was called a void, thinking that I'd fall into it, or that focusing on it would make things worse. But when I started focusing on the flame, it didn't feel so... so wrong. When I touched it, for a moment it didn't burn me... it got bigger."

Rick listened in silence, trying to keep his face neutral. He hadn't seen Melissa this serious in a long time, and her eyes wandered, never quite meeting his.

"So I... worked with that. I made the flame burn really hot for a while and just... burned the inside of the sphere until I'd hollowed out the entire thing. It did backfire when I went too far, and I'd have been in trouble if you hadn't come to help me. But..." She finally looked at him, playfulness gone to reveal vulnerability. "That wasn't wrong, was it? I didn't... break myself somehow?"

"No, I don't think so." He pulled her into another quick hug. "I'm not an expert, but what you've built feels stable. Just keep an eye on it and don't worry unless something changes drastically."

"Oh, that's good. Everyone was so happy and I was just sitting there, wondering if it was all ruined somehow. I mean, I'd prefer to know for sure, but just hearing you say that helps me feel better."

"Actually, I think I can do better than that." Rick pulled out his phone and navigated to the medical app. "If there's anything seriously wrong, this should give us an alert."

[Melissa Hunter

Lucrim Generation: 6514

Current Lucrim: 426

Ether Void: -100]

It was odd that the ether void value sat at exactly -100, but he decided not to focus on that to avoid making her nervous. Instead, he flipped to the in-depth tab that showed the value over time. "See? Last night when things stabilized, the void value jumped up - or down, I guess - to negative 100 and it's stayed there ever since."

"And that's good? You actually look at that app a lot more than I do."

"Yes, it's good. Normally even when you were doing fine there were constant little fluctuations. Earlier I spent a lot of time looking at them, seeing if there was any kind of pattern that we could use to predict when a fit would occur."

"Aww, you did? You never mentioned that!" Melissa smiled at him, some of her nervousness fading. He brushed aside the sentiment, now very focused on the numbers.

"It never did any good, but I can promise you we haven't seen stability like this before. Now, it's weird that it's at negative 100 instead of 0, but I think you don't have any reason to be nervous."

"That's a relief, it really is."

"But beyond that, your numbers are way different. Here, let me access your lucrima portfolio..."

[Name: Melissa Hunter

Ether Tier: N/A (minor)

Ether Score: N/A (minor)

Lucrim Generation: 6514

Current Lucrim: 426]

[Melissa Hunter's Lucrima Portfolio

Foundation: 1950 (Lv I)

Lucore Mass: 3464 (N/A)

Steel Lucore: 1100 (Lv I)

Total Lucrim: 6514]

He'd seen it before, but hadn't quite believed it until he saw her full portfolio. It was natural that his sister would have increased her generation rate given the high quality philosopher's elixir she'd been drinking, but this was explosive growth. That could only mean one thing.

"You've developed a mature lucrima soul, sis. You're not a minor anymore."

"Uh, it explicitly says I'm a minor."

"The ratings agencies always take time to update and they consider a whole bunch of things. Including age, so it might not change officially for a while. What matters is that your numbers went way up, which is the real sign." Rick frowned as he considered them. "Your foundation percentage is pretty good, actually - better than mine. Make sure not to lose that. If you don't pay attention, spare lucrim will go toward your foundation inefficiently."

"Oh, god, am I gonna become a numbers-obsessed guy now?" Melissa gave a mock groan, but he saw happiness underneath the act. "Are you gonna start making me come in to the gym and learn the Cosmic Fist? What if I don't want my life to be just going around Cosmic Fisting people?"

"Uh, please don't say it that way." Rick smiled and put his phone away. "You don't need to worry about it for now, and you *do* need to get to school. But since this is your health at stake, you need to pay attention to these things."

"Yeah, I'm just playing with you." Melissa had her own phone out, checking her numbers. "This 'Lucore Mass' bit is lucrim I have, but haven't invested toward anything, right?"

"That's right. Even if you're not interested in anything else, it'd be worth your while to put it toward improving your health or a bit of defense for safety."

"But what's this Steel Lucore? I mean, I guess it has to be the shell, but what does that *mean*?"

"Can't tell you for sure." A year ago he would have been clueless, but the mess with the Golden Lucore left him with a bit of information for her. "I don't know if the names are purely random or if they're descriptive, but it'd feel pointless to use adjectives if they were meaningless. So maybe we should be encouraged that it used 'Steel' for your shell."

"I choose to take it that way!" Melissa put her phone away and swung her backpack up onto one shoulder. Before she left, she leaned up beside him and kissed him on the cheek. "Thanks for everything. I'll see you after school."

With that, she was off. Rick looked after her for a while, concerned out of habit, but maybe the difficulties were finally over. It was a relief to know that she was stable, but he was also left to consider his own growth as he hadn't for some time.

He was surprised at how damaged his foundation felt. It wasn't as if he'd been pushing himself especially hard, certainly not in combat, but maybe all his work had cost him. Then again, what remained felt dense and fire-hardened, not weak. It would take some work to rebuild it for use in combat, but perhaps it would be a step forward in the end.

A notification popped up on his phone. When Rick saw that it was a request from Granny Whitney to attend another match, he didn't even blink. Compared to what he'd just been through, he could handle this.

Chapter 25: Public Techniques

When Rick showed up for his fight, Granny Whitney didn't ask him about what had happened even once. She gave him another disabling pill, but he managed to push through the fight. His victory was far from elegant, but he was the last one standing. Afterward, she handed him a bottle of 100k elixir with an odd smile on her face.

"Not bad at all, dearie. Perhaps you're ready for a higher dose."

All he could do was shake his head. "Give me some more time to work on my foundation first."

"Hmm, I suppose you do have work to do. Very well, we still have time." Granny Whitney looked like she was about to walk out again, so he spoke up to stop her.

"I'm ready to begin working on the mana leeches again. Do you think I can take out the smaller one before the competition?"

She turned back, shaking her head. "You could do that, but only if getting rid of one of them is more important to you than efficiency. The larger debt is Stage II, so it's draining you faster."

Math wasn't his strong suit, but he saw the logic: if his goal with each invested lucrim was to decrease the drain on his strength, then it should all go toward the more dangerous debt, even if it meant he had both aura leeches inside him for longer. What was the difference between one ghostly creature draining his strength and two, though? Best to focus on the long term.

"Thanks, I'll do that." Rick nodded to her gratefully. "Is there anything else I should be doing to prepare?"

"Perhaps another core? I'll leave that to your discretion, dearie. Granny Whitney needs to go on a little vacation." With that line she departed, humming a little tune to herself. He honestly wasn't sure if that was a cover for something else, or if she was actually going to go relax on a beach somewhere.

With his next objectives set, Rick threw himself into training over the next several weeks. His first goal was to fix the damage to his foundation, both because he ran the risk of taking a serious injury without it and because he wanted the spare lucrim. He put some of it toward paying off the aura leech but began gathering more of it to fashion into a new core, though he hadn't made his final decision there yet.

Though the difference wasn't dramatic, he appreciated the benefits of the Graham's Stake Lucore. The slow flow of power within him wouldn't pay a utility bill, but it left him more refreshed. Usually he had to hold back on expending lucrim while sparring or fighting, needing every iota of it until his next paycheck. Now he had the option of relying on his new core... though he still intended to save every lucrim instead, to keep fighting out of his situation.

Meanwhile he kept an eye on Melissa just in case there were any new problems, but she seemed stable. More than stable, she was thriving. She remained pale and thin, yet she was always improving her shell and took up experimenting with other types of core. Even if she joked about muscleheads and people who trained all day, it was fun to be able to discuss lucrima with her.

The main difficulty was that they were desperately poor, thanks to all their expenses during her illness. No more taxis for him - he ran everywhere to save what he could. Even once he received his next paycheck, it was immediately absorbed paying off the bills that had begun to stack up. It led to some pretty pathetic meals, but they got through it together.

Eventually he'd built up enough available lucrim that he wanted to invest it, but he wasn't sure how. He talked to Henry and even tried to get advice from Jimmy, yet didn't feel like he got any satisfactory answers. They might both be stronger than him, but that didn't mean he wanted to emulate their paths in life.

He managed to get in contact with Uncle Frank again after a while. His uncle mostly confirmed that his idea of developing a speed or ability core would be a good step forward, which was nothing new. However, his uncle also reminded him of a resource he hadn't been thinking about: the public library.

Rick jogged down the sidewalk in the middle of Branton, looking for the building he hadn't visited in years. Soon he spotted the familiar shape, heavily fortified walls along the sides with spires rising from the top for lucrima-users to use as fighting platforms. The Branton Public Library also had large open windows, which ruined the look of the fortress, but it wasn't exactly a traditional library.

Centuries ago, most knowledge had been firmly controlled by the powers of the world. They began by hoarding their secrets of lucrim techniques, but that attitude had expanded to cover all knowledge. Eventually a group of powerful warriors had banded together with a radically different purpose: to make knowledge free for everyone.

Though they faced vicious attacks from many combat sects, in the end they were victorious. The libraries didn't revolutionize the lucrim or martial arts worlds, not trying to archive every hidden technique, but they did make knowledge available to the masses. That change had kick-started the Industrial Revolution and now they received federal funding. No sect would dream of attacking the libraries now... though they didn't need to.

As he walked closer, Rick noticed that the sidewalk leading up to the entrance was in poor shape. What he had thought were random bushes were actually meant to be trimmed in the shape of famous librarians, instead allowed to grow beyond their normal shape, giving the impression that the famous librarians had the shape of balls of dough.

The internet and the increasing corporatization of lucrim had eaten into the base of support for libraries. As he walked in, he saw parents bringing children and a few teenagers who had no better options than the library's ancient computers, but almost no warriors.

Once inside, he found himself a bit uncertain where to go next. They had shelves of popular books near the front with nonfiction off to one side. No sign of lucrim technique manuals anywhere, but perhaps those were held somewhere more secure. With no clear idea where to start, Rick just headed up to the front counter.

"Can I help you?" A middle-aged man looked up from the books he was sorting and smiled warmly.

"I'm looking for techniques. Manuals, scrolls, that sort of thing... do you still have them?"

"Really?" The man's smile wavered, but soon returned. "Well, suit yourself! I don't think I can help you very much, but if you talk to Heather over here, she can probably find you what you need."

Rick thanked the man and left, wondering about that reaction. The middle-aged man had seemed perfectly nice, just disappointed in a fatherly way. He only had a generation rate around 40,000 lucrim, with little sign that he had invested power toward combat. Perhaps he didn't approve of the traditional purpose of libraries.

In any case, he had pointed him toward a young woman pushing a cart between the shelves, replacing books. Her short hair was dyed bright pink, she wore dark leather with flowery wristbands, and he could see tendril-like tattoos peeking out from her sleeves. When he approached she looked up at him, revealing that she also wore thick circular glasses.

"Hello there, can I help you find something?"

Not sure what to make of her, Rick just pushed forward. "I'm looking for lucrim techniques?"

"Oh!" Heather immediately perked up. "Wow, we hardly get anybody like that anymore! Screw all these books... let's head down to the archives and see if we can't find something for you. I'm Heather, by the way. Did I mention that?"

She led him away from the main parts of the library, which were brightly lit and in better repair, to a dusty back corridor. They reached a heavily armored door and she began flipping through keys on her ring, talking to him all the while.

"I don't like it, but that's where the funding is these days. Everybody wants name brand skills, not the old classics. Which is just absurd! Name brand skills? You pick up a technique just because some fucking celebrity did?"

"I agree that last part is illogical," Rick said, "but I think the rest makes sense. The big corporations and sects have some of the best skills. And even if there are good alternatives, there's some value in surprising someone with unusual techniques."

Heather snorted. "Half of what's written about that kind of thing is bullshit, if you ask me. Everyone is all 'This technique is optimized for 23-year-old half-Samoan half-Ugandan left-handed dentists' as if it really makes a difference. We all have flesh and blood, we all have lucrima souls. I'm not saying there are no differences, but there are only so many ways you can accomplish a goal like 'go fast' or 'blow up things' before you - oh, here it is!"

She found the key she needed and unlocked the door, then held it open for him. Rick walked in and peered through the dark shelves. Many were filled with books in the classic manual style, but he saw individual scrolls, clay tablets, and several microfilm readers. There was an enormous amount of knowledge here, even if it was knowledge that was publicly available.

"So..." Heather leaned against one of the shelves and folded her arms as she watched him. "What kind of technique are you looking for?"

Until that moment, he had still been trying to decide. Her ranting had actually been what pushing him to one side: she was right, there were limits to how much the basic techniques could vary. Gaining a well-known ability might be a liability, but gaining a classic form of speed would probably be indistinguishable from many alternatives. "I'm looking to create a speed core."

"You're gonna have to be way more specific than that."

"Something for combat, not sprinting. It should probably include some aerial agility. Doesn't need to involve flying at all. But most importantly, I want something... good." Rick shrugged awkwardly. "Sorry, that's a bad description. I just mean that it shouldn't be something that will be obsolete in a few years, or with serious drawbacks in certain conditions that would limit its effectiveness."

"Well, you're not going to find the perfect technique anywhere, much less at the library." Heather screwed up her face, thinking seriously. "But there are totally skills you wouldn't regret. My first thought for combat is always Tsai's Bull. If you want depth, I suppose you could try Bunyan's Step. If you're in a hurry, though, best to go for a generic tech like Swiftfist or Kentucky Hoof."

A few of those sounded familiar, probably from a teacher droning on in history class. It was good to have options, but... "What did you mean by depth?"

"For Bunyan's Step? Well, uh... it's one of those skills that doesn't have a million variants, just a few that can be used flexibly. It's not complex, but because of that simplicity you can do more with it, you know? Give it enough time and it can really evolve into something strong."

"That sounds promising. Let me see that, then."

"Fan-fucking-tastic! Right this way!" Heather led him through the shelves with unhesitating certainty. Her rapid pace and unwavering gaze were not at all hampered by the fact that they doubled back several times. She didn't seem to know precisely where she was going, she was just heading there with great certainty.

But in the end, she swiveled on one heel and plucked a book from the shelf. It was a rather heavy one, dusty from the years, but she presented it to him like a treasure. "Ta-dah! This one can teach you Bunyan's Step, the associated core, and all that good shit. Also some other stuff you won't need, but we'll let you check out the whole book."

Though Rick took a while to page through the book, he soon felt certain that this technique would be a good choice. It was more devoted to bursts of speed than agility, but it could be used in midair, which was a significant advantage. There were also many pages at the end devoted to implementing the skill, covering real situations instead of precise forms.

It was simple but powerful. People might scorn it for coming from the public library, but he didn't think that he would regret choosing the skill.

He said goodbye to Heather, who seemed disappointed to lose someone to talk to, and filled out the paperwork necessary to check out the book. Too eager to wait to get home, he skimmed through the important parts, then considered them carefully as he ran back.

It took him several days to master the basics necessary to create his new core, during which time he barely did anything other than eat, go to work, and train. Eventually on a day he had off while Melissa was still in school, he decided that now was the time.

Between his training and improvements in his foundation, he had 3600 lucrim capacity to dedicate to his portfolio. Perhaps not enough to impress Birthrighters, but that was an exceptional amount for him. Since much of it came from the improvements in his foundation, which he wouldn't get again, this decision would have quite some impact.

If only he didn't have so many choices. Though he regretted it a little, he decided not to spend any lucrim getting rid of an aura leech. That would have helped a bit, but it would have been shortsighted.

However, he also couldn't afford to throw it all into Graham's Stake. Yes, the core was growing on its own and improving his long term potential, but it did so very slowly compared to other factors and he needed to care about the short term.

To that end, he decided that he should invest the majority of it in Bunyan's Step, then add some more to his defensive core, since that was his greatest strength. He couldn't eliminate his weaknesses, so his strengths needed to be potent enough to give him a real edge.

It took him multiple hours to finish crafting the core to his satisfaction, but eventually he was done. Traditionally he should have drunk serum or philosopher's elixir to restore his reserves, but there was nothing like that left in the house. But when he looked over his new portfolio, he found himself satisfied.

[Name: Rick Hunter

Ether Tier: 18th

Ether Score: 193

Lucrim Generation: 24,400

Effective Rate: 17,178

Current Lucrim: 445]

[Rick Hunter's Lucrima Portfolio

Foundation: 5200 (Lv III)

Offensive Lucore: 3925 (Lv III)

Defensive Lucore: 7375 (Lv VI)

Bunyan's Step: 3000 (Lv I)

Graham's Stake: 3150 (Lv II)

Aura Leech: -4623 (Stage II)

Aura Leech: -2599 (Stage I)

Tracking Bond: 100 (Lv XIII)

Gross Lucrim: 24,400

Net Lucrim: 17,178]

Finally, his lucrim generation rate had increased past the point where he had been before his parents' inheritance had ruined him. His ether score was even recovering, apparently impressed by all his development. But most importantly, his cores had strengthened massively and he now had a complete set: offense, defense, and mobility.

Most added special abilities to the main types, but he could wait. Wanting to improve his new core, Rick began testing it, hopping around the house. Unused to his newfound speed, he slammed into the walls a few times, prompting shouting and cursing from their neighbors.

The style of movement was certainly strange, carrying him across space almost faster than he could react. That could be dangerous if he didn't get used to it, so he kept practicing.

As he did, however, he considered the numbers again. As he'd feared, they didn't quite add up. His total generation rate was over 24,000, yet the value of his cores didn't even reach 23,000. Looking the symptom up online, he discovered that this was a common side effect of mistraining, injuries, or aura leeches.

Had those lucrim been lost forever? It didn't seem possible - surely they must be floating in his system even if the app didn't categorize them. The internet gave him only contradictory answers, so he set the issue aside for the time being. What mattered in the end was his ability to fight.

When his phone interrupted his training, Rick assumed that it was Melissa, but the number was unknown. Assuming it was probably an automated call trying to sell him car insurance or claiming his demonic bond had come due, he ignored it. Yet the same number called back a second time. Rick stared at it for a while, then reluctantly picked up.

"Hello? You there, Rick?" It was Tom, from the Underground. Rick felt a sense of uneasiness as he answered.

"Yeah, I'm here. Why are you calling?"

"I want you to come to my next match. Something is wrong - Alger seems way too happy about it. I've been asking around, but I can't get any concrete information." Tom took a deep breath. "I have a bad feeling about this. If something goes wrong, I'd like to have someone I can trust."

After a long pause, Rick agreed. Hopefully this wouldn't be a mistake, but he was overdue for something to go wrong.

Chapter 26: Chaos in the Underground

The stands at the Underground were packed, but the crowd didn't seem any wilder than normal. Certainly nothing like the Slayer match. Though Rick had arrived and been able to talk to Tom a little, the other man didn't give him any information about what exactly he suspected was wrong.

So all Rick could really do was keep his eyes open. In the days before the event, he'd trained himself extensively with the Bunyan's Step, raising the core to the second stage. More importantly, he felt he had a solid grasp on how to use it, so his new speed wouldn't end up being a liability. He didn't know if that would be enough, but he'd done all he could to prepare.

If Granny Whitney had been there, he could have asked her, but she was still absent. The only person who might know much of anything was Alger. As usual, the Underground's owner sat in the cheap seats, eagerly watching through the chain link fence. Did he seem more manic than usual, or was that just the power of suggestion?

"Yo, Rick!" He heard Henry's voice and turned to see his friend shouldering his way through the crowd. "You don't come check out fights very often."

"Tom asked me to come as some sort of backup."

"Shit, you too?" Henry got close enough to him and lowered his voice to a level that could barely be heard under the roar of the crowd. "I got pretty much the same thing and I don't even know the guy all that well. The two of you at least fought together."

Rick frowned at that. "You don't suppose Tom is the one setting up some sort of scheme?"

"No idea. He's certainly been moving up the low ranks quickly, but could he really do that? I think it's a lot more likely that the owner has something weird in mind for him."

They sat down together and let their auras burn just a little, which was enough to keep the crowd from bumping into them. The match started not long after, but it was nothing special. Just an advanced melee, Tom against another group of people of comparable level.

Not identical, though - Tom was showing his skills well. In addition to bolts arcing in every direction, he had some kind of new technique that let him slide across the ground on lightning. Ever since Alger had taken him on, he'd been getting quite a few advantages and was shooting up the ranks.

Watching the fight wasn't going to do any good, Rick decided. For one, it would just irritate him. But more importantly, everybody was watching the fight. If anything was going to go wrong, it probably wouldn't happen there.

He looked around for anyone suspicious, though he wasn't sure exactly what that would look like. Lots of different people came to the Underground, but they tended not to be clean-cut family types. All he really noticed was that there was betting going on, both formally and a few men just grabbing bills and apparently tracking bets in their heads.

Would it be rational to try to bet on the matches, or just throwing money away? Uncle Frank had always said gambling was a waste of time, and Rick had an aunt who blew every dollar she got in casinos. But this wasn't exactly pure gambling, because he thought he was a better judge of strength than the average customer, both due to experience and increasing knowledge of the fighters involved.

Of course, the odds would be in favor of Tom for this match, so he couldn't earn anything that way. Could he bet on *himself*? Given how many of his matches involved him barely making it through due to Granny Whitney's handicapping, the odds were probably against him.

It was probably illegal to bet on himself, but all of the fights were illegal anyway. Even if they didn't permit it, he could make an arrangement with someone else. Yet that solution seemed so obvious that he had to figure that other people would already have considered it. Perhaps it was too easy, unless others were already doing it and just not talking about it.

Rick shook his head sharply - this was not the time for such things. He was here in case anything strange happened during the match, so he needed to stay focused.

Since the brawl was still going on as normal, Rick instead looked above the main stands, into the private boxes. By design they were nearly invisible behind the lights, but if he peered he could just make them out. All the windows were reflective enough that he couldn't see inside, so that didn't do him much good. Just out of curiosity, he began looking closer around each box, wondering how they connected to the tunnels around the arena and how close they were to the surface.

Could someone hide up there? Unless there were hidden sensors, it would be the perfect place to take a shot. Given the height of the chamber, there was always the possibility of an attack from above as well. But if he had thought of both of those possibilities in a few minutes, surely Alger had thought of them.

The Underground's owner was watching the fight, not as engaged as usual. The way one knee bounced up and down... perhaps he was impatient? That didn't bode well, but it didn't tell him anything more than he already knew from Tom.

In the end, Rick didn't figure anything out before the match ended, leaving him feeling useless. Henry gave a low groan. "Was there even any point in us being here, then?"

"I don't know." Rick kept looking around as Tom waved to the crowd and then headed out. "What else is scheduled for the day?"

"Just some minor stuff to warm up the crowd, Tom's match, then something special... wait a minute, shouldn't the entrances have opened by now?"

Rick sat up straight, realizing that Henry was right: the lucrim defenses hadn't dropped. Tom seemed a bit surprised as well and turned back, just as Alger leapt to his feet, voice booming over the arena.

"Ladies and gentlemen, we have a special treat for you tonight! We've all seen our beloved Tom rise through the ranks with pluck and vigor! But can he face our special guest, who paid for a chance to face off against our best young warriors?"

A single one of the entrances opened and a short young man walked in. Despite his height, his body was well-built, with the type of bulk that only short men could manage. He wore dark pants and a t-shirt that looked simple yet high quality...

That was when Rick recognized him: the third Birthrighter who had been with Mike.

"Please welcome Magnus Astor to the Underground!"

The crowds cheered, though not as wildly as sometimes. Plainly, this was a bit of a surprise to them too, not like the Slayer round. Magnus strolled into the arena confidently, raising a fist to the crowd, but Rick had stopped looking at him.

For this to be a coincidence seemed impossible, so the question was why. Alger had said he paid for a chance to face young fighters. If that was the truth, then it seemed as though this strategy might have been intended to find or draw out Rick. If that was a front for something else, Rick had no way of knowing what it might be. He didn't entirely like either option.

"Looks like we're about the same age." Magnus walked toward Tom, crackling the knuckles in one hand, then the other. "This is all you have to show for yourself?"

"What I have, I earned." Tom gathered his strength, electricity crackling along his arms. "It wasn't handed to me."

"Let's see if that'll make any difference at all."

Tom raised a hand and released a barrage of bolts that arced across the arena, slow enough to be visible but all converging on his opponent. Yet they exploded against a spherical barrier that had been invisible until the impacts. Magnus grinned and rushed forward.

The fight was on, but Rick barely watched it. His eyes searched through the crowds until he saw them: two figures in dark hoodies moving in his direction. Though the hoods obscured their identities, they looked suspicious as fuck. Now that he saw them, he couldn't believe that he hadn't noticed them before. Worse, they were getting close.

"Henry, he's here." Rick elbowed his friend in the side and jerked his head in their direction. "Mike is."

"What? Where's... oh, they really stick out, now that I notice them. What do we do?"

"I doubt he's coming over here for a pleasant chat. Do fights ever break out in the Underground? In the audience, I mean."

Henry swallowed. "Uh, yeah. They can get pretty ugly."

"Then let's get the hell out of here." Rick turned to go, pushing his way through the crowd... and saw the hooded figures begin to sprint from the corner of his eyes.

Though Rick got moving first, he tried to slip through the crowds while his pursuers barreled through. Rick and Henry managed to get down next to the ground floor, almost to the exit lane. There was a random well-dressed man standing there for some reason and for a moment Rick worried that he might be working with Mike, but the man only looked mildly surprised as he dodged around.

One of the hooded figures smashed through him, sending the well-dressed man stumbling to the side. The hood fell down in the rush and Rick saw that it was indeed Mike chasing him, with Glenn just after him.

Henry turned back to face them, yellow armor forming around him, but Glenn rammed into him shoulder-first. Both of them flew past, the yellow aura exploding as it was overwhelmed by the superior force. Rick wanted to help Henry, but he barely had time to look at him before Mike was suddenly in his face, grabbing the front of his shirt and then punching him in the face.

The blow hurt, but it had only been designed to stun him. Rick stared blearily at Mike, who grinned as he lifted him into the air. "I was going to come fight you in the arena, but this place is beneath me. So I think I'll just beat the shit out of you now."

As Mike raised his hand again, Rick considered his options. Most people were currently watching the arena, so only those they had knocked aside in their fight had noticed. He couldn't count on any help from Henry, given that he and Glenn were fighting. Going toe-to-toe with Mike in the entrance lane seemed like a sure way to lose. That didn't leave him with very many options.

When Mike punched forward, Rick kicked off his chest. Not only that, he activated Bunyan's Step when he did so, propelling him backward with explosive force.

His back burned as it hit the lucrim-reinforced fence, but he smashed through. He hit the ground hard, skidding across the floor with some of the broken links digging into his back. Going through the barrier had hurt more than he expected.

But he was now lying on his back in the center of the arena with everyone looking at him. Their gaze naturally went to the source of the blow and saw Mike standing on the other side of the broken fence, eyes wide in surprise.

"It's the police!" Henry pushed himself away from Glenn long enough to yell. "This is a sting!"

A moment later Glenn grabbed his head and smashed him down into the ground, but that call was enough to unleash chaos. Not only did the crowd begin running and screaming, security forces who usually lingered near the outskirts began to move in. Alger was screaming orders and it sounded like he was contradicting the lie, but it was too late for that.

While Mike stared in horror at the mounting chaos, a tough-looking woman in leather came up behind him, grabbing his shoulder. He hit her instinctively and she dropped back... but not far. Mike realized that the security might be able to overwhelm him with numbers and snarled.

The smart thing to do would have been to run, but as Rick got to his feet, he realized that Mike wasn't going to take the smart option. Rick had a split second to prepare himself and then Mike was sprinting across the arena, sending fleeing crowd members scattering in every direction.

Prepared for such a direct attack, Rick had his first counter ready. Mike launched a predictable punch at him and Rick turned the blow aside with one hand, then jerked his arm back, slamming his elbow directly into Mike's face.

The blow landed cleanly and had all of his force behind it, but Mike had a generation rate of at least 150,000 lucrim. He grunted in pain but then gave him a mocking grin. "That all you got?"

As Mike attacked, Rick did his best to defend himself. He still had an advantage in terms of skill, but that wouldn't be enough to close the power gap between them. If he was going to make it through or even win, he needed to use his environment somehow.

A bolt of lightning seared between the two of them, forcing Mike to take a step back. Rick saw that Tom had released it and the two nodded to each other, but Tom wouldn't be much help because he had his own problems. Magnus looked unharmed, his defensive sphere sparking as he charged toward them.

There were a few audience members running across the arena floor as well, though any one of them could be a fighter. Right now it seemed a general brawl had started and Rick had no idea how long it would take to stabilize. This would be ugly unless he used the crowds to his advantage. If only they would get out of the way... like the well-dressed man from before, who had blundered out into the arena.

At that moment, the well-dressed man calmly kicked Tom in the side of the knee, snapping his leg in half.

Chapter 27: The Hitman

Though he needed to stay focused, Rick couldn't help but stare for a moment. He'd assumed that the threat of this match was Mike and his cronies, yet now realized that he was wrong. Whoever the well-dressed man was, he had calmly ignored the fray, targeted Tom specifically, and broken his leg.

Tom went down with a cry of pain, but even as he did so, he released a bolt of lightning at his attacker. Yet the well-dressed man turned it aside with a flick of his hand, then kicked Tom in the side. It didn't seem like he was there to kill, but then why was he here? Rick saw that Magnus looked shocked by his arrival as well, so could it really be unrelated?

Unfortunately, Mike didn't bother to read the situation and used Rick's distraction to punch him in the face.

Rick staggered backward, tasting blood in his mouth. Even with his defenses, he couldn't afford to take blows from someone like Mike. It was the most he could do to deflect the followup attacks, his arms stinging as he retreated from Mike's assault. Just blocking would wear him down too quickly, he needed an alternative...

As Tom tried to drive off his attacker, his bolts failed to connect, but Rick realized that was his chance. He retreated from Mike, putting the Birthrighter between him and the fight. Mike grinned. "What's the matter, coward? You wanted to fight before, why not-"

A bolt hit him from behind and he pitched forward. Rick leapt in, smashing a knee into his chin as he staggered and slamming him onto his back.

That had been another clean blow to the head, but with the lucrim gap between them, Rick didn't count on it keeping Mike down. But Mike's petty vendetta didn't matter, not when the well-dressed hitman was apparently trying to disable Tom. Whatever was going on there, he had a bad feeling about it.

Rick found Tom skating back across the arena with lightning crackling underneath him. Unfortunately, the hitman was drawing a gun on his position.

If it had been a normal gun it would have been nearly useless, but based on how competent the man seemed, it had to be a lucrim weapon. Possibly even a custom one designed specifically for the hitman. Either way, it was bad news, yet Rick found himself leaping to help.

He burst toward the hitman with a Bunyan's Step, yet it wasn't fast enough. His fist missed and the hitman suddenly struck him across the head with the back end of his pistol. Rick managed to stay on his feet, but found himself facing the barrel of the gun.

An agonizing instant later, a glowing yellow figure collided with the hitman. Henry let out a roar as he punched the man repeatedly, the demonic aura around him adding extra power to his blows. Yet the most they seemed able to do was disrupt the hitman's impeccable clothes, because he calmly endured the blows and raised his gun again, this time at Henry.

Before he could fire, Glenn charged after Henry, shattering his aura again. It looked like the center of the arena would devolve into a brawl and Rick made a split second decision.

He used another Bunyan's Step to push him through the conflict, grabbing Henry around the waist as he did so. They both skidded to a halt at the side of the arena, near Tom. The large man had managed to pull himself up via the chain link fence, but his broken leg looked to be in bad shape.

Since the fight in the center was chaotic enough to buy a little time, Rick turned to him. "Is this what you were afraid of? Who is that?"

"I don't know." Tom shook his head slowly, stunned on several levels. "I didn't think..."

But whatever he had meant to say was interrupted by a gunshot that drew their attention. Magnus staggered backward, clutching his stomach. It didn't look like his defensive sphere had broken, but he seemed to have taken a serious injury. The hitman raised his gun to fire again, but Glenn grabbed him from behind and they wrestled over the weapon.

Meanwhile, Mike flipped himself back to his feet. He saw that his friends were fighting with the hitman... but turned away from them, searching for Rick.

Fighting under conditions like this was sheer stupidity. They needed to escape, it was just a question of how. One exit was clogged with audience members, another seemed to have become a brawl with Underground security, a third was too close to Mike and the hitman...

Then he saw their chance: Emily stood by another of the exits, having just knocked out several people.

Her exit lane looked clear and he thought it led to the surface fairly quickly. Rick set Henry on his feet but kept an arm around his friend's shoulders. "Guys, trust me on this." He pushed under Tom's arm, urging him to lean on him, then began to gather his strength.

Emily either felt his preparation or coincidentally looked, because she made eye contact at that moment. Understanding what he meant to do, she started to shake her head, but it was too late. Rick gathered all the strength he could, extended it around his allies, and activated another Bunyan's Step.

All three of them flashed across the arena, nearly colliding with her. Rick started to drop, having overdrawn himself - the technique wasn't meant to carry people along with him. Henry helped prop him up, leaving the three of them unsteady.

"Fine," Emily said, glaring over the three of them. "Let's just get out of here."

They pushed through the doors, rushing through a poorly-lit corridor. Henry managed to run on his own, though he stumbled, while Rick had to support Tom, who had clearly taken a serious beating in addition to his broken leg. Despite the circumstances, Rick glanced to the taller man to interrogate him.

"You have no idea who the gunman is?"

"Never seen him before." Tom winced in pain as they had to take a sharp corner, Emily leading them into the back rooms. "He could have killed me, but he shot my arm instead."

"Why *exactly* did you tell us to come? You had to know something like this would happen."

"I had no idea it would be anything like this. I just thought Alger was going to force me into some sort of special match. Which he did, but..."

Rick wasn't sure he completely believed that explanation, but there was little time. He trusted that Emily knew the back routes well enough to get them out, but they weren't making good time given their injuries. They burst through another door and for a moment he thought they'd hit a dead end, then he realized that there was an elevator at the end of the hall.

Well, not exactly an elevator. Instead of an entrance, there was just a small platform without sides, attached to an automated pulley system. It looked like it went into a shaft overhead, so small that at best two people could fit through. More like a dumbwaiter than an elevator, so he wasn't sure it would be strong enough.

"It can carry people," Emily said, almost as if she'd read his thoughts. "But not all of us at once. You, go first, since you seem to be the target."

She jabbed a finger at Tom, so Rick helped him approach the platform. Before he could get far, Henry stopped him. "Let me go first, man. I'll owe you one, but I have to get out of here."

Rick frowned at him, getting Tom onto the platform. "You still have the demonic bond to protect you. If I get shot by that guy..."

"No, I don't." Henry grimaced for a moment, the veins in his face turning a dark yellow, and Rick realized that his coworker was pale and sweating. "I've drawn the max from the bond and I'm paying for it. I can barely stay on my feet. I have to get out."

"Dammit, just decide!" Emily glared at them, her eyes briefly flicking to the door behind them.

Realizing that time was essential, Rick let Henry take over helping Tom. The two of them got positioned on the small platform - there wasn't much space due to Tom's muscular body - and then pulled a lever. The platform rose smoothly, taking them into the shaft above.

Which left Rick on the ground with Emily. He knew it couldn't be long before the platform came back down, but he found himself glancing nervously back. They hadn't been closely trailed by anyone, and if he was an optimistic person, he might have hoped that they had lost their pursuers.

Rick was not an optimistic person. He took a deep breath and prepared himself to fight again.

"What's this stupid brawl between you and Mike?" Emily's body was tense and her aura burned tightly, but that didn't stop her from glancing over at him with a scornful look. Rick sighed.

"He came into the gym where I work looking for a fight. I let him beat the crap out of me, but I wasn't subservient enough. Damaged something his father gave him, got him in trouble, and now he has it out for me."

"Huh. I can buy that, I guess." After considering that for a moment, Emily gave him a skeptical glance. "You really work at one of those human practice dummy gyms? I can't imagine anything more degrading."

Irritated, Rick glanced back at the elevator. The pulleys had stopped moving, but they hadn't begun coming back down yet, so he was stuck with her. "Look, it was one of the only jobs available to me, okay? It's not like it was my lifelong dream to work there."

"But you did make that decision, one way or another. You don't end up at one of those places if you've made good choices in life."

"That's rich, coming from you. You said you were an engineer? That means you can pretty much do whatever you want - you don't have to make hard choices."

Emily folded her arms and frowned at him. "I didn't just stumble into my work. I analyzed all my career opportunities and chose one I knew had good prospects. Anything else would have been wasting my life."

"Right, wasting your life." Rick shot her a bitter glance. "That's easy to say when your parents set you on the right path, paid for your education, and-"

"My parents didn't leave me a damn thing." She sounded surprisingly bitter, cutting into his anger, but at that moment there was a creaking sound.

When he looked up, he saw that the elevator was finally moving back down toward them. Just as he breathed a sigh of relief, he heard a second creaking.

The door behind them opened and the hitman stepped into the room, gun raised.

Chapter 28: Aftermath Coffee

Emily moved faster than he could, an aura sword blazing from her left arm, but she barely managed to raise it before the hitman turned his gun on her. She froze immediately and for a moment Rick was sure things would go poorly.

Then, to his surprise, the hitman spoke for the first time. "I have no interest in either of you. All I want is the exit route." As he spoke, the elevator finally began to come back down, not that it did them any good.

Instead of responding, Emily just kept moving her sword slowly, extended in front of her. She couldn't block bullets, could she? Aura might have no limitations to movement speed, but human reaction times simply weren't that fast. The biological limits could be changed with lucrim, but Emily had a generation rate of 85,000, not the hundreds of thousands that required.

"Stalling me is an aggressive act." The hitman raised his other hand to brace his gun and it looked like he might really fire it, so Rick spoke up quickly. He wasn't sure if there was any plan at all, but delaying him until others could arrive might be their only chance.

"We're not going to surrender when you're just going to go kill Tom."

"I don't need to do anything else to the target." The hitman finally gave him the slightest glance, as if Rick was beneath his notice. "But I don't have any instruction to leave you alive."

"How can we trust anything you say?"

"You're stalling." The hitman's eyes narrowed and his hand tensed as he pulled the trigger.

Before he could, Emily's sword went through his arm. She hadn't moved, still standing in position, but the aura blade had sliced through the gun and most of the hitman's arm. He hadn't even seen it move - did it have a ranged form?

There was no time to consider that, because the hitman only winced for a moment at the loss of his arm. He simply reached into his pocket with his remaining hand and drew a second gun.

Before he could get it into position, Rick leapt across the space between them and tackled him. Or at least he tried. Running into the hitman's waist was like colliding with a pillar of concrete and Rick immediately knew he couldn't drop him. But though his opponent burned with intense lucrim, he wasn't so powerful that he could just ignore a tackle.

Barreling forward, Rick pushed his opponent back against the wall and rammed his shoulder into the man's stomach. A moment later the hitman brought an elbow down on his back.

The force of the blow flattened Rick to the floor instantly and pain screamed through his back. Though he forced himself to move, he wasn't fast enough - the hitman was raising the small pistol directly at him.

Abruptly his arm blurred into a different position. In a flash of movement Rick couldn't follow, a blade of purple aura was embedded in the wall beside them. Yet though the aura blade had moved almost instantly, the hitman had pulled his hand out of the way. His arm was raised in a defensive position now, but it was only a matter of time before he aimed again, this time at Emily.

But that was enough time for Rick. He braced his hands on the floor and spun, driving a kick into his opponent's legs. It only staggered the hitman for a moment and he glanced down with a look of scorn...

Then there was an aura blade through his chest.

Emily tore it out through the side, leaving the hitman to collapse in a bloody mess. Some of it hit Rick, forcing him to collapse backward away from it. He hit the ground painfully, his strength spent in that attack. At least the hitman was finally dead, his aura flickering out.

But Emily stood over him, aura blade crackling as she stared down at him with a cold expression. "You saw my trick."

"Wait." Rick raised his arms peacefully, forcing himself to maintain eye contact. "Whatever you did with your sword, I won't breathe a word of it. Just letting me go would be much simpler than risking an investigation, especially because Tom and Henry knew you were with m-"

"Jesus Christ." Emily rubbed her eyes with her free hand. After that she gave him a wry look that made her seem much more human. "I was pissed that you saw the secret, not thinking of *killing* you. What kind of monster do you think I am?"

Shrugging, Rick nodded in the direction of the hitman's body. "I mean, thank you for saving me."

"No, I'd have had a difficult time without you. And you did a good job of playing support instead of uselessly throwing yourself against someone much stronger than you." Emily regarded him coolly for a moment, then lifted him up with one hand. "Come on, let's get out of here."

"Do we want to leave the body for security to find?" He went along with her to the elevator platform, though he looked over his shoulder uncertainly.

"Security in this place can be a bit indiscriminate and I don't trust Alger in the slightest. No, we need to get out."

She stepped up onto the platform and grabbed the central cable. Without very much space, it was going to be a bit awkward, but since their lives were at stake Rick just pushed through it, stepping on across from her and grabbing the same cable. Emily reached down to pull the lever and they started to rise.

The platform moved slowly and he was afraid that Mike would barge in to attack, but the room remained silent. Going through the shaft in the ceiling, they'd need to push together a bit, which might be awkward. Especially because he could imagine Emily scowling at him the entire time. To try to avoid the uncomfortableness, he decided to head it off.

"That sword technique is a good one. Nonlethal at low intensity, but it uses the same skills for lethal fighting. And not many would expect a melee weapon to be able to double as a ranged attack. You probably could have taken him off guard even without me, just because he was underestimating you."

"Oh, so you were playing dumb before." Emily averted her eyes, seeming more uncomfortable about his comments then the fact that they were brushing up against each other. "It takes too much time to generate a new blade, though, and that always gives warning that I'm preparing to attack."

"Still, those are skill and power problems you can solve. The design is good."

"Thanks." They passed into the ceiling, the world around them growing dark. While they were still passing through, Emily spoke more quietly. "It's my design, actually."

Rick's eyebrows rose and he was glad the darkness hid his surprise. She seemed to respect him a tiny bit more than before, so he didn't want to ruin that by acting like a fool. Designing new lucrim techniques was crazy to him, but he supposed not for her. "Huh, then you're a lucrim engineer?"

"Not as my main job." They reached the top, the elevator coming out in a slot in what appeared to be a small abandoned shed. The doorway lay open, letting in lights from the street outside. Emily quickly moved away from him toward it, though she kept speaking. "It's not like I created it from scratch. There are a lot of open source fundamentals to build on, and I have some proprietary designs from work."

"That just makes sense. Why reinvent the wheel?"

Originally his only objective had been to make Emily favorably inclined toward him so that she wouldn't kill him or otherwise turn on him. Now he hoped she wouldn't leave, both because she might be able to help and because it might be interesting to see what she was like when she wasn't hostile.

They headed out into the street and he felt like it was finally over. Yes, Mike could still show up and attack him, but he couldn't hear any sounds of the fight going on in the Underground. Based on the tunnels they'd passed through and the height of the elevator, they were quite some distance from the arena. Hopefully clear of the aftermath, though Emily set off down the street at a purposeful stride.

"I don't want to stalk you," Rick said, "but I'm not exactly relaxed after all that."

"No kidding." Emily rubbed her left wrist slowly. "That was... only the third person I've killed. The world of lucrim is vicious, but you don't get used to it."

All he could do was nod. "I've never killed anyone." They continued to walk in silence for a time before he decided to speak up. "Is it okay if I ask you some questions?"

"I suppose there's no harm. We're technically on the same team, or at least we will be."

"You mean Granny Whitney?" That was just a guess based on her previous comment, but judging from the way she looked at him, he'd been right. After a sharp stare, Emily turned sharply down another street and gestured for him to follow.

"This way. We need to get to a secure location first."

Security turned out to be a run-down diner on the next street, its neon sign buzzing obnoxiously overhead. Even at this time of night it had a decent number of people inside and in the parking lot. Perhaps being in public mattered more than any direct defenses.

They slipped into a corner booth where they could watch the nearby area carefully. When the waitress came Emily ordered two coffees without asking him. As soon as the waitress was gone, she turned her cool gaze to him.

"Whitney wants to recruit you as her featherweight, doesn't she?"

Rick nodded. "Yeah, she already did."

"You shouldn't trust her. She might seem kind on the surface, but-"

"The same day we met, she killed someone in front of me, then used it for blackmail."

Emily responded with a wry smile that transformed her face. "Then I see my warning is entirely wasted on you."

They were interrupted when the waitress returned with their coffee. She tried to get them to order dessert rather aggressively, but Emily glared her away. When she turned back, the smile was gone, but her coolness no longer seemed so hostile. Both of them took a sip of coffee, Rick wondering who was going to pay. Most likely she didn't even think about such things, not with an engineer's salary. Eventually he realized that he was going to need to keep the conversation moving.

"I'm guessing that Whitney didn't blackmail you?"

"No, just bribery." Emily sighed and sat back, holding her cup in one hand. "I'm not really into fights like these, but I needed to test myself in a real fight. Whitney decided to recruit me, so she offered me something valuable to be her middleweight."

Though Rick wanted to ask what it was she needed, he suspected that Emily wouldn't appreciate him prying. Better to take a different tack. "So that's what you meant about us being on the same team. Do you know any of the other three people?"

"I've met the welterweight - that's the tier between us - and he's an asshole. The top two, I have little idea. Whitney never said anything about the cruiserweight class and she hinted that everybody is going to bring in a ringer for their heavyweight."

"Everybody? Implying that she's competing against other known people in the Underground putting together their own teams?"

"So I presume. That's about all I know." Emily took another sip of coffee and regarded him thoughtfully. "I apologize for insulting you. You're obviously talented and you're smarter than I thought. What I can't figure out is how someone as smart as you ended up doing so little with his life."

Rick frowned, doing his best to hold back his irritation. "That's a crappy apology."

Emily just shrugged. "Sorry. I'm not good at dealing with people and I don't care to be. But I mean it: your generation rate is 25,000 lucrim - tops - and your effective strength is less considering the aura leeches. That's not great."

"The world isn't a level playing field." He saw that her eyes were still skeptical and so he pushed forward. "You said your parents never gave you anything. I wasn't so lucky - mine gave me those aura leeches."

"Ah." Emily nodded as if she understood and drank her coffee, though she still didn't understand.

Still not sure what to think of her, Rick drank his own coffee. She clearly wasn't someone who had just been handed a powerful Birthright Core, but that didn't mean she really understood. While she must have worked hard to reach her position and it took real talent to be an engineer, that didn't mean she understood his life and he didn't know how to explain.

"Okay, I don't think we were followed." Emily drained the rest of her cup and stood up. "Thanks for the help, but I need to get home and take care of some things. I suppose we'll see each other later."

"Uh... aren't we worried about the authorities? What's going to happen after all this?"

"Alger will make sure it gets covered up. Don't worry about it." She headed out, paying on the way before he could object and leaving him sitting there alone.

Only after she was gone did it really get through to him that he had nearly died. His hands trembled with an emotion he couldn't describe, somewhere between fear and excitement, making it difficult to drink his coffee.

It was almost like the old days, when those with power had done whatever they wanted and fights to death in the street had been common. In the modern era the law might look the other way when it came to normal fights, but people didn't just kill each other. Except, apparently, they did.

Part of him expected to see Mike again despite everything, but gradually he admitted that it probably wouldn't happen. Mike's plan to attack would have been thoroughly foiled by the chaos and most likely he wouldn't be able to try something so blunt again. Especially not because it gave the hitman an opening to attack Tom.

Except the hitman hadn't been trying to kill anyone, if Tom was to be believed. Had the hitman known about the potential disruption and used it? Could he be connected to Mike in some way? It could just as easily be a random coincidence or a complex connection based on elements he didn't even know existed.

There were no answers because the only person who knew for sure was dead. Rick quietly drank his coffee.

Chapter 29: Cleanup

Given everything that had happened, Rick expected to hear about it on the news, but instead there was nothing. Even when he headed in to work the next day, there was nothing whatsoever on the news about it, online or on local television. Had it been covered up somehow? Or did things like this happen regularly and they simply never made their way to the public news?

When he arrived, he discovered that the House of the Cosmic Fist had its sidewalk covered in broken glass and beer bottles. Right now his coworker Danny was working on cleaning it up and gave him a civil nod. They didn't have intersecting shifts much, but Danny was alright. Single and handsome in a fatherly-looking late-30-something sort of way, so he got a lot of the female clients in the same age bracket.

"We had a mess with some drunks," Danny said. "Most likely Jimmy will send you out here to help."

"Guess I'll take my chances first, but you're probably right."

"Just be glad I already got the vomit cleaned up."

Stepping over the broken glass, Rick walked into the gym. It wasn't in great shape either, dirty towels lying around and equipment not put away. Probably because Danny was busy cleaning the sidewalk and their boss was obviously not going to do any work. Jimmy sat in his usual place, paging through a magazine.

"Rick." He gave a grunt by way of greeting. "We're gonna need you outside."

"Okay, I'll head out in a bit. I just wanted to ask... was there any news about a fight last night?"

"Nope. Only reason I know anything happened is that Henry tried to call to get time off." Jimmy looked up at him, eyes revealing nothing. "A lot of stuff like that happens, kid, even in a place the size of Branton. Hell, if you get out into the country, there are lucrim duels and the police just look the other way. Relax and do your job."

Rick nodded and headed out, though it wasn't that simple for him. In addition to potential problems so serious they'd involved a hitman, Mike and his cronies were still out there. If they were willing to pay money for a shot at fighting him in the Underground, they were committed to this. He thought - or at least hoped - that they wouldn't try to target people close to him for a vendetta like this. But it was obvious that he was going to see them again.

As he picked up bottles and cans outside, Rick considered his path forward. Without expensive training options, there was no way he could simply jump in power and be equal to the Birthrighters. Hell, their parents could probably just hand them Lucores stronger than he was.

That left either recruiting more allies, or finding some other path. Rick went inside to get a broom to help sweep up the broken glass and found himself looking over the messy gym. Usually he didn't think about how small and dingy the place was, yet now he found it pressing on him.

Right now, if he was honest with himself, he belonged here. For all his skill and determination, he was exactly the sort of person Birthrighters expected to work at a little place like this. No matter how hard he worked there, he wasn't going to change who he was.

Mike didn't train at places like this. Emily definitely didn't. Lisa was only there for personal reasons and could have done better. Was this what he wanted to do with his life? He didn't want to end up like Danny, getting older and still working a job like this. The idea of being like Jimmy was even worse - his boss might own the company, but he had little ambition and spent his days sitting in a gym dealing with shitty customers.

What did he actually want, though? He'd spent much of his life reacting, whether it was to his parents, Melissa's condition, or the aura leeches. Just building a decent life for himself and his sister had been his goal for a long time, but it wasn't enough.

Being champion of the Underground had no real appeal. Goals like relationships and children might be nice, but they couldn't drive him. He couldn't afford to go back to school and try to reinvent himself. Rick kept thinking about it as they finished cleaning up, but didn't feel any closer to answers.

Just as he was heading back in, his phone rang. To his surprise, it was Tom, so he picked up quickly. "Hey, man, what's up?"

"Rick, sorry about before." Tom sounded tired but otherwise fine. "I had no idea things would turn out to be that dangerous."

"I'm not going to pretend I'm happy about it, but I understand it was beyond your control. But what exactly was going on?"

"I'm still trying to figure that out, to be honest. Everything about the Underground is strange lately. You might want to keep your distance for a little while until things settle down."

"Thanks for the warning, but you've gotta give me more than that."

"When I talked to Alger, I tried to really push him for answers. He's definitely unhappy... I don't think I've ever seen him like this." Tom paused for a long moment, then sighed. "As far as I can tell, there's a special tournament coming up. Alger and some of the biggest patrons of the Underground will be each fielding teams with dif-"

"Yeah, I... had an idea that might be happening."

"You did? Well, anyway, Alger wants me to be his welterweight. I think - and I'm reading between the lines here - that one of his rivals wanted to take me out. Not kill me, just disable me enough that I wouldn't be able to compete effectively in the event."

Though it was far from the most important aspect of the situation, Rick felt a twinge of bitterness when Tom mentioned his power class. He and Tom had started fighting in the Underground at about the same time, but Tom was considered a welterweight while Rick was a featherweight? But since there was nothing to gain from bitterness, he kept his tone light. "How fast are you going to recover? That leg looked pretty bad."

"Alger is pulling out the stops to get it healed, so I should be fine. Honestly, he's taking this way too seriously." Tom gave a low laugh. "I take that back. Given that his mysterious rival actually hired someone to break my legs and shoot me, maybe he's not taking it seriously enough."

"Yeah, it's messed up. You still fighting?"

"Definitely. I'll miss some training, but I should be stronger after the recovery. Anyway, I just wanted to thank you for helping and urge you to stay away for a bit. But next time you come to the Underground, let me at least buy you a drink in thanks, okay?"

"Sure, man. See you later." Rick hung up, beginning to scowl. He didn't want anything bad to happen to Tom, but he was irritated that someone who had been roughly on his level was now patronizing him. Given his situation, he wouldn't refuse the offer, but it still rubbed him the wrong way.

Rick stopped thinking about those issues for a while as he helped one of his usual clients and two walk-ins. He found himself actually wishing that Granny Whitney was back, though, much as that thought scared him. She could have told him who sent the hitman and how much of a threat he should expect. Most likely she wouldn't have *helped*, but information was better than nothing.

Henry came in, looking too tired to talk, and just focused on his work. They worked together for a while, focused on their thoughts, and eventually Rick's shift ended. When he started getting ready to go, however, Henry stopped him.

"Hey man, can you actually wait a bit for me? I have a thing we should do after work."

"What?" Rick raised an eyebrow. "You're going to have to give me more information than that."

"Overdrawing on the demonic bond last night... it sucked big time, man. I need to get another one, and I want you to come with me." Henry managed to grin. "And maybe you could use one too, huh? You're leaving lucrim on the table without it."

"I'll pass, and I don't know how much extra time I have today."

"Hey, wait, don't be like that. Look... this would be a big favor for me. Second bonds can be more difficult, so I might not be in a good condition to get home afterward. I'm just a bit nervous about it, and I'd feel better with you along. Come on, can you do that for a buddy?"

Sighing, Rick nodded slowly. "Alright. I guess it's just an hour before your shift ends, so I can wait."

Since he was stuck at the gym for a while, Rick headed to the aura machines and did a workout of his own. After coming into contact with so many powerful opponents, he certainly saw room for improvement. Especially that hitman... he hadn't been overwhelming, but he had certainly been professional. There was as much of a gap between his lucrima portfolio and Rick's as between Rick and average people who just collected lucrim from work.

When Rick finished all he could productively attempt that day, he sat back in the machine and waited for a bit. Henry was working with his last client, a young woman in leggings and a tight top. While Henry wasn't enough of a dick to "correct her form" unnecessarily, he definitely got an eyeful when she wasn't looking. Rick sighed and meditated until they were done.

"Yo, Rick! Thanks for waiting." Henry called to him, prompting him to get up. Rick decided that he didn't mind the extra time waiting, since he had a lot of personal training he needed to do anyway.

"Ready to go?"

"Almost." Henry looked out the front windows, watching his client's hips as she walked to her car. "Unf. I wouldn't mind doing some pairbond training with her, if you know what I mean."

Rick knew it was innuendo and decided that he didn't care. "You can't pairbond via one night stands. That would royally screw up your lucrima."

"You wound me, man!" Henry drew himself up, pretending to be offended. "Just because I want to get my dick wet doesn't mean

I'm looking for just *anything*. If it's somebody like her, I don't mind getting married and all that. Hell, that sounds pretty good."

Jimmy snorted from his position by the counter. "It only sounds good from that side, kid. Most of what you'd want ends after the honeymoon."

"Maybe for you, old man, but I'm serious about this. Do you know how effective pairbond training can be? I'm not even talking about with someone stronger than you, though I wouldn't mind that. The growth numbers can be fantastic."

"You have no idea, kid." Jimmy looked up wearily and shook his head.

Rick glanced between them, actually a bit curious. Based on how Jimmy occasionally complained about his ex-wife, he suspected there was a history there, but he'd never gotten the full story. Pairbond training wasn't something that particularly interested him, but he decided to speak up to find out more. "You're saying there are disadvantages, boss?"

"Hell yes, there are disadvantages. When things don't work out and the pairbond gets severed, what are you gonna do then? You stand to lose more than you gained, believe me. And that's assuming the damn courts don't force some kind of lucrim alimony. Take it from someone who fucked it up once: it's not worth it."

Henry laughed. "Okay, okay, you don't have to bare your heart or anything. Agree to disagree."

Jimmy grunted and went back to his magazine.

"Alright, Rick, you wanna go?" Henry turned to him and jerked a thumb toward the door. "This should be fun, but we've gotta hurry before the demon office closes."

"Yeah, alright." Rick fell into line beside him. "How long will this take?"

"Oh, just 15 minutes or so. It's way easier than you'd think. Honestly, man, you should consider getting one while we're there. There's no way you're going to get as much power fast, at least not for people like us."

The way Henry was pushing for it, Rick had to wonder if he had an ulterior motive. There was no chance Rick would actually get a demonic bond, but he'd agreed to go with his friend, so he'd follow through. It would be his first time in a place like that, so it might be interesting.

Time for a business meeting with some demons.

Chapter 30: Sealing a Demonic Bond

They had to go halfway across Branton to reach the demons' offices, since demons didn't set up shop in the lousy parts of town. As far as Rick knew, there was a huge demonic firm that owned one of the central buildings and a few significant clans that owned entire floors of some of the other large buildings. But they were not going to visit one of those clans - people with ether scores as low as theirs wouldn't even be let in the door.

Still, the clan they visited had a nice office in a decent part of town. Rick actually worried that they might not allow him in, since his ether score had only recently gone above 200. If the clan hadn't updated their records, they might still think he was in the bottom fifth.

At the door they were met with a security guard who was permanently bonded, his eyes blood red. Little more than a shell for the demon inside him - Rick didn't want to think about what he or his family might have done to end up in that situation. But regardless of his nature, the man was ultimately just a simple employee: he checked them for weapons, noted their IDs, and let them in.

Inside, Rick discovered a pleasant lobby with a fountain in the center. Yes, the fountain had liquid that looked like blood, but that was to be expected. Almost everyone they saw was permanently bonded, though there were a few human employees working at the desks.

Before they got far inside, a demon manifested in front of them, one that Rick could only call a succubus. Other than her bright red skin and horns, she looked like an exceptionally curvy woman, wisps of cloth floating around her and improbably managing to always hide just enough that she was technically clothed, if not safe for work.

"Henry, baby!" She gave him a brilliant smile and a wink. "So glad to see you back!"

"Glad to be back, Lilith." Henry turned to Rick and gestured in her direction elaborately. "Rick, this is Lilith. She takes good, good care of all the new clients."

Rick frowned. "Lilith as in the mythological Lilith? That's an important name... what are you doing in Branton?"

His words were downright rude, by design, but Lilith just gave a throaty chuckle. She floated forward and ran a finger up his chest, though she couldn't really - the tip of her finger passed through him, barely perceptible. "Hmm, do we have a skeptic? And one who's never been bonded before..."

"Ah, he's just with me." Henry quickly stepped in, getting her attention again. "I'm here to see about getting a second bond. Any chance I could get approved for one of those Ruby Bonds you told me about?"

"Hmm, let me see..." Lilith's eyes went white and she froze for a moment, then as she returned she folded her arms and made a pouting expression with her lips. "Sorry, Henry, but there's nothing I can do. As a special service to you, I can find you someone for a second bond, but it will still be from the subprime tier. I am *so* sorry about this, Henry."

"Hey, you did the best you could. But, if I can ask, what goes into the decision?"

"We're always looking for something special in our clients." Lilith floated around behind Henry, wrapped her ghostly arms around his neck. "But I'm afraid it mostly comes down to tier and ether score in the end, baby. You'll get there one day."

"Yeah, definitely. What can I get today?"

"Let me introduce you to a personal friend of mine..."

Lilith began to guide Henry into one of the back rooms, but he turned back to wave at Rick. "Thanks for coming with me, man, I'll just be a bit. While you're out here, maybe you can look at their brochures and things? Seriously, give it some thought."

Rick nodded and watched them go, wondering if this was something he should stop. Obviously not, because Henry could make his own choices, but the whole thing felt strange to him. Once they were out of sight, Rick headed to one of the counters.

Though he looked through the brochures, they struck him as cheaply advertising just a few things: power, wealth, and sex. Less of the last one than he'd expected, given how Lilith acted, but he wondered if the demons tailored their approach to each client. Getting tired of hype he didn't entirely trust, Rick glanced up at the permanently bonded man behind the counter.

"Do you have anything more straightforward? Just information about what you offer?"

"Yeah, sure." The man might be a demon controlling a flesh puppet, but he helpfully pulled a booklet from out of his desk and handed it to him. "This one will tell you all you need to know. Feel free to keep that one if you want."

"Thanks." Rick accepted the booklet and took several steps back to get out of the center of the foyer, then began reading through it.

Almost immediately he confirmed what he'd strongly suspected: Henry was *not* being bonded to a demon like Lilith. The lowest tier of bonds was all with little gremlin-like demons that were mixes of chitin and slime. According to the booklet they didn't even have the intelligence of dogs. That seemed a bit insulting, but if their fellow demons said so, it was probably true.

In fact, he couldn't find any concrete information about succubi. The brochures definitely promised "special services" by implication, but the booklet was business-like. Which made sense: the demons were running a business. There had been wars in the distant past, but these days they found war less effective than capitalism.

What surprised him was how complex the system was. Multiple different tiers of bonds available with a variety of different perks. The absolute lowest options were called "subprime" and everything else had elaborate names designed to sound prestigious. Not vaguely seductive to him, but he could see how some people would take on a bond to become Golden Diamond Preferred Members.

"Reading anything interesting?"

He jumped and found Lilith just over his shoulder, her voice a low purr. "I'm not interested in getting a demonic bond, I'm just walking with Henry."

"Are you sure there's nothing I can do to change your mind?" Lilith floated around in front of him, bedroom eyes practically glowing. "We could give you a great starter bond, better than we gave your friend. I gave your profile a look on the way in, and your score is... not bad at all."

"My ether score is exactly 201," Rick said. "That's two points above pathetic."

"Oh, but we have a proprietary algorithm for soul evaluation. It takes into account more than your current ether score, including your trajectory and other conditions. You have a few factors knocking your current score way down, but other factors are rather promising. Enough that you have a decent trust score for the future."

Hearing that stream of words come out of her mouth took Rick aback, though he quickly realized that he was being closed-minded. Just because Lilith dressed like a prostitute and practically moaned some words didn't mean she was incompetent. Given that she apparently had a major role in a business like this, she was likely very competent.

Still, her act rubbed him the wrong way and he gave her a skeptical glance. "I'm still not sure I believe your name is really Lilith. Unless that's just become a common demon name now."

"It's a title, actually." The demoness gave him a mischievous wink. "I'm not going to use my real name at work, but let's just say it's less elegant."

"Huh. Was Lilith a real demon at all?"

"That's just one of your stories, I'm afraid. We know we don't have the best reputation, so we do our best to make people... comfortable."

"I'm not sure taking such a hard approach is the best way to be accepted by, you know, the female half of the population."

To his surprise, Lilith - or not Lilith - gave a low laugh that *didn't* sound like it was trying too hard to be sexy. "It's part of the job, hon. But if you want to talk brass tacks, you are underestimating two things. One, the number of bisexual women in the world. Two, the variety of demons we have on staff. Trust me, we have incubi for those who are into that, and fluffy demons for families. Really, we try to make everyone comfortable with us."

Rick found himself relaxing a bit, though he folded his arms and examined her cautiously. "Your goal is still to absorb power in our world via bonds, though. And I hope you won't pretend that people don't lose their souls. Hard to build a reputation from that."

"Sure, but those are all in the terms of the contract." Lilith rolled her eyes. "Is it really our fault if some people make terrible decisions and go too far? Our job is to provide a service, and believe me, we like responsible people who draw on the bond reasonably for many years more than those who burn themselves out."

Somehow, he found himself nodding along. What she said made sense, and some of the better bonds he'd found in the booklet didn't sound so bad. Maybe there were hidden traps in the fine print, but she had a point that demons had no reason to try to take over.

She was actually pretty cute now that she wasn't draping herself over him... and Rick immediately realized what was happening.

Since the start of their conversation, Lilith had changed. He had been too distracted to notice, but her tone had become more business-like and her vocabulary had improved. The way she rolled her eyes from before was nothing like she'd acted with Henry. Even her outfit had changed, the ribbons closing around her for a look that was definitely sexual, but a restrained sexuality instead of flaunting herself.

Damn, she was good. Rick wondered just how much more she would change if they kept talking for a long time. No doubt she'd change into the kind of smart girl he liked, slowly convincing him to take on a bond. Well, he wasn't falling for that.

"This isn't happening, is it?" Lilith must have seen the change in his expression, because she smirked and seemed to relax. That only made him wonder if this was yet another ploy. "Don't worry, I'm not going to waste my energy on a lost cause. Your friend just won't get his referral."

"Referral?" Rick stiffened, wondering if it was a distraction for only a moment before he became concerned.

"It's in that booklet, if you read far enough. If you convince a friend to sign up with us, you can gain a bonus to your maximum bond limit. 250 lucrim at signing, up to 1000 depending on how heavily they use the bond."

"I see." Rick had to take a mental step back to think about that. That explained why Henry had been so insistent about making him come along. The referral system struck him as an abhorrent method, but honestly the demons had probably learned it from human businesses.

After that Lilith left him alone. Rick looked over the booklet a little longer even though he had no intention of taking any kind of bond, then wandered a bit. Fortunately, Henry had been telling the truth about the process not taking long, so soon enough he returned from the back rooms.

"Double bonds!" He pulled up his sleeve to show the opposite bicep from before, this one with a stylized toad demon tattooed on it. "Shame I couldn't get you on my arm, Lilith."

"Oh, you naughty boy!" Lilith flirted with him shamelessly for a while and Rick tuned them out entirely, just lingering near the door. Henry made one more attempt to convince him to get a bond, but Rick rebuffed it coldly. Eventually they headed out, Lilith giving Henry a seductive wave and - he thought - casting an amused glance toward Rick.

Once they were out, Henry scowled down at the payment. "They always act like you're going to get a succubus, but the demon this time was this awful frog thing."

Rick sighed. "But it was worth a decent amount, right?"

"Since it's a second bond and I'm stretched thin, this one is only worth 4000. But it's better than nothing."

Quite a bit more than nothing. Rick checked his friend's new numbers out of habit:

[Name: Hendog69 (pseudonym)

Ether Tier: 15th

Ether Score: 211

Lucrim Generation: 34,250

- Demonic Bond: 12,000

- Demonic Bond: 4000

Current Lucrim: (private data)]

Not only had his generation rate shot up another 4000 lucrim, nearly half his strength was built on demonic bonds. It was enough for Rick to feel a bit jealous, but not enough for him to consider getting one, even for a second.

Admittedly, the demons had seemed more human than he expected. But Rick knew a scam when he saw one, and everything about Lilith had set him on edge.

Unfortunately, he was going to be facing opponents who didn't care about that, and the temporary power they received would be considerable. These were probably nothing compared to the demonic bonds that someone like Mike would receive. Rick stared downward, trying to come up with a way to bridge that gap and finding nothing.

Chapter 31: Silver Linings

Without Underground matches to fill his schedule, Rick wasn't entirely sure what to do with himself. It hadn't been that long ago that he hadn't had fights at all... what had he done before then? He had a few hobbies, mostly ones that didn't cost anything, but he couldn't fill his entire schedule with just those.

There were clear limits on how long he could train effectively. It might sound dramatic to meditate for years, but studies showed that the efficacy of each hour of meditation was less than half of the previous hour. Likewise, his body wore out and needed time for recovery after physical training. If he'd had an infinite budget, maybe he could have accelerated those processes, but for now he needed to work with them.

Rick ended up going back to the library a few times, asking Heather for more books. Though he had enough techniques he needed to progress that adding more would split his efforts, that didn't mean he couldn't improve his knowledge base. He spent a while reading about the complex interrelations between lucrim, ether, and aura, which he'd thought he understood but actually only had a vague sense for.

For a while he also got further into the Graham's Stake core. It was remarkable how it grew without him needing to do anything, providing him with a steady, if small, supply of energy. Apparently Perpetual Souls used similar techniques to provide their endless energy, though that status was absurdly far off.

Though he was tempted to invest more in the core, since he enjoyed the internal supply of lucrim, he thought that his core combat abilities were more important for now. Besides, the books revealed that there were many other techniques aside from Graham's Stake, some with extremely complex results or huge risks that could make or break someone's entire lucrima.

All of that would have to be figured out later. For now, he focused on the few things he could control.

No training was going to transform him overnight, but he slowly realized that he did have useful options. Maybe not directly related to power, but he could remove certain inefficiencies in his life, he could improve his overall situation. The only challenge was finding them.

That day at work he had a chance, if he dared. Rick struggled to stay focused during the dull hours of normal clients until Lisa showed up. She smiled brightly when she saw him. "Hey, Rick. Ready for our sparring today?"

"Absolutely."

They went through their usual routines, pressing one another hard. Though she was still unquestionably stronger than him with 54,000 lucrim, the gap in their combat ability had declined. He still lacked the overall grace and edge of her high total, but his offensive and defensive cores had vastly increased in strength. Not to mention that he had been throwing himself against powerful and experienced fighters over and over again, which had significantly sharpened his skills.

In a real fight, the winner would probably be determined by psychology, not strength. But this wasn't a real fight, just sparring. The point was to push each other to the edge, to exercise both body and lucrima to the limit. Now that he was strong enough that she didn't have to hold back so much, it was actually more fun.

When they finished sparring, they were both sweating and gasping for breath, so they just dropped down onto the mats. Lisa grinned over at him, flush from the exertion, and he had to resist the urge to grin back. If he did, Jimmy would roll his eyes and make cracks about not getting involved with their clients.

Actually, Rick had in mind something that Jimmy would hate much more. He wasn't sure how to bring it up, but Lisa made things easier by starting the conversation. "How is Melissa doing?"

"She's still well - not only is her condition stable, she's strengthening the shell." The void also seemed to be growing in strength, but since it hadn't had a negative impact so far, he tried not to worry about it.

"That's a relief to hear. She's a great kid, so I wish her all the best."

"On that note..." Rick lowered his voice, speaking just loudly enough for Lisa to hear. "She does still have problems with holding her lucrim too tensely. She could probably use your help again."

"Oh, I'd be happy to!" Lisa lowered her voice automatically to match him, but judging from her expression she didn't get why.

"I've been thinking about that. I'd prefer to be able to compensate you for your work - don't object, I'd feel more comfortable that way." Rick took a deep breath and, after a glance toward Jimmy, just went for it. "It occurs to me that you also want something from me, but maybe we could arrange to... do things directly, without anyone in the middle."

Now she got it, her eyes flickering to where Jimmy read unknowingly. "You're suggesting trading sparring for massages?"

"Those two probably aren't equivalent, but we could figure out some sort of exchange rate, right? I never see you use any of the other equipment here anymore, so you'd save money on your gym subscription."

"It'd also be easier if we could meet anywhere, anytime." Lisa was nodding slowly and he let himself feel a bit of relief: it seemed like she was open to the idea. "Maybe we should discuss the exact details somewhere else, but... yeah, I think this could be better. Thanks for the idea, Rick."

With her smiling at him, he decided to keep going. "I hope this doesn't make it creepy, but... you do have massage techniques that can restore lucrima damage, right? I've been trying to make plans, and some of the best ways to develop might be pretty rough on me..."

"You thought that was going to come off as creepy?" To his relief, Lisa gave him an odd smile. "For one, it's my job. For another, I spend a lot of time going into homes that are armored little fortresses with guards. By comparison, visiting you and your sister is downright homey."

"Good. Then... you'd probably better go for now, but you have my number, so we can figure things out when we have time."

"Sounds good. I look forward to it, Rick."

With that, Lisa left the gym for the day. Rick was afraid that Jimmy might figure out what he was doing somehow, but the next week Lisa canceled her subscription while he wasn't in, and the day after that Jimmy didn't say anything about it. Though

Rick had expected that losing money would get through to him, perhaps Jimmy really didn't care about that, either.

In any case, once they got the details figured out, that was a straightforward improvement to his life. He and Melissa got access to an excellent massage therapist in return for doing what he'd been doing anyway. Since Lisa really did benefit from their sparring, he didn't even feel like it was cheating, just a fair exchange.

Unfortunately, he hadn't come up with too many other improvements that were such obvious win-wins. Life tended to be a zero sum game in a lot of ways, and he lacked the resources that made it easier. Without the additional money from matches in the Underground, he didn't have much extra to work with, so he couldn't buy philosopher's elixir or even serum to recharge himself.

Just when he was starting to think things were going too well, he got a strange letter in the mail: a note from Melissa's principal. Apparently Melissa had been involved in some kind of fight, though it was unclear about the exact nature of it.

Governing her behavior wasn't his job, but legally he was responsible. Rick puzzled over that note while he trained the rest of the day until Melissa got back home. He waved the note in her direction when she entered and she let out a groan.

"Oh, god, they really sent you a note? If it was anybody else, I'd be so embarrassed."

"I'm not really sure what even happened." Rick held the note in front of his face and let his eyes run over it, as if it would say something new. "I guess if you don't want to talk about it, that's fine. Did they deserve it?"

"Haha, not really. But I want to talk about it." Melissa threw her backpack on the floor and plopped down onto the couch. "Okay, so... there's this girl called Jenn who is kind of a bitch. Not like over-the-top bitch, but I've never really liked her. When we were in L.E., we ended up on opposite sides of this lucrim dodgeball match. You know what that is?"

"Everybody who has ever been in school knows about lucrim dodgeball. It's the easiest way for the teachers to do nothing for a whole period."

"That's true," Melissa said, "but I don't mind, because it's fun. Anyway, Jenn really went after me this time for some reason - actually, the reason was that I snapped back at her for making fun of my clothes, but whatever. The important thing is that she decided to cheat. Her lucrima got fully developed early, so she likes to use it on people. But this time..."

"Well, it didn't go well for her." Melissa hesitated in her story, glancing at him. "She used lucrim to throw a ball really hard, so I used mine back to stop it. She figured it out and got pissed, and... that's when... basically, Jenn tried to knock me over with her aura, but instead I kind of... burned it. She ended up falling down and losing a chunk of lucrim."

Rick had been listening quietly, obviously supportive of his sister, but as he understood at the end his eyes widened. "You mean that you used your ether void to destroy some of her lucrim."

Melissa winced. "Yeah, I guess so. I mean, I didn't intend to, it just happened naturally. Do... uh, do you think I could end up doing that accidentally to people? Would that make me a threat?"

"It's not very likely. Most likely it only worked because Jenn is untrained and the best attack she can manage is just flooding aura. That's not much different than when I flow some lucrim to you." What he left unsaid was that such a flow shouldn't have been able to hurt Jenn. He wanted to say something more, but had no proof at all for his instinctive reaction.

"Do you think I'm gonna get in trouble, Rick?"

"No, you're probably fine." He passed the principal's note over to her. "They didn't say anything about further disciplinary action, and in any case they already know about your condition. If Jenn tried to press charges or anything like that, she'd have to deal with the fact that she attacked someone who's 'disabled'."

"Dyurr, that's me! I'm differently abled!" After crossing her eyes and sticking out her tongue, Melissa returned to looking serious. "But what does it actually mean? The idea that I have a little flame inside me instead of just a soul-sucking void... well, it might seem dumb, but it feels a lot more pleasant. I never thought that it could hurt anybody..."

Rick considered the matter for some time, his theoretical knowledge insufficient to make a judgment. Eventually he decided that it might be better to simply perform an experiment. "Let's try to recreate what happened and see how it goes."

They gave it a few attempts, but as he'd suspected, they all failed because Rick's strength was refined for combat. Yet when he felt his sister's aura, he did feel as though something was wrong. Though it might come off as merely her condition to anyone else, he knew that it was more.

The ether void that had once threatened her life was growing. More than that, it was developing in a new direction. He had no idea what that meant, if it would be fatal or possibly even beneficial, so he just told Melissa what he knew. She listened somberly, then spent a while thinking.

"Rick... I'm not an expert on this at all, but I can tell you how it feels: this feels right. I don't think I'm going to get myself killed this way and I feel healthier than I have in years. But if there's a real risk to you or anybody else..."

"No, I don't think that's likely. Come on, let's try something else."

This time he tried harder to lower his defenses, let her aura slide into him. It didn't work, because she lacked the experience. Frowning, Rick tried a different tactic. He extended lucrim to her, as he had once done in order to alleviate her condition, but instead of raw lucrim, he tried to connect a channel directly to his Lucores.

Instantly he felt a scorching and tearing sensation. Rick reacted so violently that Melissa shrank back with a high-pitched noise, eyes wide. He rushed to apologize, but to his surprise she grinned.

"Whoa, that was crazy! A bit like what happened with Jenn, but yours was *way* more intense!"

"I think we replicated it, a bit." Rick had to shake his head as he accepted that his theory was at least slightly correct. "Basically, it seems to me that you're in control of the ether void."

"Really? If that was true, I should be able to throw it at people or drain all their lucrim or other awesome things."

"Not like that. But instead of the void consuming you - or maybe cannibalizing would be a better word - it's maintaining a stable nature. Your shell is holding firm, but you can still pass lucrim to and from it - you'd die otherwise. If you ever end up with others' lucrim, it gets sucked in."

"That's crazy." Melissa sat back and thought about it. "You never did answer: does that mean I'm a threat to people around me?"

"I don't think so. The same skills you need to keep yourself alive are the ones that you need to keep this under control." Rick smiled encouragingly at her. "But you might have stumbled onto something useful. Let's repeat the experiment."

"But... won't that hurt you?"

"Yes, but training hurts too. Every time my lucrima is exposed to intense conditions, it grows back stronger once I recover. Well, your ether void is a condition that it's barely experienced before, so I have a lot of growing to do."

Grinning as she understood, Melissa quickly cooperated. For once, things went as smoothly as he'd hoped. Though it took effort to lower all his defenses and make contact, once he did, his lucrima faced an entirely new type of damage. The first day he had to spend time recovering after only the third attempt, but he did better the day after that.

Over the next week they modified their usual schedule, adding the strange form of training to their usual chatting and TV watching. Each session left him feeling a bit scorched, and threads had been torn from his foundation, but he rebuilt each time. It was like a more controlled version of the damage she had done to him during her crisis, and it had equivalently impressive effects.

Though the effect declined over time as he adjusted to exposure to the ether void, it still left him with a far denser foundation. Not only had it increased its rank classification, he had a great deal more lucrim to invest. Since he hadn't been planning on such a benefit, he decided to put it all toward Graham's Stake. That was an investment in both their futures.

Maybe it wasn't a legendary technique or an overpowering Birthright Core, but it was nice to have an advantage all his own. Smiling to himself as he repeated his exercises, Rick brought up his profile again:

[Name: Rick Hunter

Ether Tier: 17th

Ether Score: 215

Lucrim Generation: 26,300

Effective Rate: 19,310

Current Lucrim: 201]

[Rick Hunter's Lucrima Portfolio

Foundation: 3100 (Lv IV)

Offensive Lucore: 4500 (Lv III)

Defensive Lucore: 8000 (Lv VI)

Bunyan's Step: 3650 (Lv II)

Graham's Stake: 5275 (Lv II)

Aura Leech: -4504 (Stage II)

Aura Leech: -2486 (Stage I)

Tracking Bond: 100 (Lv XIII)

Gross Lucrim: 26,300

Net Lucrim: 19,310]

He couldn't be sure exactly what had done it, but he'd moved up an ether tier as well. This was pretty good for growth mostly on his own, and it would create a strong basis for development in the future. If he did ever gain wealth or unique medicines, he'd be able to take advantage of them instead of the benefits draining into his flaws.

The improvement in his foundation was especially satisfying: it now used only 12% of his total generation rate. After so many years being told his foundation was sloppy and inefficient, it now felt solid and powerful. He actually found himself wondering what the end goal was, since surely it didn't make sense to keep reducing the foundation further and further. It was the basis for the rest of his power, after all, so it was necessary to some degree.

Just as he pulled out his phone to research the subject, he received a text message. As he read it, Rick realized that his time of relaxation had ended:

I'm back, dearie. I expect to see you in the Underground as soon as possible.

Chapter 32: Granny is Back

Since Granny Whitney's message seemed serious, Rick headed straight to the Underground. He was on edge as he approached, expecting to get attacked by Mike or for hitmen to jump out of the shadows, but the neighborhood appeared no different than usual. When he got close and found the entrance warehouse the same as it had always been, he allowed himself to relax a little.

Hopefully things would be more secure from now on. Alger ran his arena casually, but he had to care about the damage the incident had done to his income and reputation. Presumably there were more security measures in place.

Other than passing through some sort of lucrim scanner on the way down, Rick didn't notice anything different, but presumably the best security measures wouldn't be obvious. He glanced into the arena itself, but it was completely empty, since there weren't fights during the day. No one but a janitor mopping at a stain on the floor, which was oddly prosaic.

Instead of entering, he headed off the entrance path to the offices, since he couldn't think of many other places Granny Whitney might be. As he headed through, he found himself wondering if he shouldn't try to memorize the tunnel layout. Not knowing it had been a disadvantage during the chaos, even if it had worked out in the end.

Soon he came to Alger's office and finally saw her. Granny Whitney was speaking to Alger, who wore a flashy new suit. Standing in between them was another man, built like a tank. He wore simple dark clothing and had black hair that hung down around his head randomly.

The man looked up and for a moment Rick stopped.

Even though they only locked eyes for an instant, all of Rick's instincts screamed at him that he was in mortal danger. The man's eyes burned like molten fire, carrying a force that flattened him with a gaze. Though his muscularity might have seemed thuggish on most people, in this man it carried an animal ferocity.

Rick had no idea what the man's generation rate might be or if his conceptions of lucrim even applied. He realized that he was facing the strongest person he had ever met. Over his life Rick had a solid sense of what humans could normally do, how much strength it took to generate an aura or fly. But this man struck him as entirely superhuman.

"Oh, there you are, dearie!" Granny Whitney turned from the two and smiled at him. "I didn't expect you to come quite this fast, so why don't you wait just off to the side there?"

Feeling a bit weak, Rick nodded and moved. The inhuman man had already stopped looking at him - in fact, he had barely glanced at him. It had felt like a stare, since that moment had seared through him, but he realized that from the man's perspective this was just another ordinary encounter with someone far beneath him.

Though Rick headed into the room Granny Whitney had indicated, he paused at the door, glancing back again. Partially to listen to the conversation, partially because he wanted to see their interactions, partially because he wanted to feel that intense power again, so he'd be better prepared the next time.

Despite the man's power and ferocity, Alger and Granny Whitney didn't seem cowed. Alger was even arguing with him, something to do with whether or not the man's past history in the Underground still applied. The man didn't speak, letting Granny Whitney do the arguing. She seemed calm as well, though Rick noted that she never patted the man, called him dearie, or otherwise belittled him. Whoever he was, they took him seriously.

Eventually Rick stumbled into the other room and sat down. For a while he just stared. He knew that certain CEOs, celebrities, and sect leaders had truly monstrous levels of power, and he'd seen some impressive feats on television, but he'd never met someone like that in person.

The higher tiers of warriors really were different. If he continued training, could he eventually become like that? Would he feel like a god, or just himself with more power? The idea boggled the mind and he soon set aside such fanciful dreams in favor of the steps he could take directly in front of him.

Shaking himself, Rick tried to refocus. The room he'd entered was another one of the back offices of the Underground, comfortable and weirdly like a living room. This one didn't have any other entrances and appeared to be some sort of waiting room. Other than a water cooler and some furniture around a low table, there wasn't much in it.

On the other end of the table, however, he saw a number of items. Judging from the handbag and knitting, they were Granny Whitney's things. As if she had set them down when interrupted by something else, which meant he had an opportunity to investigate without her influence.

Was that foolish? Rick decided that he wouldn't touch anything, just examine it carefully. He held his hand over the knitting, doing his best to sense it. There was concentrated lucrim built into the needles, which suggested that they could be used as weapons. The knitting itself, however, just felt like ordinary yarn. Maybe she just liked knitting.

Among the other objects he didn't find anything of obvious informational value like a phone or notebook. Besides, he doubted that Granny Whitney would be so sloppy as to leave that kind of thing behind.

There were several bottles in a row, mostly synthetic drugs to enhance lucrim training. One of them appeared to be an ordinary calcium supplement. The strangest was a pharmaceutical designed to alleviate some heart condition he'd never heard of. Based on the number of warnings on the bottle's instructions, it was a highly potent medicine - he didn't even want to think about how much it would cost.

Within the bag he could see several stranger objects. There was a small satchel that felt like it contained lucrim stores, a long reed that hissed with potency, and a plastic bag filled with white powder. Examining them closer, Rick thought he had a vague idea about the first two, but the powder puzzled him. Presumably it was for training, but he didn't feel any lucrim from it and he wasn't sure of its nature...

"That's cocaine, dearie."

Rick jumped up from the couch, startled and a bit ashamed to have been caught snooping. He realized that he should probably be worried, given who he was dealing with, but Granny Whitney just shuffled into the room. Her kind smile was actually kind instead of threatening, or at least he hoped it was.

"Since that's Granny's cocaine, maybe leave it alone? I have some goodies for you too, don't worry." She came to sit down opposite him and began to sort through the items. It seemed like she was going to speak about other subjects, but Rick had to ask.

"Just who was that with Alger?"

"His name is Teragen. It took me a great deal of effort to convince him to be my heavyweight, so I'm glad that dear Alger saw reason and allowed him to participate. Would have been such a terrible disappointment otherwise."

"I heard a little... he was a fighter here once?"

"That was a very long time ago, in a different Underground." Granny Whitney looked wistful for a moment. "He was such a precocious young man, then. The years have really changed him."

"He looked young, though. Is he...?"

"Immortal? A Perpetual Soul? He's both, but you don't worry your head about that." She reached over to pat him on the cheek. "His job is to win me the heavyweight division, yours is to win the featherweight. They both count for the same number of points in the end, so you can just put him out of your mind, dearie."

Rick slowly shook his head, coming to grips with the fact that he would be on the same team as that man, even if only technically. But he didn't want to let the matter go and to fall into her plans, so he made himself speak up. "Did you hear about the incident while you were gone?"

"Yes, so shocking." Granny Whitney clicked her tongue sharply. "I can't believe someone already tried to use a hitman so far from the competition. Not only is it sloppy, it will prevent me from using the same tactic. Really, whoever was behind it ruined the fun for everyone."

"So, you don't know who it was?"

"I have my suspicions - there are only so many of us who are serious contenders, and Gerald likes this sort of thing. But you shouldn't worry about that. Now that we're getting closer, everyone will be under more scrutiny. There will be last desperate attempts to interfere with one another on the final days before the event, but otherwise you can focus solely on training."

While her reassurances were never entirely reassuring, Rick felt that he had to accept that for now. "While you were gone, I met Emily. Apparently you're recruiting both of us... or do you have an even larger pool of people you're considering? Am I just one of many possible featherweights?"

"That would be too tedious, dearie. No, I've invested money and blackmail in you, so I expect you to do your part."

Rick didn't like to think about what Granny Whitney might do if she didn't need him at all, but having that much pressure on him was uncomfortable as well. This competition was looking more serious all the time: not only was a rival team willing to hire a hitman, she had recruited someone like Teragen. The idea of watching the heavyweight match both excited and terrified him. "How many do you have?"

"Hmm... normally I would say better not to distract yourself with such things, but you're a bright enough young man. And I do have the leverage I need on you, so I suppose there's no harm in sharing." Granny Whitney took a small piece of paper from her cardigan and set it down on the table.

[Featherweight: Rick Hunter

Welterweight: Anthony Taylor

Middleweight: Emily Park

Cruiserweight:

Heavyweight: Teragen]

While that didn't tell him anything too essential, it was interesting to learn the identity of his other teammate, as well as Emily's last name. Teragen apparently didn't have one, or was too important for it to be recorded. But more importantly... "No cruiserweight yet?"

"No, I'm afraid not. I have my eye on someone, but it might be a bit difficult to convince them." Granny Whitney sighed and began packing up some of the medications. "Plus there's the difficulty of getting all of you enough points so that you can participate. You're going to need to take part in some big matches to catch up, by the way."

"I'd have more points if you didn't handicap me every match."

"But that would slow down your development, dearie, and Granny Whitney needs you at the top of your game when it's time for the match."

Rick considered that for a time, eyes running over the list. "So I take it there's no danger that I'll improve too much for the featherweight category? What are the limits to each, anyway?"

"For the Underground, the limit is a crude measure of lucrim generation rate, but I wouldn't take that too seriously. The power classes are different for other professions, anyway, Alger just likes his little games." She gave him a little smile. "In any case, don't you worry about that. Granny Whitney will make sure you end up just where you need to be. Now, let me get a good look at you!"

She poked at him experimentally, testing his lucrima. Occasionally she told him to activate his aura, once she hooked a knitting needle into his mouth to open it, like he was a horse. Rick honestly had no idea if she needed to do all that or if she was just humiliating him, but in the end she sat back, satisfied.

"You haven't been wasting your time in my absence. That foundation of yours has particularly improved, which will save me time and money in your training. It's good to see diligence in young people these days."

"So this is about preparing for the match? Do you have some kind of specific plan for it?"

"Oh, it's still too early to be blocking out your days by the hour or anything. But I do have a number of interesting ideas." She looked through her bag for a time, then pulled out one of the bottles. "These are for you now - take one of them every day, not too soon after eating or drinking. They'll tear up your insides something fierce."

Rick stared at her flatly. "...for a reason, right? They're not just torture?"

She chuckled and didn't explicitly answer. "In my absence, it seems an old friend of mine has come up with a good candidate for the featherweight tier, a martial artist with a soft style that damages the internal organs. If you aren't ready for it, well, then

Granny wouldn't get a return on her investment. Why don't you start with one now?"

For a brief moment, he considered disobeying. It had been a long time since the Slayer incident, and given how casual Alger had been about the hitman, perhaps he didn't care so much. But then again... if she knew people like Teragen, he couldn't underestimate her. Worse, she was going to all this effort just for a competition. Testing how far she would go if snubbed seemed unwise.

Rick swallowed the pill.

For a while he felt no different and Granny Whitney nodded her approval. "Very good, dearie. I'm afraid I can't afford to invest too much in you, but this should get you part of the way there. The question now is how to make up for your other flaws."

"I noticed that my numbers don't add up," Rick said. "There's been lucrima damage... is it possible to fix that?"

"Not yet, not yet. Everything in good time. Hmm, what other options do we have? I could try to get Emily to help out, but she didn't really take to Anthony, no, not at all..."

"We worked together during the incident. She might be willing to help me."

Granny Whitney's eyebrows shot up. "Is that so? Well, then, perhaps I'll set something up! Just give me a little time to check on some other things..."

Though he had more questions to ask, at that moment Rick felt his stomach wrench. It started out like a bad stomach ache, then felt as if something was tearing. He clutched his stomach, first in surprise and then in agonizing pain. His stomach seemed to be tearing in half and he tasted bile on the back of his throat. When he slumped over onto the couch, he saw Granny Whitney shaking her head.

"Oh dear, it seems that's doing a number on you. We need you to be able to shrug off pain like this, okay, dearie?"

"Okay." Rick used the last of his strength to flip her off.

Then he fell unconscious to the sound of the old woman chuckling.

Chapter 33: Side Effects

He'd expected it to get easier, but it never did. Rick stared at his seventh pill for a long time, trying to psych himself up to take it. Sometimes he tried to tell himself that it wasn't that bad, but he never really believed it. The pain from each one was just as agonizing as the last.

Keeping the pill held in his palm, Rick went through his full set of meditation and exercises again. Partially to delay, though he justified it by thinking that his motivation to do all that work would be significantly reduced after so much pain. Just enduring each one of the pills felt like all the work he should need to do for a day, but unlike his other work, he couldn't choose to stop the pill half-way.

Finally he forced himself to swallow it quickly. It didn't kick in right away, but he just lay down on the couch and waited for it.

Sometime later he found himself staring up at the ceiling. He hurt all over. Well, not precisely all over, more in all of his inner parts. Usually he was bruised everywhere, but his skin felt fine. It was more like he had twisted every muscle in his body. For a while he thought about how exactly he hurt, then he fell unconscious again.

When Rick woke up the second time, he had a feeling that something was wrong. It had never been this bad before, or this long. But had it been long? He wanted to get out his phone to check, but his arms wouldn't cooperate. Again he faded out.

The third time he ached a bit, but the pain was gone. There were also the sounds of movement and someone humming. He'd have panicked if he hadn't recognized Melissa's voice a second later. That was good, because getting up quickly might have split his head in half.

"Oh, you're up!" Melissa's head popped over the back of the couch. "You didn't seem well, so I decided to make you soup. I mean, it's ramen, but soup feels like the thing to make."

"Thanks, sis." He sat up, very slowly, and realized that he felt okay... except for a growing discomfort with how much time had passed. "How long was I out?"

"I have no idea, but I got home about 30 minutes ago."

He swallowed, trying to remember the exact time he'd gotten around to taking the pill. That meant he'd been barely conscious for several hours. Was something wrong with him, some unintended consequence of the pills? Granny Whitney had implied that it should feel the same every day, but she might have lied. Given the pain, that might have been a necessary lie.

Eventually Melissa brought him a bowl of soup. It was simple, but it felt good to get something hot in his stomach. He supposed that was a good sign, given that if his insides were in terrible shape, eating something would have made things worse.

Soon after, Melissa dropped down onto the couch with a bowl of her own, steam from it fogging up her glasses. "I thought about moving you to the bed, but I wasn't sure I could lift you. I was sure if I tried, I'd end up dropping you and whacking your head on something."

"I'm okay... there's no need for that."

"Yeah, but I'm enjoying it. It's nice to take care of you for once." She grinned, but then her expression became more serious. "Are you okay? Anything strange going on?"

"It's just those pills." He gestured at the unmarked bottle with his spoon. "They're involved with training, but they're pretty unpleasant. I don't recommend taking one."

Melissa's eyes went wide. "Do you mean that I shouldn't have eaten them all while you were asleep?"

"Ha. Ha. But seriously, people said good things about the work I've done on my foundation, and that's largely thanks to you."

"Oh, good. I'm not saying I'm sitting around moping about it, but I do wish I could do more to help you sometimes. Glad I didn't cause any harm somehow."

"If anything is causing harm, it's these pills. But I'll deal with it." Rick ate in silence for a while, watching himself carefully for any signs of something wrong, but he felt better the longer he was awake. "So, has anything special been going on with you lately?"

"Nothing actually special, but I do have one thing that's very, very 'special' if you know what I mean. It's amazing, you'll love it."

Melissa set aside her bowl and hopped up, running over to her backpack. She pulled out a DVD case and thrust it toward him like it was some great treasure. Rick blinked as he looked over the over-dramatic cover, poorly dressed actors horridly edited into random position. And based on the title... "Fist of the Sublime? What is this?"

"Basically the worst movie ever, or so I hear. They apparently had zero special effects budget, so they just got the best lucrim-users they had nearby - who weren't very good - to pretend to do all the fights. I hear you can see stuff catch on fire in some scenes. They actually end up getting arrested at one point, so a scene just cuts off abruptly and then starts again in a completely different location." His sister's eyes sparkled. "It sounds amazing."

"Heh, that does sound fun." He turned the case over to see if the back side mentioned how long it was, but it only talked about the "fist-pounding action" in oddly inconsistent fonts. "You're wanting to watch it sometime? How long is it?"

"About two hours, I think. I actually don't have time to watch it tonight because there's a ton of homework I've gotta do. But we can find the time, right? You're not too busy to manage a movie?"

Rick blinked, wondering if he really did seem that busy. Between work, training, and his matches, perhaps he was. Immediately he decided to make time for the movie, though it was just a question of when. "Let's definitely find the time. Friday evening I have to work late, though."

"Ugh, your job is the worst. Next week is going to be really busy for me, so it probably needs to be this weekend or the next one. I suppose you have to work both of them?"

"This weekend is busy except for Saturday morning. Next weekend I'll get off by Sunday evening, but..." Rick checked his phone and noted the reminder. "No, I have to meet Emily then."

He realized that was a mistake the next second, but it was too late. Melissa drew both hands to her mouth in mock surprise. "Oooh, Emily. I don't even know who that is, so I'm going to assume the worst possible things!"

"Yup, it's definitely whatever you're imagining."

"How scandalous! I think I might faint!"

Rick rolled his eyes. "Really, it's more training. This upcoming tournament thing is the entire reason Granny Whitney is pushing me through all this. If we win, then I can pay her back and we'll finally be even. Then the two of us can make our own decisions and figure out where we want to go."

"That sounds nice." Melissa drew her legs up against herself and wrapped her arms around them. "Are you completely sure that she'll let you go, after the tournament? Is it possible that she'll go back on her word or rope you into something else?"

"Yeah, I've thought about that, but I hope not. Everything with her is a double-edged sword, but she's not completely unreasonable. From what I've seen the reward for this event will be pretty substantial, plus I think it's an ego thing for her. If I help her win and surrender my winnings, she has no reason not to be favorably inclined toward me."

"Hopefully so."

"I do want to watch this gloriously dumb movie, though, so let's figure out a time." Rick thought about his schedule again and sighed. "And I might as well just preempt you on the joke, because the reason we can't watch it Saturday morning is my meeting with Lisa."

Melissa shed her concern and punched him playfully on the arm. "You literal canine!"

They took it easy the rest of the night, chatting with each other before they had to get back to their work. Melissa stayed close to take care of him if anything happened, but he felt better now that he'd gotten through the effects of the pill.

The fact that the seventh pill had been worse made him anxious about the eighth one. Just in case, he took it while Melissa was home, but this time he didn't fall unconscious. It did seem to last longer than the first six had, however. He also thought it might have been more painful, though that might have been just his imagination.

While doing his work, he did his best to look up what he could about the pills. There seemed to be several different formulations, which made it much more difficult to know for sure. Almost everyone seemed to say that this type of training was dangerous, which wasn't exactly comforting. The only people he found who approved of its use said that it was good for "cleansing spiritual toxins" and sold the pills for hundreds of dollars each, which just made him more anxious about it.

After that, the next pill was worse, he was sure of it. When he trained that day, he had significant muscular fatigue in his core. So it was getting worse.

But what could he actually do about it? If Granny Whitney wanted to kill him, she could find an easier way. If she had malicious non-lethal intentions, she would certainly have a way to find out if he was obeying her instructions. And if she was telling the truth, then taking the pills could actually save his life later when he fought an opponent who did damage to internal organs.

In the end, there wasn't much he could do except push forward and hope he wasn't moving toward a dead end.

Chapter 34: Public Park Training

The plan was to meet Lisa at one of Branton's public parks for their informal sparring sessions. Rick sat on the bench by their usual place, looking around and trying to remember the exact name. It was named after a famous duel between two grandmasters, he was pretty sure, but the name escaped him. Everybody usually just called it Eastpark, for the uninspired reason that it was the easternmost of them.

Dressed casually as he was, he looked like many of the other people in the park to exercise. Yet he didn't feel the same as the people he saw, even if many of those going past had generation rates of 40,000 or more. They might outclass him in lucrim generation, but he was starting to realize how that measurement was only of limited use. Since so few shielded their lucrima, he was able to get an impression of them.

A woman jogging along had an impressive 60,000, but over half of that was consumed by her inefficient foundation. At the other end of the park, a man smoking a cigarette had 50,000, but his cores were a wrecked mess. When a pleasant-looking couple walked past with a stroller, Rick was surprised to see that they had over 40,000 lucrim in demonic bonds.

They were all just trying to get by in their own way. It was remarkable how people with so much more strength and money than him could still be struggling, but apparently that was just how life was.

Still, it was a relief when Lisa appeared beside him. Not only was he glad to see her, the lucrima aura around her was much more pure and stable. Even if she wasn't a fighter by trade, he'd bet on her over most of the people they'd seen in the park, even those who were sparring.

"You ready?" Lisa hopped back and forth a bit. "I jogged over here, so I'm restless."

"Sure, we can start now."

They headed off the main path and away from the family areas to begin sparring. Everyone could use the public parks for training, and since it was a nice day, many were. Mostly not seriously, and there was a couple being unnecessarily flirtatious as they did their exercises.

Thankfully, Lisa dropped into a crouch and came at him seriously. He removed such thoughts from his mind and just focused on sparring, which helped clear his mind. Lisa had stopped lowering her generation rate artificially, since it wasn't needed for him to keep up anymore. That meant some of her blows hurt a lot, but he'd faced worse.

As they moved they actually tore up some of the grass, however. That was one of the things that could get people kicked out: the authorities didn't want people having huge brawls that destroyed half the park. The general assumption was that if you were that powerful, you could afford a proper training facility. Unfortunately, he and Lisa might be getting into an uncomfortable zone between those two.

When they finished, they dropped onto the grass to catch their breath. Lisa fell back and caught herself with her arms, staring skyward. Rick closed his eyes and took a moment to collect himself before speaking.

"That was pretty good. I know you're not interested in the combat side of things, but you're getting a lot better about counter-attacking. Not much hesitation and over-defending now."

"Thanks." Lisa shot him a smile. "To tell you the truth, I actually put a bit of effort into my combat core. I figure if I spar this often, I should get better at it."

"Hmm, how is your portfolio organized, then?"

"You know, I should just give you access to my profile. Kind of silly that I haven't done it already, given that you're my personal trainer and everything." Lisa tapped on her phone and transferred permissions over to him, so he brought up her profile.

[Name: LisLis (pseudonym)

Ether Tier: 13th

Ether Score: 626

Lucrim Generation: 59,500

 - Demonic Bond: 6500

Current Lucrim: (private data)

[LisLis's Lucrima Portfolio

Foundation: 12,000 (Lv III)

Professional Massage Lucore: 31,800 (Lv VII)

Transportation Core: 5000 (Lv IV)

Legacy Core: 6200 (Lv III)

Combat Core: 4500 (Lv II)]

Though he kept a neutral expression, Rick found himself a bit intimidated. Lisa had over 30,000 lucrim invested in her occupation - she was definitely a professional, probably worth more than he was as a trainer. Even adding up all of his combat cores, he didn't have that much in his profession.

The presence of a demonic bond surprised him, but he decided that he couldn't hold it against her. He'd never gotten the slightest sense that she drew off one and she definitely wasn't dependent on it. Perhaps she just had it as a backup source of lucrim or for security. Uncle Frank said that some people viewed them that way, though he thought they were still an accident waiting to happen.

In any case, he realized that he was spending too long staring at her portfolio and she was watching nervously, so he glanced up and smiled. "Not bad. I see it classifies your main core as Level VII - I don't have anything ranked that high."

"Thanks, I've put a lot of effort into it." Lisa shook her head and then dropped back onto the grass with her hands behind her head. "I've been there for a while, though. It seems like it will take a lot of work to break into Level VIII."

"This general 'Combat Core' is probably fine for your purposes. I... actually don't know what this 'Legacy Core' is, though."

Lisa glanced up at him in surprise. "Really? Your parents didn't always bug you to be investing more in your Legacy Core? Mine never shut up about it. Not only is it one of the best ways to leave a Birthright Core to your descendants, it can really improve your health when you get older. I try to put some into it every month, but... well, you know how life goes."

His parents had not exactly been the type to invest money for the future, but Rick held his tongue about all that. When he reached out toward Lisa's portfolio in real life, instead of via the app, he thought he had a sense for it. The Legacy Core was actually similar to Graham's Stake, in that it slowly gathered strength over time. He could definitely see the benefits, though he was a bit irritated that things he'd never heard of were common clichés to people of higher classes.

"Plus, having one improves your ether score," Lisa went on. "It's one of those things people bug you about, but it really does make a difference. I couldn't have gotten my current apartment without a 600+ ether score."

"Actually, I was going to ask you about that, too. Yours is really high... I don't suppose there's any trick to it?"

After looking at him for a while, Lisa closed her eyes with an odd expression. "I'm not sure what to tell you, Rick. If you asked my parents and their friends, they practically believe that ether score is just how good of a person you are. They always told me you just need to be responsible and you'll get a good one. But you're one of the most responsible people I know and that hasn't worked out for you."

She'd put effort into not insulting him, but it still stung a bit. Rick forced himself to focus on her words instead of the gap between them. "My parents never talked about that kind of thing. I... don't think the companies that calculate the score really care about certain kinds of responsibility."

"Yeah, it seems that way."

They had fully recovered by then, so they both got back up. In the time they had been working, the park had cleared out a bit. As they headed back to the sidewalk, Rick found himself wincing and holding his stomach. Just a cramp, or an aftereffect from the pills?

"Are you okay?" Lisa moved up to him, putting a gentle hand on his shoulder.

"It's some medicine I'm taking for training. Really does a number on me."

"Oh, I've seen similar things before. I have clients that are just horrible to their bodies, then expect me to come in and make things better like I'm a mystical healer or an actual doctor." Instead of removing her hand from his shoulder, Lisa stayed touching him. He felt warmth spreading from her as she activated her primary lucrim core and he didn't resist. "Hmm, you have a lot of tension and you've been hard on your lucrima. I trust you to know your limits, but... keep an eye on it, or you'll injure yourself."

Rick sighed. "It's about the same as you and your Legacy Core. I always intend to do the right thing, but life keeps interrupting."

Lisa took her hand off his shoulder but stayed close, giving him a smile. "You know, you've been fulfilling your side of the bargain, but I haven't really given you much in return. Literally just one massage for Melissa. Are you sure you don't want one yourself? It'd probably do you some good."

"I..." Part of him wanted to because she was offering a valuable service. Another part wanted to find out how her hands would feel kneading his muscles. But the part that won out was the one who thought it would end up really awkward. "Thanks for the offer, but I'm under too much stress right now. Maybe once I get through some issues I'll have time to relax."

"Personally, I think you could use a massage more while you're under stress, but suit yourself." They started walking again, but as they went, Lisa looked over at him in concern. "I'm not a doctor, so take this with a grain of salt, but I didn't like how your lucrima felt. Be careful with all the stuff you're doing, okay? People can permanently injure themselves with aggressive over-training."

"Yeah, I'll keep that in mind." Rick smiled at her, grateful that she cared, even if it didn't matter.

This was like everything else. The best of intentions didn't really matter when life got in the way.

Chapter 35: Power Budgeting

The next time Rick had a match, he tried to decide whether to take his pill before or after. In the end he decided to take it before, just in case he was severely injured during the match. Though enduring the pain of his insides tearing apart wasn't a pleasant way to prep for a match, he disliked the idea of feeling that pain after a difficult fight even more.

As if that wasn't enough, Granny Whitney still gave him one of her foundation-damaging pills from before. So even though his internal injuries felt like they had recovered, he went into the match dizzy and drained.

Fortunately, he felt as though he had improved, or at least improved at fighting under such unfavorable conditions. It was far from a glorious victory and he fell multiple times, but he was the last one standing. Granny Whitney just smiled at him and wrote a note in a small book.

With the match complete, he had a bit of free time. Though he used some of it to recover and then train more, he also got the chance to watch Fist of the Sublime with Melissa. It was as gloriously stupid as promised and they quoted each other lines from it excessively until the jokes got old.

After that, however, he had an uncertain engagement: meeting with Emily. He hadn't seen her since the incident and he wasn't sure if she would resent being forced into it.

On that day, he got a text from Emily saying to meet him at some place called the "Recluse's Retreat." He hadn't heard of it before, but some checking on the internet gave him the address and a description. They had a fancy website that looked like it was designed to impress wealthy clients, emphasizing the luxury of the place without telling him overly much about what it was actually for.

In any case, he needed to hurry to get there in time, even using a taxi. Rick scrambled out the door and used the ride over to collect himself. Given how he'd fought alongside Emily, he trusted her - at least more than he trusted Granny Whitney - but that didn't mean their meeting would be easy.

The Recluse's Retreat was a boxy U-shaped building in the center of the city, unlike what he'd seen on the website... at least until he got to the main gate. There was a garden within, completely walled off by the front gate and the building around it. All of the photographs on the site had been cleverly staged to make it seem more expansive than it really was, though even the truth was more peaceful than the street outside.

When he stepped up to the gate, a man in a uniform he'd seen on the site stepped into his path. The man had a polite smile, but he also had a generation rate of over 50,000 lucrim and an active aura. "Excuse me, sir, but I don't believe I've seen you before. If you want to apply for our services, simpl-"

"He's with me." Emily stood up from one of the small ponds, having been so still that he'd missed her until she moved. The doorman immediately nodded to her and bowed away, then Emily waved a hand indicating that Rick should enter. "Let's get this over with."

"What exactly are we doing here?" He knew it made him look ignorant, but he couldn't help but look around as they walked into the garden.

"You haven't been to a place like this before? Well, maybe not. Basically, this is the modern version of going to train alone on a mountain. You can't find privacy like that in a city, and even the mountains are crowded with tourists these days. But what you can get are heavily secured, completely private rooms. Most of the space in the building is dedicated to those."

That made sense to him, and the prices on the website hadn't been ridiculous, but it was still a level of luxury he'd never even considered. Would his training have been more productive if he'd done it in a specialized chamber instead of at his strip mall gym, or in his crappy apartment? He wasn't actually sure, but it was obvious why people would prefer this.

One of the side doors led into what looked like a fully-equipped gym, but when he glanced toward it Emily waved him away. "That's just a secondary service. We're here for the place to train."

He followed her, looking over his shoulder as they went. This gym looked far nicer than the House of the Cosmic Fist, everything in pristine condition and waiting trainers who had probably been selected for both skill and attractiveness. It didn't need to give itself a grandiose name, just called itself the "Branton Recluse Center Gym" and let the quality speak for itself.

Trying not to let that get to him, Rick followed Emily into the building on the other side. She spoke briefly to the woman at the desk, then received a key and led them into a hallway that wouldn't have been out of place at a decent hotel. But when they stepped inside their door, it was obviously no hotel.

There was no free-standing furniture at all, just a set of cabinets built into the back wall. The walls, ceiling, and floor were all heavily ether enchanted, and when he tested them, they had just the right amount of give. Unless you were unleashing massive amounts of power, you could train in here without concern.

"If you don't have access to a corporate or university training facility," Emily said, "I find this is really worth the money. Aside from the obvious, the privacy shielding is excellent. Nobody can observe any techniques you use in here, so it's the perfect place to prepare in private."

"Does that mean a lot of crimes are committed in here?"

His question prompted an odd look from Emily, but then she tilted her head to consider. "Most likely, though I'd imagine they'd be white collar crimes. It's not like you could cover up a murder in a place like this. Plus, they do record everyone who enters and exits."

"Yeah, it was just a question." Rick pulled off his jacket and set it down in one corner. "I'm happy to learn, but I'm not sure what Granny Whitney wants you to teach me."

"A little more meditating or sparring isn't going to help you all that much. We need to make a qualitative change to have an impact." As she explained, Emily sat down with her legs crossed, so he went to sit across from her. "I thought we'd start with lucrim budgeting, unless you already know it."

Rick watched her thoughtfully. It sounded familiar, but... "I don't know the technique."

"It's not a technique so much as a method of organizing your techs. Most people who focus on lucrim generation rate are shortsighted about this sort of thing, so they often don't wield as much power as you might expect. For example, someone who is rolling with 100,000 lucrim might generally have a lot of power. But when they exhaust themselves and only have a little left, they won't have enough to keep their cores operating at full power and major weaknesses start to appear."

"And this 'lucrim budgeting' helps with that?"

"Essentially, you plan out exactly how much energy you're going to devote to each aspect of your lucrima portfolio. That way you won't overextend yourself and waste all of it on an excessive technique. Likewise, when you're running low on power, you're prepared to operate with less overall while keeping yourself balanced."

As she explained, Rick felt a growing level of resentment rise within him. While admittedly he'd never heard of this exact technique before, it was based on the idea that he was an idiot who wasted any power that was given to him. He'd never had an excess of lucrim, so how could he waste it?

Seething internally, Rick threw himself into the exercise. It started with mentally considering the exact proportions necessary and then modeling it in his aura, but he skipped all that. He'd been using those skills for years to get by. Instead he switched directly to modulating his lucrima as she'd instructed.

Emily frowned and tilted her head at him. "Hmm... reduce yourself to 50% of your maximum generation rate."

He did so without blinking.

"10%."

That took a little more effort, but he managed it without too much difficulty. Emily gave him a long look, then sat back. "Maybe you don't need this exercise after all."

"Do you really think I have enough lucrim to be throwing it away?" His voice sounded angrier than was polite, but Emily didn't flinch even slightly, so he pressed on. "I don't have some amazing job that pays 80,000 lucrim a year and my Birthright Core was a net negative. Operating on low energy is what I do."

"That isn't a universal law. I've seen fighters with only 10,000 lucrim who manage to squander half of it on unnecessary aura flashiness. But... that isn't a problem for you." While she didn't look exactly apologetic, Emily did give him a respectful nod. "It looks like your balance is already very efficient. You might be able to gain a little from the exercise, but not much."

To prove that he could, he lowered himself to 5% and stayed balanced, though that proved difficult. It wasn't that this "budgeting" technique offered no benefits at all, just that the approach treated him like he was a fool. Though it wasn't as direct as clients like Darin, it was still blaming him for the situation he had been born into as if it was his fault.

Emily sighed and held up her hands. "Alright, you've made your point. I can see that I've offended you. But I'm just as tired of people treating me like I was handed all the power I've worked hard for, especially when they're as sloppy as some."

"That's..." His instincts were to argue back, but after having grown up with people like his parents and Uncle Alan, he couldn't deny it. "I'm not saying you're entirely wrong. I'd just prefer to spend this time on something more useful instead of Baby's First Aura."

"Fair enough. If you had your choice, what would you want to learn?"

Rick hesitated, wondering if that was a test. Obviously she wasn't going to teach him any of her own skills, and though the room was equipped for sparring, based on her attitude he thought she didn't want that. He was tempted to ask for everything he could, but instead decided that this was a time for humility. "You and others have talked about how lucrim generation rate isn't a good measure of strength. I'm afraid I still don't understand why."

"Ah. That's not so much wrong as it applies less and less the further you go." Emily sat back, considering it for a moment. At least she didn't find the question stupid or insulting, even if it seemed like a simple subject for her. "Basically, novices gather as much lucrim as they can and expend it just as fast. That's why generation rate is a good measure of their strength."

"But even I invest what I can into cores, and I'm no expert."

"That's right, you're a step up from novices. But the stage beyond that is to supply your own lucrim with cores that can generate it." She held up a hand quickly. "Now, I know you've already started on Graham's Stake. That's good. But you're still dependent on salary or purchases for your lucrim, which limits you."

Though that was obvious, he didn't think she was talking down to him anymore. "I can see how it would make a difference once you have that established. How do you measure strength, then? Is there another shorthand, or do you just have to evaluate everything in a more complex way?"

"Based on how well you fight those above you, you should already know that more complex evaluations are more valuable. But yes, there's another way. You can't usually do it at a glance, but once you have experience with it, you can evaluate someone's entire lucrima portfolio. That gives you a much better approximation of strength."

"What about me, then?"

"Go back to full strength." Emily closed her eyes for a moment, considering, then nodded. "Roughly... 22,000 lucrim invested. Then we add your generation rate on top of that, though since yours is hindered by the aura leeches... about 42,000 total."

Rick considered that quietly. That was getting into respectable territory, though he wasn't sure about this new method. "I don't really have a point of comparison... your generation rate is about 85,000 lucrim, but what's your portfolio?"

Instead of answering, she taught him the basics of how to approximate it. Though he didn't feel like he would be comfortable using it in real life for a long time, in conditions like this, he was able to get a better sense for Emily's strength. It was higher than he expected and he paled a bit.

"Yours is... high. Hundreds of thousands."

"That's right." Emily nodded, only slightly self-satisfied. "For comparison, Glenn has a generation rate of 110,000 lucrim, but he blows most of it. In terms of invested cores, he only has 25,000 or so. Now, his overall threat would still be evaluated as 135,000, since he can pour an enormous amount of strength into his cores, but you see the difference."

That explained why Glenn had seemed to defer to her, since Emily's overall threat was much higher than that. But he found himself more curious about something else. "So... just theoretically, if Glenn and I had both nearly exhausted all our energy, we would be about equal?"

"More or less. The lucrim intensity he regularly deals with has a quality of its own, but there's also intelligence and skill and other factors. Of course, since he can afford to restore himself regularly, you aren't going to fight him at low strength."

It was still something to think about. Emily seemed to relax as they continued the training session, and after a while he figured it out: she'd been dreading giving a remedial lecture to him, but now that he'd earned a bit of respect, her irritation faded. She was sharp-tongued and not exactly kind, but she knew what she was talking about and he found himself enjoying talking to her.

They didn't spar or do any explosive training, yet he found it more useful than many hours in the gym. She taught him a few useful tricks that could spike his generation rate a little more - and more importantly, how he could apply that strength toward increasing practical power.

She had less to say about how exactly to deal with his foundation, just confirming that it was probably fine for now and he could focus on other things. On the subject of the aura leeches, she had suggestions for how to pay them off faster that surprised him, making him wonder if she had experience with them. It must have shown on his face, because she gave him an odd smile.

"How do you think I paid my way through university? Sure, I still have a few normal loans to pay off, but the biggest debt is always based in lucrim. I graduated with a nasty set of leeches."

He hadn't considered that before, but considering the cost of good schools, it made sense. "How many have you paid off?"

"Actually, I tried something else: I reconsolidated most of the leeches into a single one at Stage II. It's a huge leech that will take a while to pay off, but the overall drain is much less than multiple leeches. I don't recommend you do that, by the way, since you can just get rid of the ones you're carrying without excessive trouble."

"But if your generation rate is really 85,000, couldn't you get rid of it fairly quickly? Especially given how efficient you are with everything."

"I could, but a Stage II leech isn't that big a deal. Right now, it's more important for me to invest in other cores - some of them generate lucrim faster than the leech can drain it, so it's actually a net positive to keep the leech. That's a bit advanced for what you're dealing with, though."

She sounded condescending, but he'd come to understand that she was just blunt. The concept seemed easy enough and he accepted that it was indeed more advanced than he needed at the moment, so he set it aside. "I think I understand everything we've talked about, but it's a bit difficult to put together. Will you give me permission to check your profile so I can see your portfolio directly?"

"No." Emily didn't sound angry, but he didn't think that answer would change.

"Okay, that's fine. Just asking."

"I'm not offended, just private." She tilted her head at him curiously. "I think we've done enough for today, but I wanted to impose on your own privacy. It's fine to refuse the questions."

"No harm in asking."

"Why exactly haven't you developed more? I've been running numbers in my head based on your efficiency levels, and you should be further along, even assuming you were less efficient in the past. Getting about 20,000 per year from work should add up..."

Rick shook his head. "No, the gym where I work pays about 15,000 lucrim per year."

Emily's eyes widened just a bit. "That's... I don't see how you manage with that little, but I suppose that explains why you're so efficient."

"My sister also has a medical condition... instead of a normal soul, she has an ether void that burns up her lucrim. Though her condition has improved now, for most of her life I needed to drain a lot of lucrim to keep her healthy."

She didn't answer for a long time, staring at him with a look he couldn't quite interpret. After a while she closed her eyes. "I... apologize, Rick. I made a lot of assumptions about you, and even after you disproved some of them, I kept making others. This is no comfort at all, but... you've been dealt a pretty bad hand by life. That you've come this far is impressive."

"You're right: it's no comfort at all." Rick smiled to soften the words. "I just hope I can do enough that Mike and his buddies don't end up killing me when he gets his revenge."

"Life isn't fair." Emily stood up, stretching her body after sitting for so long, and glanced at him through her hair. "Realistically, Mike and Glenn are going to be handed a lot more things in life, so it'd be hard for you to catch up. But if you had the same advantages or were on a level playing field... I'd definitely bet on you."

"Thanks, Emily." He stood up as well and went to get his jacket. "At least I'm catching up a little, thanks to Granny Whitney wanting to use me. Most of her training is double-edged, but at least... oh, no offense."

"None taken. However much you trust her, you should trust her even less. For whatever it's worth, she didn't have any ulterior motives sending me to help. I'm not going to bail you out or shower you in lucrim, but I'm happy to help."

"I appreciate it. On that note..." Rick reached into his pocket and pulled out the bottle. "Do you think I should be concerned about these? She has me taking them and the side effects are pretty bad. Nothing I've read has been able to tell me if those are normal or if I'm going to cause problems for myself."

Emily barely glanced at the bottle, instead opening it and examining the pills before looking back to him. "I'm no expert on medicine, so I can't tell you a lot. But based on some research

I've done for myself... maybe you're right to be concerned. If there was a medicine that gave you an immediate benefit and caused long term damage only after the match, Whitney wouldn't hesitate to give it to you."

"Yeah, that's what I was afraid of."

"I suggest getting a full medical exam. Ideally as soon as possible, but it might make sense to wait until you can stop taking the medicine. Then you can probably get the damage healed before things go on a bad path. You need to be careful about any training that alters your physical fundamentals."

And like that, a bit of distance appeared between them again. Emily lived in a world where she could just get a medical exam if that was best for her health. That wasn't an option for him, and the surgery or healing would probably be far beyond what he could afford.

Still, he thanked her as they headed out. It might not be enough to bridge the gap, but now he felt like he could at least see how far away his opponents stood.

Chapter 36: Fight Patrons

As Rick signed his name on the form, he reflected just how many decisions in his life were controlled by circumstances. Yes, he was technically signing up for this Underground match of his own free will. But given how strongly Granny Whitney had suggested that he take it, and the fact that she needed him to get more points before the big match, it wasn't really his choice.

Rick slid the paper across the desk to Alger, who beamed with his usual cheerfulness, but Rick could barely focus on him. It wasn't just the blackmail keeping him in the Underground. Joining a combat sect or a university had never been options for him. He'd ended up stumbling forward into whatever jobs he could get, leading to his present situation.

Strangely, even though his life was so restricted now, in some ways he was more free than he had been before. He had the strength to stand on his own and he'd managed to help Melissa gain control of her condition. Once he was done with this, he might be able to make his own choices.

"Boy? You still with us?" Alger peered at him and Rick realized too late that he had been spacing out. "This is a wonderful opportunity for you! I don't give fighters on the lower tiers named matches very often!"

"Yes, I'm very grateful." Rick did his best to push other thoughts aside and just smile. "I want to participate in the upcoming tournament, but it's looking like it might be a struggle to get to 250 points."

"I have no doubt you will, my boy. You have the pluck and good heart to make it." Alger paused, glancing toward the arena itself. "But you know, you still have some time until the match itself begins. Would you be willing to listen to an old man for a moment?"

"Sure." Though that made Rick a bit nervous, he absolutely needed to stay on Alger's good side... though the strange man's favor had problems all its own.

"I understand you are thinking about fighting for Granny Whitney in the little tournament coming up. As it happens, I will be fielding a team myself, and I could use a good featherweight. Tom is developing much too quickly to compete in that power class, I'm afraid."

That made him wonder about Tom's development and Rick wanted to check the other man's profile, but he resisted and just stayed focused on Alger.

"You seem like a promising young man and, though it pains me to say this, I'm afraid that Granny Whitney is really not a very good role model for you. I think you could do much better if you were to work with my team. Trust me, I would take care of all the details, and I do very well for those who are working for me. What do you say?"

For a moment, Rick considered it. Though Granny Whitney had multiple potential threats to use against him, the initial blackmail had been over the death of the Slayer. But she couldn't go to real authorities with something like that, which meant she'd go through Alger. If Rick jumped ship and went all-in with Alger, perhaps he could negate that threat and get out of the tormenting relationship.

But of course it couldn't be that easy. Granny Whitney would come after him, since he'd be effectively stealing what she'd given him at the beginning. Rick also wasn't sure that Alger would necessarily be any better - better the devil he knew. No, better not to take the risk.

Keeping all of that off his face, Rick responded with a generic smile. "Sorry, sir, but I gave my word that I'd help her. And I like to think I'm a man of my word."

"I see." For a moment, Alger stared at him, his eyes no longer dancing. But a moment later he smiled broadly. "It's good to see a lad with some backbone! I regret I didn't get to talk to you earlier, but that's how it goes. Have fun in your match!"

That was obviously a dismissal, and if not, Alger made it obvious by getting up and rushing from the room. Rick didn't linger, trying to refocus himself as he prepared for the match. Though there was more time before the multi-tier event, he wanted to reach the 250 point entrance requirement today, so that he'd have plenty of time to prepare for the tournament.

As he headed out toward the arena entrance, he discovered one more obstacle in his way: Granny Whitney stood beside the double doors. She smiled pleasantly at him, but he could only groan.

"This time too? I thought the point was to do well and get enough points to qualify."

"If you can't make it with a handicap, dearie, then you won't stand a chance in the tournament." Her smile broadened and she handed him another pill. "Now take your medicine."

He swallowed it as usual, trying to focus on the benefits to his foundation instead of the impending dizziness and weakness. Yet this time, after he took it, she handed him a second pill. This one was pitch black and much larger than average, enough that he wasn't sure if he'd be able to swallow it.

"This should help a little. Just be quick, dearie." With that ambiguous suggestion, she pushed the pill into his hands and waited expectantly for him to swallow it. He needed to work up some saliva, but he managed. With that, she gave him a pat on the shoulder and pushed him toward the arena itself.

Within, he found that the crowd was surprisingly large and raucous. Most likely that wasn't for his match - given how things had gone the last time they were like this, he hoped not - but the fact that a match he participated in was part of a major event night indicated how his status had changed. Unless this was going to be another unpleasant surprise, of course.

But this time, he didn't see anything amiss. The match was supposed to be three on three, a competition between some of the newer members of the Underground. According to Emily, it was also likely to be for the purposes of hyping up the lower tiers that people wouldn't generally care about. Alger really wanted this next event to be a huge one.

Tom and Henry already stood on his side of the arena, waiting for him. Rick headed to join them, looking to the other side. At least he wasn't last: one of the other team hadn't arrived yet either. He didn't recognize one of them at all, a slightly older man, and the second was someone he'd seen in a few melees, a ranged aura attacker he couldn't name.

"Oh, thank god, it's you." Henry glanced at him and grinned. "Based on what he was saying, I thought the third person would be some loser."

Rick raised an eyebrow. "Was that an insult or not?"

"I really didn't know, man. Think we can do this?"

Before Rick could answer, Tom stepped in, frowning at Henry. "Just who was saying that? Did you get a patron?"

Henry gave them both a sly grin. "Maybe. But does it really matter? We need to focus on winning this fight."

"It does matter." Tom glanced once to the other side of the arena, then turned to face the other two. "This isn't really the best time to discuss this, but I guess we're waiting anyway. I've come to believe that there are three real contenders for the victor of the multi-tier match. Alger, Granny Whitney... and someone from the criminal underworld."

As he said the names, Tom pointed to himself, then Rick, then Henry. Getting it several seconds later, Henry glared at him. "Are you suggesting something? Look, I don't really know my patron, I just know that he's a big deal. And that he helped me get a new bond to bail out my previous two. What does it matter?"

"Because according to my research, the hitman wasn't sent by Granny Whitney. And unless you think Alger is playing fourth dimensional chess attacking his own fighter, then there's only one major source left."

"You don't know that! There might be only three major contenders, but there are way more minor ones, and any of them could have been behind the attack."

Tom frowned and stepped up to Henry, who began summoning his demonic shell. Before things could get out of hand, Rick stepped in between them. "I'm not saying this doesn't matter, but whatever the truth is, we all need to finish this match. If we can't work together, that doesn't help anyone."

They glared at one another one more time, but they both stepped back. Hopefully they'd be professional enough to work together, because he didn't relish the idea of trying to carry this match. At least one fighter on the other side was in the welterweight tier, so Rick was overall out of his weight class.

The only bright side was the fact that he didn't feel too bad. Though the first pill seemed to have kicked in, his vision only swam a little and the drain was perfectly manageable. Whatever that second pill was, it was canceling the side effects of the first... or delaying them. Based on Granny Whitney's warning, he wanted the match to be over as soon as possible.

Fortunately, they didn't have to wait too much longer before the final contestant arrived, and he realized that he actually recognized her. It was the young woman with the spiked club, who he hadn't seen in quite a few matches. Did that mean anything? Possibly that she'd been recruited by someone else, but otherwise it didn't make a difference.

"Finally, it is time!" Alger stood up from his usual position, arms spreading wide. "Six of the finest new warriors in the Underground, all joining within the past year. This is their last chance to win glory for themselves through their grit and determination! Fight!"

Nobody expected his speech to turn into the fight declaration so quickly, but the sound rang through the air. The fight had begun.

Chapter 37: Three on Three

Before any of them could move, the old man stepped forward, one foot stomping down on the floor. Light green aura spread from his foot, a spiderweb of lines that raced across the floor toward them. Tom jumped aside, summoning his lightning, while Henry tried to move and didn't quite escape in time.

The aura lines leapt from the floor, snapping around his leg and binding him in place. Since they didn't appear harmful, Rick decided not to dodge: the beginning of the match was the best time to take his opponent's measure.

When the aura snaked around his legs it burned a little, but it wasn't an attack. Instead he struggled against the lines of power, testing how well they bound him in place. Meanwhile, the old man's teammates wasted no time attacking, as if they'd planned this. Perhaps they did, spending their time coordinating instead of arguing.

While Rick tested his strength against the aura bonds, everyone else began to attack. The enemy aura user began hurling spheres at them, but Tom made all of them explode early with a few bolts of lightning. Meanwhile, the woman with the bat leapt at Henry, who barely managed to activate his demonic shell in time. He rocked backward from the first blow, cracks beginning to form in the shell, but then struck back and the two of them began fighting toe-to-toe.

Taking a deep breath, Rick leapt upward, tearing free from the enemy aura. It hadn't been all that strong in the end, though if it caught him unawares it could hinder him at a critical moment. So long as he kept moving, he didn't think the old man's aura would be a problem.

But the aura user targeting him would be. Since he was suspended in midair, he was the obvious target, and several explosive spheres hurtled in his direction.

Fortunately, he'd chosen Bunyan's Step for exactly this purpose. It propelled him through the air, past the spheres before they could explode. The aura user had only a moment to look shocked before Rick rammed into him shoulder-first.

His opponent staggered back into the chain link fence and bounced off toward him. Rick tried to meet him with an elbow to the face, but the man sent his aura bursting in all directions, providing a cushion that pushed Rick back.

Not by very much. He'd expected to have been thrown back or stunned, yet Rick felt fine - he'd experienced much worse than this. While his opponent looked on in shock, he reached through the man's aura to grab him by the neck, then slam him to the ground.

Though he'd planned to hit him while he was down, the old man was advancing on them and he was extending a lot of tendrils along the ground. Even if they were individually weak, if that many grabbed him, it could be difficult to break out. Not willing to risk getting trapped on the enemy's side of the arena, Rick leapt back across.

That didn't mean retreating, though. He struck at the bat wielder from behind, and though she sensed his attack and pulled her weapon back to block it, the blow staggered her.

She lashed out with her spiked club and he managed to block the blow, but he regretted it - one of the spikes tore through his sleeve and drew a line of blood across his arm. Clearly, she'd been increasing her offensive abilities considerably. It looked like she'd dealt so many blows to Henry that he couldn't even take advantage of her back being turned.

A moment later lightning crashed down where she stood. Somehow she leapt back to her allies, so it only served to blind all of them. Rick stumbled through the blindness, grabbing Henry's shoulder under his crumbling armor.

"Get it together, man. They'll come again soon."

"Yeah, yeah..." Henry shook his head sharply and restored the yellow shell of aura, but he didn't look well. Had some of her blows gotten through?

Both sides took a moment to recover, but the rest wouldn't last long. In the brief pause, Rick realized how much the crowds were cheering. It seemed that the six of them had advanced enough for their fight to be interesting to watch, even if it wasn't exactly a heavyweight bout. Perhaps that was why the multi-tier event started with the featherweight class.

Then there was no more time for idle thoughts, because the other side was attacking. Surprisingly, the old man began, not with the aura tendrils but with aura bursts. They were weak and slow compared to his ally's sphere attacks, so Rick just dodged to the side.

Henry let out a roar and charged directly at them. His demonic shell looked impressive, but charging into fire was a bad move. Rick was too surprised to provide support, so aura tendrils soon began snapping up around Henry's legs.

Though Henry broke through them, he wasn't so lucky when the aura user attacked. Sphere after sphere slammed into his armor, increasing the cracks through it. Henry got off a wild blow that knocked the old man backward, but his armor was taking heavy damage and the woman with the spiked club was getting ready for a counterattack.

Before she could, Tom clapped his hands together, releasing a lightning shockwave just in front of Henry. It knocked all their opponents back and drove the old man to the ground, but Henry also staggered back. He didn't look well at all, yellow veins standing out on his face.

By that time Rick had moved to support him, trying to intercept the woman with the spiked club. She redirected to attack him with a clumsy swing. He easily deflected it... and realized it was a feint.

As soon as he lost his momentum to deflect her swing, she sprinted directly at Henry. Tom launched a bolt of lightning at her, yet she spun aside to dodge it and came back around just in front of Henry. He let out another cry, flooding more power into his shell and swinging down.

Her blow shattered through the shell around his fist and kept going, smashing through his helm as well. As pieces of solidified aura rained throughout the ecstatic crowd, Henry crashed back to the ground, his shell crumbling.

Rick darted in, grabbed him, and rushed out with another Bunyan's Step. He was still nearly struck by the aura user's spheres and more tendrils, since it looked like the old man was back up. Dammit, then both sides still had three fighters.

When he got back across the arena with Henry, however, he realized that even odds might be over-optimistic. Henry looked horrible and his lucrima portfolio felt utterly drained. It felt as though... no, hopefully not. While Tom kept the enemy at bay, Rick tried to slap him back awake.

"Stay with us, Henry!"

"...nothing left." He shook his head. "I drew all the bonds to the maximum... they won't give me any more... damn demons..."

From the corner of his eye, Rick saw a sphere of aura moving toward him, passing Tom's lightning defenses. If he grabbed Henry he just might be able to make it... but Rick realized that his coworker was down for the count. He leapt away on his own just before the sphere hit.

The explosion sent Henry sliding across the arena to the fence, where he lay still. That meant it was three to two, so they-

Out of nowhere the woman with the club was swinging at him. Relying on his defenses, Rick managed to fend her off, but each of her blows was heavy. Now that she was in range she could wear him down, so unless Tom...

At that moment Tom released a bolt of electricity at her back. Yet she again moved with impressive agility, ducking beneath it so that the bolt hit Rick's chest.

Where it had always been intended to go. Rick channeled the current through his body and slammed his knee up into the woman's chin.

The explosive force sent her stumbling backward, dropping her club. It was impressive that she didn't fall, but she was stunned long enough for Rick to close in and deliver several quick jabs that dropped her. Good, perhaps the most dangerous of the enemy was down. Without her, the ranged attackers...

Rick wavered on his feet, suddenly overwhelmed by a surge of nausea. He pushed past it, looked toward their opponents, but the room was spinning more. Was the effect of the suppressant Granny Whitney had given him wearing off?

Somehow he missed the tendrils creeping across the ground until they gripped his leg. He tore free from them easily, yet instead of dodging away, he ended up staggering and nearly falling. His stomach was churning and it felt as though he might vomit at any minute, but that was nothing compared to the disruptions flowing through his lucrim. What was wrong with him?

Intellectually he knew that the aura user would be targeting him soon, but he felt as though he was moving in slow motion. A sphere slammed into his chest and he couldn't stop himself from falling. Even his defensive core seemed to be spluttering, refusing to work properly.

Another sphere flitted toward him, but at that moment Tom smashed down into the ground, releasing a wave of lightning that annihilated the sphere and drove their opponents away. But when he turned back, his expression was deeply concerned.

"Rick? Are you still in this?"

"I... I'm not sure..." Struggling to make the arena stop spinning around him, Rick gripped the floor and tried to push himself up. "Something's wrong. I'll be done soon, then it's up to you."

"What?"

There was no time to explain, though. Rick stumbled out toward their opponents, barely able to see. Whatever was happening, it was getting worse. If he wanted to have any more impact on the battle, it needed to be right that moment.

Of course, his clumsy stumble made him an easy target. As both opponents focused on him, Rick forced his way through all the chaos in his head with raw willpower to use a single core: Bunyan's step.

As he activated it, he threw himself sideways. His body collided with both opponents, sending them all tumbling like bowling pins. It hurt like hell, especially since his defensive core was still faltering. Though his vision was growing dark, Rick saw bolts rain down on their opponent, dealing serious damage since they were off guard. They wouldn't recover from that.

Another victory that left him half-dead. As he passed out, Rick hoped it wasn't becoming a habit.

Chapter 38: Consequences

When Rick woke up, he could feel that he'd received some healing, but he still felt like shit. Now that he had some perspective and wasn't in the middle of combat, he felt as though the side effects had been a greatly amplified version of the usual handicapping pill. They didn't just disorient and exhaust him, they'd disrupted his lucrima down to the foundation.

He'd been moved to the dingy hospital building, but no one else was currently in the room. Rick forced himself to sit up and discovered that his things were beside him, including his phone. Though it hurt to stretch far enough to reach it, he got his phone and checked the results of the match.

[Special Match Performance:

Participation +10

Opponent KO +10

Assist +2

Knocked Out -3

Total Reward: 19

Cumulative Points: 252]

Then he'd just barely made it: he could participate in the multi-tier tournament without needing to enter any more matches.

Presuming that Granny Whitney had been honest about her intentions there. He looked forward to it - as much as the fights honed his edge, he liked training that didn't leave him hurting this badly.

As he looked at his match performance, he found himself wishing that it gave more information. How many points had Tom and Henry received? Most likely Tom had gotten a lot of credit again, but Rick didn't really care about that. Arbitrary points didn't matter, only what he'd learned from the match.

Henry concerned him more. If what he had said was true, then he'd severely overdrawn his demonic bonds. That would have nasty long term consequences, unless his patron somehow bailed him out. But after the match had gone poorly, Rick had to wonder if Henry's patron would want him at all. If it was really the same person who had sent the hitman, then he was ruthless.

"Not bad at all, dearie!" Granny Whitney tottered into the room, beaming. "You have enough points to qualify now!"

"Barely." Rick rubbed his forehead to try to massage the pain away. "When the second pill you gave me wore off, it was almost worse than the effects of the first one. I wish you'd told me it had such a tight time limit."

"Oh, no, it's not like that at all. The second pill didn't activate until most of the way through the match, after you'd used most of your lucrim." She beamed even brighter, not even bothering to lie. "You managed to struggle through, though! I honestly didn't expect that."

At this stage, he barely even sighed. "That would have reduced my score even further... so you didn't expect me to qualify after this match?"

"No, I expected it to take another one or two fights. But since you've done well, I guess that gives you extra time to prepare yourself."

"Can I have medicine to repair lucrima damage now?"

"Hmm..." Granny Whitney grabbed his chin, turning his head left and right as she analyzed him. "No, not yet. This is going to be much closer than I'd hoped, but I suppose that's the risk we're taking. For now, just keep doing what you've been doing, dearie."

"Really? More of the same?"

"I think you'll find some nice benefits after having endured that last match! I'm not trying to poison you, after all... just use you."

Rick sighed and accepted it. "Alright, fine. Just tell me what you need me to do. Then once we get past this tournament, we're done."

"That sounds about right. For now, just take these." Granny Whitney dropped several items beside him, then turned and bustled out. "Lots to do, lots to do! I've told Emily to work with you, and there are enough pills there to last until the event. Don't bother me unless there's an emergency, dearie!"

With that, she was gone. Rick took a moment to collect himself as he put away the new items she'd given him, then finally headed out himself. He felt a bit better now, and she was right that the disruption could lead to some new improvements, but he wished there was a better way to train.

Though he intended to head home and sleep for a while, on his way out he checked into all the rooms with lights. He was looking for Henry, but he ended up stumbling across his opponents first: the old man lay unconscious, while the woman with the spiked bat - currently leaning beside her bed - grinned at him.

"That was one hell of a hit!"

"Thanks. You have a lot of lucrim in that club of yours, it was rough to block."

"Haha, you're way too casual about that. I'm used to smashing straight through people."

They went silent for a moment, so Rick decided to just move on before it got awkward. "Listen, it's nice talking to you, but I want to check on my friend."

"I assume you mean the one with the demonic bonds?" She bit her lip and peered into the hallway. "Just left of here - no, right from your perspective - and down the hall. I saw them take him somewhere around there, anyway."

"Thanks." Now that he had a direction, Rick headed to find his coworker.

Inside, he found Henry lying on his back, apparently unconscious. It looked as though a machine had been attached to him, but it had recently been removed. His life wasn't in danger, but the condition of his lucrima was shocking. Henry was deep in the grip of his demonic bonds, paying for all the power he'd been loaned for so long.

To Rick's surprise, Henry opened his eyes and looked at him, so Rick walked in. "You were right in the thick of things back there, man," Rick said. "You doing okay?"

"Of course I'm not fucking okay." Henry practically spat out the words. "I can't draw my usual power anymore, and on top of that they penalized me for it. There's probably no chance in hell I can get into the big event. And if I don't, how am I going to pay off the bonds?"

"That's rough. When I had the aura leeches implanted, I felt-"

"Don't pretend they're the same." Henry glared at him and turned away, staring toward the wall.

For a time Rick just stood there, wondering if it was worth trying to reach out again. Maybe what Henry needed was time, though it seemed more like he was embracing the bitterness. Rick had wanted to learn more about the exact penalties, but realized that since he still had permission to view Henry's profile, he had an easier method than asking him.

[Name: Hendog69 (pseudonym)

Ether Tier: 17th

Ether Score: 94

Lucrim Generation: 18,500

 - Demonic Bond: 12,000 (overextended - 20% repayment penalty)

 - Demonic Bond: 4000 (overextended - 23% repayment penalty)

 - Demonic Bond: 7000 (overextended - 35% repayment penalty)

Lucrim Generation with Penalty: 12,730

Current Lucrim: (private data)]

Rick refreshed the profile, just to be sure he was seeing the correct numbers. It looked like the power granted him by the demonic bonds had been entirely removed, actually reversed to drain his strength until the debt was repaid. While the impact might not be quite as immediate as the aura leeches, this would be a huge obstacle to any training Henry wanted to do.

It seemed like it had knocked him down a couple tiers as well, and his score was below 100, which was truly abysmal. All because he hadn't kept the bonds under control... now Rick understood just why his uncle was so adamant about not using them.

If Henry didn't want help, Rick didn't intend to force it. Instead he headed out, trying to decide how to spend his last month before the event. He texted Emily a few times to find out her plans. Apparently she was trying to lie low in her last matches and sneak over the 250 point mark, so she would be busier than usual. But she said they might be able to find time, and he learned from her that Granny Whitney might require their presence for more than the single day of the event itself. He'd have to rearrange his schedule around that.

Could he get off work? Technically he'd be making more money with all of his matches, even with Granny Whitney taking most of the winnings, but he couldn't just ignore his boss's demands. Marching into the gym and loudly quitting might be a fun fantasy, but he had a sister to support and needed to fund his progress somehow. He couldn't do something that reckless.

On his way out, he found Tom waiting for him. Though he had a bandage around his waist, he otherwise looked in good shape after the match. The taller man gave him a grim nod when he approached and fell in alongside him, as if he'd been waiting.

"Good job during the match." Tom glanced down at him thoughtfully. "I'm almost a bit disappointed we won't be able to fight each other during the event."

It didn't sound like Tom intended to jibe him about being in different power classes, so Rick just nodded. "But we're technically going to be on different teams, huh? You went all-in with Alger."

"He's done well for me since I joined the Underground, yes. But it's not a real loyalty." Tom shrugged. "Granny Whitney strikes me as a shady character, but she hasn't done anything to me. The one who bothers me is the third player, assuming he was the one who sent the hitman. I want to take his fighters down. Hard."

"Are you suggesting some kind of alliance?"

"No, just talking aloud. Honestly, I'll be rooting for you more than Alger's featherweight, if it comes to that." Tom turned abruptly and stuck out his hand. "Good luck out there."

"Sure, you too." Rick shook his hand, squeezing back to avoid Tom crushing his grip. They let go and turned in opposite directions, almost as if they'd planned it that way.

So far he knew someone in four out of the five tiers, knowing absolutely nothing about the cruiserweights. Part of Rick wondered if he should do more research into the welterweights, meet the person Granny Whitney had found for the tier above his. In theory he might be able to give them suggestions about fighting Tom.

But that only made sense if his goal was to win, and it wasn't. Granny Whitney wanted to win, but he just wanted to fulfill his obligation and be done with it. Yes, he'd watch Emily's match, and he was curious to see what the fight in the heavyweight division would look like. Beyond that, investing too much in the event was only a distraction. This was just part of his life, he didn't live for the event.

Once he finished, would he really leave the Underground behind? He'd gotten used to having the fights as part of his schedule and could almost imagine missing them. Without medicine painfully handicapping him, and with the ability to choose his own matches, maybe it could even be fun. Then again, someone had hired a hitman to disable Tom, so maybe even considering it was reckless...

Deep in his own thoughts, Rick didn't notice that anything was wrong until his instincts warned him of power flaring ahead. He took a cautious step back and found himself looking at Mike and Magnus. Both Birthrighters were at full power and flaring their auras.

"You've been running around for a while, and Father says I should end this." Mike stepped forward with a smug look on his face. "So we're going to do this the old-fashioned way: a challenge."

"That's a lot of lucrim just to issue a challenge." Rick kept his hands in his pockets and tried to look casual. They were in between the Underground and the illegal clinic, so in theory he had multiple allies nearby if things went bad.

"I, Mike Maguire, formally challenge you to a duel of honor." Mike took another step forward and extended a legal document to him. "A battle to surrender or utter defeat, to end the conflict between us once and for all. You can see the time and place on the paper, and if you do not arrive, you will forfeit."

Rick stared at it for a moment, then looked up. "Nah."

"What?" Mike's face went red and his aura spiked dangerously. "You... you can't just ignore a challenge! Are you a sniveling coward?"

"I'm not required by law to accept it. Maybe that would be a big deal if we lived in a village where everybody cared, but this won't even make the news."

"So you are a coward!"

"I'm not the one challenging people with a tiny fraction of my power just so I can feel better about myself."

Mike let out an angry roar and swung wildly, but Rick had predicted it. He slid just to the side of the first punch and took a step back from the second, letting him seem completely calm compared to Mike's rage. The truth was that despite all his progress, getting hit by a blow like that would be a serious problem, but he didn't think today would turn into a fight, so he could stay in control.

"Calm down, man." Magnus grabbed one of Mike's arms and tugged him back. "If you brawl with him now, it'll just get worse. Do what we planned."

"Right. The plan." Mike let out a breath angrily and drew himself up. For a moment he just tapped a message on his phone, then he looked back to Rick and his expression became much less pleasant. "I figured you might try to take the coward's way out. But believe me, you'll accept the challenge."

Rick thought about snapping back, but the change in Mike's attitude made him too nervous. He didn't like the fact that Glenn was missing, either. If they ambushed him here, the situation could turn bad, but he thought he could Bunyan's Step away before they dealt serious damage.

Consumed by thoughts of battle, Rick was taken entirely off guard when his phone rang. It seemed entirely inappropriate for the situation, but Mike didn't look irritated, he just smiled smugly.

Suddenly chilled, Rick checked the number. It was Melissa.

Mike's smile widened.

Chapter 39: Ultimatum

"Rick?" Melissa's voice was quiet and frightened. "Somebody just b-broke down the door... blew it off the hinges. I'm hiding, but I can see him in the entrance..."

For a time, Rick couldn't say anything. The phone almost slipped out of his hand as he stared at Mike, who kept watching him with that same smug look on his face. But he heard the desperation in his sister's voice and couldn't let himself stay silent. "Melissa, I'm sorry. This is my fault. Just stay there and things will be okay."

"What's going on? Are you okay?"

"Please. I'll talk to you soon."

When his sister went silent, Rick lowered the phone, though he kept the call going just in case. Then he looked up at Mike, staring directly into the smug bastard's eyes. The Birthrighter looked pleased with himself, not cruel, so he could hope that this was only a threat.

As his fear for Melissa faded, Rick found it replaced with rage. It burned coldly within him, not changing his expression in the slightest. He was at a disadvantage now, so he needed to wait for a better opportunity. But simply letting this go was no longer an option.

"I wouldn't have had to do this," Mike said, "if you didn't act like a little bitch. You should be grateful that this is all I'm doing. There was a time when I could have killed you for what you did to me, but I'll settle for humiliating you and making sure you never fight again."

"Just give me that." Rick took the legal document and began looking over it. Most of it was unsurprising, the challenge terms that everyone knew well. But the limits... instead of going until a fall or first blood, the match would continue until surrender or unconsciousness. Someone could deal permanent injuries under terms like that. Of course, the match would likely not be fair, so a brutal beating would only happen if Rick lost.

"I tried to remove the surrendering part, to keep you from being a little coward again, but the lawyers said it was legally required." Mike wiggled his phone and smirked. "But you know what will happen if you don't fight to the end."

"I accept the terms - if you call off your goon."

"Fine, fine." Smug in his victory, Mike tapped another message. After a while, he heard Melissa let out a sigh of relief. Though the threat still hung over them, Rick was fairly certain that Mike had only intended an empty threat and wouldn't push it further.

But that left Rick with little choice. The most he could do was buy a little time, which he needed to do given the date on the paper. "This will interfere with the tournament, which I can't cancel."

"Fine, move it after." Mike shrugged scornfully. "It doesn't matter how long you delay, it's going to end up the same."

According to the terms, he couldn't delay the date more than a month, so Rick put the challenge off as much as he could. He bit his thumb hard enough to draw blood, then pressed it down onto the document. Immediately Mike snatched the paper from him, grinning. "Signed and sealed! You're not getting out of this one, you bastard!"

"I'll see you there, and I'll fight to the end." Rick wanted to glare at Mike, but knew it was a better tactic to look cowed for now. "Just don't hurt my sister."

"Believe me, you're the only one I want to hurt." With that, Mike and his friend strutted away, clearly viewing this as a victory. Rick stood in the street, watching them go.

Now he was backed into a corner, so he had no choice. Feeling as much fury as he currently did, he wanted nothing more than to go to the match and pay Mike back for this. That would be difficult, likely impossible, yet those cold flames felt as though they could burn anything.

"Rick?" His sister's voice was distant until he brought the phone to his ear. "God, Rick, I'm so sorry about this..."

"It isn't your fault. He was going to force me into this one way or another."

"Can he really do this? Threatening someone is illegal, can't we just turn him in or something?"

Truthfully, he hadn't considered that. Rick thought about it for a moment, but it wasn't really a choice. "No, it wouldn't do any good. The combat sects occasionally kill people and have the authorities look away, and a company like Maguire Incorporated is even bigger than most of them. They can get away with this, at least as far as the law is concerned." Not as far as he was concerned.

"Well... get home soon, okay?" Melissa took a slow, shuddering breath, then forcibly lightened her tone. "Wow, he really did a number on our door. These hinges are... yeah, that's not getting fixed. Think we can get the landlord to fix it?"

"I think combat damage isn't covered by our lease, and even if he did, it would take him a month. If he's in a hurry."

"Guess we'll have to buy another door, then. You know, I have absolutely no idea how much those cost."

"Neither do I, but I suppose we'll find out." Talking about petty details with his sister helped him come down from the intensity of the confrontation, at least a little. Rick and Melissa stayed on the line, by unspoken agreement moving to talking about anything other than the threat. They'd see each other shortly, but they needed to talk.

When he reached the parking lot outside their apartment, his eyes were immediately drawn to their door. It looked like Melissa had propped the door up in the frame, but it was obviously in bad shape. Suddenly Rick felt heavy and mounting all the stairs to the apartment seemed impossible.

"Fuck, man." One of the methheads loitering by the base of the stairs gave him an odd look. "Crazy fucking shit man. Whatever's going on with you, real sorry about it, mmkay?"

"Uh, thanks." Was that a display of solidarity from the local methheads? Rick gave him a weak smile and the man shuffled away, presumably to smoke meth. The strangeness of it broke Rick out of his funk and he took the stairs several at a time, hurrying to his apartment.

"Was that one of those guys by the stairs?" Melissa asked through the phone.

"Yeah, apparently people saw the Birthrighter break the door."

"It was pretty loud, so I'm not surprised. Not that they did anything. I mean, not with somebody that dangerous..."

Finally Rick arrived, moving the door out of the way with his free hand. He found Melissa on the other side, waiting for him. They stood there for a while, both still holding their phones to their ears uselessly, then they leapt to embrace one another.

"God, that was awful." Melissa pressed her forehead hard against his chest and gripped him tighter. "When he broke the door down I had no idea what was going on and I was just..."

"Don't worry, it's over now." He wanted to comfort her, but his mood darkened. 'They have what they want."

"Yes, I heard." She pulled back and drew him into the apartment, staring into his eyes seriously. "So you don't have any choice but to fight him? When does the challenge happen?"

"Barely two weeks after the end of the multi-tier event. So I need to get through that without getting too injured, because I doubt I'll get any help once Granny Whitney gets what she wants."

"But... can you beat him? Not that I don't believe in you, bro, but they're Birthrighters with over 100,000 lucrim, right? And won't his father just hand him a bunch more power to make sure he wins?"

Rick considered the question as they sat down. "I hope that last part won't happen. I met Mike's father very briefly when I gave the core back, and he seemed a bit irritated at his son. Though this challenge must have gotten his support, for it to happen at all, I don't know if he's fully invested in it. I hope not, because if he does go all-in, then I don't have a chance."

"But even so, that's a really huge gap in lucrim..."

"It is, yeah. But fighting him one on one in a formal challenge is better than him ambushing me at any time with his friends helping. The smart thing to do would be to let him beat me until he's satisfied. If I focused on defense until then, I could probably avoid permanent injury." Rick took a deep breath, forcibly relaxing his fists. "But I want to win."

Melissa hugged him tightly. "I don't know what the right thing to do is. Your life is most important, so I don't want you to risk yourself at all. I hate the idea of people like him being able to just walk over us, so... I'd love to see you beat the shit out of him."

"Language, language."

She stuck out her tongue at him. "So it becomes wholesome to wish terrible violence on somebody if I say 'beat the poopy out of him'?"

"Yes, that's very wholesome." The absurdity of it made him finally smile, which let most of the tension ease from him. It didn't improve the facts of the situation, but he couldn't face those facts if he was still wrapped up in emotions. "Let's go get this door fixed before too many bugs come in. I'll try to come up with a plan while we work on it."

The mundane activity gave him something to do with his hands and took his mind off his new problem, for at least a little while. Time was precious, but rushing into things would accomplish nothing. He needed to remain calm and use the days he had efficiently.

Currently he had about a month before the multi-tier match, then two weeks after that before the challenge. Focusing on them one at a time was simply not an option, which meant he'd need to split his attention. Life would be easier if he could devote himself entirely to a series of individual goals, but that wasn't how life worked - he should count himself lucky if he didn't run into several brand new problems before the challenge fight.

But how was he going to fight someone with as much power as Mike? There was no magical solution that would transform him and no medicine that could grant him that much power. He could make progress in his remaining time, but he couldn't depend on that.

Once they had the door roughly repaired and made calls about getting a replacement, Rick pulled up his profile to consider his options.

[Name: Rick Hunter

Ether Tier: 17th

Ether Score: 229

Lucrim Generation: 27,650

Effective Rate: 21,636

Current Lucrim: 2408]

[Rick Hunter's Lucrima Portfolio

Foundation: 3050 (Lv IV)

Offensive Lucore: 4700 (Lv III)

Defensive Lucore: 8400 (Lv VI)

Bunyan's Step: 3950 (Lv II)

Graham's Stake: 5500 (Lv II)

Aura Leech: -3554 (Stage II)

Aura Leech: -2460 (Stage I)

Tracking Bond: 100 (Lv XIII)

Gross Lucrim: 27,650

Net Lucrim: 21,636]

For a moment the sheer size of the lucrim gap depressed him, but he pushed past that by remembering what Emily had said. What mattered was how much of their power they had invested and how well they had invested it. He did have useful assets to bring to the fight, and he could strengthen them, particularly if he focused on combat cores instead of Graham's Stake.

Mike was certainly going to enter the match fully charged. Thanks to extra money from the fights, Rick could afford enough philosopher's elixir and serum to do the same. Endurance would be key, because his only chance was to make his opponent exhaust himself.

If so, he needed to get rid of the aura leeches. Rick seriously considered whether or not that was a good idea, because it would lead to more lucrima damage and might have lower returns than focusing on combat. Yet he knew there were drugs to deal with that and Granny Whitney might even give him some before the tournament, so he would have to take the chance.

Getting the leeches out of him would greatly improve his stamina.

He had one major advantage: he was very familiar with fighting opponents more powerful than him. His opponent was doing this for the sake of his ego, while Rick was doing it to survive. That was an edge that Mike could never purchase.

Yet that might not be enough. Rick moved from thinking about what was reasonable to what was possible, no matter how desperate...

Chapter 40: Planning Recovery

After several days training his fundamentals, Rick had advanced as much as he thought he could for now. Fortunately, he'd also developed a plan that might give him the edge he needed against Mike. The difficulty would be surviving his plan.

The first step involved checking what resources he already had. He had scheduled a sparring match with Lisa for that day, so he headed out to meet her at the park. Doing some research online suggested that high end lucrim massages could do a little healing work, and they definitely helped with recovery, but he didn't want to depend on the impossible.

"Hey, Rick!" Lisa greeted him with her usual smile. "You ready to spar?"

"More than ready. I need to update you on some things, but let's do it while we're recovering."

They started sparring in their usual location, though this time Rick didn't hold back. He was interested to see that Lisa responded easily, pulling out a technique he'd never seen before. Every time he made contact with her aura, he felt slightly numb. Though he could push through the numbness, by the end of their match his entire body tingled as if it had fallen asleep.

"That's new." He shook his hands, trying to get sensation back into them. "At a higher intensity, that could be disabling, maybe even lethal."

"Actually, it's not new - and I didn't mean it to be dangerous. You were just taking it really seriously, so I reacted automatically." As they sat down, she glanced over at him in concern. "Are you alright? Usually you don't let your emotions get to you."

"Well... that's a bit of a story."

He told her about the upcoming fight against Mike briefly. Though he'd intended to skip anything related to Melissa, somehow he ended up telling Lisa about that as well. It didn't matter, since she'd probably learn by implication the next time she gave his sister a massage.

When he was finished, Lisa shook her head. "That's awful. I wish... well, there's no point saying it, but I wish we lived in a world where things were fair. If everybody had equal amounts of lucrim somehow, or aura didn't exist..."

"I don't think it would change anything." Rick slowly rubbed his eyes. "Some people would still find a way to gain an advantage and then lord it over others. If it wasn't lucrim, it'd just be money or something else."

"Yeah, but I imagine the fact that the powerful can become immortal and blow up mountains doesn't help."

"Heh, that's fair."

"So why did you tell me all this?" Lisa put a hand on his shoulder. "If there's anything I can do, I'm happy to help. It's just... there's no way I can fight, if that's what you were asking. I might be an okay fighter thanks to you, but I don't think I have it in me to be in a serious fight."

Rick quickly shook his head to ward off that suggestion. "No, I wouldn't ask you to do that. But since I'm going to get heavily injured during this, I wanted to ask you about your limits when it comes to healing. I know massage therapy isn't meant for that, but I had to ask."

"I'm better with internal problems than anything external." Lisa shifted away, tugging a few blades of grass out of the ground and slowly tearing them apart. "I mean, nobody can massage a wound back together. Most of what I do isn't exactly repairing damage so much as helping the body function better. But when it comes to damage to your lucrima, I can help with that. So if you have a broken leg, you want a hospital or a healer, but if you're trying to regain strength in the leg you broke, maybe I can help."

"Hmm. How long would it take to do the majority of the recovery? I know it's a long road to get back to 100%, but what about being fighting ready?"

"The most extensive course of therapy I offer is two four hour sessions in one day. That's what I do for professional fighters who need to get back on their feet as quickly as possible."

Rick nodded. "Good. I don't know if our sparring is worth enough for that, but I think I'm going to need it. Hopefully you'll give me an advance."

"Sure, but..." Lisa tossed her pieces of grass aside and focused fully on him, her face filled with concern. "I hope you're not doing anything too crazy, Rick. The way you're talking about this makes me think you're going to get yourself almost killed."

"Yes, most likely. But since I don't have a choice, I'm doing my best to prepare for it."

She shook her head slowly. "I know they threatened your sister, but... surely there's another way? I'm not saying that I have an alternative, and I'm not judging your decisions, just... do you really think Mike is going to beat you that badly?"

"I don't intend to give him a chance." Rick sighed and got to his feet, forcing himself to smile again. "Thanks for sparring, Lisa."

"Aren't I supposed to be thanking you? I mean, I will, if you need the recovery."

"If you still have time before you need to go, I actually wanted to ask you several other questions."

"Yeah, sure." Lisa got up and walked along beside him, guiding them toward the walking path that circled around Eastpark. "What's up?"

"One of the most obvious components of recovery is medicine, but trying to research about it, I feel... well, dumb, to be honest. There are so many different sources online and I don't know enough to be sure which ones are accurate. Practically any herbal supplement or mystic herb site starts setting off bullshit alarms for me, so I can't judge between them."

To his surprise, Lisa laughed oddly. "Oh, you don't want to get me started on that. My mother is really into certain treatments and... really, don't get me ranting."

"I don't mind. It might be educational."

"Well... if you say so. Not exactly sure where to start, though. You're looking for medicine that can bring you back from serious injuries, right?"

"And ideally help me grow stronger from them, yeah." Rick shrugged. "I realize that's asking a lot, hence why I kept finding suspicious-looking products and sites."

"That's not asking the impossible, though. Some of my clients look for general health advice, or at least talk a lot about it, so I think I can give you some good suggestions. But I'm not an alchemist or a doctor, so you should take everything I say with a grain of salt."

"No, you know a lot more than me. Even just simple things... I see arguments about natural herbs versus synthetic versions and I just don't know who's right. Are the synthetic versions really inferior to the traditionally-grown plants? Or is that just being stubborn in the face of progress?"

"It's both!" Lisa smiled and began explaining, gesturing expressively while she spoke, though he couldn't derive any meaning from her gestures. "It depends on the plant, so you have to follow the research. In a lot of cases, the synthetic versions are just as as good as the traditional versions, just cheaper. You're right about those: people just like paying more to think they're getting a better product. But in some cases, the best synthetic attempts don't do as well in head-to-head tests, so the original plant has some emergent property they haven't duplicated in the lab yet."

"Hmm, then I'm going to have to rely on you."

"Don't worry, I waste a lot of time reading up on these things! Well, I guess not wasting... anyway, there are actually some cases where the synthetic version isolates the active ingredient from the original and is thus much more effective... though that means it's also more expensive. So sometimes a premium price is just for suckers, but sometimes it's because of a superior product.

"Fun fact: the most successful synthetic was so massively successful that the 'natural-only' crowd can't compete and people don't even think about it: serum. Go back thousands of years and only kings and queens drank it, and even a few centuries ago it was valuable. But now you can buy it in a 6-pack from the store, and even the cheap stuff is more potent than the serum kings and queens got. Isn't technology amazing?"

It was interesting to hear her speak about a subject with such passion, so Rick found himself smiling as he listened to her. Though it wasn't relevant to what he needed, he decided he might as well ease another curiosity. "What about all the family-exclusive or hidden sect formulas? Is there anything to them?"

"Those are really a mixed bag." Lisa gave a formless shrug. "There are some groups that have incredibly powerful formulations, without question. Some are actually state secrets.

But the world is just chock full of special families and combat sects, and all of them wanted to pretend they had hidden knowledge."

"So some of them are worthless?"

"Absolutely. There have been a few clinical trials that went really poorly, the 'powerful secret medicine' not doing much better than the commonly available alternatives. A few did even worse than placebos! Or there was one that only did as well as common medicine because it was literally just a mix of aspirin and serum. Apparently they'd made the creation process so opaque, even their alchemists didn't know that's all it was."

Rick chuckled, for the first time seeing how reading a bunch of scientific literature could be fun. "I'm guessing they don't let people test their secret medicines very often, then?"

"You got it. But if you want a rule of thumb: be skeptical of hidden secrets. A few medicines are so powerful they're kept secrets, but for many, ask this question: if their medicine was so good, why don't they gain more power by just patenting and selling it?"

"Good point. Trying to keep all of this in mind, though... I feel like it's a bit overwhelming. It will be hard to make a good choice."

"It might seem that way, but you can really sort through the options." Still walking, Lisa pulled out her phone and began to navigate somewhere. "Here, let me show you a site where you can order most things at wholesale prices."

"Wait, you can buy lucrim medication online?" Even as he said it, however, he felt dumb for assuming you couldn't. Why wouldn't the industry have modernized, given the profitability of their field?

"Oh, the internet actually made things way easier. It's a stereotype, but a lot of alchemists are introverts, if not full misanthropes. The people who are really crazy about developing their medicines are happy to support themselves via online sales and never have to interact with people."

She showed him a website and he pulled it up on his phone. It looked like any other online store, simple to navigate and remarkably clear about the contents of each product. Now that he saw the name, he thought he'd seen a few people talking about getting their medicine from there, but he had assumed it was a secret location, not just a website.

"So..." As Rick paged through lists of healing medications, he found himself overwhelmed by the choices. "Is there any way to get a good deal? Because I need as much as I can get, but I don't have a lot of money to burn."

"There actually is one easy win: generic medication." Lisa poked at his screen to navigate somewhere else. "When the patents run out, companies make way less money on a drug, but it's still perfectly good. Usually they find a different way to get the same effect and thus get new patents. They pretend the new drug is an improvement, but often times it doesn't do any better in tests."

With Lisa's help, Rick found and identified several generic medications that provided rapid healing. They were still expensive, given their powerful effects, but nothing like he'd been expecting. Certainly nothing like what he'd expected could be shipped directly to his house.

Buying generics meant that he had more money left over than he expected. Though it would mean lean times for the next month, he decided to spend everything except his emergency fund on one final medication: something that would help him grow from a near death experience. After considering several different options, he found what he wanted.

It had a long scientific name, but in ancient times it had been called Deathbane and recently it was marketed as "Life's Edge." Just buying a small package of one dose would cost an obscene amount, plus it required a more expensive shipping option so that it wouldn't be stolen or damaged in the mail. But the lucrim numbers it gave looked promising, the user reviews were solid, and Lisa didn't have any objections to it.

When he prepared to place the order, however, she looked at him in concern. "This is so... I mean... again, I'm not telling you what you should do. Do you really think you're going to come that close to death, Rick?"

"That is the plan." He placed the order, trying not to think about how much money he had just spent.

It would be worth it. Hopefully.

Chapter 41: The Gifts of Family

All the medicine had arrived without incident, but the Deathbane had arrived with instructions. Not a few lines on the side of a bottle, but multiple pages in a glossy booklet. Reading over it, Rick discovered that it was half warnings and half suggestions for how to get the most use out of such a medicine. Clearly, they understood their customers.

The suggestions included a large number of different exercises that would prepare a person to benefit from their near death experience. Some were too far on the mystical side for him to handle, dealing with abstract matters of lucrima that most modern lucrim-users ignored. Though he logged the exercises away for future reference, there simply wasn't time to learn such difficult exercises.

Many he had already mastered, however, so he repeated them a few times just to make sure he was fresh. That left a few that were within his ability but he hadn't done extensively, so he focused on those. If all went well, he should be in the state the instructions regarded as "optimally prepared."

One of those involved raw perception, extending his senses not inward, but outward. Such exercises had been about communing with the natural world in the old days, but there wasn't a lot of natural world around these days, not in a city. Instead he extended his focus outward, feeling the lucrima of the people in the apartments around him. It was a grim experience, repeated encounters with desperation and poverty, but he pressed on.

Strangely, there was a pulsating source of instability. When Rick focused on it exclusively, he discovered that it was closer than he had thought. He'd never felt anything quite like it and had to wonder if it could be a threat. Either a pending attack, or something left behind to track them.

Setting aside the exercise entirely, Rick devoted himself to tracking down the instability... and almost immediately found the source.

"Hmm?" Melissa looked up at him from her lotus position on the bed. "Something wrong?"

"Not unless that's unintentional. You're feeling okay?"

"Oh, this isn't my condition flaring up. I'm in control of it." She gave him a smile and cupped her hands in front of her stomach. Immediately he felt the instability again, though now he realized that it was a flickering... like a flame. Within her lucrima, yes, but also within her hands. "This is all I'm doing, see? Just something I'm trying for fun... unless you think I shouldn't?"

"With anyone else, I'd say it's a bad idea. But I think you know yourself better, and you still seem stable, so I have no problem with it."

"Thanks, Rick. My L.E. teacher is always getting after me for bad lucrima form, but this feels a lot more comfortable to me."

"Wait." Rick sat down on the bed beside her and locked her gaze with his. "Are you being completely honest with me, Melissa? If you don't want to talk about it, you don't have to, but I don't believe you're doing this randomly."

She stared back at him for a while, then sighed. "Yeah, sorry. It's not that I wanted to lie to you or that it's a big secret, just..." His sister lowered her head so that her hair partially covered her face. "When the Birthrighter attacked, I felt... I mean, it's not like I didn't know I was vulnerable. But I didn't like being in that position..."

Unable to find words to help her, Rick hesitantly touched her back. She didn't move away and instead shuffled over to lean against him, so he just rubbed her back.

"Honestly, it made me really angry. I know you're just going to fight Mike in a formal challenge, but I wish you could beat the shit out of all three of them. I wish I could. I know that it isn't possible to gain that much power that quickly, but... there are other assholes out there. I want to be ready."

Though the idea of his little sister fighting made him a bit uncomfortable, he couldn't deny the anger she felt. "I think I understand some of what you mean. If you want ideas about getting started with combat Lucores, I can make some suggestions."

"Thanks. Really, I mean it." Melissa let her body relax a little more, but still didn't look at him. "For now, I've been focusing on the void inside me. Letting the flame shrink and grow. At first it was simple tests, because I didn't want to accidentally hurt you or any of my friends. But now..." She finally looked up, eyes uncertain. "I want to hurt him. Is that wrong?"

"I don't think so." Rick was no moral exemplar and felt strange answering such a question. Who was he to give her an answer like that? But he saw the pain in her eyes and couldn't leave her question unanswered. "Can I see what you were doing before this?"

"Hmm? Oh, sure." A moment later, he felt her lucrima shift. He had become used to the feeling of an ether void within her, so it was surprising when it disappeared. No, it shrank to nearly nothing. When his eyes widened Melissa smiled and expanded the flame again.

"Wow. It really does seem like you have it under control."

"Before, it was always burning me. But thanks to what you taught me... well, I'm not sure exactly what it is, but I feel a lot better this way."

"And you were trying to find a way to weaponize it."

Melissa looked away shyly. "Yeah, I guess. I figured that if it could help your foundation, and if it hurt my classmate... maybe I can do even more with it."

"I think it would be good to talk to more experts," Rick said, "but I think it's fine. I've paid a lot of attention to your lucrima over the years and it feels healthier than it's ever been."

"If that's true... could you teach me how to use it more effectively?"

"I'm honestly not sure." Both if he had the knowledge to teach her and if it was a good idea. Now that he understood her intent, her technique actually tickled something in the back of his mind. Many elements were completely unfamiliar to him, but perhaps...

Before the conversation could go further, he heard a notification tone from his phone. Normally he would have ignored it, but they could both use a bit of a break. When he checked the notification, to his surprise it was from their uncle. Melissa noticed that it had drawn his full attention and perked up.

"What is it? Not something bad?"

"For once, no." He stood up and smiled. "It's Uncle Frank - he wants to video chat."

"Oh, great!" Melissa pushed past him to fire up their laptop.

Soon they were waiting for the program to load, crowding together so they would both be seen in the cheap webcam. The computer took longer than usual, as if taunting them for being eager, before everything loaded and the connection finally came through.

"Richard! Melissa!" Uncle Frank looked very glad to see them, pretending to hug the camera. When he sat back, he looked healthy but a bit worn. Not only had he clearly been working in dirty conditions, Rick thought that he might have a few recently healed injuries. "It's always wonderful to see the two of you. God, I know I always say this, but you're growing up so fast."

"What's the occasion, Uncle Frank?" Melissa leaned forward, peering at his image. "You're not getting into anything dangerous, are you?"

"No more than the job description, don't you worry. No, I actually wanted to call to apologize. It doesn't look like I'm going to get back to the States this year at all, which means I'm going to miss your graduation, Melissa."

"Oh, gosh, you don't need to apologize for that. It's not like it's that big a deal."

Their uncle shook his head. "It'd be better if you had family supporting you. I hate to say it, but you're not likely to get many people from your local family."

"I'll have one!" Melissa wrapped one arm around Rick's neck and shook him a bit. "Seriously, Uncle Frank, we're just glad to talk to you. You don't have to worry about being away with work."

Rick nodded in agreement. "You said you wouldn't get back this year - does that mean you might have a chance to visit next year?"

"That's right." Uncle Frank nodded, a big smile on his face. "We're getting close to a big discovery, I'm sure of it. After that, I'll definitely be due for some rest and relaxation. Can't think of any better way to spend it than with my favorite niece and nephew."

It would be a long time before he arrived, long enough that it would be completely irrelevant to all Rick's present problems, but he was still encouraged to hear the news. He was glad to hear that he'd get a chance to spend some time with his favorite uncle again and wondered how different things might be now that he was much more experienced with lucrima souls.

Well, unless the difference was that he was injured or dead.

That thought aside, they had a good time doing nothing but chatting and catching up on various events. Rick decided not to go into more detail about his problems than he already had: his uncle knew most of it and had given him enough advice. If Uncle Frank had been nearby, Rick definitely would have depended on him, but for now he didn't want to risk his uncle abandoning important work to come and deal with problems like his.

Eventually, with the sunlight ebbing on his end, Uncle Frank sighed. "As much fun as this has been, you two, I think I need to go soon."

"Thanks for taking the time, though!" Melissa beamed at him. "I'll consider this an early graduation present."

"That's very sweet, but your present should be the actual gift I sent." Abruptly their uncle's expression darkened. "You did receive it, didn't you? There was some money, a few things I thought Melissa would like, and some useful medication for you too, Rick. Did you get them?"

Rick and Melissa looked at each other. His sister was completely confused, but Rick was slowly coming to a painful realization. He swallowed and spoke. "When was it supposed to arrive?"

"Should have been around this time. I wanted to time it to be the same day that I called you, but the call got delayed by a couple days, so I assumed you already had the package. While I have internet I guess I should check the tracking again, because last I checked it was en route..."

"What address did you send it to?"

"I used the private family channel, since the contents were valuable..." There was a split second of their uncle cursing before he cut his mic. After venting his anger with several words Rick could almost lip-read, Uncle Frank turned the mic on again. "I'm guessing that one of my brothers changed the private channel to redirect to their address instead?"

"Most likely." Rick ran his hands through his hair in frustration, trying to think back over the documents he'd signed before the Birthright Cores. Had they talked about this? "Dammit, I should have checked for this... of course they'd be able to change it after our parents died..."

"No, don't blame yourself. These things happen."

Melissa did her best to smile, though he could see the anger in her eyes. "It's the thought that counts, Uncle Frank. Honestly, I'm really glad you were thinking of us."

"I wish I could be there more for both of you. But I'm proud of you - you've done so well despite facing so much."

They spoke for a little while longer, dragging out their goodbyes, but Rick had trouble focusing. The pleasant warmth of spending time with his favorite family members was gone now, and anger over what had happened rose within him.

As soon as the call was over, he was going to visit the rest of his family.

Chapter 42: A Family Visit

As the bus headed to the suburbs of Branton, Rick tried to get his anger under control. Not to suppress it. Just make sure that he used it instead of the other way around.

The idea that Uncle Frank's gift had been stolen by the rest of their family was infuriating, but there was only so much he could do. Technically he had their phone numbers, but he decided not to call them. If things had gone the way he suspected, then it would be better not to give them any warning.

He was fairly certain that the person behind it would be Uncle Alan. After all, he had been the one to go after Rick's parents' Birthright Cores. Had his uncle done this in retaliation for losing them, or just to try to steal whatever he could? Presumably there would be answers soon.

When Rick got off at the last stop, he was still some distance from his family's neighborhood. Though part of him wanted to sprint, Rick made himself walk to stay focused. Whenever the package had arrived, it had been long enough ago that a few extra minutes would make no difference either way. What mattered was that he arrived in a clear state of mind.

Average suburbs gave way to the trailer parks. He felt a brief flicker of nostalgia for the first of them, still the same after all these years. The people in this neighborhood were alright and a few even nodded to him, as if they vaguely recognized him. None of them were rich, but many had painted their trailers, set up flowers, actually worked on the broken cars nearby, and generally still kept trying.

As he walked further, he reached his family's old neighborhood. These trailers were poorly maintained and rusting, TV antennas the closest anyone came to ornamentation. He stepped off the main road onto a dirt one, littered with trash and broken glass. A few people sat outside, drinking shirtless and just staring at him, but he ignored them.

Finally he was within sight of his uncle's trailer. He and several other relatives had pushed all their trailers together for some long past reason that didn't matter anymore. Even the same dog was there, a mangy creature tied to a post. When he approached, it both whimpered and snarled.

Rick walked up to knock on the door, but at that moment several of his cousins slouched around the sides of the trailers. They looked unkempt, but it was an organized movement. All of them were burning with lucrim as well, making it obvious where Uncle Frank's gift had gone.

"We figured you'd come, Dick." One of his cousins taunted him, but Rick ignored him, just looking around at those approaching. Three of his cousins moving in front of him, an aunt and two more cousins now approaching from behind to surround him.

Not thinking about them as family, Rick just counted lucrim generation rates:

[Area Lucrima Analysis:

Opponent A: 12,500

Opponent B: 18,000

Opponent C: 11,000

Opponent D: 27,750

Opponent E: 14,000

Opponent F: 19,250]

"What's the matter, Dick?" A cousin from behind punched at his shoulder, a mockery of the friendly gesture. Rick let the blow bounce off. "Not going to greet your family?"

"You know why I'm here." Not letting them cow him, Rick turned slowly in a circle, looking at all of them. Yes, they knew. "You stole Uncle Frank's gift."

His aunt smacked her lips. "And it tasted good, boy. Thanks to him, we all ate well and we have the strength to win a few more brawls. You can't take that away from us, so what are you going to do?"

"There should have been more: a letter and objects without value. Please give them to me and I'll walk away."

The tallest of his cousins, about his age with 18,000 lucrim, laughed and stepped up to him. "You're gonna walk away no matter what, Dick. Make it easy on yourself and just do it now." When Rick didn't back down, he stepped up so they were eye to eye. "Don't be stupid. We've been spoiling for a fight and we're packing 100,000 lucrim between us."

"No, you're not." What Emily had told him about the limitations of generation rate had never been more obvious to him than in that moment. Over the course of their lives, his family had possessed hundreds of thousands of lucrim, but what had they done with it? They'd let it all run through them like water, spending it on small luxuries. A few of them had cores, but most of them just pooled the lucrim inside their lucrima until they spent it.

"Are you high, Dick?" His aunt came closer, smirking at him. "You went off and acted like you were better than everyone, but what have you made of yourself? Still working at that shitty little gym?"

Rick closed his eyes and took a deep breath. "Please give me whatever is left of Uncle Frank's gift. This is the last time I'm asking."

"Ooh! He's asking, boys, because he learned fancy manners in the-"

She cut off as Rick reached back and grabbed her by the head with his left hand. Though his aunt had the strength to resist him, she was taken entirely off guard by the abrupt movement. Before she could recover, he pulled her directly into his elbow as he slammed it into her face.

His aunt dropped like a stone and everyone else stared in shock. Given that she'd held slightly more lucrim than he did, she should have been able to fight him for a long time. But none of that lucrim had been packed into an effective core, rendering her nearly defenseless to his strike, honed by combat in the Underground. It hadn't even been a fight.

And his aunt had been the strongest of them, which was why he'd taken her out first. There were still five of them surrounding him, but that wasn't enough.

One of his cousins let out a yell and struck at him from behind. Predictable. Rick stepped back toward him so his cousin's fist sailed past his head harmlessly, then struck his cousin on the head without even looking. Again, he dropped in a single blow.

Three of the remaining four lunged at him, striking from all sides. Rick simply braced himself to endure the clumsy blows. Compared to the attacks he'd received from so many in the arena, much less Mike and his cronies, these were nothing. With attacks coming from all sides, his efforts to land another decisive blow didn't get through, but he just needed to wait for his moment.

Eventually one of his cousins tried to kick him in the crotch. Rick grabbed her leg in one hand and jerked her off her feet, swinging her directly toward the remaining three. One managed to dodge, but the other two went down, tumbling into the dirt.

The last rose, thinking he'd dodged, but Rick was already there, grabbing him by the front of the shirt. It took surprisingly little strength to fling him to the side, his cousin smashing into one of the trailers so hard that it rocked on its foundations. That left all but one of them down, and though some were conscious, they didn't look like they were going to get up to challenge him again.

What had the last of them been doing? Rick turned to find his tallest cousin grinning savagely as aura rose around him. It was built to create explosive spheres, but what had he been doing all this time? Gradually Rick realized that it had actually taken him this long to gather his aura and prepare for an attack.

"You're gonna regret this, Dick." His cousin smirked and raised his hands to either side, beginning to gather aura spheres. "I'll blast you t-"

Rick used a Bunyan's Step to cross the distance between them in an instant. Before his cousin even realized that he had moved, Rick grabbed both of his wrists. The aura burned, but it was practically tickling compared to what he was used to.

His cousin flinched in shock as he caught up to the movement, his smirk gone. Rick hadn't intended to smirk back, yet he found himself grinning savagely. Panicking, his cousin dropped his aura and tried to struggle away.

Using his wrists, Rick pulled his cousin closer and slammed their foreheads together. His cousin went down hard and lay groaning in the dirt.

After confirming that none of them were coming after him again, Rick stepped over his cousins and reached the door to the main trailer. It was locked, but he snapped the cheap lock and tore open the door.

He entered cautiously, not letting his easy victory get to his head. Though Rick had defeated his Uncle Alan before, his uncle was still more dangerous than all the others put together, thanks to his fighting experience and developed cores. There wasn't much space in the trailer home for an ambush, but he needed to be prepared.

Yet almost immediately he realized that there would be no ambush. His uncle sat in a recliner that looked brand new, eyes bleary and unfocused. Judging from the spoon and syringe on the table, he hadn't invested the money.

When Rick approached him, his uncle flinched. "Boy... you gotta understand... things are rough here..."

"So you spent what you stole on drugs and... a new chair?" As Rick stared at him, his anger faded. Not only did his uncle feel weak and drained, his generation rate had declined to just under 30,000. Clearly the aura leech had not been kind to him.

"Richard... Rick... we just wanted..."

"Shut up." Rick looked around the filthy home for anything that might remain. "Is there anything left?"

Uncle Alan refused to meet his gaze. Of course the money was long gone, and it felt like his aunt and cousins had absorbed all the lucrim that had been sent. But there should still have been the gift for Melissa... surely they couldn't have pawned it so quickly, especially because Uncle Frank would have sent something of more personal value.

Abruptly he saw them: several glass figurines lay broken on the floor. Rick bent down and picked the pieces up, turning them over in his hands. He didn't recognize the figures, but based on the robes they must have been Asian grandmasters. The quality of the work was amazing - exactly the sort of thing Melissa would have loved. She would have known who they were, even broken like this.

"Why?" Anger gone, Rick looked up at his uncle. "What could you possibly gain by breaking them?"

"No... was an accident..." Uncle Alan shook his head blearily, then reached for the syringe. Before he could reach it, Rick grabbed him by the neck and slammed him back into his chair.

"That isn't good enough. If there's something else and you didn't tell me, you'll regret it."

Rick had never threatened someone like that in his life, much less expected it to work. Yet to his surprise, his uncle flinched and shivered, and not from withdrawal. "Please... there was some plant... weird lucrim shit... I ate one of them and I almost died... others are in the kitchen."

Dropping his uncle back into the chair, Rick looked toward the small area they called a kitchen. Yes, there was a box there that looked too good for the house. Before moving to it, he glared back at his uncle. "Pick up every one of the glass pieces and put them back in their box. Unless you already destroyed the box too, somehow."

When Rick approached the box in the kitchen he was afraid that it would be empty, but he found that his uncle had told the truth. The interior was spaced into four different sections, each of which had held a dried black root. Rick didn't recognize them, but his uncle had implied that they were for lucrim development. One of the roots was gone, but he still had three. That would have to be enough.

Turning back, Rick discovered that his order had been obeyed. Uncle Alan fumbled the glass pieces a few times, but put them all into a box. It still had a few shreds of tape and wrapping paper, remnants of the gift for Melissa that it should have been.

"Thank you." Rick spoke the words as coldly as he could and was gratified when his uncle flinched. "You are going to change the family channel to redirect to my apartment. When I check tomorrow, it better be done."

With that, he took both boxes and walked out the door. No one moved to stop him.

Chapter 43: Researching a Solution

Though tracking down Granny Whitney wasn't easy, she was predictable when it came to managing fights in the Underground. It had taken Rick some time to set things up properly, but he did some of his training at the Underground instead of at home and eventually he got lucky.

He spotted her getting involved with another match and eventually figured out her interest: a woman in her late thirties who had a generation rate of well over 150,000 lucrim. Perhaps she was Granny Whitney's cruiserweight candidate, then. The match itself was intense and Rick almost got sucked into watching it, but he recalled his purpose at the end. When the two women met after the match, he followed them, preparing for his chance.

Rick noted with only a little bitterness that Granny Whitney didn't seem to be handicapping her newest candidate, and in fact seemed very helpful. There was tension between them, though, so he tried not to make judgments about the exact situation.

In the end, what mattered was getting a chance to talk to the old woman. He fell in beside her when she tried to slip out of the Underground. "So, is that our cruiserweight?"

"That she is, dearie." But Granny Whitney didn't smile as much as usual, a hard light in her eyes. "It's wonderful to talk to you, my dear boy, but I'm afraid that I really have a great deal to do. Just focus on training until the event, won't you?"

"That was actually what I wanted to talk about. I've been pouring most of my strength into getting rid of the aura leeches, but I've picked up a lot of baggage along the way. There's a nearly 6000 lucrim gap between my portfolio and my generation rate."

"Well, you've become a bit more sophisticated about such things! Never fear, dearie, Granny Whitney will take care of that."

"Wouldn't this be the time to try to purify those problems? I understand the methods can take a week or more to work." The size of the gap actually bothered him, since it reminded him of the rest of his family and their inefficiencies. Yet Granny Whitney didn't seem to care, just shaking her head.

"Purifying all of that is both difficult and expensive. There is a simpler solution, a medicine that will briefly bring out your full potential. I intend to give it to you just before the match."

Rick nodded in understanding, swallowing his disappointment. Perhaps that had been too much to hope, then. He'd known that Granny Whitney didn't care about his development, just wanted to use it, but he still slipped up and forgot sometimes. Her solution to the problem was best from her perspective, but useless for his challenge against Mike.

"Is that all, dearie?" She sped up, trying to leave him behind in the corridors. "I really must be going..."

"One more thing: if you wanted to really hurt someone in a single blow, how would you do it?"

That brought her up short and she turned back to him, eyes twinkling merrily. "Don't ask questions if you don't want to know the answer, dearie." But when he didn't back down from her gaze, she shrugged and went on. "Your question isn't really about me, of course, and you couldn't use most of the techniques I would. Frankly, that isn't a very good objective for the match."

"This isn't for the match." Rick folded his arms and stepped into her path so she couldn't move away. "Answer this last question and I'll leave you alone."

"Alright, dearie, alright. Settle down. If I were you... hmm... what you want to do is find your enemy when they're weak, then strike not to cause physical damage, but to push your aura directly into their lucrima soul. If you choose the right location, they'll be feeling it for a very long time. Look up what they call the 'dantian' in the east." Abruptly she reached up and patted his cheek. "You're a smart boy, you'll figure out the rest. Have fun, dearie!"

With that, she slipped past him and vanished. When Rick started to move, he found that his entire body had locked up. It faded after several seconds, but he realized that she had somehow disrupted him when she patted his cheek. That was frustrating, but at least she'd given him the answer to his question.

Since he hadn't expected a full answer, that was acceptable. Rick glanced at the time and left the Underground to visit the library again. If Heather was on staff at this time, she'd probably be able to teach him what he needed to know. He didn't need to develop a brand new technique, just understand enough for one good blow.

As he headed to the library, however, he found himself disappointed that Granny Whitney wasn't going to give him purification medicine. He'd looked it up online and found that it was absurdly expensive. It would have been worth it, to recover the large amount of strength lost in impurities and inefficiencies, but even if he saved everything he earned in the last month and spent it all on one dose of medicine, he'd only be able to afford sub-standard purification. Given his circumstances, better to keep slowly improving his strength with philosopher's elixir.

He thought about it, but couldn't come up with any real solution. It was a difficult problem and he realized that there might simply be no good solution. His life didn't have many of those. Perhaps all he could do was leverage the resources he had and make as much progress as he could.

The roots his uncle had sent him were potent, but nothing magical that would transform his life. Using them to charge his training, he'd increased his generation rate by over 1000 lucrim, yet almost all of it had gone directly into getting rid of the larger aura leech. Even focusing on it, he'd only managed to get the debt down to 549. He was going to have to accept that the last leech would stay with him, because there was no way he could make enough progress to get rid of it as well.

There would be no dramatic transformation there. If he wanted a qualitative difference before the fight, he needed to take more drastic steps. Hopefully the library would help him get a bit closer to another one of those.

When he entered the library, he asked around after Heather and was pointed toward the computers. She was helping someone get a document printed and looked utterly bored, but when she saw him she grinned. Rick nodded to her and headed back toward the lucrim section, and she caught up to him before he arrived.

"Hey, it's you again. Fuckin' A. I hope you have more interesting questions for me than basic computer problems?"

Rick nodded. "Yes, are there any lucrim techniques that let you update printer drivers?"

She punched him in the arm, not lightly. "Don't even fucking joke like that. Seriously, what's your question this time?"

"Someone I work with told me that I should look up information about dantians."

"Oh, sure. I can get you some books right away." Heather got the door opened and led him into the lucrim section, moving randomly but finding books in the end, as usual. "Kind of an odd research topic, though. They're really not part of modern lucrim theory, and I didn't take you for the type to be interested in historical curiosities."

"Really?" Rick frowned. He was no expert, but he didn't think it was purely historical. "I thought it was still a part of certain lucrim arts. People still believe in them, right?"

"People believe in a lot of things. Tell me, what do you know about dantians?"

"Well... they're body parts that supposedly gather and collect lucrim. I'm unclear on if there's one, three, or more."

"Typically people say three: one in your head, one in your chest, and one just below your navel. And it's true that those parts are critical to your lucrima, so an injury there is serious." Heather stopped with a book in hand, using it to point at him. "But think about it. That's your brain, your heart, and your gut. How could those areas not be important to the process?"

Having no expertise on the subject, Rick could only shrug and accept what she said. "As it happens, I'm most concerned about injuries there."

"Sure, I can find you some resources about that. Just because some writers were a bit off base about this sort of thing doesn't mean they were spouting nonsense. I haven't actually looked too deep into this myself, but I can get you started."

Before long, Heather had a small stack of books for him and took them to a small desk hidden away in the archives. She'd finished her job, but she stayed and slipped down into the chair opposite him. As he began looking through the books, she leaned forward, giving him a curious look.

"What's this about, anyway?"

Since he didn't intend to tell her the truth, Rick had a lie ready. "My sister has been sick her entire life. Do you know anything about ether voids?"

"Hmm, only a little." Heather sat back and considered him seriously. "I don't think you're going to find an answer here about that. If somebody told you that her dantian is broken or something, they have the wrong idea."

"No, I understand her condition. At least I understand a little. I'm just trying to understand more about these sorts of injuries in the abstract."

Heather grinned and nodded. "Yeah, I know about just needing to sate curiosity sometimes. Actually, I read one of these... just a sec, let me find the right page." She grabbed one of the books and began flipping through it, still speaking. "You might learn some interesting things, but I hope you don't try anything here with your sister. Letting lucrim flow into her would help her condition, but if you tried to insert it straight into the void, that would be bad for her."

Though he latched onto that statement, Rick kept himself from looking too eager. Instead he waited until Heather found the page she wanted and slapped the book down on the table. It appeared to be a diagram of the body, lucrim flowing in various passages. However, instead of focusing on the three points she'd emphasized, the central core of the lines seemed to be a spot between the heart and the stomach.

"Okay, this guy was practically thrown out as a fraud in some places, but he was right about a few things. The core of most people's 'soul' - if you're okay with calling it that - is right here. There's no organ there or anything, but it's the point where all the flows come together in most people."

"And? What about it?"

"Most likely your sister was born with it, but if it happened because of an injury, it'd be right here. So yeah, if you want to learn more about it, keep reading about this stuff."

"Got it. Thanks, Heather."

"No problem!" She beamed at him and seemed to want to linger, but instead sighed. "Welp, I gotta get back to the old fucking grind. You bring any questions you have, okay?"

He agreed and smiled at her as she left, then began to read the books. Though he didn't have time to read all of them, he didn't need to. It might be interesting to learn more about the theory behind Melissa's condition, but he suspected that she herself might be a better source of information. From what he'd read, a lot of ancient sources were based around finding universal truths about lucrima, which led to flattening natural human differences.

In any case, Rick was interested in causing injuries, not healing them.

Combining what he'd learned from Granny Whitney and from these sources gave him the final pieces he needed. It would take him a while to work out the details, but he thought it was possible: a blow to the chest that would ram aura straight into the heart of the opponent's lucrima.

Just surviving the match against Mike wouldn't be enough, since another challenge could easily follow. No, he needed to end it decisively. Since it was impossible for him to gain so much strength to dominate the match, what he needed to do was focus on one strike at the end. This one would leave Mike with an injury that would make him hesitate to ever attack Rick's family again.

And that would be the end of it. Hopefully.

Chapter 44: Sibling Technique

Without fights in the Underground to occupy his schedule, Rick should have felt more free overall. Instead he found himself entirely consumed with preparations, not just for the coming multi-tier tournament, but for the confrontation with Mike after it. Nearly every waking moment he wasn't at work, he was training for the inevitable or at least thinking about it.

He had never trained this hard in his life. Lisa warned him that he was dangerously close to over-training, which would actually begin to reverse his progress if he kept forcing it. The body wasn't made to work constantly, needing time to repair itself, and the soul wasn't made to meditate constantly. Without substance to meditate on, it could quickly become useless or worse.

But for now, he pushed on. Most likely he would need to spend a while resting and reflecting after this, but he would be grateful just for the opportunity. If he didn't make it through, there would be no rest at all.

To put off over-training as long as possible, he alternated between three exercises: expanding his lucrim via philosopher's elixir, doing exercises to prepare for the Deathbane, and developing his new finishing technique. The first was limited by his paychecks, since he wasn't willing to put Melissa at risk, and he'd done enough of the second for the day, so at the moment he was focused on the third.

There wasn't time to develop it to the point where he could use it as a primary combat technique, but he thought he was close to making it functional. If anything, the problem would not be finishing the technique, but finishing it and finding the result underwhelming. He'd likely only have one chance to strike...

An idea slid into his mind and Rick found himself considering something new. He glanced over his shoulder, where Melissa sat at the little table, doing her best to glue the figurines back together. They would never be anything like they were meant to be, of course, but she seemed to find it calming to place the pieces back into their proper formation. She'd already repaired one of the figures, a robed woman who was heavily cracked, but still recognizable.

"Are all the pieces there?" He leaned down over her shoulder, watching her work. Melissa gave him a brief smile before gesturing with the pieces she was holding.

"I've got all the big pieces, but I'm missing some chips. Those chips are actually the biggest problem, since it's easy to misjudge and glue them wrong. That can be a real pain." As she continued working, she glanced back at him again. "Anyway, what's up? You're way too focused to just amble over to chat."

"You mean I can't want to take a break with my dearest sister?"

"Nope. It's in one of the clauses of the Super Serious Training Guy contract or something."

Rick sighed. "Am I really getting that bad?"

"You're fine, I'm just teasing you." Melissa stopped working and set down the glass figurine to look at him. "I mean, if you were like this all the time from now on, I wouldn't like it. But I understand why you need to work so hard. If there was ever a time to go overboard, this is it."

Yes, she would understand more than anyone else, having been drawn in herself. Remembering that made Rick get over his discomfort with asking what he'd been thinking. "You remember that exercise you did where you drained my foundation to make it more efficient?"

"Sure, but I thought that wasn't helping much anymore."

"What I need is for you to combine that with the offensive technique you were working on earlier."

"Eh?" Though Melissa gave him an odd look, as he began to demonstrate what he intended, she quickly caught on. Much sooner than he expected, she managed to manifest what he'd hoped. She cupped her hands in front of her, an invisible flame burning within.

While she worked on that, Rick formed spare lucrim into a shell similar to her own. It wouldn't serve to contain the flame in the same way, and he didn't think anything would keep the flame in its place in the center. That was a problem that he hoped he could solve, however, and the important thing was to test the concept.

"Okay, so..." Melissa extended her cupped hands toward him. "Now I try to... hand it off, I guess? How can I put it into the sphere thing without burning through the side?"

"This is lucrim, not physical matter. You should be able to pass through."

Due to her inexperience, the flame did deal some damage, but Rick managed to accept it from her. He rebuilt the sphere around the flame and tried to pin it in place with aura pressure. All his instincts screamed to push the whole thing away from himself, that it was dangerous, yet he suppressed those and kept trying. If he could sustain it inside himself in a balanced way...

Without warning the flames licked the side of the sphere and his lucrim began to burn away. Rick let out a cry and dropped to one knee, grabbing the side of the table. Before much could burn, Melissa reached out a hand and the void flame snuffed out immediately.

"Gosh, I'm sorry... should I have made a smaller one?"

"No, you did fine." Rick took a deep breath and got back to his feet. "I was the one who screwed it up. Next time I'll do better... though I don't know if I want to try again just now."

"We're not going to try again at all unless you explain what you're trying here." Melissa put her hands on his shoulders, making him look at her. "I'm just coming to grips with my condition, Rick. If I end up hurting you with it, that's going to... well, it'd really mess me up."

He considered in silence for a moment, then decided that there was no harm in explaining one of his core plans. In fact, given that his plan now included her, it would be downright foolish not to. "If we do this right, the one you'll hurt will be Mike."

"Ooh, do tell." Melissa moved away from the little table, vaulted over the couch, and patted the seat beside her. "Tell me everything."

"Basically, I think we should assume that the match won't be fair. If Mike is winning, he'll do as much damage to me as he can. But if I gain the advantage, he'll call it off. Maybe not right away, since he has an ego, but he can just give up before I can get back at him, then try again later." Rick sat down and smiled at his sister. "So before he does, I need to hit him with something he'll remember."

Melissa gave him a vicious smile. "I like the sound of that. I'd love to do it myself, but it's obvious that I can't actually harm someone with developed lucrim defenses. Not right now. You think you can use my skill somehow?"

"I can't use it, but I can carry these... void flames you create. At least, I think I can. What matters is that I've been working on a technique to do aura damage to someone's lucrima. I was planning to use my own aura... but using yours would be much more effective."

"Wow, so you'd... punch the flame into him? That sounds like it'd hurt a lot." His sister sat back, smile softening. "I really like that idea, Rick. I mean, I'd prefer for us to take out Glenn, but since Mike is the one ultimately responsible, I'll settle for that."

"Maybe you can hit Glenn yourself someday." Encouraging his sister to get into a feud with a powerful Birthrighter was probably not a good big brother move, but he liked seeing her so optimistic.

The two of them worked together on the basics of the technique. Though Rick realized he'd need a lot more time to safely carry one of his sister's void flames, it was easier with her helping directly. Even if successful, the result would basically be a bomb inside him that she could explode whenever she wanted, but he had no concerns about making himself vulnerable to her.

Eventually it grew late and Melissa said she needed to get working on homework she'd been putting off. It was just as well, because it was getting close to his appointment with Emily. Rick headed out to the Recluse's Retreat.

Though they couldn't meet often because she was busy with work, he and Emily had set up a training schedule. Emily's defensive core had much more lucrim than his, but it was actually rated lower, so she could learn from him. It was a fairly equitable agreement, so he was glad that she wasn't just pitying him.

In return, she helped polish his offense. Her aura blades were incredibly sharp and he was still in awe of how much force she could put into a blow. Even if he couldn't attain that level, he could make his offensive skills less lackluster. Their relative weaknesses made the training mutually beneficial, so he was always glad when she had time.

Usually when he arrived at the Recluse's Retreat, the guard waved him through. But this time, the man stepped into his path. "I'm sorry, sir, but only clients and their guests are allowed inside."

"Come on," Rick said, "don't you recognize me by now? I work with Emily."

"And she didn't say anything about a guest today. I'm afraid you'll have to wait, sir."

That was frustrating, and it implied worse possibilities, but he wasn't going to get in a fight with the retreat staff. Rick stepped back and shuffled his feet while he waited, wondering what the problem could be. As conscientious as Emily was, he didn't believe that she could have simply forgotten. She also wasn't the type to simply snub him, so he was left with grim possibilities.

At last he saw Emily approach, her usually stern expression more serious than normal. Instead of waving him in, she left the retreat. Without saying a word she jerked her head down the street, so he followed her. They walked out of earshot before she glanced to him.

"Did you get a message from Whitney?"

"What? No."

Emily sighed. "I was afraid of that. I'm not sure if she expects you to run, but she doesn't give you the same respect she gives the rest of us."

"So she told you something? What?"

"There are signs that one of her rivals is trying to target her chosen fighters. Outside of the Underground, just whenever he gets the chance. As such, she's going to take all of us early. In about a week we'll all be taken three days early, kept under lock and key until it's time for the event."

"Huh." Rick considered that revelation. He didn't like the idea of Granny Whitney kidnapping him, since that was likely what would happen, but he also didn't like the idea of hitmen coming after him. Much less coming to his apartment and targeting Melissa. "So that changes things?"

"It's very inconvenient for me, but I can't afford to fight her on this. I need to work this whole week to prepare, so I'm afraid our training is canceled for now." Emily stopped walking and turned to him. "But then we're going to be stuck together for three days while we wait for the event. I'll prepare some final exercises for you and I expect you to do the same."

If all the fighters would be forced together before the event, then his schedule had just gotten rearranged. Hopefully it would still work, but... "I'll prepare some defensive exercises so you don't waste your time, but I don't know how much time I'll have for yours. I'm likely to be injured for much of that time."

Emily raised an eyebrow at him, but didn't ask questions. "Fair enough. I'll see you there, Rick. Don't take any unnecessary risks."

With that, she turned and walked away. From her, that was practically a warm farewell. Rick stared after her for a moment before realizing he had no time to space out.

He had almost no time at all. Soon he would be facing three major threats in succession and he could only hope that his preparations had been enough.

Chapter 45: Granny Whitney's Team

When the day arrived for him to be kidnapped, Rick was ready. Melissa had argued that she should come along, that it might be safer for her to be with him, but he had refused. It might have been nice to have her with him, and he respected her desire to see the fights... but he didn't want her to be in the same room with Granny Whitney, ever.

Even if it was just instinct, or unjustified paranoia, he wanted to be careful. So Melissa had gone to stay with a friend for a while. Once he was gone, he'd text her, presuming that he'd be allowed to do that. In any case, he waited alone as he felt lucrim concentrate outside his apartment.

There was a knock on the door. Rick picked up his backpack with all his things in it and walked out. Unsurprisingly, Granny Whitney stood at the door. She looked mildly irritated to see him prepared, but covered it with a warm smile.

"I see someone warned you, dearie."

"I agreed to fight in this match for you," Rick said, "and I'm not going back on my commitment. Besides, if your rival is really targeting your fighters, I'm safer wherever you're taking me."

"You're a very reasonable young man." Her next smile looked authentic, though that didn't make it comforting. "And for the record, I have no plans to imprison you or anything of the sort. We're merely all taking a little retreat together, to make sure there aren't any... last second surprises. From anyone."

As she stepped away from the door, Rick looked beyond her, wondering how she had arrived. Soon he got his answer as Granny Whitney pulled a pair of car keys from her handbag and lifted them before her, lucrim pulsing through them.

Aura slid between the different elements of the keychain, powering the external Lucores there. The power quickly multiplied, arcs of light showering through the air by the balcony. The arcs grew concrete, forming a shape that floated there, like a bird opening its wings to fly. Rick had seen lucrim vehicles before, but never one this intense, so he watched curiously as it manifested...

As a car. A little blue economy car, just floating in the air beside his apartment.

"Get in, dearie." Granny Whitney hopped over the railing easily, sailing toward the car. The door and upper part split open to allow her to enter and she landed on the seat with her purse in her lap.

Rick followed more slowly, a bit disoriented by the whole thing. He wasn't exactly concerned about the gap, since the fall wouldn't really hurt him, but he wasn't used to just throwing himself over the railing. But since keeping her waiting might go poorly for him, he forced himself to jump into the car, which opened to swallow him as well.

Then he found himself floating in the air... in what felt like a very ordinary vehicle. It was more spacious than a normal car and the seats were much nicer quality, but otherwise it was bizarrely ordinary. There was no steering wheel, of course, and the dash had a few pictures of children, a stuffed sheep, and a pair of knitting needles.

Humming to herself, Granny Whitney set her keys into the ignition, imparted a command, and then sat back. The vehicle smoothly flew away from the apartment parking lot, then began to climb rapidly. He barely felt the movement, as if the lucrim shell around them was compensating for it somehow.

"Now, I wasn't going to trouble you with details, dearie, but it seems that you've already learned some of them, so we might as well." She smiled over at him. "Yes, I fear one of my rivals is indeed targeting my fighters. Not that I wouldn't do the same in his position - it's rather difficult to replace fighters at this stage. I just wanted to be sure everything went smoothly."

"Just who is this guy sending hitmen? And is a random match in the Underground really this important?"

"It's more important than you know. Branton may not be the largest city, but the Underground is a rather notable fighting arena. As for your first question... his name is Gerald. He's a nice enough sort, he just likes using hitmen a bit too much. Oh, but I suppose you'd know him as the American Basilisk."

Rick stared at her. "You're telling me that a notorious mob boss is competing in this event so seriously that he's sending hitmen to disable the competition?"

"That's about it, dearie. And there are hitwomen, too. Don't be closed-minded."

"That... you still didn't really answer my question. I don't see why this is worth so much trouble from everyone. The rewards can't be that amazing."

Granny Whitney chuckled like he was a child making an amusing spelling mistake. "Oh, the rewards are rather good, but you'll recall those are mine. But no, they aren't the reason. This is about honor, about respect. When it comes to the world of lucrim, that is ultimately the currency of power. Yes, this little fight is just a game, but it is a game about control."

Her voice went hard at the end and Rick swallowed his remaining questions. If Granny Whitney was someone who casually spoke of competing against a person as dangerous as the American Basilisk, then she was even more of a threat than he thought. He realized that Henry had probably dodged a bullet getting taken out of the competition - working for a mobster had to end poorly.

Then again, perhaps Rick was in exactly the same position. He glanced at the old woman from the corner of his eyes, wondering if she was running part of the criminal underworld. Based on what he'd seen... he doubted it. Not that he thought she couldn't, but he felt like her interests lay elsewhere. Hopefully not with him, once she got what she wanted.

If two such important people were competing in this event, then who was Alger to host it? Rick had always assumed he was just a local fight enthusiast, but perhaps there was more going on. He vowed that once he got out of this, he was staying far away from this kind of shady business.

Rick had a feeling he wouldn't be able to keep that vow.

In surprisingly little time they began to descend again, breaking through the clouds. He looked out the window and saw that they were already outside Branton, flying over empty fields. The vehicle might look ordinary, but they had made very good time.

As they descended, he saw that what appeared to be an ordinary farm house from the air was actually a much larger complex. That wasn't a barn, it was an armored bunker. Rick swallowed and tried not to let it get to him.

When they landed, Granny Whitney recalled the lucrim vehicle almost immediately, forcing him to rush to land on his feet instead of being dumped on the ground. Once he had his balance, he tried to check his phone, only to find that he had no reception. They should have good reception even out here, so he could only assume...

"That isn't going to work, dearie." The old woman began walking away from him toward the central house. "Take some time away from all these modern screens and enjoy nature, okay?"

That was obviously not the purpose of all this, but he had no choice but to humor her. They walked up toward the large farmhouse, which looked to be much more elaborate than he'd thought at first. This place had never been used as an actual farm, that much was obvious.

Still, it was strange being out in the country. It had a different smell, more different than comparing the city center to the suburbs. An earthy smell, but more pleasant than what he'd grown up with in the trailer park. Above all, it was silent, just the sounds of the wind in the trees. He'd spent some time outside the city visiting distant relatives, so it wasn't exactly shocking, but out here the stillness of it all was eerie.

As they reached the door, it opened and a young man pushed through. His lucrima felt strong but disrupted, in the 60,000 lucrim range but difficult to evaluate. Though he wore training gear, it was old and stained. When they approached, the man smiled and rushed to shake his hand.

"Hey, man, how's it going? I'm Anthony, nice to meet you."

"Uh, nice to meet you too." Rick shook his hand and tried to pull back, but Anthony wouldn't let go. Instead he kept a grip on his hand and pulled him out to the edge of the porch, movements a bit jerky and manic.

"This is a nice place, you're gonna have a good time here." When they got a short distance away, he leaned closer and spoke in a lower voice. "Listen, man, do you got any elixir?"

Rick realized what was happening and forcibly pulled his hand away. Anthony was a power addict going through withdrawal -

now that he was looking for signs of addiction, he spotted them immediately. The other man twitched in response and frowned.

"Come on, I need-"

"Anthony." Granny Whitney spoke warmly... from just behind them. Rick hadn't heard her move and Anthony jumped in place. "You know this is for your own good. Just calm down and get through it and you'll feel much better in a few days."

"Yeah... yeah, Granny, you're right. Let me just take a walk around, clear my head..." Anthony nodded and headed out into the farm, entirely too quickly.

Granny Whitney floated behind him, her knitting needles sliding smoothly from her handbag. As graceful as her movements looked, they weren't slow: Rick could barely follow them with his eyes, much less avoid them. She struck Anthony in the neck with her needles as she landed behind him and his entire body went limp, slumping to the ground.

"He's a good lad, just a bit mixed up." The old woman turned back to him and smiled. "Would you carry him in for me, dearie?"

Rick headed back to pick up the power addict, carrying him over one shoulder and hoping the man didn't vomit down his back. It seemed like whatever Granny Whitney had done to him had disabled him completely, because he didn't respond at all.

Inside, Rick found the house to be well-furnished, if a bit rustic. The living room was to the left, so he headed there to set Anthony down in one of the overstuffed chairs. He almost didn't see Emily there, since she sat with her legs crossed in a dark corner. When he smiled at her she just nodded in acknowledgment - clearly she wasn't in the mood to talk.

Since Granny Whitney had vanished, Rick decided that he was probably free to spend his time how he wanted. Three days in this place... that would be extremely strange, if he didn't already have plans for it. But for now he needed to get his bearings and find the other fighters.

Leaving the living room, Rick headed in the other direction, to a kitchen area. It appeared to be devoid of most of the items he'd expect in a kitchen, but a woman sat in one of the chairs, staring out the window. He realized that he recognized her: it was the woman he'd seen with Granny Whitney, presumably their group's cruiserweight.

"Hi, I'm Rick."

"I'm Malati." She shook his hand reluctantly and then pulled back. "No offense, but I don't want anything to do with you fighters. I'm just doing what I need to do, then I'm getting back to my life."

Not the best start, but he didn't need to engage her in a long conversation, so Rick just nodded. "I'm here under duress too, for whatever that's worth. Rest assured, I'm not trying to pry into your situation, I'm just noting who's here since we'll be fighting together."

"We won't actually ever fight together. Our points count toward the same ends, but otherwise we aren't involved."

"That was what I meant, but fair enough. I won't bother you too much, but I'm curious: how does someone who isn't interested in fighting end up in a situation like this?"

"There are certain bills I need to pay and my options were limited. Eventually you get... stuck in a rut." Malati fixed him with a stern gaze. "I guess you're better than Anthony, but if you keep talking to me I might revise that opinion. Are we done yet?"

"Fine, just one more question: have you seen our heavyweight? He's... uh, I think you'd remember him."

"Back porch." Malati pointed into the hallway, then turned back to staring out her window. Rick nodded his thanks and went in the direction she'd indicated, though his thoughts stayed with her a moment longer.

Could he sense a slight disruption in Malati's lucrima? It might be presumptuous of him to draw conclusions when he was still a novice at sensing lucrim portfolios, but he thought there might be. Perhaps something like a chronic illness... it wasn't like his sister, but in a way he was reminded of her. He wondered if that was the source of the bills she needed to pay and if Granny Whitney had either offered her a way out or forced her into it. Either way, he should ask Emily later.

The fact that Malati had apparently stumbled into this role bothered him more than whatever her personal situation was. She had a generation rate well above 150,000 lucrim and felt strong enough, far above his power class. How did someone just wander into a life like that? Yet he knew that many of his own decisions had been determined by the ruts he'd worn for himself...

Well, he was going to be getting out of one rut. It might be stupid, but whatever was left of him would definitely be out of the rut.

After a couple wrong turns that revealed empty bedrooms, Rick discovered which of the halls led out to the back porch. It was actually more of a deck, an expanse of polished wood that looked out over the nicely cut lawn.

Teragen sat there, just as inhumanly intense as he had been before, even though he was just sitting in a chair. Granny Whitney stood beside him, speaking softly, but he could barely hear her as he reached the doorway.

"-know you don't need it," the old woman was saying, "but it's better to be certain about these things. I don't want you starting a war with the American Basilisk."

Instead of answering, Teragen just looked up at her. Granny Whitney sighed.

"I don't care what you want, that fight gains me nothing. Just cooperate, or our deal is off and you'll have wasted all this time."

Rick wasn't certain if her words got through to Teragen, because at that moment the huge man looked back, straight at him. Not as if he was surprised, but as if he'd known Rick was there from the beginning. As Granny Whitney turned toward him, Rick decided to just head out onto the deck, since he would look like a childish eavesdropper trying to hide.

"We were in the middle of a conversation, dearie." Granny Whitney seemed truly annoyed with him, perhaps worn thin from dealing with someone she couldn't bully. Rick raised his hands and sat down in one of the furthest chairs on the deck.

"Don't mind me, I just need a few minutes to collect myself."

Clucking disapprovingly, the old woman lingered a while longer, then wandered out into the yard. He realized that she was checking invisible lucrim defenses, so subtly woven into the hedges of trees around the farm that he hadn't even noticed them. But that was a distraction, since his real purpose was finally within sight.

Instead of paying attention to her, Rick ran through his exercises again. As he did, he took the Deathbane out of his backpack and slowly opened its special case. He turned the potent bottle over in his hands as he continued meditating.

Was this stupid? Undoubtedly, but it might still be his best option. Rick stared at Teragen, trying to read him. His body seemed to be built entirely from tightly corded muscle, bursting with power, but he might be tense beyond even that. Or perhaps bored, not wanting to waste time in this hiding place. He wanted to fight - hopefully that was a good thing, not a bad one.

When he finished his exercises, Rick drank the Deathbane. As he swallowed it, he realized that he was fully committed now. Fear or caution had nothing on his desire to avoid wasting that much money.

Rick stood up and walked across the deck toward Teragen. It became more difficult to walk as he drew closer, the air itself resisting him. Not the man's aura, which was suppressed, but some kind of secondary aura that bent the world around him. He was unquestionably the most powerful person Rick had met directly.

When Rick got close, Teragen looked up at him. The power in those eyes nearly froze him in place, leaving Rick with only a few seconds of movement before he was overwhelmed.

So he used them to punch Teragen in the face.

Chapter 46: Deathbane

The punch did not go well.

Before his fist could reach Teragen's face, it was brought to a painful halt by a wall of aura. That aura immediately closed around his fist, binding his arm in place and then pinning his entire body there. Teragen rose to his feet, towering over Rick and staring down at him.

"Why?" The word was so chillingly calm that Rick could barely even hear what the man sounded like. But he'd been prepared for something like this, and extended his other hand, holding the empty Deathbane bottle.

"I want to train to fight a wolf by attacking a bear."

For a long moment Teragen just stared down at him, utterly expressionless. Rick forced himself to stare back, though he was dimly aware that Granny Whitney had noticed and was approaching. That could be a problem. Likewise, it would be an even bigger problem if Teragen decided to just kill him. The tension stretched and his entire body cramped.

Then Teragen let out a snort of amusement. Somehow Rick found himself staggering back, his ears ringing. He hadn't even seen the blow, was barely catching up to feeling it now.

"That's enough!" Granny Whitney was moving toward them, eyes burning as she reached for her knitting needles. She was too late.

When he moved, Teragen seemed to entirely vanish, leaving his chair falling backward in his wake. But Rick had barely registered that fact when he felt a blow strike his back.

It wasn't just overwhelmingly powerful, it was complex. At first he felt the blunt force smash through his aura as if it wasn't there, then collide with his back. Yet even as his body started to fall away from the impact, there was a secondary force, a sharp blow piercing through his lucrim defenses. Rick had been focusing entirely on defense, yet it wasn't enough. He desperately threw everything he had against the blow, trying to resist the third element: a shockwave that threatened to shatter him.

Yet even as that blow ended, he glimpsed Teragen again, this time in front of him. Rick still had no chance of following his movement, he just felt his head snap back as a fist collided with it. Again he threw everything he had into defense, trying to resist the overwhelming power.

The blow knocked him off the ground so quickly that the air burned against his skin, yet it was the same instant his feet left the ground that he saw Teragen above him. Nearly at the same moment, a foot collided with his chest, yet another explosive three-part attack.

Somewhere in his mind he knew that the movements must be happening terrifyingly fast, yet in his consciousness it was a slow agony. He had expected it to all be over in an instant, yet as his mind struggled to react, he needed to throw his will into his defenses with each and every moment. This wasn't a sprint over lava, it was a marathon through it.

Impossible as it seemed, he didn't give in, maintaining his defenses as well as he could. Through his agony he recognized that he was plummeting down toward the deck, but before he landed, Teragen had already moved back down, kicking upward directly into his spine.

From there Rick lost all conscious control, lost even the ability to mentally follow the attacks against him. There were only the overwhelming blows from every side, tossing his body through the air like a ragdoll. The whiplash alone should have been life-threatening, yet somehow he held on.

It ended with a searing pain in his chest, different than all that came before it. Rick's mind caught up and he realized that he was almost standing, or at least his feet were pointing down. He couldn't really feel his body.

Except for Teragen's palm stabbing into his chest.

The warrior's fingers were crooked like claws and they went straight into his chest. As if his aura, his lucrim, and his flesh were no more than hot butter. He could feel every finger digging into his body, even the palm pushing into him like white hot plasma. That blow could have torn straight through him and left nothing behind.

Instead, Teragen used his bloody grip to knock him backward, sending Rick flying back through the air. As he sailed back, Rick had his first moment of true clarity since the assault began. Judging from how he was falling, he was probably going to break his neck and die. He saw Granny Whitney, still on the yard staring in surprise.

And he heard the chair hit the deck with a dull thunk. No, surely the entire attack couldn't have taken place in such a short time...

Rick wasn't sure whether or not he blacked out before he hit the ground. He simply ended.

~ ~ ~

Pain and darkness.

~ ~ ~

Lucrim and fragments of consciousness, trying to force their way through the emptiness...

~ ~ ~

Rick faded in and out of consciousness several times before he finally came to enough to register and remember his surroundings. It seemed that he lay alone in a large bed. He didn't recognize the ceiling, but based on the quiet outside, he guessed that he was in the farmhouse.

Movement was impossible. At first he was concerned that he had been paralyzed, yet he couldn't move his mouth or face. How had he opened his eyes? Even blinking was difficult, struggling through some power that kept him bound firmly in place. His eyes were growing dry by the time someone came into the room.

"Oh!" It was a woman who he dimly remembered as one of the Underground's doctors. She moved closer to him, looking him over somberly. "Are you feeling well?"

He couldn't answer and couldn't even convey that to her, but she remembered a moment earlier.

"Right, we needed to do a complete aura suspension. I'll ease that off so you can relax while I get Granny Whitney. Uh... good luck."

With that ominous note, she rushed from the room. Rick did feel a bit less stiff, as if the invisible bonds around him had eased. But instead of relaxation, the new freedom just brought pain. It was worse than any wound he'd ever felt before combined with the internal injury pills he'd taken. Yet he didn't think that he had been permanently disabled and the presence of the doctor supported that theory.

Yet he had to wonder if that would last as Granny Whitney entered the room. "My, my... you're a problem child, aren't you dearie?" She seemed even sweeter than before and it was honestly terrifying. The old woman sat down in a chair beside the bed and pulled out some knitting, her needles flashing in a silver blur. "Just what were you thinking?"

When Rick tried to answer he found that his throat ached and he couldn't speak. Clicking her tongue impatiently, Granny Whitney stabbed a needle into his neck. Suddenly his throat felt clear - much worse, but clear. "I... I need to get stronger."

"You were already strong enough, but I suppose that's what I get for recruiting your type." Her needles went back to flashing back and forth, scraping against one another sharply. "I saved your life, but it will require more than that to put you back together in fighting shape. I'm not sure that's worth my investment."

"You..." Rick swallowed painfully and just pushed forward, since there was no way back. "You always made it clear that we're not friends, and we're not allies. I decided that I was willing to bet that you wouldn't be willing to throw away or replace me this close to the tournament."

"Yes, yes, you're very clever. Don't overestimate your own value."

"I made preparations. Took Deathbane... there's more medicine in my backpack... and I have a deal with a lucrim therapist..." Though he wasn't sure how things would work with Lisa. His original plan had been to challenge Teragen after the tournament, in a more public location. That was a concern, but when he saw Granny Whitney sigh in resignation he began to feel relief.

"If you hadn't taken those precautions, you would be dead. Even if Teragen had left you alive, I would have ensured it." The old woman's fingers finally slowed, no longer knitting at a terrifying rate. "I suppose I can tolerate this as overzealousness, which is a common failing of your type. But as soon as the tournament is over, we are done. I had been planning to heal any injuries you sustained during the matches as thanks, but... I no longer feel so generous."

"Thank you."

She snorted and left the room without answering. Rick spent a while just staring at the ceiling, wishing he could fall unconscious but hurting too much to slip away.

Eventually the doctor came back in and began to give him some of his own medication, along with something that made him sleepy. He drifted in and out of consciousness, mostly waking to be given water or more medication.

They had drawn the curtains, so he had no way of measuring time. Seconds felt like hours, so he gave up even trying to pass time via hours or minutes. All he could focus on was the pain, which changed as he progressed. It began as aches and pains everywhere and slowly became a cool, liquid pain that flowed through his veins. Though it hurt, he could feel himself adapting, transforming...

When he finally checked his lucrim portfolio, he was surprised to find that it wasn't destroyed. If he had wanted to, Teragen could have shattered every Lucore he possessed. The fact that he was still alive meant that he had been spared, as he had hoped.

As the pain progressed, a few others occasionally visited him. Emily came once to confirm that he was alive and would recover, but otherwise seemed entirely preoccupied with her own concerns. He blearily taught her the defensive rituals that he had planned, even though she objected that he wouldn't be able to learn from her. That was fine - he'd gotten what he needed for the tournament.

One day Granny Whitney came in along with the doctor, carrying something that hung loose. He looked at it nervously until he realized that it was a rough yarn sweater. The doctor tugged off his shirt and replaced it with the sweater, leaving him a bit stunned.

"Uh..." Rick pulled at it weakly, both trying to find a comfortable position and to determine if the sweater was created with lucrim. "Is this part of the recovery?"

"No, it's part of your punishment." With that, Granny Whitney swept out of the room again, leaving him partially baffled and partially concerned that she'd left some horrible trap for him.

As his recovery continued, he gradually realized that this was neither something to help him nor a trick to drain his lucrim. But it was both a malicious scheme and revenge.

The sweater was extremely itchy.

~ ~ ~

Every time Rick awoke he felt a little better, though utterly distanced from the world. Once he was surprised to see Lisa there, apparently tracked down and brought to the location. He worried that something might be done to her, but she seemed more concerned about him than for herself, so perhaps they were merely letting her honor the deal.

He had a vague impression that her hands were strong and gentle, but he drifted in and out of consciousness while she worked. The first time he actually accepted a massage from her, and he was barely able to feel it. But when he woke up with her gone, he could feel a significant difference.

Piece by piece, he was being put back together.

Eventually, Rick woke up and he felt fine. Everything about him seemed to have been scoured clean by fire, but there was no more pain, at least not compared to before. When he flexed his aura, everything in his lucrima responded appropriately. When he tried to sit up, his body obeyed and he didn't feel anything tear inside him.

Dammit, he was still wearing the sweater. Rick tugged it off and threw it aside, noting that there was a terrible hand print scar on his chest from the final attack. Ignoring it, he pulled on one of his shirts from his backpack. It was light now, all the medicine that he had brought with him consumed in his recovery. But it would be worth it. Right now he was too exhausted to properly appreciate his own power, but once he restored his energy, it would be worth it.

As rough as it had been, he could feel that the Deathbane had done its work. Instead of breaking, his lucrima had struggled to adapt to the overwhelming power set against it. They stood no chance, but now the bar for raw power that his body understood had been greatly increased.

He padded his way from the room, not bothering to find his shoes. It seemed his room had been on the third level of the house, so he headed down to find the others. But when he found the stairs to the first level, he discovered that Granny Whitney was coming up the stairs toward him. Something in her gaze told him to wait for her.

"Finally, you're awake. I was beginning to worry that all of this was a waste."

"Is it that close to the tournament?"

"We leave in an hour, and you need that time to restore yourself. There's also one more thing." Her friendly smile turned sharp and she grabbed him by the collar, pulling him into one of the side rooms. Since she had helped heal him, he didn't resist, but he also strongly disliked the look he saw in her eyes.

"What is it?"

"You see, dearie, in all your frenzy to train as much as possible, you've been rather an inconvenience. I estimate your lucrim generation rate to be nearly 35,000 now. Even with that last leech of yours, that's rather impressive."

Rick was surprised to hear it and almost smiled - he hadn't expected to make that much progress - yet the way Granny Whitney spoke of it made him nervous.

"Here's the problem: I needed a featherweight, and the maximum generation rate for that power class is 30,000. All this extra power you've worked so hard for is useless to me."

He froze, instincts warring within him. The way she spoke so coldly, part of him was certain that she intended to kill him now that he was useless to her. Yet he knew that she wouldn't have paid to help heal him if that was her intention, so he forced himself to remain still.

"So Granny Whitney had to come up with a solution. What's one more expense before the end, hmm?" From her handbag, the old woman pulled out something new: an aura leech. Unlike the others, this one was pale white and pulsed softly. It strained through the air in his direction, revealing serrated teeth that he hadn't seen on the others.

"That's going to handicap me down to the class limit?" Rick asked. "Is that legal?"

"Within certain limits relative to total portfolio size, leeches are considered just part of a natural lucrima. If you had increased your power too much I would have had to cripple you permanently. Fortunately, this will suffice. Unlike legal aura leeches, this one will restrain you to the exact generation rate limit and no more. You won't have to pay it off, but I leave figuring out how to remove it to you."

Swallowing, Rick pulled his shoulders back and braced himself. "Well, go ahead and use it. I won't run."

"After all this trouble, dearie, you don't have a choice." She gave him a kind smile and then let the leech burrow into his chest.

The pain was intense, and a few days ago he thought it might have made him black out. Yet after what he had been through, Rick just swayed on his feet. Pushing through the pain with sheer willpower, he ignored the leech tearing into the heart of his spirit and focused on the old woman in front of him. "If we're being honest with each other... why have you been handicapping me since the beginning?"

"It's a trick." Granny Whitney gave a little shrug, just watching the leech to make sure it implanted. "I knew that Gerald and Alger would be carefully watching every candidate and making their own schemes, so I had to counter. For example, I kept my deal with Emily secret until the last second. With you, I made sure that everyone only saw you at your worst."

"Oh..." Rick thought back over the matches, how she'd given him pills that simultaneously helped him train and made him perform poorly. "And you made me collapse in my last match so I would seem like less of a threat?"

"That's right, dearie. I had a decoy fighter I was making a show of talking to as well, just to make them discount you completely. But I meant what I said the first time: you're a promising young man."

"Did... did you have to go this far? Surely just taking a few steps to hold me back would have been enough."

"Well, it isn't just the mind games." Granny Whitney smiled cheerfully and rubbed the fingers of one hand together. "There's also the betting... and the odds on you have become long indeed. The money doesn't mean very much to me, but Gerald always prides himself on beating the odds. This should be quite an embarrassment for him."

Learning that he was basically just a gimmick in Granny Whitney's arsenal should have upset him, yet Rick found that he didn't care. Yes, she had used him, but in a way he had used her. Provided that he could get rid of the leech in his chest - and assuming she really wouldn't come after him - he would end their relationship in a much stronger position. He'd definitely paid for it in pain and suffering, but now that he was on the far end, he would accept the progress.

"There's also this." She pulled some dark cloth from her bag and handed it to him. Rick realized that it was a high quality aura suit, designed for easy movement and manifestation of combat aura. Suits like these did a good job of absorbing aura, potentially becoming as durable as the fighter themselves. "I can't have you representing me in those shabby clothes."

"I... thank you. Anything else?"

"Just this."

Granny Whitney's hand snapped out and he felt her poke him in several places. His lucrima immediately screamed, beginning to burn in a way he'd never felt before. He dropped to one knee in pain... yet through the pain, he actually felt better. Broken and inefficient lucrim began to swirl, temporarily unlocking strength that had been restricted within him. Strange how Granny Whitney both helped and hindered him, so that he was restricted to the power class, yet fully able to use every lucrim within that limit.

"There! Now that's everything, I suppose!" The old woman smiled at him and began making her way down the stairs slowly. "Get dressed and come down as soon as you recover. No more time for games or preparations. The tournament is about to begin."

Chapter 47: The Multi-Tier Tournament Begins

This time, they didn't take the grandma car. Instead, Granny Whitney manifested black arcs of lucrim that solidified into an enormous black hawk. It shifted almost as if it was alive, but the side opened like a door, revealing a conventional interior. A normal vehicle could never have functioned that way, but as the hawk flapped into the air, Rick barely felt any disturbance.

It was all rather ostentatious for Granny Whitney, but Rick realized that her purpose now was to make an entrance. For her this fight wasn't about any of them, instead solely about making a statement to her rivals. As they soared over Branton, Rick tried to get himself into the proper mindset.

He'd been given enough philosopher's elixir to charge himself to full strength, but no more. Barring an emergency during the tournament, he'd received the last gift Granny Whitney would ever give him. Now he needed to pay his debts to her.

While he put on his seatbelt, he noticed Teragen glance at him briefly. The superhuman man seemed mildly amused, then he went back to staring at nothing from the floor of the vehicle. Rick decided that was probably all he was going to get out of him, and offering thanks would be useless.

As Rick looked around the interior of the lucrim vehicle, he found himself doubting that he belonged there. Even though intellectually he knew that his job was to compete against people in his same power class, he couldn't help but reflect that he was weaker than everyone there. Teragen was obviously above him, while Emily and Malati were a clear step above and even Anthony had twice his lucrim generation rate. He might be a power junkie, but that led him to develop a dangerous lucrima.

Granny Whitney had closed herself off somewhere near the head of the hawk, leaving the rest of them in the compartment. Rick realized that he had entirely missed the time spent together on the farm and wondered if the others had gotten to know one another. Based on the utter silence, maybe not.

"Alright!" Anthony stood up, which he wasn't supposed to do, and pumped a fist in the air. "We are going to crush this tournament!"

Malati frowned at him. "Sit down."

"Come on, aren't you psyched? Even the third prize rewards aren't bad, and I think we have a shot at winning the whole thing! This is something to celebrate!" Anthony leaned an arm on Emily's chair, leering down at her. "You are really wound up, babe. Maybe you can sustain that for now, but afterward... we're going to need to celebrate, yeah? I guarantee, I can help you relax."

Emily just... didn't respond. Not as if she was ignoring him, but as if she hadn't heard him. The entire time since Rick had woken up, she'd been in some sort of trance. Her aura whistled around her, sharp as a blade. In the face of her all-consuming focus, Anthony gave up and stopped hitting on her.

"Fine, be that way. What about you, Malati? Not that I'm propositioning you, but you can cut loose, right? I don't want this victory party to suck."

"I can relax just fine, but I'd rather not do it around a pig like you."

"Oh, come on. I don't have to take that from you." Anthony turned around to glance at Teragen, who still sat on the floor against one wall, because nobody was going to make him put on a seatbelt. "What about you, big guy? Any chance you're a 'work hard, play hard' type of guy?"

Teragen glanced at him and Rick was gratified to see that Anthony wasn't immune to the force of his presence either. Then Teragen looked away without saying anything.

Groaning, Anthony rolled his eyes. It was obvious who he'd approach next, so Rick preempted him. "I'm glad you're trying to take our minds off it, man, but I can't stop thinking about the tournament. I won't be able to think about anything that happens afterward until the fights are over."

"Guess that's just how it is." Anthony sat down in his seat and stopped trying to start conversation. It seemed like he'd gotten over his withdrawal, not displaying any of the symptoms from earlier. But Rick had known enough addicts to guess that Anthony was eagerly awaiting his next fix - the fact that he was addicted to raw power didn't change anything.

To take his mind off such things, Rick turned to look out the semi-transparent parts of their vehicle. Given that it flew at good speed, he would have expected them to arrive already. Actually... when he looked at the landscape more carefully, it didn't seem like they were going back to Branton at all.

He glanced around at the others, wondering if he should be concerned. Most of them were looking outside as well and didn't think it was worth comment. After staying silent for a while longer, he decided that he didn't want to sustain that much uncertainty.

"Are we not going back to the Underground?"

Anthony chuckled. "You don't know? For the actually important matches, they have a special arena. It should be coming up soon, I think - I never could keep all the generic countryside straight."

Peering ahead, Rick saw only one likely destination: a massive abandoned factory. It was probably part of the old Branton, the original small town that had been dominated by manufacturers. When the manufacturing jobs dried up, the original community almost died and the modern city had become the main heart of Branton.

As they circled overhead, Rick could hear the roar of a crowd. Were there really going to be that many people? He had been counting on the relatively small crowds of the usual arena, so the idea of going before a huge crowd brought back his concerns.

Forcing himself to look away, Rick instead pulled out his phone to remind him of what he had to work with.

[Name: Rick Hunter

Ether Tier: 16th

Ether Score: 238

Lucrim Generation: 34,850

Effective Rate: 29,999

Current Lucrim: 29,999]

[Rick Hunter's Lucrima Portfolio

Foundation: 3100 (Lv IV)

Offensive Lucore: 5500 (Lv IV)

Defensive Lucore: 11,300 (Lv VII)

Bunyan's Step: 4900 (Lv IV)

Graham's Stake: 5950 (Lv II)

Aura Leech: -2460 (Stage I)

Faux Leech: -1641 (Stage IV)

Tracking Bond: 100 (Lv XIII)

Gross Lucrim: 34,850

Net Lucrim: 29,999]

The familiar numbers helped him regain his calm, even if he didn't like being reminded of the new leech inside him. He might be weaker than the other fighters in the plane, but he was not weak. His foundation was more compact and efficient than his original had been, despite the huge increase in his generation rate. His primary Lucores were well-balanced for combat, and over 10,000 lucrim invested into defense was nothing to be easily ignored.

That was what he had earned with all his work so far, and he'd earn more. Hopefully removing the leech and absorbing what he learned in the tournament would help him prepare. During the tournament he'd be facing opponents of a similar class, but when he fought Mike there would be no such fairness. He didn't just need to win, he needed to win without being injured and while increasing in strength.

But none of that mattered now. Rick cleared his mind of everything but the tournament as they came down to land.

As their vehicle began to circle downward rapidly, he realized that they were not going to be simply landing on a strip somewhere. No, it looked like they were heading toward the entrance itself. Before he could ask anyone about that, a door formed in the wall ahead of them and Granny Whitney walked out with a serious expression.

"It's time to make an entrance, dearies. Don't make me look bad."

Though the internal compartment shifted to stabilize them, the hawk pulled into a dive. Rick gripped the armrests of his seat, expecting to collide with the roof, but instead saw that it had been removed. Within the factory's old walls, he could see an arena surrounded by huge stands. This didn't help his nervousness.

He wanted to ask how they were going to make their entrance, but the chairs and seatbelts dissolved into the lucrim vehicle, forcing them to their feet. The entire vehicle shifted as the hawk dived, becoming a single corridor. When the hawk finally landed dramatically, wings outstretched, the door lowered for them to exit and the crowd's roar swept in like a wave.

Going out there was the last thing he wanted to do, but Rick found himself swept along with the others as they marched out. They weren't the only team arriving, but in their complex lucrim hawk, they definitely attracted a lot of attention. It was uncomfortable to think about the crowds looking at him, so Rick just tried to stick close to the others. He noted that all of them had been given aura suits as well, though Teragen still wore his own clothes.

Anthony was raising his fists and playing to the crowd, while Malati just gave a polite wave. Emily and Teragen didn't respond at all, so Rick decided to take a page from their book. He noted that Granny Whitney didn't come with them, but the others seemed to know where to go.

From the central arena, which was a massive octagon surrounded by a cage of silvery lucrim chains, they headed toward the stands. A narrow pathway underneath led into a concrete area that seemed to extend below the stands. To distract himself from all the attention, Rick marveled at how much had been built. They had kept the overall structure of the massive factory, but replacing everything within must have been nearly as expensive.

Eventually their group passed beneath the crowds and entered a dimly lit concrete corridor. Granny Whitney met them there, nodding slightly as if their entrance had been acceptable. She led them up a stairwell to a row of structures built from the wall.

When they came out at the top of the stairs, Rick realized that they were now above and behind the audience. From this position, they had a commanding view of the arena. They passed one room with a large team inside it, lushly appointed with even recovery equipment. But the one Granny Whitney led them to was utterly spartan, just a set of chairs facing the windows, with viewing screens beside the windows for close-ups of the fighting.

"These are our headquarters," she explained. "When it's your turn to fight, there's a special passage to get down beneath the arena. Everyone stays until all the matches are done, then what you do is up to you. Until then, no celebrations, no distractions."

They all nodded, her seriousness infecting them. Emily went to sit first, taking the chair on the far left, so Rick sat beside her. She didn't seem to object, which was good enough in her current state. Anthony sat on his right, Malati sat at the end, and Teragen ignored the last chair, sitting down against the wall and closing his eyes. Granny Whitney had a chair for herself behind them, but stayed on her feet, staring out the window with bright eyes.

Though the chairs looked simple, they were more comfortable than he expected. He settled in, letting himself get used to the new scale of the event. After all the preparations he'd done, he could deal with a few crowds.

It seemed they had timed their entrance well, because they didn't have to wait very long before the event began. Fireworks exploded around the arena, and when they faded, Alger stood in the center of the octagon. He gave everyone a dramatic bow, then swept upright and spoke in a loud voice.

"Ladies and gentlemen, welcome to the Underground Arena!" The crowds roared out approval and he raised his hands as if drinking them in. "If I attempted to introduce to you everyone who will be taking part in today's competitions, I would be standing here all day! You will see young warriors beginning their path, journeymen with developed skills, and masters at the peak of their ability. If you are interested in pursuing this adventure with me... I can only refer you to the next match. Let the tournament begin!"

With that he disappeared in another burst of fireworks and a roar of the crowd. Rick found himself wishing that he'd mastered the rules of the event in greater depth. He knew that everyone would need to fight more than once, in melee matches that would be scored similarly to the normal Underground matches. Beyond that, he really wasn't sure how the event would proceed.

A screen above the octagon lit up, or rather a series of screens that faced every direction so the whole audience could see. The display began spinning through several symbols and words, quickly at first, then slowing down so that he could read them. They were all power tier names, rolling past the screen with flashing and noises until finally settling on a result:

Featherweight tier.

Granny Whitney struck his shoulder. "Rick, you're up. Don't disappoint me."

Chapter 48: First Round

Instead of getting a chance to see how the tournament matches operated, Rick found himself pushed down a confusing set of corridors toward the arena. He realized that the route was actually logical, as a way to get multiple fighters down into the arena without congestion, but that was little comfort as he was rushed out.

Several other fighters joined him in the area below the arena, preparing to take the stage. All of them had lucrim generation rates in the 25,000 to 30,000 range, which made sense since anything less would be a disadvantage in this power class. With generation rate out of the picture, it would all be about skill and lucrim portfolio, but he was too frazzled to analyze anyone in greater detail.

"You're still alive?" One of the other fighters, vaguely familiar from his time in the Underground, looked at him with a bit of pity. "Do you need money so badly that you're willing to suffer in front of everyone?"

Part of Rick wanted to snap back a reply, but most of him was numb and distracted. Trash talk was irrelevant, all that mattered was getting his head in the game. When a ramp up to the arena floor lowered from the ceiling, he followed in the middle of the group.

They came out in the arena, the lights overhead blinding and the crowd roaring from all sides. Actually, the lights prevented him from seeing the crowd unless he particularly focused, so Rick tried to ignore them altogether. He let the crowds become a hum in the back of his mind and just drew his aura up around him as he prepared to fight.

The arena floor was covered in about a foot of tough rubber, heavily reinforced by ether enchantments. Not a comfortable place to fall, but better than the concrete floor of the Underground. It spread out to the edges of the octagon, where there were pillars at each of the points. Overall, it was much more open than the previous arena, with the thin lucrim chains barely visible in the light.

Once everyone had arrived, they began to spread out. Eight different fighters, looking rather small in the huge octagon, which rose up to three times his height. Presumably the size was better-suited to the higher power classes, who might find the arena too small if anything. Still, the size gave mobility an advantage, which should work for him.

A horn blared out, signaling the start of the match, and everyone leapt to attack at the same time.

They leapt rather slowly. At first Rick thought that his mind was too numb, showing him the world in slow motion. Yet when he began to move, he felt light on his feet. It was more than just an issue of speed: his mind had transformed, ready to fight at much higher speeds.

He had grown used to fighting Emily and Lisa, who were substantially faster than him, and he had seen true speed when confronting Teragen. Compared to them, these other contestants seemed to be moving with exaggerated care. Not absurdly slow, but he felt as though he had plenty of time to react.

Some had already begun to attack each other while he was thrown off by the speed of combat, so he needed to get involved. This wasn't the time for flashy or dramatic moves, just earning points. Two fighters were struggling near him and he attacked directly with blows to the head.

They were completely taken off guard and his earliest blows landed easily. Though the two fighters were too tough to go down with single blows, they reeled away from him. Rick kept up the pressure, raining down blows and preventing them from recovering until they both dropped to the arena floor.

Behind him, he heard a rush of flame. When he turned to look, he saw the man who had mocked him was now encased in flame. Almost the definition of a flashy move. When the man swept a hand toward him, releasing a sphere of fire, Rick considered dodging and decided against it.

Instead he struck aside the first flaming sphere, sending it to scatter against the barrier at the edge of the arena. Rick was actually taken off guard for a moment at how easy it had been.

More than that, he marveled at the fact that his hand didn't hurt at all. His aura was powered by a defensive core of over 10,000 lucrim, and that meant more than he'd expected.

So Rick charged in directly, barely dodging the flames released toward him. He felt the heat, but he didn't think the flames would have harmed him even if they struck directly. His opponent became more and more desperate, hurling a last spread of spheres and then drawing up all his power to expand the flames around him.

Not that it mattered, since Rick charged straight into him, slamming him back into one of the eight pillars around the arena. The flames licked at him harmlessly, no hotter than a campfire.

Before his opponent could recover from the shock, Rick lunged up, slamming an elbow directly into his chin. In an instant the flames went out and then his opponent dropped.

Turning away from him, Rick examined the rest of the arena. Three more people on their feet, one of whom he recognized as the old man from his three-on-three match. He was sending out tendrils of aura again, but they seemed no stronger than last time. Rick instead focused his attention on the others. One of them was an aura sphere user who seemed to have invested a lot of lucrim into the skill, so she was the next priority threat.

Except that some obscure instinct told him to jump.

Rick leapt away from the aura tendrils that approached him, uncertain if he was being unnecessarily cautious. A moment later he realized that he had been right: the tendrils leapt up around the aura user with surprising ferocity. They squeezed hard enough that she grunted in pain, then they contracted and smashed her into the ground.

As Rick landed at a safe distance, he realized that the old man had been hiding his power. The same strategy Granny Whitney had forced on him, but intentionally using a weaker version of the skill so that people would underestimate his binding ability and not dodge. Rick still couldn't identify what exactly had stuck out to him as wrong, but some part of his brain had identified that there was a hidden threat.

More tendrils were coming for him, so Rick considered his strategy quickly. If his opponent needed to trick people to catch them, then he must not be confident in his technique's speed. Rick prepared a Bunyan's Step, then flashed over the arena.

Though he reached his opponent instantly, already punching, the old man reacted in time. Tendrils extended from his body, wrapping around Rick's arm even as he struck. His body strained as he reversed direction, tearing free from the aura tendrils with difficulty. More were grabbing at his legs, forcing him to power through and leap away.

Okay, so that hadn't been successful. Rick bent down and grabbed one of the unconscious fighters, then hurled her at his opponent.

The old man managed to push aside the body with more tendrils, but couldn't react fast enough as Rick used a Bunyan's Step to get behind him. He started with a blow to the man's back, which staggered him but prompted more tendrils to grasp at him.

Rick jerked his arm back and tugged the tendrils with it, pulling the old man off balance. While his opponent was stumbling, Rick swept his legs, then brought both hands down on his chest, smashing him to the ground. The old man hit hard and groaned, still able to fight, so Rick prepared to leap away...

Except the tone sounded again. Suddenly he realized that the match was over and he was the winner.

Should he have held back more and pretended to struggle? Surely the odds would shift in his favor now, so Granny Whitney might not make as much betting. Then again, perhaps his top priority was to gain as many points as possible. More importantly than either of those: Rick was done losing with a handicap. He was going to throw himself into every single match with all the power he possessed.

The crowds were cheering for him, but he had already begun tuning out their noises. There was no point boasting or getting their attention. Now that he was done with his fight, Rick was abruptly very much done with the spotlight. He waited for the ramp beneath the arena floor to open and walked down into the space beneath without looking back.

Once he was out of the blazing light and the sounds of the arena were muted, his head spun. He found himself trembling slightly, though not in shock or fear. Though he'd needed to expend much of his strength, that had been easier than he expected. Yes, some of it was Granny Whitney's strategy, but he'd still won.

A tournament official walked up beside him, giving him an odd look. "Uh, sir? The victors are actually supposed to leave through the exit ramp."

"Huh?" Rick looked up as if he would see it there, then realized the official was talking about a ramp above. "You mean walk off the field instead of going below again?"

"That's right. Everyone already made their entrances, but victors get to make exits."

"Oh. I'll... keep that in mind next time, I guess."

"Good attitude. Get back to your place and enjoy your rest, then." With that, the official gestured him toward the corridor and Rick began heading back.

Okay, so he'd won and then immediately made a dumb mistake. Would the crowd know he'd gone the wrong way, or did he get away with it because he was the first match? After a little thought, Rick decided that it didn't matter at all: he'd won. Smiling to himself, he sped up to a jog as he returned to his team's room.

When he entered, everyone seemed to be focused on the arena, where another match had already started. He'd wasted too long returning. But when they noticed him, Malati gave him an encouraging smile, while Anthony raised a fist for him to bump.

"That was great, man! Got us off to a fantastic start!"

"I did what I could." He glanced around the room and found the others present, it was just that Emily remained focused internally and Teragen ignored everyone. "Who's fighting now?"

"More featherweights, dearie." Granny Whitney's smile seemed authentic as she approached and handed him a can of serum. "You didn't think you won the whole class, did you? No, your next match will probably be more difficult, so get ready."

That raised more questions about the exact mechanics of the tournament, but there were more important questions. Not wanting to seem ignorant, Rick first checked the screens and quickly found what he wanted: a scoreboard. The results of his match were listed there, though thankfully he was listed as "Granny's Underground Featherweight" instead of his full name. According to that, he'd earned 10 points for the team, the highest score from the first round.

Beside that box, there was another that listed team scores. It seemed like there were 24 teams overall, meaning there were over a hundred fighters total. More importantly, over a dozen rival featherweights he hadn't fought yet. It looked like eight more of them were fighting now... no, at that moment the battle ended. Two were still standing, having fought each other to a draw.

"Which of these are your rivals?" Rick asked as he looked at the team scores. He wondered for a moment if Granny Whitney wouldn't answer him, but she didn't hesitate.

"Alger named his team after himself and Obsidian Thirty is Gerald's team. There are a few others who will be contenders as well, but we're the main three."

With that in mind, Rick checked the screen of rankings. It displayed the top ten teams prominently, though at the moment many of them were tied. All the other teams were listed in smaller font, but he ignored those.

[1) Obsidian Thirty - 11 pts

2) Granny's Underground - 10 pts

3) Serpenza - 8 pts

4) Alger's Heroes - 5 pts

5) Branton Bulldogs - 3 pts

5) Chayichita Clan - 3 pts

7) Verdant Mountain Sect - 2 pts

7) Graham's Gym - 2 pts

9) Branton Chamber of Combat - 1 pt

9) Swiftfist Sect - 1 pt]

Rick frowned. "How does his team have more points than ours?"

Malati shook her head as if he was supposed to know these things. "They've finished two rounds already and his featherweight fought in both rounds. It's randomized, so sometimes things like that will happen. He didn't do as well in the second round because you hit him pretty good - only 3 points - but the combined total is still higher."

"Don't worry, dearie." Granny Whitney patted him on the cheek. "This sort of tournament isn't decided in one round. You drink your serum so you're ready for your next fight. We've only just begun."

As Rick got back to his seat, he saw that the signs of the arena were rolling through the power classes again. He braced himself to get unlucky and have to go straight back out, but it wasn't his class.

Middleweight. Emily was up next.

Chapter 49: Cheating Randomness

As the next round of the tournament set up, Rick tried to get comfortable to watch. He'd never been very fond of watching professional fighting on television, since it felt strange without sensing lucrim along with it, like mere special effects. This was nearly the same thing, since their room was rather far from the arena, but he kept his eyes glued to the screen because Emily was participating.

Realizing that he was still just holding his can of serum, Rick popped it open and began drinking. Since the next time he fought was apparently random, he needed to be fully rested and recharged. Before he got halfway through the can, he saw Emily walk from underneath the arena along with the other contestants. They weren't given long before the buzzer sounded and the match began.

Before the buzzer had even faded, Emily had already leapt at her nearest opponent and swept her aura blade straight through him. It was in non-lethal mode, so it didn't cut flesh, but the man's aura was cleanly severed in two. The shock of it made him drop, but Emily was already moving on her next opponent.

But as effective as her first attack had been, none of her opponents were weak. The second managed to repel her sword with a burst of aura and a third counter-attacked, forcing her to retreat. Not just retreat, but leap across the arena to attack another opponent who was engaged in a melee.

This blow was more successful, though not enough to take him down. As Emily retreated and again struck opportunistically, Rick tried to get a proper sense for the fight. She certainly wasn't holding back in terms of raw strength, but she hadn't used her ranged ability at all. He wasn't sure if she was holding that in reserve or if she didn't want to use it at all in public.

In any case, he had to admire the sheer focus in how she fought. Whatever meditation she had been doing, it had effectively given her an edge. There were other fighters stronger, or equally skilled, but none approached combat with the same intensity.

Five of the fighters fell relatively quickly, leaving Emily and two others cautiously testing out one another. Rick was curious to see who would win, only for the buzzer to sound again. Already declared a tie? Though he found that disappointing, perhaps for the the sake of the audience the tournament organizers wanted to keep things moving forward.

All three victors returned along the routes back, receiving some cheers, but not overwhelming praise. Rick glanced back at Granny Whitney. "Do they usually cut off rounds that quickly if there isn't a clear winner?"

"They want the tournament to escalate in intensity, but that's hard to orchestrate." She answered without taking her eyes away from the screen where the results would be displayed. "So they manipulate the early rounds to weed out the weaker fighters and set up better final matches."

Then it was all entertainment, to some degree. Even though he shouldn't care about the results, he disliked that idea. How far would the tournament organizers go in order to package all the fights as an entertaining product? He even wondered if the randomization was rigged, though if that was the case, surely statisticians would notice and object. There was money riding on the results, after all.

Before Emily got back, the results from the fight appeared. Emily had earned them 6 points, with the other remaining fighters getting 5 and 4 based on how well they had done in the early part. Not overwhelming, but Granny Whitney seemed satisfied. Perhaps because they were now tied for first place.

Rick glanced at the screen again, this time focusing solely on the top five groups.

The screen wheeled through the tiers again, coming to rest on the welterweight class. Anthony hopped up to his feet. "Alright, time for me to get us the lead back! I'll carry you all if I have to." As he turned around to go, Emily entered the room. He raised a hand for her to meet. "Passing the torch, eh?"

Emily ignored him and went back to sit down in her seat. Rolling his eyes exaggeratedly, Anthony headed out to the arena. Rick wasn't sure if it would be better to ignore her, but when he gave Emily a respectful nod, she nodded back.

When Anthony came out in the octagon, he seemed twitchy and unsteady on his feet, as if his withdrawal symptoms had returned. Though Rick spent a moment wondering if the prospect of the fight had somehow triggered his addiction, he realized there was a simpler explanation: it was an act.

Anthony held back as the match started, but when an opponent approached him, he reacted with shocking speed, releasing an aura sphere. Most such attacks just burst and did damage to aura defenses, but Anthony's exploded, sending his opponent flying backward. Immediately the act dropped and he began to aggressively attack the other fighters while Granny Whitney smiled.

His initial attack was very effective, but it wasn't enough to take the match. Another fighter using a style that looked like judo managed to "throw" his spheres, redirecting them to explode harmlessly at a distance. It seemed an effective counter, but the match was ended before either of them could adapt or pull out any other techniques.

When the results were displayed, Anthony had earned 8 points... but his remaining opponent had earned 9. Surprisingly, the victor was from the team called the Branton Bulldogs, which seemed like a boring local group not associated with any of the major players. Yet this victory had catapulted them higher in the rankings.

[1) Granny's Underground - 24 pts

2) Obsidian Thirty - 18 pts

3) Branton Bulldogs - 14 pts

4) Serpenza - 13 pts

5) Alger's Heroes - 9 pts]

Before he could voice a question, Malati did it for him. "Who are they? Some local club?"

"They're irrelevant, dearie." Granny Whitney seemed pleased now that they were firmly in the lead, beaming at all of them instead of pacing behind their chairs. "They have some strong fighters in the lower tiers, but they struggled to fill the classes above middleweight."

"We're winning, though."

"That doesn't mean anything, while the matches are still unbalanced. Every fighter matters in the end."

As if to make her point, the welterweight category came up again, this time without Anthony being included. That was twice in a row that the same category had come up - surely that couldn't happen randomly? Rick took a step back, remembering how Uncle Frank sometimes ranted about how people didn't understand randomness. In a truly random sequence, it would be more suspicious if there weren't a few oddities.

Still, he had to wonder if the organizers were leaning on or faking the randomized choice of power classes. So far they'd had multiple rounds at the lower classes, as if to get them out of the way to lead up to more exciting fights.

"Aww, yeah, who's the man?" Anthony came back into the room with a smug look. "I'm the man! We've got this now!" Most of them ignored him, but Granny Whitney handed him a drink and patted him on the cheek.

"Very good, dearie."

As the next fighters moved out, Rick went back to wondering if the randomization was being manipulated. Just as he was about to ask about it, he saw that he recognized someone in the next match: Tom. He towered over the others in the same match, wearing a sleeveless leather jacket and looking like he would come out swinging with his fists. Anyone who hadn't seen him fight in the Underground was going to be very surprised.

When the match began, several fighters immediately ganged up on him, charging from multiple sides. Tom simply exploded in a massive aura of electricity that sent his opponents flying in every direction. The electricity seemed to linger with him, crackling around his body, as he began to aggressively release more bolts of lightning at those who remained.

These weren't controlled bolts, just the slightly random but instantaneous ones. Some missed, but Tom released such an enormous torrent of them that some still landed. Rick realized what he was doing: expending all of his available power on a shock and awe offensive.

It worked. When Tom stopped unleashing lightning, every single one of his opponents was down. The repeated attacks had used up most of his reserves, but that wasn't obvious to most of those watching. All they saw was one fighter utterly annihilate his opponents, so they cheered raucously.

Malati turned to Anthony with a smirk. "You're the man, huh? Well, you'd better be ready to face that man, or you won't be carrying this team anywhere."

"Just a bunch of flashy shit." Anthony sat lower in his chair, glowering resentfully. "And a cheap surprise trick. I'll be ready for him."

The results came in and Granny Whitney frowned at them. Tom had received 12 points - the most from any single round in the tournament so far. It wasn't enough to unseat them, but it put Alger's team up near the top and proved what she had said about the matches just beginning.

Relative score didn't matter at this stage so much as who had the advantage in each power class. None of the other top contenders had been in this match, so their scores remained unchanged. The result was a rather impressive leap:

[1) Granny's Underground - 24 pts

2) Alger's Heroes - 21 pts

3) Obsidian Thirty - 18 pts

4) Branton Bulldogs - 14 pts

5) Serpenza - 13 pts]

That might matter a great deal to Granny Whitney and her rivals, but Rick tried not to get caught up in the results. He did need them to win for Granny Whitney to forgive his debts, but all he could control was his own matches. Instead, he focused on the randomization question.

"Is the match order really purely random?" he asked, watching as the tiers began to cycle past again. "What happens if it keeps coming up with the same power class over and over? Wouldn't that add a huge component of randomness to the tournament?"

"It doesn't work quite like that." Malati started to answer, but was cut off as the cruiserweight class came up on screen. "Well, that's me. Wish me luck."

She left without answering his question, and Granny Whitney didn't seem inclined to pay attention to him. Rick was surprised when Emily spoke up.

"The screen displays a wheel with five classes, but that's just a graphic displayed over the real calculation." Emily's voice was flatter than normal and she didn't look at him while she spoke. "Each selection is taken from a pool of remaining matches, which is weighted so that those who have fought most recently are less likely to fight again."

"That makes sense, thanks. Is there any chance they weight them to start with the lower tiers first? In general, I mean."

"Hmm. Possibly." Emily considered the question and retreated into herself, but he decided to try for the most relevant question.

"How often are each of us going to fight?"

Granny Whitney spoke from just behind him, making him a jump a bit. "It depends on how many fighters in your power class are eliminated, plus random chance. Most likely two times, but once if you're unlucky, three times if you're lucky. Lucky from my perspective, of course... more points for me, more injuries for you."

While they spoke, Malati's match had begun. It started with a few attempts to dominate the arena, but when none were successful, the fighters dropped back. They all had generation rates over 100,000 lucrim, so when fighting cautiously, they didn't go down easily. Though there were subtle shifts in the balance, the fight was actually a bit boring.

When he saw movement in the stands across from them, Rick tensed up. Had a brawl started? Was the American Basilisk using more hitmen during the event itself? A large group of people rose up, almost like a panic, but then they sat back down... and the group beside them rose up, waving their arms...

Were they doing the Mexican Wave? An audience at a high level combat tournament was doing the freaking wave?

While Rick was vaguely irritated by this development, no doubt the tournament organizers were deeply frustrated by the slow match. They didn't seem willing to cut it off early, however, so it stretched out. Only after three of the fighters fell did the buzzer finally sound. Malati was part of a three-way tie for first and no team was awarded very many points, so the rankings didn't change much.

Now that he understood the rules of the tournament better, Rick was feeling a bit more comfortable. He'd finished drinking his serum and felt like he was fully recovered. If he had to fight an average number of times, he was already half-way done. Things were going pretty well.

His stomach still flipped when he saw his power class come up on the screen again. The tournament wasn't even half over and it was already time for his second match.

Chapter 50: The Verdant Mountain Sect

Though Rick was still apprehensive about his match, he was nowhere near as disoriented as the first time. Now that he understood the passages between their room and the arena, he was impressed by how easy it was to get from one to the other. No doubt that made the space underneath the stands a mess, but it kept the matches moving quickly.

When he came out beneath the arena, he saw someone he recognized from the Underground: the woman with the spiked club. They randomly ran into each other often enough, maybe he should learn her name. But when he started to ask, she saw him and sighed.

"Oh, god, I got you already? Just my luck."

Rick blinked, not being used to anyone worrying about his strength. He tried to play it off with a shrug. "I'm not going to go straight for you or anything - that bat hurts."

"Still, there's no chance of getting points for sweeping the round. Alger is not going to be happy with me."

"Ah, he recruited you? I was wondering who he chose for his featherweight."

The woman sighed. "Honestly, I think I was like his third choice. But I get paid for each point I earn him, so it's better than nothing. Plus, it's fun to fight on such a huge stage, you know?"

It didn't strike him as fun at all, but at that point the ramps descended for them to walk up to the arena. As they did, they naturally moved in opposite directions so they wouldn't be right next to each other at the start. While Rick thought he could take her, he didn't think he could do it quickly, so it was better to take a chance on some of the fighters he didn't know.

When he looked around the octagon, he saw a few people he vaguely recognized from the Underground. If they hadn't stuck in his mind, they probably weren't overwhelming, so they'd make good targets. Then there was a man wearing formal green robes, looking like he'd stepped out of a combat sect from an old story. He stared around the group as if he was superior to all of them, even though his generation rate was just around 29,500 lucrim, same as most of the fighters.

Then the question was whether to play it safe with the robed man, or aim to earn points by taking down weaker opponents quickly. When the buzzer rang, Rick was still trying to decide between the two. He reprimanded himself to be more decisive, but then the choice was taken out of his hands.

The man in the green robe clapped his hands together and his aura exploded in all directions. At first Rick thought it did no harm whatsoever, but then he saw other fighters beginning to drop. A little later he began to feel sick, head spinning as nausea welled up within him.

Several fighters dropped immediately, but some remained on their feet. One staggered toward the man in the green robe, but was too dizzy to fight effectively and was felled by a series of rapid blows. Meanwhile, the woman with the spiked club didn't try to attack him, taking down other staggering fighters to earn points before she fell.

Yet Rick felt fine. It wasn't pleasant, but it was nothing like the nausea that Granny Whitney's pills had forced on him. He launched himself toward the man in the green robe, trying to take him out with the first blow. His fist struck his opponent's chest, but the other man only grunted and fell back.

Though the man in the green robe seemed startled that his technique had been overcome, he wasn't incompetent. Rick traded several blows with him before he managed to kick his opponent's shin. The other man winced and dropped slightly, leaving an opening for Rick to kick him in the chest. As the man flew backward and collapsed to the arena floor, the effect vanished, leaving only lingering nausea.

Just before the club struck, Rick heard it whistling toward his head. He blocked the blow with his forearm, surprised that it only stung instead of breaking his skin. The woman with the club still looked a bit nauseous, so she failed to defend effectively and he swept her feet, dropping her to the floor.

That was apparently enough to end the match, again with him the victor. This time Rick didn't blunder by going back down the ramp, instead observing that small doors opened in the lucrim boundaries. He walked through the one pointing toward his team and headed toward the stands, surprised to hear the crowds cheering for him. They might not know his name, but they'd seen him win two matches, so they might be starting to remember him.

As Rick began to smile, he looked up and saw that Mike was watching him.

It nearly made him stumble, but Rick kept moving, pretending he hadn't seen. The Birthrighter sat in one of the expensive seats, staring down at him viciously. Rick kept up the pretense, refusing to make eye contact, but internally he was shaken. Now he had to worry that Mike was planning to sabotage him, though more likely he was just there to observe him in preparation for their match.

Ultimately, it changed nothing. He still had to do his best in the fights, and his purpose was still to fight Mike after the tournament was over. His opponent observing him was a disadvantage, yes, but Rick didn't use any fancy tricks.

He tried to put Mike out of his mind and just headed back to his team's room. Once there, he discovered that both he and the green robed man had received 8 points. That struck him as a bit unfair, since he'd won, but he supposed the other man had dropped more opponents. The woman with the spiked club had received 4, which he hoped was enough for her.

Almost everyone was absorbed by the next selection, but Granny Whitney turned to nod at him. "Another good match, dearie. I'm not regretting the money I invested in you so much anymore."

"Was that why you made me nauseous in so many matches? So I'd be prepared to fight him?"

"It was for your health, dearie." Her eyes twinkled. "But let's just say I had some idea what you might face."

"That was one of your rivals, then? Which one?"

Granny Whitney shook her head. "No, that was actually the Verdant Mountain sect. They always participate in the large events in the region, and though they rarely win, they tend to dominate certain matches. Neutralizing them is good enough, because they're not as strong on all tiers."

Usually Rick just paid attention to the top teams on the scoreboard, but when he looked lower, he saw that the new group was indeed getting close:

[1] Granny's Underground - 35 pts

2) Alger's Heroes - 31 pts

3) Obsidian Thirty - 26 pts

4) Serpenza - 19 pts

5) Branton Bulldogs - 18 pts

6) Verdant Mountain Sect - 15 pts]

As he looked at the list, Rick realized that someone was missing. "I met Alger's featherweight during that fight, but what about the American Basilisk's? Have I already fought him?"

"No. You haven't met him yet, but you will."

Rick sat down heavily, not feeling quite as well as after his first fight. The nausea was fading and Granny Whitney gave him a serum and some medicine, but there was still growing fatigue. It was impossible to fight this intensely and not take some attrition. Given how the match choices had gone, he felt certain that he was going to have to fight again. He'd already done well for his team, but the third match might end up being the one that mattered.

The next round was revealed to be for the heavyweights, so Rick sat forward eagerly as Teragen finally moved from his spot on the floor. This would be the most powerful melee he'd ever seen, and much more authentic than the professional fights, since there were few rules.

When all eight heavyweights assembled below, Rick was grateful that they weren't all as overwhelming as Teragen. Oh, they were all far stronger than him, but only a few seemed inhuman. They all stood still, then when the buzzer rang, the arena exploded.

Yet as Rick watched, he found himself disappointed. The fight was impressive as far as spectacle went, the fighters flashing around the arena so quickly they were almost invisible, trading blows that sent shockwaves rippling through the air. One of them actually summoned some kind of dragon, which arced over the arena breathing fire on the fighters before another heavyweight sliced it in half. Another fighter manifested a lucrim machine gun and sprayed bullets all through the arena and it didn't tip the scales at all, none of the others even blinking.

The problem was that it was all too far above him. He couldn't sit back and enjoy the intensity of it, he wanted to understand and follow the lucrim techniques. Yet before he had even begun to catch up to the overpowering fighters, the match was already over.

One had fallen, two were injured, and the other five looked untouched, including Teragen. He realized that one of the survivors wore the Verdant Mountain sect's traditional robes. Perhaps a long fight would have ended differently, but it was over rather soon. Not that many points were awarded, either, which mirrored his sense of anti-climax.

"Is that usually how heavyweight fights go?" Rick glanced at the others, some of his disappointment showing. "Or will they fight to the finish later?"

Anthony sat back and propped his legs up on the window. "Nah, the pros don't like to lose publicly. This is like a chance to show off for them, not a serious tournament. They prefer the invitation-only, one-on-one type deals."

"That's right," Malati said. "In these multi-tier tournaments, the top power classes often cancel each other out. That's why you need a strategy for all the tiers."

Rick glanced at Granny Whitney, but she had nothing to add, watching the scoreboard. Though her team was still in the lead, she seemed more tense than before. He looked to the listing and saw that the Verdant Mountain sect had knocked the Branton Bulldogs out of the top five, but otherwise nothing had changed.

The next class selected was welterweight again, so Anthony left with his usual bravado. When he got down to the arena, Rick saw that Tom was in the match too, as well as a green-robed woman.

At the edge lurked a man in a long coat who looked strong as well. Since all the most powerful welterweights were thrown into this melee, it seemed like this match was meant to finish the power class.

When the match started, Tom began with an explosion of lightning, but only one of the weaker fighters was hit by it. Judging from the strength of the blast, Rick thought that Tom had anticipated that and not put much strength into it. The green-robed woman faced off with him, extending an aura that seemed to suppress Tom's lightning entirely.

Then the man in the long coat shot Anthony in the back.

It looked like a lucrim bullet, too, which would have shocked Rick if he hadn't just seen a machine gun used in the previous match. Anthony grunted in pain and dropped to one knee, but pushed himself back up. He hurled one of his explosive spheres, but the man shot straight through it.

This bullet hit Anthony in the chest. He staggered a step back, aura failing, and a third shot knocked him flat on his back.

Seconds into the match, their fighter had been taken out. Granny Whitney released a slow breath that hissed through her teeth. Below, Anthony began to bleed out on the arena floor, yet she gave no instructions.

Though the Verdant Mountain sect member pressed Tom fiercely, her aura proved ineffective against the lucrim bullets from the man who Rick assumed was from the American Basilisk's team. Her body was immediately pulled from the arena by other green-robed figures and taken for treatment. In the end Tom faced off with the gunman, but his lightning proved overwhelming and he was the only one standing at the end, though injured.

They all looked to the screen for the scores, recognizing that this was their first major loss. Anthony's performance earned only a single point, while Tom and the gunman both received 7 points. As the results were displayed, the rankings shifted as well.

[1] Alger's Heroes - 42 pts

2) Granny's Underground - 40 pts

3) Obsidian Thirty - 37 pts

4) Serpenza - 25 pts

5) Verdant Mountain Sect - 23 pts]

Granny Whitney clucked her tongue and shook her head slowly. Before she could say anything, an official leaned into their room with a look of concern. "Uh... we've stabilized your fighter, but he needs more treatment. If you tell me wh-"

"No." Granny Whitney didn't even look back at him. "We have no additional treatment to offer. Do your bare minimum and then turn him out. He isn't to be allowed into the contestant area again."

The official's eyebrows rose, but he nodded and slipped out. Once he was gone, Granny Whitney turned to them all and smiled gently.

"Well, this is a setback, isn't it? Please do your best from now on."

Chapter 51: Closing In

Their room had never been exactly festive, but after Anthony's defeat and dismissal, it became much grimmer. Malati was digging her long fingernails into her own arms, struggling with the tension. Teragen and Emily seemed mostly unaffected, but when the screen declared that the middleweight class was next, Emily couldn't escape it.

"Take out Alger's fighter." Granny Whitney grabbed Emily's arm as she stood up, staring at her. "He needs to take a hard loss now, or he'll extend his advantage."

"I can try." Emily still seemed focused, though the recent events had weakened her concentration a bit. "Which one is he?"

"He's an old hand at the Underground, with a strong Turtle Lucore. You're a good match-up for him, which is part of why I recruited you. Don't disappoint me."

Instead of answering, Emily just headed toward the arena tunnel. Rick found himself on the edge of his seat, hoping that she'd do well. Though she had more resources than some of the rest of them and could recover without Granny Whitney's help, he didn't want her to end up injured because the old woman pushed them too far.

The match started intensely, but this time Emily didn't jump into the fray. Instead she crept around the side of the octagon, repelling anyone who tried to engage her with rapid swipes of her aura blade. The fighter with the "Turtle Lucore" turned out to be an older man who could rapidly convert his aura into some sort of defensive shell, hence the name.

Emily rushed past his defenses and swiped for his neck, but her blow was repelled by the defensive shell. She fell back, taking fire from another one of the combatants, and then the man charged, slamming into her.

One of Emily's arms was burned and she should have been disoriented from the burst, yet her unnatural focus held. She struck out at her target again and the man retracted his aura into his defensive shell, just as before.

Except her other hand swung out first, a second aura blade cutting through the outer part of his aura. The man winced and his control faltered, the shell dropping away to expose one of his legs. She struck it instantly, her blade sweeping through his leg. As he cried out in pain, she slammed both blades into his chest.

Even in non-lethal mode, two blades like that going through a person's torso must have been painful. It was unquestionably a disabling blow and the man dropped, but Emily was entirely committed to the movement. When others struck her from behind, she went flying across the arena and smashed into one of the pillars before falling to the ground.

Rick gripped his armrests tightly, willing her to get back to her feet. She gradually did, stabbing her aura blades into the arena floor and levering herself up. But when Emily staggered back to her feet, her eyes had changed. The meditative trance that had taken her that far had been broken.

That didn't mean she was weak, as one of the other fighters learned when he attacked from the side and got a blade to the face. But it took obvious effort for her to straighten after the blow, struggling to move past her injuries and the fatigue. Worse, in the time it had taken her to get up, a lean woman in a black coat had taken out all the other fighters except a man wearing a dragon mask.

At the beginning of the fight, Rick would have guessed that Emily had a good chance against either of them. But now, they were both in good condition, while she was struggling. Just when he started to worry... the buzzer sounded. Emily looked upward, as if slightly surprised, then began limping her way back to the room.

Meanwhile, everyone looked to the screens to see the results. Emily had scored 4 points, which was only the third most in that round. However, Granny Whitney seemed pleased enough. Apparently taking out Alger's fighter really had been her top priority, even if it hadn't regained them the lead.

[1) Obsidian Thirty - 45 pts

2) Granny's Underground - 44 pts

3) Alger's Heroes - 43 pts

4) Serpenza - 31 pts

5) Verdant Mountain Sect - 24 pts]

Now he saw the core three competitors pulling ahead of the others, neck and neck as they moved toward the finish. The single point difference between the three groups meant almost nothing, so perhaps Granny Whitney was right to focus more on taking out one of their opponents. Their job was to make her happy, after all, not to win.

When Emily returned to the room, she was limping but didn't show any pain. Malati got out of her seat to help support her, but Emily just looked to Granny Whitney. The old woman gave a slight nod, and after that Emily seemed to relax.

She didn't let Malati help her for long, however, and instead of returning to her seat, she sat cross-legged in one corner of the room. Rick glanced back at her a couple of times before he decided that it was worth going to talk to her. He'd just have to hope that he wasn't annoying her.

"Hey." He sat down a short distance away from her. "Are you okay?"

"I will manage." She was silent for a long time, then spoke softly. "Your defensive techniques were useful in limiting injury. Thank you."

That seemed to take a lot from her, so he shrugged it off. "It was a fair exchange, or if anything I got the better end of the deal. Will I be bothering you if I stay here?"

"No. It is fine."

Emily didn't say anything more than that, however. After they sat in silence for a while, Malati's power class came up and she headed out to the arena. Though Rick wouldn't have minded seeing her in combat more, he didn't want to just walk away from Emily. After a bit of awkward silence, he decided to just satisfy his curiosity.

"What was that trance-like state you were in?"

"Part of my discipline." She paused long enough that he thought she might not provide any more of an answer, but eventually she continued. "It was necessary if I wanted to perform at an adequate level as a melee fighter, if you understand me."

He nodded to let her know he understood: she didn't want to show her ranged attack in front of so many people. Rick found himself wondering if that was simply for self-defense, or if she had other reasons. "It seemed pretty impressive. Are you trying to regain it?"

"If possible. It would help with the pain."

"Shouldn't Granny Whitney be providing you healing, anyway?"

Emily shrugged. "I'm done fighting for the day, so she doesn't have any motive to help me. But the rewards include a number of valuable items that would help me recover, so I am not concerned. It's just an issue of pain-management until then."

"Let me know if there's anything I can do, okay."

"Yes... I will." She actually gave him a slight smile, and then opened her mouth to say more, but at that moment a gasp of surprise went through the audience.

Both of them stood up to see what was happening. All the screens displayed different angles of the same thing: the center of the arena was smoking from some sort of impact that left several bodies crumpled nearby, one of them bent in half. It looked like the man's back might be broken, brutally enough to provoke the reaction, but Rick found his attention drawn elsewhere:

Malati lay at the edge of the blast radius, unconscious.

The fight ended soon afterward and Rick glanced toward Granny Whitney. She looked furious, and he wondered if she would abandon Malati as well, but after a pause she moved to the door and gave a command. Several people in healer's outfits moved out to recover Malati and took her beneath for treatment.

It took everything a while to get back to normal, since the man with the broken back needed serious medical attention. The results also seemed to be delayed, though Rick wasn't sure if it made any difference. Unless the injury had been done via an illegal method, there probably wouldn't be any penalties. Or maybe the tournament organizers were drawing it out, since the crowd was abuzz with talk of the previous match.

When the large screens began cycling through the tiers again, the results popped up on screen. As expected, Malati had not done well, leading their group to drop back more.

[1] Obsidian Thirty - 49 pts

2) Alger's Heroes - 47 pts

3) Granny's Underground - 46 pts

4) Serpenza - 33 pts

5) Verdant Mountain Sect - 28 pts]

That was bad news, but they were still not far from the other main contenders. Yet Rick's attention was drawn away from the scores by a gasp from the crowd. There was no one fighting, what could have drawn such a reaction? He saw it a moment later:

The screens had selected middleweight again. Emily closed her eyes and took a slow, shuddering breath, then began to move toward the door.

"Wait." Granny Whitney moved to block her path and pulled something from out of her handbag. "Take this."

"Have I fulfilled the terms of our agreement?" Emily accepted the object, but looked down at her with a neutral expression.

"Well enough. But I expect you to give this everything you have."

"I'll try." With that, she headed out to the arena, still limping. Rick rushed to take his seat and watch the match.

When Emily walked up the ramp onto the arena, she was no longer limping. In fact, she looked as calm as before, though he suspected that was partially an act. Whatever that trance technique was, it couldn't be dropped and resumed on a whim.

This time there were only four fighters, the three survivors of the previous match and one from the previous middleweight match. He was the freshest and knew it, immediately rushing to attack the others while they were still reeling from their injuries.

In a less experienced group, it might have worked, but those who remained were all veterans. They actually briefly aligned in an unspoken truce against him, striking back and rapidly dealing several injuries. As he fell back, they turned on each other, but Emily slid free of the combat, her aura blade held in defensive position.

The woman in the black coat - presumably affiliated with the American Basilisk - kept targeting her, but she did so predictably, thus opening herself to attacks from the other two. Rick was starting to hope that the battle would reach equilibrium and be ended... then one of the fighters went down.

Immediately the American Basilisk's fighter lunged for Emily again. The other remaining fighter tried to take advantage, but it was all a feint - the woman turned on him and raised a finger, firing several aura bolts that pierced her opponent. Even as he fell, she turned on Emily and rushed in to end the match.

Though Emily swung at her, the other woman dodged and then grabbed her arm. Her fingers bit through the aura blade and then somehow she snuffed it out. Emily jerked back, but too late: the other woman aimed at her with two fingers and fired multiple aura bolts through her stomach.

Emily summoned an aura blade around her other hand and cut through her opponent's arm - or tried to. Instead of sliding through and dealing lucrima damage, the edge actually bit in, causing blood to flow from the woman's coat. She fell back with a cry but then struck back, dropping Emily to the ground.

Rick found himself hoping that she'd stay down this time, let the match end without any more serious injures. Yet somehow Emily pushed herself upward again, weak but refusing to surrender. Her opponent had been cradling her arm but turned back angrily, raising her good hand to release more of the aura bolts.

The buzzer sounded.

A second after it went off, ending the match, the woman in the cloak fired several more aura bolts anyway. Emily collapsed to the ground, barely evading them, and lay still. Rick honestly wasn't certain if it was an intentional dodge or if she had just run out of energy.

Though Granny Whitney gave orders to retrieve Emily and help heal her, she was obviously focused on the screens, waiting for the results. They took a bit longer than usual, and Rick was surprised to see that Emily received the second most points. Their opponents had pulled further ahead, but only by one more point, and the fact that Alger's fighter had been eliminated made him plummet.

[1] Obsidian Thirty - 54 pts

2) Granny's Underground - 50 pts

3) Alger's Heroes - 47 pts

4) Serpenza - 34 pts

5) Verdant Mountain Sect - 28 pts]

"Four points." Granny stared at the screen for a long time, then turned to look at them, first at Teragen and then at Rick. "You need to close that gap, somehow. Alger will be throwing everything into the last matches as well, so you can't get complacent."

Though she spoke to Teragen, she seemed to be focused more on him. After all, the heavyweight class was likely to mostly cancel out again. Now he understood why she was willing to invest time and money into the lowest power class. He didn't like it, but he did understand.

Rick wanted to find out if Emily was okay, but knew he couldn't go meet her. Not with the screens lighting up and running through the wheel of power classes again. Though they displayed all five, Rick remembered what Emily had said. Based on how many fighters were down, there were probably only two options. That gave him a 50% chance of having more time.

And even when it was just a coin flip, his luck couldn't let him rest.

The last featherweight match was about to begin and all the pressure was on him. He couldn't just win, he needed to win decisively. As he started to walk down to the arena, Rick tried not to think about Granny Whitney's eyes drilling into his back.

Chapter 52: Rick's Last Fight

When Rick reached the chamber beneath the arena, the ramp didn't lower as quickly as before. Perhaps they had more cleaning work to do. In any case, he didn't want to waste that time, so he ended up looking over the others more carefully. After the previous rounds, he actually didn't recognize any of the remaining featherweights, and he struggled to accurately evaluate their lucrima portfolios.

While he was watching, one of them approached with a smug look on his face. The man was several years older than him and wore a black coat that looked of a kind with the other fighters who worked for the American Basilisk.

"I've been looking forward to this, kid. Your defense is good, for a featherweight, but we'll see how well it holds up against me."

It was obvious he was talking trash, but Rick decided to just smile back. "Sure, should be interesting. Out of curiosity, do you work for the American Basilisk, or did he just recruit you for this?"

"Our boss prefers to stay in-house." The man cast him a scornful glance. "Unlike the old woman, who just uses whatever pawns she finds lying on the street. What did she promise you? I wouldn't count on getting it."

"If you're all official... did he give you those coats as uniforms, or did you all just independently think that the best look was running around like you're in a movie?" Rick fixed a smile on his face, which became easy when he saw the irritation in the other man's face.

"Keep talking like that, kid, and see where it gets you. I've been looking forward to this."

"You the final boss, then?" Rick stepped up to him and poked him in the chest. "Then I'll take you down and get everything that's coming to me."

They might have said more, but at that moment the ramp finally descended into their space. When Rick moved to walk up, his opponent shadowed him, glaring. Soon they stood underneath the glaring light, roughly in the center of the arena, facing one another. Rick put up his fists, his opponent dropped into a fighting stance with open palms, and they both awaited the signal.

The buzzer sounded and Rick used a Bunyan's Step to run away.

While the cloaked man stared in surprise, Rick instead rushed another opponent. The other man hadn't been expecting him at all, allowing Rick to land a jarring elbow strike to the skull. Wasting all his strength on the person who was likely the strongest opponent was stupid, especially given that his goal wasn't just to win. He needed to earn points by taking down others first.

Unfortunately, none of the remaining fighters were weak. Though Rick tried to land followup blows, his opponent pushed him back with a rush of aura. A moment later he was drawing a gun, but Rick didn't have time to think about it, because the man in the cloak was rushing at him.

Dropping back to the floor, Rick barely avoided the hand swiping at his face. Damn, this opponent was fast. Worse, the other man nearest them was now aiming down at him. Rick used another Bunyan's Step to throw himself across the arena, evading the gunshots and getting further away from the man in the cloak.

When Rick hopped back to his feet, he saw that another of the fighters was rushing them, cloaked in a flaming aura that seemed to cause pain just by entering it. Though Rick pretended to be watching that fight, he actually monitored his surroundings, looking for other opponents.

One of them was creeping up behind him... carrying an actual sword? Rick pretended he didn't notice until the blade thrust at his back, then he spun to the side. It cut just past him, glancing off his arm, and then he slammed an elbow into his opponent's face. The woman tried to raise her sword and cut again, but she didn't have the speed for it. He kicked her hands, knocking away her blade, then took her down with several more blows.

Yet as he turned back, he was surprised to feel a line of pain across his chest. Somehow she had dealt another blow, one he hadn't even noticed. It was fortunate that he'd been able to turn her ambush against her, or he might have taken even more injuries.

In any case, the remaining three fighters were still clashing. The man in the cloak managed to peel away from the other two and came for him. Rick smirked and raised his hand, gesturing for his opponent to come at him.

Then he sprinted straight past him in another Bunyan's Step.

He nearly collided with another one of his opponents. Though Rick dealt a blow to his neck, he was surprised when it glanced off. Whoever this man was, he was tough, with a defensive core that might be better than Rick's.

But Rick didn't need to fight him. The man launched a wild haymaker, so Rick redirected his movement to send the man stumbling behind him, nearly colliding with the man in the coat. That gave Rick time to-

There was a gun in his face, held by the last of his opponents.

His mind froze, yet his body moved on instinct. Somehow Rick slapped it aside before the man could fire, then reversed and smashed his elbow into his opponent's face. Worn down by his fight with the others, the gunman finally went down.

Finally free for a few seconds, Rick caught his breath and got his bearings. To his surprise, he discovered that the large fighter was staggering back, bleeding from his ears. As Rick watched, the man in the cloak attacked again. His hand just seemed to slap his opponent in the chest, doing no damage to the man's muscular body... yet a moment later he spat up blood and collapsed onto the arena floor.

The man in the cloak turned to him and Rick felt a moment of concern. He knew that Granny Whitney must have been preparing him for this man's technique, yet the idea of taking this risk... no, it was nothing compared to the risk he'd taken attacking Teragen. Rick pushed aside his misgivings, instead putting on a smirk.

"You think that's gonna work on me? Come on, then!"

"Oh, I will." The man in the cloak abruptly surged forward, moving with even more speed than he'd displayed before.

Rick tried to meet him with a punch, only to have his arm swept aside. He had planned to leave an opening, but it turned out to be unnecessary: his opponent was inside his guard in a single movement. Then the palm hit his chest and his insides twisted painfully.

Pushing through, Rick rammed the base of his palm straight into his opponent's nose. As it snapped, he saw the cloaked man's shock over the pain. He was used to disabling targets with blows like that and wasn't prepared for someone as apparently normal as Rick to have trained internally. Instead of tearing apart his internal organs, after all of the painful pills, his body merely twisted in response before resisting the energy.

While his opponent was stunned, Rick managed to land a blow to the stomach. Yet his next attempt was blocked, his opponent grabbing his arm, wrenching it aside, and striking him several times on the chest. The pain was worse, but nothing like what he'd been forced through.

Spinning backward with the force on his arm, Rick flipped into the air, slamming a knee into his opponent's head. That made the man in the cloak stagger further, but he stayed on his feet. In fact, he was only stunned long enough for Rick to land safely, then they were trading moves again.

The blows had weakened his opponent, however, so the man's movements were no longer as smooth as they had once been. Rick managed to land a brutal kick to his knee, opening him up for another blow to the skull.

It still wasn't enough. The man in the cloak responded with a flurry of sweeping movements, forcing Rick to back up. How long could his opponent maintain such an assault? Normally Rick would have wanted to fall back and find an opening, but he was exhausted and beaten from the fight, not to mention the internal damage. He needed to end this, so he had to make an opening.

When another palm rushed at him, Rick stopped trying to block or dodge. Instead he traded blows, his elbow striking his opponent's face at the same time the palm hit his shoulder.

Finally the man in the cloak fell and didn't get up. Yet Rick felt something horribly painful in his gut and the world spun around him. When he fell, he tried to catch himself with his left arm, yet it hung limp, as if damaged by the final blow. He barely managed to prop himself up with his other arm.

Letting himself fall to the ground and rest would have felt so good, and forcing himself to straighten up was agony. Yet Rick slowly got back to his feet anyway. Not for the sake of winning more points in the match, but because he wanted to be standing at the end of it.

The crowds cheered as he straightened up, yet he didn't feel any sense of pride. This last opponent might actually have been stronger than him, and his hand-to-hand skills were definitely superior. That was even before his ability to cause internal damage was considered. Without Granny Whitney specifically training him to resist it, and the surprise blows that advantage had allowed him to land, he wouldn't have been able to win.

In a way, he was just a weapon being wielded by another. So his opponent had been right, but it didn't really matter. Rick didn't care about the glory, only the results. If being used as a tool was the price he paid for survival and steps toward a new life for himself and those who mattered to him, then he would pay it.

Now it was finally over. Rick tried not to stagger as he left the arena and walked between the stands, but he was exhausted. When he licked his teeth, he discovered that there was some blood in his mouth. The rest of him didn't look great either, the blood from the cut covering his chest and waist. But that was fine - there was no one else in his power class left standing, so he was done.

Except as he walked out, Rick saw Mike watching him, and remembered that he wasn't done at all.

For him, the true final round would come in two weeks, when he fought Mike. There would be no buzzer to end that fight and no allies to help him. The Birthrighter sneered at him, but Rick realized that was just fine. Mike had come to check his progress, but he saw only Rick at his weakest.

For the next fight, he would create his own advantages. Hopefully it would be enough that he could defeat someone well above his power class.

As he painfully mounted the steps back to the team's room, Rick found his mind wandering. Had he earned enough points for their team to catch up? Would it matter at all, since the last match would be Teragen's anyway?

Who would be waiting for him when he came back? He hoped that Emily had recovered from her injuries, and wished Malati a swift recovery as well. His mind wandered to Anthony before he remembered that Granny Whitney had abandoned him for his failure. How had he forgotten that? Rick's thoughts spiraled out lazily, then he clutched at his stomach as it cramped up.

His foot missed the next step and his face slammed into the stairs. Rick's body went limp and he collapsed, alone in the stairwell.

Chapter 53: The Tournament Ends

Rick drifted in a warm space, unconsciousness wrapping around him softly... until something lanced straight through his heart.

He jerked upward, wide awake in an instant and completely disoriented. If not for a hand pushing him back down, he might have ended up thrashing wildly. Yet as his brain caught up to his body, he realized that there was no need to panic. Emily was the one pushing him down, though she took her hand off his chest now that he was awake.

Currently he lay on the floor of their room. He felt a bit beaten up and everything in his chest hurt, but he didn't feel anything that felt like a mortal wound. In fact, the worst pain was on his face. Only then did he remember falling down in the stairwell.

"I fell..." He touched his face and his fingers came away with blood. "What happened?"

"I saw that you didn't arrive and suspected that you hadn't made it up," Emily said. "Don't worry, you seem to be in decent condition. The worst-looking wound is actually the one you got from the stairs, and that's superficial."

Though he was grateful for that, Rick realized that there was something much more important. "What about you? You look... completely fine."

"I am." Emily raised her hands in front of her, flexing them slowly. "Whitney had some of her specialists take care of me. I'm not sure what they used, but I've never been healed so quickly."

"And Malati?" He realized that he could look and saw that the other woman was sitting in her chair, watching the arena. "Same for her, I take it?"

"That's right. I'm not sure why Whitney didn't heal you."

"It's because of the stunt I pulled back at the farm." Rick painfully shifted so he could rest his back against the wall. "She said she wouldn't help me anymore."

"Hmm. Well, I was concerned that you might have a concussion, so I shocked you back awake. You seem to be fine as far as I can tell, but you should really speak to a medical professional."

Rick nodded slowly. Now that the important issues had been addressed, his mind wandered back to the tournament. "What about the match? How many more fights are there?"

"It's already over." Malati called from her position, finally turning around to look at them. "I'm just watching them set up for the final ceremony. You missed a pretty intense final heavyweight fight, but as usual, they didn't go long enough for any decisive finishes. Teragen managed to earn us one point on the competition, but that was it."

"Then... the final score?"

Granny Whitney marched into that room at the moment, a smile on her face. "It was enough, dearie. You earned 4 points over Gerald's fighter, which was enough to tie up the score. Then Teragen won the final round for us, so we finished on top."

His reaction wasn't so much victory as relief. Not only was it over, he had succeeded. Granny Whitney would finally forgive his debt, remove his tracking bond, and let him go on his way. It wasn't true freedom, since he still needed to fight Mike, but it was a huge step forward.

Feeling better, he managed to get to his feet and check the screens, where he saw the final score displayed:

[1) Granny's Underground - 62 pts

2) Obsidian Thirty - 61 pts

3) Alger's Heroes - 55 pts

4) Serpenza - 41 pts

5) Verdant Mountain Sect - 36 pts]

Seeing the numbers listed so clearly helped him relax another notch. When he found the previous match's scores and added those points to his previous two... he had earned 24 points for his team, just over a third of their total. There was no way Granny Whitney could claim that he hadn't pulled his weight. Most likely no one would remember him compared to all the other fighters, but he'd made a difference.

"Yes, Gerald is very unhappy about all this." The old woman chuckled maliciously. "He left without even claiming his reward. And Alger won't be able to preach at me for at least a year. Yes, this is quite a victory for Granny Whitney."

Malati shook her head. "That's well and good, but is it a victory for us? You know I have my own priorities."

"Never fear, dearie! I was actually just coming to tell you that we should all get ready to go down and receive our rewards. It won't be too dramatic of a ceremony, and there are no medals, but I think you'll enjoy the gift baskets."

There wasn't time for him to do much more than step into the men's bathroom and clean his face. He looked like a bit of a mess compared to the others, who seemed almost as fresh as when they'd started. Though the worst injury was the damage done to his internal organs, the most obvious one was the line cut into his face by the stair step. If he hadn't been completely exhausted, it wouldn't have done any harm at all, but at the very end, he took such a stupid injury.

Yet it didn't matter. As he cleaned up quickly, Rick found himself smiling. After the end of the day, he would be able to leave behind a major set of obligations. That was a better prize than all of the rewards he would have been given.

When he stepped out of the bathroom, he found Granny Whitney waiting for him, hands clasped together on her handbag. "I took the liberty of claiming all of your rewards, dearie. Just in case you were thinking of making any... final adjustment to our deal."

"You made it clear you wouldn't help anymore." Rick touched the cut on his face, which still bled a little from the deepest part. "This is what I get. Don't tell me that you're going to exact more vengeance?"

"I thought about it." She gave him a grandmotherly smile and her eyes glittered. "But you helped carry our team to the end, and that counts for something. As I said, you're a fine young lad."

"This fine young lad wants nothing more to do with you, once his obligations are fulfilled."

Granny Whitney chuckled as if she knew something he didn't. "Fair enough, dearie. I'll just have that tracking bond off and then you can be free of me. There's going to be a celebration afterward, though, and you can attend if you like. It's up to you."

She reached out and grasped his wrist, but this time instead of pain, he felt something leave him. It was a complex process of unraveling, yet it seemed that the tracking bond was finally gone. When he confirmed with his phone, he let himself smile. Then this part of it was over.

Though part of him wanted to go straight home and begin preparing for his next fight, Rick realized that he was tired. Not just from the combat, but from all the tension of the tournament. Considering that he still needed to speak more with Emily and others, he could afford to spend a little time unwinding afterward.

Rick went down with the others and they marched out the main gate, victorious. The crowds cheered them wildly as they headed out to the arena, where Alger stood with the tournament organizers. Even though his team had come in third place, he seemed honestly excited to congratulate all of them.

Each of them received a basket filled with valuable items: potent philosopher's elixir, special medicines, training manuals, and more. Rick received a basket, but his was empty, as per the agreement. Alger went out of his way to shake his hand, though, telling him what a good job he'd done. Really, he seemed entertained by the whole event itself.

His smile faltered only briefly, when he greeted Granny Whitney. Rick couldn't hear what was said between them, but Alger handed her something with a sour expression on his face and turned away.

It was Rick's first time in front of a cheering crowd like that, yet he found himself mostly unmoved. That kind of praise and adoration didn't do much for him. He took the same approach as Teragen, who seemed to ignore all of it, impatient to go.

Yet when they left the stage, they were swept away by a crowd of officials and fans. Without warning, Rick found himself with women surrounding him, which was more alarming than anything. "I thought you did great!" one of them said, beaming at him.

"Yeah!" Another latched himself onto his arm, then oohed as she felt his muscle. "Wow, your arm feels so strong..."

Disoriented, Rick just tried not to be separated from the others as they were led into a large room overlooking the arena. It was lavishly furnished and decorated, with a table filled with food and drink. As he looked around the room, Rick saw a large number of women he suspected were escorts, but also serious-looking businessmen and others who did not seem likely to celebrate.

"Typical." Malati brushed past some of the women to stand beside him, rolling her eyes. "I expected there'd be people here trying to sign fighting deals, but of course they just throw a bunch of paid women at us. Even though half the remaining team is female."

Rick had absolutely no idea what he was supposed to say to that, plus the women were still latched onto him. Before he could look too stupid, Granny Whitney appeared beside them with a sly smile. "No one here is that closed-minded, dearie. Look that way."

Several handsome and gratuitously shirtless men appeared behind Malati, smiling broadly. She gave a little laugh. "Well then, don't mind if I do!" Hopping into the air, she made one of the men catch her, then directed them to carry her off as she laughed.

Frowning, Rick glanced at the woman groping his bicep. "Is it true that you're paid to be here?"

She giggled. "We're here to provide companionship, sure, but we were the ones who chose you specifically."

"Then thanks, but no thanks." Rick pulled away from them and they whined, but they let him go. Granny Whitney saw and chuckled.

"Suit yourself, dearie. But I think there's no point being young if you aren't going to enjoy yourself a bit." She then turned around to one of the women and patted her on the head. "I'll take a private room and one of each, dearie!"

With that, Granny Whitney left the party, a scantily clad woman on one arm and a shirtless man on the other. Rick stared after her for a very, very long moment before deciding that he didn't need to think about that ever again.

He had more escorts eyeing him, so he went on the move. Even if there was no ulterior motive, Rick was troubled by their attention. This party was phrased as a reward, but it was a trap. Maybe some of the people there just wanted to recruit able fighters to their programs, but he had no doubt that they could also be ruthless. There had been a time when being a professional fighter had been a dream for him, but now... having seen the type of people who operated in that world, he didn't want to blunder into it.

However, without any reward, he was still dirt poor. Rick ignored his way through the party to the refreshments table, where he grabbed a bottle of philosopher's elixir. It was just 10k, but they were giving them away like they had no real value.

Maybe not to most, but he needed to restore his reserves. Pulling out the cork, Rick just drank straight from the bottle. Not classy, but if they were going to throw women at him, then they weren't going to object if he acted like a brute.

As he drank, he scoped out the room and found few familiar faces remaining. Alger and his team were present, clearly enjoying attention even if they hadn't been first. Tom was seated on a couch with his arms around two women, though he wasn't going off with them. Teragen was nowhere to be seen, probably having left to return to his training. He also couldn't find...

"Why'd you turn them down?" Emily appeared beside him, carrying a delicate elixir glass in one hand. She looked way classier than him swigging from a bottle, but he pushed that aside to try to focus on her question.

"Honestly... I feel strange being around someone who's paid to pretend to like me. I don't think I could ever get it out of my head."

"Hmm." She took a sip from her glass, eyeing him over the edge.

"I think I'm going to go pretty soon, but since Whitney took my reward, I need to take what I can get."

"On that note, I had something to give you." Emily slid a hand from her pocket, holding something out for him. When he extended his hand, she dropped a blood red sphere into it. "This was one of the rewards. It will help purify lucrima inefficiencies."

"You aren't giving this to me, are you?" Rick examined it, marveling at how heavy it felt in his palm.

"I don't really have problems with inefficiency, and I figure that I owe part of my reward to your work. It isn't fair that you had yours stolen."

Rick sighed. "That's the deal I made. But... thank you. This will make a difference."

"You're welcome, Rick." Emily gave him another of her slight smiles. For a moment, despite the uncomfortable circumstances and the party buzzing around them, he actually felt a warm connection.

Then another scantily clad woman approached them. Whatever she had been about to say, Emily interrupted it with a glare of death. The escort retreated rapidly, but the mood was lost.

"You're going to fight Mike soon, aren't you?"

"Yeah." Rick put the sphere away in his jacket and took a long drink. "In theory he can't cheat much and can't kill me even if things go wrong. Hopefully that will be the end of it, but I'm concerned that he'll bring his friends and just turn the match into a beatdown."

"Don't be." Emily turned away, refilling her glass. "I get the impression that his father is annoyed by the matter and wants it ended. If you can end the challenge decisively, that might actually finish it for good."

Now that he was past the tournament, older plans and concerns began to crowd in. His matches that day had been difficult, but what he faced next was going to be completely different. "That's my hope, anyway. I'll try."

"Good luck." With that, Emily moved away from him and disappeared into the crowd.

Rick stayed by the table for a while longer, drinking, then decided to just grab another couple bottles of elixir. Who was going to stop him, after all? He tucked them under his arm and marched out the door, ignoring offers of all kinds until he was back outside.

Without the lights blazing down on the arena, it was very dark outside. Though there were people heading to their cars, he felt mostly alone for the first time since the tournament began. Rick took a moment to just breathe, letting some of the stress melt away.

When he rubbed his wrist, he imagined that he could feel the absence of the tracking bond. There was still the matter of the faux leech, but he could figure that out later. He had fulfilled his obligations, getting out from under the threat of blackmail and the requirements of fighting in the Underground. That left him free to make his own path.

As he stared out over the parking lot, Rick realized he had a more immediate problem: how was he going to get home?

Granny Whitney was obviously busy and probably wouldn't offer him a ride anyway - they were done, after all. He considered bumming a ride from Emily, but they had parted on good terms and he didn't want to ruin it in such an undignified way. Some of the people going to their cars might recognize him, but he wouldn't embarrass himself by hitchhiking.

So the winner of the tournament's featherweight division wandered away from the arena, walking to take the bus home.

Chapter 54: Purifying Lucrima

"Are you telling me that your biggest injury was caused by stairs?" Melissa fell back onto the couch, trying to stifle her giggles.

Rick stared down at her and groaned. He was glad to be back, but as soon as Melissa had gotten over her real concern, she had to ask about the cut on his face. "Look, a bunch of people beating the crap out of each other in an abandoned factory isn't as glamorous as it sounds, okay?"

"Oh, but it should be! You can tell everyone that you received that scar while fighting the Bolivian ninjas that killed our parents!"

"Why Bolivia?"

"Are you telling me that Bolivia isn't known for its parricidal ninjas?"

"It's only parricide if you kill your own parents, so I'm going to say no."

Melissa grinned and sat up, moving over to hug him again. "Seriously, Rick, I'm glad you're alright. When you didn't call, I got really worried, even though you said that might happen."

"Yeah, I'm sorry about that." He patted his sister on the back and then shifted back to his side, relaxing into the couch. "Lisa updated you, at least?"

"Yeah, though that actually made me worry more. She said you were in really awful shape... oh, you should probably call her so she knows everything is okay. When we last talked, she was thinking about trying to go out to the tournament herself, though she decided against it."

"I need to talk to her anyway about purification rituals, so maybe I'll wait until the Bolivian ninja scars fade." Rick closed his eyes and was surprised how good it felt. He had felt exhausted the entire bus ride back, especially as the strengthening effect Granny Whitney used on him faded, but he hadn't let himself relax. Hadn't been able to.

"Wow, you look super tired. Can you finally rest for now?"

"It isn't really over. I only have about two weeks before I have to fight Mike. But... yeah, I need sleep. Sorry if I'm kicking you out the living room."

"Oh, I was staying up waiting for you. I'll be glad to finally go to bed too." Melissa got up and went to get his pillow, tossing it into his face. When she got out his blanket, she came closer, handing it to him directly as she spoke in a softer voice. "Rest well, okay? And try not to go overboard. I'd rather you surrender than be all brave and have something happen to you."

Rick mumbled his thanks as he slumped over onto the couch. The various subjects that had been swarming in his mind fell away one by one and then he was out.

It felt like only seconds, but then he was forced to open his eyes again. He felt a bit more rested, but that also meant that he felt new aches and pains from all the blows he'd taken the previous night. When he scrabbled for his phone, he hoped that he would find it was still the middle of the night... but no, it was already 10:00 AM. Even sleeping in hadn't been enough.

Part of him wanted to go back to sleep, but he knew that he would probably end up lying there half-awake for a long time and it wouldn't be restful. Instead he forced himself to go through his usual exercises and meditation. At least his lucrima was still in good shape. In fact, after facing so much combat, it was ready to grow.

Going through all of that had woken him up, so he stood up and stretched. For a moment he wondered why Melissa wasn't there, then he remembered that it was Monday and so of course she'd be at school. He had asked for Monday off work, since he'd expected he might need to recover, but he'd need to go to work on Tuesday.

That reminded him that he'd need to ask to get off work so that he could attend the ritual combat challenge. Because of course he did.

When he began walking around their apartment, he discovered that Melissa had left a note for him on the little table, complete with a drawing of a hamster punching a cat. It was actually pretty well-drawn and he found himself wondering when she'd taken up art. Though he smiled at the picture, he also felt a sense of loss that he hadn't even noticed that part of her life.

Hopefully things would be different soon, once he finally got past all this conflict. He'd survived his insane plan with Teragen and gotten free of Granny Whitney, which was a good start. Now he just needed to deal with all the impurities in his lucrima, get rid of the faux leech, and then hope it was all enough for him to fight Mike.

The last stage of preparation would be far easier thanks to Emily's generosity. Rick went to get the heavy red sphere from his things, only to find that it wasn't there. He flinched, desperately searching other pockets. Could he have put it in the wrong place in his exhaustion? Might Melissa have moved it somewhere? Was it possible that it had been stolen? He began to search frantically, coming up with worse and worse scenarios.

...it had rolled under the couch.

Brushing some lint off the sphere, Rick examined it carefully. This was a valuable piece of medicine, one that would make a huge difference for him, but he wasn't actually sure how to use it properly. Rick got out his phone and began checking around, eventually finding the name of the medicine and instructions on how to take it.

He learned the basics easily: shave pieces off the sphere, dissolve them into water, and drink the result as soon as the water changed color. That was good, since he didn't think he could possibly swallow something that large. But the online sources he found didn't contain very much about how to properly optimize the process.

After trying unsuccessfully for a while, he decided to call Lisa. She was glad to hear he was alright and he repeated some of the conversations he'd already had with his sister. It was good to hear her voice, though, and they arranged to meet up at the end of the week to work on the purification process.

The first thing he did after that was get the faux leech removed. Though he'd worried about it at first, when he went into the clinic, they quickly confirmed that it wasn't an official leech paying off a debt. Once that was determined, the old man in the cowboy hat easily removed it.

For the rest of that week, he focused on solidifying all his progress from the tournament. It had been a good test of all his skills, after all, even if it hadn't stretched his lucrima as much as the near-death experience with Teragen. In the end, he made solid improvements, but he continued eyeing the overall numbers and noting the discrepancy.

His overall generation rate was 35,600 lucrim, yet the total value of his lucrima portfolio was only 31,475. That left a gap of just over 4000 lucrim, which was no small amount to him. There was also the last aura leech, still formidable at -2453.

It would have been appropriate if he had gotten rid of the leech before the fight with Mike, but as he considered his options, he decided that it just wasn't possible. Not for someone with his resources, at least not without a miracle, and those were a bit scarce in his life. That meant he would need to take the expensive purification medication, only to cause more residual damage later when he got rid of the last aura leech. Not ideal, but it was the best option available to him.

Eventually he went to meet Lisa in the park as usual. When he saw her, he was surprised when she rushed up to him and hugged him tightly. "Oh, god, I'm so glad to see you're actually alright!"

"Uh, thanks." No, that was a dumb thing to say, but it was too late. Rick hugged back a bit, realizing that while the tournament was already firmly in the past for him, she hadn't seen him since then. Lisa pulled back and peered at his face.

"Huh, that's odd. Melissa said something about a huge scar from the tournament?"

Rick rolled his eyes. "That's a joke. I did get a cut, but it's mostly gone now." The only remaining injury was the burned hand-mark on his chest, which ignored all treatment.

"Yes, your lucrima is healthy enough that you shouldn't scar." Lisa set off down the trail, smiling over at him. "Today we need to find a new place, somewhere quiet where you can focus. I find it's best to do this sort of thing out in nature. I've only used purification medicine this potent a few times before, but the same principles should apply."

"We're actually doing it outside? I was under the impression that my body, uh, would need to expel a lot of impurities. And that the process could get pretty messy."

Now it was Lisa's turn to roll her eyes. "Those are mostly scams. They're as bad as the people who want to sell you really expensive methods of purifying your body of toxins, as if your kidneys don't exist. No, if you want to do it right, the process is a little different."

"But I saw videos online. People were in a pool and shed enormous amounts of black goo."

"Still scams - some of those companies actually get investigated by the government, though they're always moving slower than the advertisers. Often it's actually a trick - whatever medicine they give you has an active agent that reacts to water by forming that type of goo, thus giving the impression that you're purging your body of all kinds of things. I can show you debunking videos later."

"That might be interesting, but I believe you." Rick spotted a grove of trees near the end of the park, where the path curved back around. Not exactly an isolated retreat, but there were no picnic tables nearby and it looked peaceful enough. "How about there?"

"Yeah, that will do."

They got set up there and Lisa began filling water bottles from one of the public drinking fountains. It wasn't exactly training in a remote mountain waterfall, but it would do. As they set everything up, Lisa explained the purification process.

"As you fight or focus lucrim, especially when you use it to do things like get rid of aura leeches, some of your strength gets invested wrong. Instead of joining your Lucores, they form little clots that float within your lucrima. These don't do any real harm, but they represent part of your total potential strength that's being wasted."

"Can't they grow bigger and cause health problems?"

Lisa shook her head. "Those are lucrim blockages, and they're different things. Similar in nature, but you can't get rid of them in the same way. With those, the problem is that they're tough and fused with your main Lucores. With the tiny clots, the problem is that there's a ton of them and they're difficult to find."

"Hmm. So we can filter them out, somehow?"

"That can be done, and some schools have suggested it, but it's not a very efficient process. This baby operates by entirely different principles." As they headed back to their chosen location, Lisa hefted the blood red sphere in one hand. "This is going to send a steady surge of energy through you. It will melt your cores, and yes, you might be able to improve a bit from that. But the real benefit is that it separates out the different elements in your lucrima. The clots will float to the surface, where they're easy to identify."

Ah, that sounded more like what he'd read about. "Once they're there, I can burn them off?"

"Exactly right. It will hurt a bit, but with the clots gone, your lucrima will recover to use the strength they were wasting. In a few days, you'll be better than new." Lisa took out a knife and began carefully shaving off peels of the sphere into the first water bottle. As Rick watched her, he found himself smiling.

"You know, you should think about starting a vlog or writing a book or something."

"Huh?" Lisa was so startled she almost sent the next shaving to the ground, but she lunged out and caught it. "What do you mean?"

"You did a really good job explaining that. I spent a while looking on the internet and there were a lot of competing explanations, most of them confusing. A few might have been trying to make the process more mystical than it really is, but some were just bad at explaining. There's value in being able to do that well."

Lisa considered that in silence for a while. "I... had honestly never considered that before. I guess doing that sort of thing is a way a lot of health people make extra money. Hmm." She set the matter out of her mind, then handed him the first of the water bottles, which turned red, then pitch black. "Enough about that - bottoms up!"

Rick sat down, drank the bottle, and welcomed the pain.

Chapter 55: Final Preparations

The first bottle went down easily enough, filling him not like water, but like a solid mass slithering through his body. Not enough. Lisa was already handing him the second bottle she'd prepared, so he accepted it and began drinking. Even before he finished, he felt the heat building in him, but he forced himself to drink all of it before tossing the bottle aside and focusing his entire mind internally.

Just as Lisa had explained, the liquid seemed to course through him, heating everything in his lucrima. It felt almost like an attack designed to soften his defenses, but he accepted it and just focused on holding onto the cores he wanted, letting the rest dissolve into a mess of gooey lucrim.

When he was handed a third water bottle, he drank it automatically and the heat grew. Sweat beaded all over his body, but that was nothing compared to the raw heat inside him. He could almost imagine that he felt the clots of misused lucrim floating to the surface, but ignored the sensations. What mattered was sticking to the plan, staying focused until the first stage was done.

"Okay, Rick, now!"

When he heard Lisa's words, he let his senses expand outward. Yes, he could feel the impurities at the edges of his lucrima, floating like tiny flecks of trash in a peaceful pond. Rick gathered his strength and threw it against them, burning away the clots. Some of his good lucrim burned as well, but that pain was part of the process.

He finished feeling raw and a bit tired, but Lisa immediately handed him another water bottle. Rick drank the pitch black liquid and felt it burn through him. That had been the first step... now to repeat the process until he had cleared out everything.

At first he focused on the free-floating impurities, but as the blood red sphere dwindled, he let the heat rush into his Lucores as well. He would need to rebuild them afterward, but he felt the brittle fragments work their way out of the core of his being.

When it was finally over he fell onto his back and just breathed for a while, staring up at the sky. Even though he'd drunk an enormous amount of water, he felt empty instead of bloated. The emptiness was strikingly pure, and even though he was tired, his body felt light. Right now he had drained himself of energy, and his defenses were soft and pliable, but he could feel the new strength within him.

"Congrats! You did a great job with that." Lisa sat down beside him, handing him a bottle of serum - higher quality stuff that they sold in glass bottles instead of cans. "I've had professional fighter clients who whined way more about the process, but you really threw yourself into it."

"Well, I knew this was my only chance." Rick drank eagerly, then wiped off his mouth as he had to stop to breathe. "It's not like I can keep purifying myself on a regular basis, given the cost."

"I think you will." Lisa gave him an encouraging smile. "Things might be rough now, but you're really improving, Rick. I expect you to keep getting better, and I'm sure your life will improve. With all the work you put in, it would be unfair if the universe didn't reward you eventually."

Rick had no confidence in the universe's justice, but he appreciated the sentiment. They chatted casually as he finished the bottle of serum, taking a while to rest after the intense experience. But eventually their time came to an end, and Lisa obviously knew it.

"Rick..." She lowered her eyes and shook her head. "I'm not sure what to say. I hope you make it through this match and things go well. If you do get injured, don't be all prideful, okay? You can call me and I'll do what I can to help."

"I appreciate that, Lisa." Rick smiled at her and they headed out of the park by the same route they came in. Once there, Lisa lingered a bit, but Rick had to say his farewells and leave.

In part, it was because he wasn't sure what to think of their conversations. Honestly, another aspect of it was that he was eager to test his new strength. And another part of him was already fixated on the upcoming battle with Mike.

But another piece of it was much more mundane: drinking all of that liquid might have purified his lucrima, but he really needed to go to the bathroom.

It took him several days to fully recover from the purification process and re-solidify his Lucores to his satisfaction, but the process was easy because it was so much fun. Usually he put himself through hell just for small improvements, but now he felt new strength surging through him. Except it wasn't really new strength, just strength he'd earned and lost somewhere along the way.

Not only did he recover over 4000 lucrim in impurities, the process had improved his maximum by another 1250. Once Rick properly invested all of that, he was proud of his results:

[Name: Rick Hunter

Ether Tier: 16th

Ether Score: 243

Lucrim Generation: 37,500

Effective Rate: 35,047

Current Lucrim: 37,500]

[Rick Hunter's Lucrima Portfolio

Foundation: 3200 (Lv IV)

Offensive Lucore: 6875 (Lv IV)

Defensive Lucore: 15,525 (Lv VII)

Bunyan's Step: 6400 (Lv IV)

Graham's Stake: 6450 (Lv II)

Aura Leech: -2453 (Stage I)

Gross Lucrim: 37,500

Net Lucrim: 35,047]

He'd invested the majority into his defense, even though it felt excessive. But he reminded himself that as much as he'd improved, he was planning to face someone who was regularly handed far higher quantities of lucrim than he possessed. Though he planned to win, when he was done, he wouldn't have expensive medical care to help him. More important than winning was being able to move on after the fight, to regain his health and spend time with those who mattered to him.

All the remaining time he had, he spent adjusting to his new power. Rick had seen new Birthrighters injure themselves, clumsily using power and speed they weren't accustomed to. While he would never perform that poorly, he needed to perfect his understanding of his limits. No overextending himself, no using less than his full capacity, just precise use of his exact abilities.

In the evenings he made sure to spend time relaxing, since he didn't want to burn himself out before the challenge. That was easy enough, since Melissa was happy to spend time with him. They divided their time between practicing his theoretical new technique and messing around as usual.

On Friday night, they tested the basic principles of it one last time. Melissa extended her hands, carrying the void flame to him. Rick closed his eyes and accepted it, wrapping the flame within a sphere of aura. Unlike before, it no longer threatened to burn him. Even when he trained or sparred while holding the trapped flame within his lucrima, it managed to sustain itself.

"Wow." Melissa sat back and watched with an odd expression. "I know it's been a long road, but I'm still surprised you can do that. The flames tend to burn up everything, yet you've adjusted."

"It's partially thanks to you learning how to create more stable flames."

"Maybe, but I think you deserve a lot of the credit. Not like you're a super genius - no offense - but I feel like you're well-suited for it. Maybe because you're my brother?" Melissa switched from contemplative to grinning at him. "Was that your scheme this whole time? You were just pretending to be a loving older brother to get a hidden technique from me!"

"Indeed. My machinations lay undetected for years." Rick smiled at her, but his mind couldn't stay light for long these days. "I'm sorry if I haven't been paying as much attention to your things these days. My problems recently... they've been a bit all-consuming."

"Oh, don't talk like that. You've been great."

"But you're getting within a few months of graduation, and I just realized that we haven't really talked about it much. Do you know what you want to do next?"

Melissa sat back, considering the question... or perhaps considering him. "I've given it a lot of thought, but I'm still not sure. Get a job as soon as possible, obviously: I've been sponging off you for long enough. Do you think you could get me a job at your gym?"

Rick immediately shook his head. "You could, but you don't want that. Female trainers usually get more creepers, at least at a little place like ours. Even if you want to go into training, you shouldn't settle for a gym that's in a strip mall. You can do better."

"You really think so? They've done some job fairs at school and... well, a lot of the entrance requirements are higher than I thought. You need certificates from a combat sect, college degrees, special training... without those, I don't have so many options."

"Why not go for those?" Rick sat forward, locking his gaze with his sister. "You said you were sponging off me earlier, but that's wrong: I'm glad to be able to help you. We're family. Now, I might not be able to afford the full fees for university or a combat sect, but you've done well and you can probably get scholarships. Don't set your sights low just because you feel you have to."

Melissa stared at him for a moment, then to his surprise, jumped forward to hug him. "Thank you, Rick. I'm... not sure what I really want in life. But I'm glad you're here with me." She pulled back and smiled at him. "I love you, bro."

"Love you too, sis."

"Now..." Her sincere expression dissolved into a smirk. "How are you going to spend your last night before the big fight? I'm thinking the best use of it would be to watch Fist of the Sublime for the third time!"

"Oh, god, no."

"But don't you care about fist-pounding action?"

Joking aside, they didn't actually watch it again. After Melissa went to bed, Rick ran through all his exercises for the last time before the big match. He would meditate a little before the fight started, but otherwise the time for preparations had ended.

As he went to sleep, he considered final desperation options one last time. What he had done was impressive, yet he was still outclassed by his opponent. If he wanted more strength, he still had the option to take a demonic bond. Given how his ether score was improving, they would probably give him a decent one. That could make up a large portion of the gap, especially if he overextended the bond.

But no. This wasn't just a grudge match to him, not an issue of ego like it was for Mike. Rick realized that the things that truly mattered to him were more important than simply winning. He fixed that thought in his mind as he fell asleep.

Hopefully he wouldn't regret that decision by tomorrow evening. One way or another, it would be over.

Chapter 56: Grudge Match

Rick woke bright and early on the day of the challenge. Melissa was already dressed and ready, leaving no question about whether or not she was coming with him. That was probably just as well, given that it would be a risk to carry the void flame longer than necessary. When he didn't object, she nodded and went back to reading, letting him prepare himself mentally.

He took his clothes into the bathroom, carefully cleaned himself, and changed. For a moment he considered wearing the suit Granny Whitney had given him, but he decided against it. Instead he just wore a pair of pants loose enough to move in and a blank gray t-shirt. Though he wasn't going to win any fashion contests, they were comfortable for combat movement and they wouldn't distract him.

For a while Rick leaned on the sink, staring at himself in the mirror. There was no trace of what he'd been through in the tournament - in fact, there was no trace of most of what had happened to him. Would he look any different than he had the day Mike wandered into the gym looking for a fight? He was a little more muscular and his aura burned more intensely, but on the outside, he looked unchanged.

Yet that wasn't true. Rick smiled as he realized that however the day ended, he knew that he was no longer the person he had been before. He would not be content with accepting life as it came to him.

"Ready to go?" He came out of the bathroom impatient to reach their location. Fortunately, Melissa was just reading on the couch and hopped up instantly.

"Let's do it! But... I guess I should have asked this first, but is it far? These shoes aren't great for a long walk."

"If there was ever a day to splurge on transportation, it's today." At the moment he felt completely fresh and relaxed, so he wasn't going to risk fatiguing himself. As they left the apartment, Rick showed her the address on the formal challenge papers. "I looked it up online and it says it's a random field, but the satellite photos show that there's some kind of ruin. I think it was the headquarters of some old group."

"Hmm, that's a ways out of town. Are we sure that we're not walking into an ambush?"

"He did everything formally, so the challenge should be listed with the government and everything. I don't think he can really cheat that." At least, he hoped not. While there were tales of poor fighters proving their worth in such challenges, there were always tales of corruption as well. But there was little he could do about that, so all they could do was move forward.

They tried to joke a few times on the taxi ride, but they were both too tense. He saw the uneasiness in his sister's eyes and wondered if it was purely concern for him, or if she was overly invested in this fight herself. Mike's friend had threatened her because of this conflict, after all, so perhaps she needed to see it happen in order to move past it.

Maybe he was imagining it all. But Rick decided that it was another reason he needed to win.

Their car passed the suburbs, then entered the fields outside Branton. It wasn't long after that they neared their location. Rick peered out the window to see if there were any surprises, but it looked just like he'd seen online. There were odd structures from the ruin that couldn't be properly seen from the street pictures, and so far they were still ambiguous, just spires rising above the grass.

When they stopped, Melissa got out and surveyed the area while Rick found change for the driver. The man didn't even ask before driving back to town. That could be a problem, but Rick put it out of his mind. He couldn't concentrate on anything but the fight set before him.

"There you are!" A short man in an ill-fitting suit moved to greet them from the side of the field. "I'm telling you, I hate these challenges at strange locations. Okay, so your great-grandfather fought an important battle here... who really cares? It's just costing the taxpayers money..."

Rick stared at him, not having expected this. "You're the challenge official?"

"That's right. You and your guest seem to be right on time. Five minutes early would have been better, but it's acceptable. We can start as soon as your opponent gets here."

"We're not just fighting in this field, are we?"

"Of course not." The official shook his head as if the idea was absurd. "This way, I'll show you the ruins."

They headed out on a small path through the grass that Rick hadn't seen from their previous angle. The official led the way, bustling as if late for a meeting. Rick followed him with Melissa shadowing him, both of them looking around curiously.

As they drew closer, the shape of the ruins became obvious: it was an ancient combat arena, a large rectangle of stone. Most of it was obscured by the tall grasses, but he could see ornate carvings on the side, worn by the years but still intact. The top was covered in dark-colored flagstones, worn smooth by the wind. What he had seen from the road were four spires at the corners that curved up toward the center.

So this was their arena. A bit more grandiose than he'd expected, if far from modern. Did Maguire Incorporated own this land? Did it have some meaning for Mike? Rick decided that both of those questions were distractions and just walked up the stairs on the side, then stood in the arena silently, getting a feel for the place.

It was like a platform of stone floating in the grasses, which flowed around them in smooth patterns. They were strangely beautiful, so he let the wind patterns relax him as he slowly walked the arena. This place had a sense of deep peacefulness that he tried to absorb into himself.

When he finished a complete circuit of the arena, he was blocked by Melissa. She glanced to the road, then the official, before leaning closer and whispering. "Perhaps we should set up now? I mean, we don't know how long we'll have to wait, but could that guy consider it cheating?"

"It's not cheating," Rick said, "but... yes, let's do it now."

Melissa took a deep breath and drew a flickering flame from within herself. This one seemed particularly compact, a dangerous fragment of utter void. If it hadn't been from her, he would have hesitated, but Rick accepted the flame, built his usual shell, then let it submerge into his lucrima.

Before the end of the day, he'd use it for real.

They stood near each other for a while, and Melissa looked like she was about to say something, but at that moment Mike finally arrived. A black speck on the horizon grew in size surprisingly fast, revealing itself to be a dark limousine as it glided toward them. Without a sound, the lucrim vehicle came to hover just beside the challenge platform. Of course Mike wouldn't walk through a field.

As his rival stepped out of the vehicle, Rick actually looked past him first. He caught a glimpse of several people, including Mike's two cronies, but beyond them sat his father and several assistants. That was what Rick had needed to know. The CEO of

Maguire Incorporated didn't get out of the car and seemed focused on other things, but he had decided to come. That was a small comfort.

Meanwhile, Mike swaggered into the arena, Glenn and Magnus behind him. They were actually in exactly the same formation as they'd entered the gym, so many months ago. Rick almost commented on it, not that it really mattered. Hopefully this time would end differently.

"Is everything ready?" Mike shot a scornful glance at Rick, then looked to the official. "I don't want to waste any more time than necessary with this scrub."

Rick resisted the urge to laugh. "Is that what you tell yourself?"

"Shut up, I'm not talking to you. I'm not here to talk to you at all, just beat you down." Mike advanced on the official, glaring down at the shorter man. "Come on, are we ready?"

The official sighed. "Yes, yes, I was ready at the appointed time. You both already signed, so you only need to have your witnesses sign, then you can begin. Can we at least be prompt about that?"

They needed witnesses? Rick realized that perhaps his view of challenge fights was shaped by movies and TV, where they probably skipped past such details. Glenn and Magnus moved up to the official, using a small blade to cut their thumbs and apply their marks to the paper. Before Rick could say anything, Melissa stepped up beside them. She cut her thumb with her teeth and applied her blood on his side of the contract, not dropping eye contact with them the entire time.

All the witnesses retreated to the sides of the arena and the limo floated a short distance away. There were no barriers at the edge of the arena, unlike in the Underground or the tournament octagon, so there could be potential collateral damage. He was glad that Melissa had started training, as she should at least be able to avoid injury.

His sister gave him an encouraging smile when he looked toward her, and Rick nodded back, but then he tried to set her out of his mind. He couldn't afford anything but pure focus for this match.

As everyone cleared away, Rick walked to the center of the arena. Mike walked opposite him, seething at him the entire time. Yet though the Birthrighter looked furious, it was a controlled rage. He wouldn't be flying off the handle and leaving himself open. No, it seemed like Mike had been waiting for this moment a long time, probably planning for it.

Rick reached out to get a sense of his opponent's generation rate and immediately regretted it. Mike felt like he was wielding over 200,000 lucrim, which was just too large a gap. Keeping his cool, Rick repeated to himself that lucrima portfolio mattered more than just a person's available power.

Unfortunately, Mike had a solid core in the center of all that lucrim. He wasn't like Rick's relatives, wasting any lucrim that came to him. It was impossible to sense exactly through all the power, but Rick thought that Mike had invested lucrim into multiple cores totaling at least 50,000 lucrim. Even by that standard, he was outmatched.

"I'm gonna enjoy this." Mike put a hand to his neck and cracked it in both directions. "You're going to be begging me to stop by the time this is over."

"Just so long as it's over." Rick kept his body loose, just staying alert in case Mike tried a surprise attack. "After this, your vendetta ends."

"Oh, it'll end. I'll pay you back for all the suffering you've put me through."

They stared at each other from opposite sides of the arena. Between them, the official raised a hand and then backed away from the center. "Alright, you can begin. As agreed, the match goes until verbal surrender or unconsciousness."

Mike let out a roar and rushed at him, a clumsy charge that Rick couldn't help but take advantage of. He dodged aside from the wild haymaker and delivered several blows into his opponent's side, not getting through his aura but softening his defenses.

A moment later, Mike's movement's changed. He lunged out, fingers almost reaching Rick's neck. Rick's instincts allowed him to jump away and evade them, but he realized that it was too late: lucrim were closing around his throat.

He started to resist it until he realized exactly what the technique did: locked his vocal cords. The skill had been so fast and light because it didn't do any harm, just prevented him from speaking. Rick's mouth opened silently as he tried to test it and he saw Mike smile viciously. So that was his plan - keep his opponent from surrendering.

Though he kept his face neutral, Rick actually found it encouraging. He didn't need to speak to fight, so he simply wouldn't resist the technique. All it represented was strength that Mike had wasted on overconfident cruelty, bridging another sliver of the gap between them.

Now that his trap was set, Mike stopped pretending to blunder into combat. Instead he dropped into a fighting stance, fists raised like a boxer. Before Rick could do more than prepare himself, Mike's aura exploded into a raging inferno and he rushed forward in a barrage of blows.

The strikes came quickly and aggressively, but the platform gave Rick a lot of space to dodge. He kept moving backward, ducking away from blows and forcing Mike to keep pursuing him. It might look like cowardice, but he could dodge all day, while Mike was burning lucrim with every strike.

As his back got closer to the edge, Rick tried to edge to the side. Mike countered aggressively, his footwork getting markedly faster. No matter how Rick tried to evade, Mike penned him in, herding him closer and closer to the corner. Soon his back was almost up against the spire.

Rick activated Bunyan's Step and flashed to the side... and saw Mike's fist flying at his face.

Instinct made him bend backward, the fist almost grazing his nose. Rick tried to counter with a kick, but it was easily blocked because he was so taken off guard. Had Mike managed to keep up with Bunyan's Step with raw lucrim alone? His reaction time shouldn't have been good enough, yet he must have noticed Rick using the technique during the tournament and been prepared for it.

With his balance ruined, Rick wasn't able to dodge back so easily and Mike attacked with renewed fury. For the first time Rick had to directly block an attack, wincing as he felt the impact vibrate through him. With his defensive core vastly improved, he could block a lot of blows like that, but they would still hurt like hell.

Mike smirked and kept attacking, certain that he would soon be victorious. Yet as the aggressive exchange of blows continued, Rick found himself speeding up. His opponent attacked with great power, yes, but it was nothing like the ferocity he had experienced when Teragen had struck him so many times in a single instant. Compared to that, his mind could cope with this, and he was gradually adapting.

Finally one of his kicks landed, hitting Mike's shin. His opponent only winced slightly, his aura mostly protecting him, but that wince delayed his barrage of attacks. Rick delivered an elbow to his stomach with all the force he could muster.

It hurt his elbow, but he was glad to see Mike stumble backward, clutching at his stomach. His eyes were open wide, shocked that he had actually been injured. Rick should have used that moment to press the attack, but his body refused to react, having pushed itself to the limit keeping up with the aggressive melee combat. So he just stood there, recovering for the next attack.

"You little shit..." Mike straightened with a growl, and the look of hatred in his eyes confirmed for Rick that the next attack would be soon. "You're a decent brawler, but that's all you are. You have absolutely no chance!"

Mike began to lift into the air, and though Rick was trying to play everything cool, his eyebrows still shot up. That Mike could fly wasn't too shocking, but the way he was levitating... his aura shifted to green and a pair of glass-like wings extended from his back.

Without warning, something rushed at his stomach. Rick had no time to register it, he just automatically countered with his knee. The impact sent a shock through his entire leg and he dropped back, only then catching up.

Sweeping away, Mike soared higher into the air, hung suspended for a moment, and then flashed down with the same blinding speed. Rick had his guard high and managed to deflect it, but his forearms both ached. He couldn't keep fighting like this... if Mike could really just pull out a skill like this, then Rick wasn't sure there was any way he could win.

"You like that?" Mike floated back up, raising his arms to either side. "You have no idea the resources I have access to!"

Something in that stuck in Rick's mind. He had little time to think about it, but the next time Mike swooped at him, he managed to dodge to the side. Mike's third attack missed as well, as Rick began to catch up to the speed of his new technique. It was fast, but like his Bunyan's Step, it moved mostly in single rushing movements. Mike couldn't react fast enough to change course in the middle of them.

Irritated, Mike floated down until he almost touched the edge of the arena - then he flashed forward, his wings scraping the arena floor. Rick managed to dodge the charge, but one of the wings clipped him, sending him tumbling to the ground.

He heard mocking laughter as he scrambled back up, but Rick found himself having to resist the urge to smile. After experiencing multiple attacks, he had finally understood his intuition earlier: Mike was attacking more simply and formulaically than before. Not just because it was difficult to react at that speed, but because he wasn't familiar with it.

As Mike levitated to the ground again, preparing for another charge, Rick braced himself. It would be a risk, but he could do this. This skill was just something Mike had purchased, not an art he had spent years training. Though it might have great power, there would always be limitations in how he used it.

When Mike swept at him again, Rick activated a Bunyan's Step the instant after, the two of them flashing toward each other faster than they could react...

And his elbow connected with Mike's neck.

The blow sent the Birthrighter spinning end over end, and when he struck the arena, his aura and wings shattered. Mike struggled to his feet, clutching his throat. It looked like his windpipe might have been broken, and Rick hesitated for a moment before deciding that this was no time for mercy. His opponent had too much lucrim left for that.

When Rick attacked, Mike managed to fend off the first few blows before Rick began connecting. But he only dealt two strikes to the head before Mike's aura exploded, back to blood red. The burst of it sent Rick sliding back across the arena.

It took him a moment to struggle to his feet, stunned by the overwhelming aura. When it became a conflict of raw aura versus aura, his opponent's lucrim would always come out on top. Still, as he struggled to his feet, Rick decided that it had been worth it to land those blows.

Though Mike was still clutching at his throat, something had changed. He was no longer panicking, and when he pulled his hand away, his throat appeared to be intact. After coughing a few times, Mike looked up and gave him a bloody grin.

"You see that? I can heal whatever you do to me!"

But his boast had the opposite effect, since Rick could feel just how much lucrim Mike had drained in order to heal the injury. Though he still had more than enough to fight, he couldn't keep healing injuries like that forever. If the fight extended to the point where they both had little left, that was when he'd have a chance.

When Mike rushed at him again, this time Rick didn't back away. He met the other man blow for blow, deflecting his attacks until he finally broke through with a blow to the chin.

Though Mike fell back, he barely staggered, landing a wild blow to Rick's chest. The force of it sent him spinning backward, nearly falling. Somehow he managed to regain control, turning his spin into a kick that forced Mike to retreat a step. But he was off balance and his opponent was coming again...

Rick got his fist into position and used a Bunyan's Step to throw himself forward with more force than he could normally manage. His blow struck his opponent's chest and he felt the flesh give way... but Mike didn't fall back. Something about his aura had changed, something that resisted the impact.

Mike lashed out, grabbing one of Rick's arms. He tugged him closer, aiming another blow for his face. Rick barely ducked beneath it, turning the movement into a shoulder ram. Yet this failed to budge Mike as well, and his arm was still grappled. Before Rick could find a way out, Mike's knee hit his stomach, sending him staggering to the side, only to be jerked back for another blow.

It wasn't a conscious decision, yet Rick found himself thrusting a hand forward, his fingers jamming directly into his opponent's eye. That finally made Mike cry out in pain and stumble away, though Rick collapsed once his arm was released.

He got to his feet painfully, watching Mike as he clutched his eye. The wound was healing, drinking in another large quantity of his lucrim, but Rick didn't feel like that was a victory. Not only was he unable to heal his own injuries, this new art was a problem. It was more subtle, somehow preventing Mike from staggering from attacks. Though it felt like it drained considerable lucrim, which was why he hadn't used it earlier, that was no comfort when it nullified Rick's primary strategy.

Though he tried to come up with a solution, Rick couldn't think of one. He didn't have any trump cards that could deal with this or any hidden potential to unlock. Instead he fell back as Mike began attacking him again, roaring in rage and yet still not getting sloppy.

The gap between them was just too wide. Rick fell back from the heavy blows and missed his opponent's kick when it struck out at his ankle. Rick's leg buckled, but he'd barely even dropped to one knee before Mike smashed into him, driving him to the ground.

Suddenly he was on his back, Mike looming over him and raining down blows on his face. On instinct Rick raised his arms to defend his head, but the repeated attacks were turning his arms into a mass of solid pain. And it was just going to continue, since his opponent still had enough lucrim for the continued aggressive attacks.

Even as he defended himself, Rick experienced a moment of clarity: his only chance was to use his new skill now. He hadn't wanted to do it like this, and knew it was a risk, but if he kept enduring this barrage of blows, he'd be defeated before he ever got a chance.

So he drew the core containing his sister's flame into his hand, then drove it into his opponent's stomach.

The strike didn't seem to do much at first, Mike simply grunting and then landing a blow directly to the face. Rick's vision flickered painfully and his defensive core shuddered. For a moment he thought the fight was lost... but then Mike grimaced in pain and clutched at his stomach.

Forcing himself to push just a little further, Rick lunged up, landing an elbow directly to his opponent's face. After that he collapsed and needed to slowly pull himself back up, but Mike fared even worse.

The Birthrighter was stumbling to his feet, staring down where he covered his stomach with both hands. It was more than shock in his eyes, it was as if he'd never felt anything like it before. His aura, already drained by excessive technique usage and constant attacking, began to flicker. From the sidelines, Melissa pumped a fist happily.

"You... what did you do?" Mike stared up at him in horror.

In response, Rick merely tapped his throat, pointing out the silencing technique.

As he'd hoped, Mike roared and attacked him again. But though the Birthrighter was still able to launch powerful attacks, his concentration had wavered. Rick stayed purely defensive, dodging away when he could and turning aside blows when necessary. This time, he didn't let himself get pinned to the side of the arena.

The flame kept burning inside Mike's core before it eventually went out. That had been what he would have expected - it would have been nice if it could keep burning away his opponent's lucrim forever, but he'd predicted that it couldn't last. Used this way, he wasn't sure if it had actually been a debilitating blow. Still, it had been worth it, to escape sure defeat.

On top of that, his opponent's lucrima was in bad shape. Mike kept attacking aggressively, apparently not realizing that the lucrim that powered him to such levels were running out. Rick was exhausted too, but he was used to fighting with no strength.

Finally Mike went too far, lunging in an aggressive attack that his strength could no longer back up. Rick deflected it with one arm, surprised at how light the blow felt, and slammed an elbow into his opponent's throat. Not a devastating blow, but enough.

Mike staggered a step back, automatically beginning to heal the injury... and finding that he didn't have the strength. His eyes went wide and he started to evade, but not fast enough. Rick closed on him, dealing a brutal series of blows to his torso and face, battering him backward. With each one, he could feel his opponent's defenses weakening even further as he struggled to pull himself together with less power than he'd ever experienced before.

"No!" Mike drew on the rest of what he had left, his explosive aura pushing Rick back, and lunged forward in a kick to the stomach.

Rick caught his foot. Not using his full defensive core, simply blocking the physical blow. He saw Mike realize in horror that he had nothing left, not even enough lucrim to reinforce his body. With only his remaining cores, he was little stronger than an untrained human.

Keeping his grip on Mike's foot, Rick lunged forward and brought an elbow down on his opponent's knee hard enough that he felt the leg snap.

Mike released a scream of pain and clutched at his leg. Though Rick's instincts told him to keep going, to beat his opponent until it was over, he held back to catch his breath. He had taken himself to his limits and he couldn't afford to get overconfident.

"I... I surrender! I surrender!" Mike thrashed backward, scrabbling over the ground to get away from Rick. His cries of pain dissolved into blubbering as he desperately called out his surrender repeatedly.

Though Rick watched him without expression, he had to admit that he felt a flicker of satisfaction at that. Maybe it wasn't the disabling injury he'd wanted, but he knew that Mike would remember this. For the rest of his life, no matter how much lucrim he drowned himself in, he would remember what it felt like to be powerless, what it felt like to lose to someone weaker than him.

Thinking that Melissa should be celebrating the victory as well, Rick turned toward her... and saw Glenn and Magnus advancing on him, auras kindling around them.

Rick tried to curse, though no sound came out. They weren't much weaker than Mike and fighting two of them at once would have been impossible even at his best, much less drained like this. Though the official objected and started to get in their way, they sidestepped around the man. Did they plan to injure him while they had a chance and damn the consequences? As Rick tried to summon enough strength for another Bunyan's Step, he didn't think he would make it...

"That's enough." The voice rang out with such clear authority that everyone stopped. Mike's father stepped from out of the limo onto the arena. Even without his aides following him, the sheer aura he radiated was intimidating. "Don't be sore losers, boys. Go."

Glenn and Magnus retreated like scolded puppies. The CEO gestured at his aides to stay back, then walked forward. His gaze fell on Mike and in that moment Rick was infinitely glad that he wasn't the Birthrighter.

"You're a disgrace to this family. All of this childishness ends at once."

Mike groaned and slumped to the arena floor. Several aides came to drag him away, but Rick could barely look at him, his attention forcibly drawn by Mike's father. The older man examined him for a moment, then gave him a polite nod.

"I can't say I'm glad to see my boy beaten, but you did well. As a small token of apology for your trouble, let me give you a ride back to town."

"...th..." Rick struggled to purge the lucrim binding his voice, tired enough that it was difficult even though Mike was down. "That's very kind, but we can't..."

"Oh, take it. You're obviously exhausted."

"I..."

Without warning Mike's father stepped up to him, all trace of a smile gone, eyes like steel. "Let me be perfectly clear. My son is an embarrassment to me personally, but that is a personal matter. Perhaps this will be good for him. But if you ever say or do anything that would embarrass our family... you will find out that Maguire Incorporated does not play games such as these."

Rick stared back because he didn't have a choice, captured by the CEO's intense gaze. Yet he wasn't overwhelmed. Not only had he faced worse, this was what his life had always been, with companies and other forces more powerful than him trying to control him. He gave a false smile and nodded. "Understood. All I want to do is go home and rest."

"Very good, then." Mike's father stepped back, once more all polite business smiles. "One of my aides will get a car for you. Have a nice day."

With that, the CEO of Maguire Incorporated ducked into his limo, already returning to his business. One of the remaining aides got out a pair of keys and summoned a lucrim vehicle, a small dark car with the kind of simple elegance that characterized everything about the family.

Since the threat had already been delivered, Rick thought there was no harm in accepting the ride. He started to walk toward it, but his leg gave out. Before he could fall, Melissa rushed to get under his arm and hold him up.

"You did it! And..." Her eyes flickered to the aide before she tried to suppress her smile. "And it worked!"

"Yes. I'd have been in trouble without your... moral support."

"Haha, that can totally be the official name." Melissa supported him into the car and he gratefully eased down onto the comfortable seats. "I can't believe it's really over. I mean, I'm sure he hates you even more now, but it felt like his father will end it for good."

"I think it's truly over." Rick felt his body relax and realized that he actually believed it. "I'm going to sleep for a solid week."

For once, things would go according to plan.

Chapter 57: Life Has No Epilogues

Weeks later, Rick was back to work at the House of the Cosmic Fist, staring out over the crappy little strip mall.

Walking into the gym and quitting dramatically was a nice fantasy, but not one he entertained for very long. He had bills to pay and a sister to support. One day he would definitely move on to better things, but he would do it when the time was right, not on a whim. Life didn't give him miracles, after all, so it paid to be cautious.

Part of him had been worried that he was slipping back into old ruts, but many elements of his life reminded him that wasn't the case. He continued training privately with Lisa, and he'd received an invitation to meet with Emily the day before. When he went home, he and his sister were working on strengthening her void flame, not weakening it. And now that the constant threats had passed, he was enjoying developing his lucrima even more.

Not only that, the ratings agencies had caught up to his progress and he'd been raised to the 15th tier. That took him out of the lowest quarter - he didn't think anyone in their family had ever done that other than Uncle Frank. But given his good mood these days, he expected that to be just the start.

After standing on the sidewalk for a while, Rick decided to go back inside and train on his own. Compared to the rewards he'd received for matches in the Underground, a tiny bonus for bringing in a new client didn't seem to matter much. He sat down in the center of the gym and began to meditate, satisfied that he was being paid for training he intended to do anyway.

"You know we always need more clients." Jimmy looked up from his magazine and gave him a skeptical look. "Don't start slacking off, now."

"I think I'll do more to bring in clients by demonstrating our discipline, don't you?" Rick smiled back at him, keeping his face neutral.

Though Jimmy stared at him in mild annoyance, he also disliked putting effort into things, so he might just drop the argument altogether. Before it could go anywhere, the doorbell rang again. Not a client: instead it was Henry, marching in with a confident look on his face.

At first glance he seemed better, without signs of having overdrawn his demonic bonds. Yet when Rick sensed his lucrima portfolio, as had become his habit, he felt that something else was wrong. It was actually nothing he'd ever felt before, so despite his coworker's cheerful expression, Rick got to his feet, preparing just in case something was wrong.

"Have you guys seen those Advanced Lucrim stations?" Henry flexed his arms, apparently enjoying his strength, though it didn't look impressive compared now that Rick's standards for physical size had been set so much higher. "God, just one loan and I feel incredible! I knocked all three demonic bonds way down and I'm even better than before!"

Rick's first instinct was to get out his phone and check, but he held it back. There wasn't a need for it, not really. He could feel that Henry was being overoptimistic: his bonds were still draining his strength, and whatever this "Advanced Lucrim" was, it was only a temporary boost to his power, not an investment. Strong as he seemed, that appearance was hiding a weak foundation.

"That's a great story," Jimmy said. "Now get to work."

"Nope. That's actually the opposite of why I'm here." Henry slapped Jimmy's magazine out of his hands and pinned it to the table. "I quit! I can make way more money fighting in the Underground, anyway."

Jimmy stared at him, then jerked his magazine out from under his hand. "Suit yourself."

"Wait, that's it?" Henry leaned forward on the desk, the wind leaving his sails. "Come on, man, I worked here for like three years. You don't have anything else to say?"

"If you want to hire one of our trainers, you can see our programs on the paper there. Otherwise, get out."

Henry stalked away, muttering curses. Rick decided to go after him - even if he wasn't truly friends with his coworker, he didn't want to let him leave that easily. Also... he was curious about this new method that had given him so much confidence.

Rick caught up to his coworker and matched pace with him. "Hey, man. Are there that many good fights in the Underground?"

"New events are happening." Henry grinned over at him as they walked. "If you're willing to take a few risks, you can do pretty well for yourself. And that's just for me! Since you were part of the tournament, you could probably make even more."

"Nah, I think I'm done with that, at least for now." Something about the offer bugged him, anyway. They wouldn't start offering more money for no reason, so there had to be a catch. "What was that you were saying about Advanced Lucrim stations, though?"

"Oh, those are fantastic! They set up one not far from here, we can check it out."

Several blocks away, down a street Rick usually didn't go, they found it. A building that had once been an abandoned gas station had been refurbished. The sign declared "Advanced Lucrim" in bold letters and there were a few flashing lights welcoming people in. A woman with a disturbingly white smile greeted them from behind the counter as they entered, but Rick looked in the other direction. The aisles of food and drinks had been replaced with several large circular machines he couldn't quite figure out.

"Yeah, those are the main event." Henry moved up to one of the machines, stepping into the circle. "You put your hands in here, run through the process, and bam! Sudden burst of strength. It somehow reaches forward and grants you strength that you're going to earn. Isn't that incredible?"

Rick didn't answer, but he thought that "incredible" was exactly the right word. All around the store, he saw flashy posters declaring the store's services. Money for nothing, it pretended to offer. Families waving bundles of cash. The money of tomorrow, today. He had to search a long time to find the fine print that made it clear the boost was effectively just a loan.

Though the machine hid the lucrim mechanisms deep within, he knew exactly what he'd feel: the same model as the Golden Lucore he had carried so long ago. This was what they had been designing: a way to harvest lucrim from those who had none. Desperate people would come in here and receive immediate lucrim, most selling it for cash. Thus squeezing even more profit from them.

Looking around the side of the machine, Rick soon found it: the logo of Maguire Incorporated. He smiled down at it oddly.

"You okay, man? You're spacing out on me." Henry waved a hand in front of his face.

"Sorry, I was just looking at the machine."

"I get it, this is fun new stuff. Anyway, you want to give them a try? You'd probably see a pretty big benefit, given how lucky you've been lately."

Rick shook his head and began walking out of the store. "No thank you."

"Are you sure, man? This really-"

"Do you get a bonus if you bring someone in?"

Henry started to object, but when Rick looked back at him, his words petered out. The silence stretched awkwardly between them, yet Rick found that it didn't touch him. He wasn't the one who had set it up and he had more important things to think about.

Eventually Henry walked in a slightly different direction and gave him a half-wave. "I guess we won't be seeing each other at the gym anymore, huh? But I'll see you around, alright, man?"

"Sure. See you around."

As they walked in separate directions, Rick thought back to what he had seen. It wasn't exactly an evil scheme, since everything Maguire Incorporated had done was perfectly legal. His involvement in the new technology had been incidental, for all the conflict that it ended up spawning. Yet it still felt strange to learn that all of this had developed in the background while he was absorbed in his own problems.

But wasn't that always the way the world went? Granny Whitney had been playing her own games, competing with Alger and the American Basilisk and probably others. All of that passed on above him... or at least it had once. Now, he found himself wondering.

Obviously he wasn't going to take on a corporation, just like he wasn't going to go challenge everyone in a combat university to a fight. But all of those ideas no longer seemed so far above him.

When he walked back into the gym, his boss looked up and grunted. "He's gone for good, huh?"

"Looks like it." Rick walked over to the counter and smiled at Jimmy. "It seems to me that you're going to be a bit shorthanded here."

Another grunt.

"I think I would like a raise."

That got his boss to slap his magazine down. "Absolutely not. You think I'm made of money?"

"No. But I think you recognize that I'm capable of working with a wider variety of clients now. If you want me to take on extra shifts and abandoned clients, I think I deserve additional compensation."

Though Jimmy obviously hated that idea, he remained silent, not having a direct way to rebut the argument. Rick just smiled and headed back to train, but before he could get to his place, the door opened again.

Darin, one of Henry's old clients. The gruff man scowled and looked around. "Where's the kid? Isn't he supposed to get here about now?"

"He quit." Jimmy grunted and looked down, though he gestured at Rick. "Take over."

"What have I always said?" Darin shook his head. "That's the problem with kids these days. And you... I remember you, arrogant little prick. Trying to tell people how to conduct their business even though you've never made anything of yourself. You think you can train me?"

Rick just smiled at him. "You said I was just a human practice dummy, right? If that's all you need, I'll do my best."

"Heh. You'd better not regret that, kid." Darin pulled off his jacket and moved out onto the mats.

Following at a slow pace, Rick considered if he was really going to do this. But as he analyzed Darin, he realized that he could. The man had stockpiled a great deal of lucrim over the years, but he just used it as money, didn't invest it into power. In fact, his generation rate was exactly the same as it had been at the beginning of all this: 55,000 lucrim. That was more than Rick, but numbers like that weren't exactly intimidating anymore.

"Let's see how long you can last when the going gets tough." Darin began to hop back and forth in a boxer's stance, shadowboxing the air. "If you keep wasting what little you've got and folding when life gets hard, you'll never make anything of yourself."

With that, he launched a wild haymaker. Rick took it directly on the face.

And didn't move.

Darin's eyes widened and he pulled his hand back slowly, shaking it subconsciously. Rick smiled at him, then raised his hands to start sparring.

Even though Rick didn't actually attack, their sparring session didn't last for very long. Darin soon left the gym in a huff, grabbing his jacket and storming out without making eye contact. Jimmy watched him go and let out a low groan, while Rick just walked up to the counter.

"So, how about that raise?"

X X X

Thank you for reading my book! If you enjoyed it, please consider leaving a review. ^-^ This book was originally posted chapter by chapter online and chapters of the sequel are currently being posted early on my Patreon:

https://www.patreon.com/sarahlin

Here are some other ways you can keep up with my work:

Mailing List: http://eepurl.com/dMSw2A

Blog: http://sarahlinauthor.blogspot.com/

Facebook: https://www.facebook.com/Sarah-Lin-1041738042689736/

It means a lot to me that you read one of my stories all the way to the end! If you believe in my work, please consider supporting

me via Patreon, leaving a review, or dropping me a note. ^-^
Thanks for reading!

Acknowledgments

Thank you to all my alpha and beta readers for their feedback.

Thanks to Cultivation Novels and GameLit Society for the community.

Thanks to Ian Mitchell for an editing note.

Appendix: April Fools' Day Chapter

(On Patreon I posted a joke chapter for April Fools' Day, just as a silly joke. It has been reproduced below in its awful glory. This chapter "occurs" after Chapter 18 of the real story.)

The poison in his body made Rick feel weak, but he forced himself to enter the Underground arena anyway. He wouldn't give up, no matter what. All the other people in the arena had generation rates of 100,000 lucrim or even more, but he got ready to fight them anyway.

Suddenly as soon as the battle started, the nearest warriors sent massive blasts of power directly toward Rick. They would tear his body apart into shreds of flesh, but he stood tall and faced them bravely. Even faced with impossible odds, he was too brave and noble to bow down to anyone.

At that moment, Lady Lysanderoth from the Purple Moon Clan happened to be descending from the Divine Heavenly Realm. When she saw how brave and handsome Rick was, she paused time and came down to stare at him. Her alabaster skin glowed in the light, especially her DD breasts.

Suddenly Rick wasn't stopped in time anymore. Everything else was, but he wasn't. He stared around in surprise until he saw Lady Lysanderoth, who nodded graciously to him.

"Noble Richard, I have been touched by your bravery. I have never seen the like, even in the Divine Heavenly Realm. To face overwhelming odds and stand against them nonetheless is the mark of a true hero."

"Uh, thanks," Rick said humbly. "Is it really that rare?"

"I have seen one quadrillion million googolplex dozen people across countless realms, and it turns out most of them are bums." Lady Lysanderoth shook her head sadly. "For your courage, I will bless you with the True Heart of Lucrim."

"Thanks," Rick said humbly.

Lady Lysanderoth reached forward and touched Rick's chest with her alabaster fingers. He felt a warmth growing inside him as his true power awakened inside him. Though he wanted her to keep touching him forever, soon after she pulled away.

"Go and live a life worthy of a hero," Lady Lysanderoth said.

"Will I ever see you again?" Rick asked humbly.

One crystalline tear rolled down Lady Lysanderoth's alabaster cheek and into her DD cleavage. "I am sorry, Richard, but it cannot be... my father will..." She could say no more. Though she knew that her love for this brave and humble young man would only grow, her father and the other members of the Purple Moon Clan would never smile upon their love. Because it was forbidden for people from Earth and people from the Divine Heavenly Realm to ever be in a relationship.

With that, Lady Lysanderoth ascended back to the Divine Heavenly Realm, with only one last longing look backward.

Time stopped freezing and suddenly Rick was being blasted again. Yet he knew that something had changed within himself. He suddenly dodged to the side, grasping the blasts of power in his hands and redirecting them toward his opponents. Every one of the blasts that had been intended for him instead blew away one of his opponents. Several of them flew into the crowds, vaporizing spectators.

Rick landed back on his feet and smirked humbly. Everyone in the crowds was flabbergasted that a man with only 15,000 lucrim could defeat warriors who were so much more powerful with only his brilliant wit.

Afterward, Rick went up to the owner and demanded his reward for the fight. He received 12 billion dollars.

On his way out, Henry suddenly ran up to Rick. "That was amazing!" Henry shouted. "I can't believe you did that, man, how did you think of it?"

"Oh, it was nothing," Rick said humbly. "I just realized that if I redirected their power against each other, I could defeat them even though I don't have as much lucrim."

"That's genius!" Henry shouted.

Suddenly, Rick had an idea. He walked into a nearby store and purchased a bottle of 1,000,000,000 lucrim philosopher's elixir with a fraction of the money he had received. As Henry watched in flabbergasted awe, Rick drew the lucrim into himself to increase his power.

Instead of simply making himself stronger, Rick increased the density of his lucrim with a special lucrim technique he had just invented. Now each individual lucrim was worth 2x a normal lucrim. He did it again and again until each lucrim was worth 64x a normal lucrim. Suddenly his growth would become 64x more potent. The power of it made him glow with power.

"That was amazing, man!" Henry shouted. "What did you do?"

"I realized that if I increased the density of my lucrim, it would become more powerful. It wouldn't work if I had trained more, but because I was weak until now, I can get started with far stronger lucrim than a normal person."

"That's fucking amazing! Nobody else has ever thought of that before!"

Rick looked at his phone and saw that his generation rate was now 300,000 lucrim, which was actually 18,600,000 because his lucrim were 64x more dense than normal peoples. He smirked and decided that it was time to head to work and teach his boss a thing or two.

When Rick suddenly entered the gym, Jimmy looked up at them and glowered. "You're late to work, boy! I oughtta beat you for this!"

"You're not going to insult me anymore!" Rick said. Jimmy immediately flushed and drew himself up, enraged that one of his employees would humiliate him by talking back to him.

"That's it! I'm going to-"

He didn't get a chance to finish his sentence, because Rick activated his new lucrim and suddenly slapped his boss across the face. The slap was so powerful that everyone in the gym with less than 50,000 lucrim died instantly.

Jimmy staggered back, flabbergasted that Rick could have struck him so easily. Rick sneered at him and pulled off his badge, dropping it onto the floor.

"This is the last day I work here - I quit!"

Jimmy just stared at him, flabbergasted that Rick would quit.

Lisa was watching from the corner of the gym and was amazed at how different Rick seemed than before. She hurried up to him while blushing and threw herself against him, rubbing her DD breasts against his arm. "Oh, Rick, you're so manly and alpha!"

"Haha yeah I guess," Rick said humbly.

"Way to go, man!" shouted Henry, who was also there.

On his way out of the gym, Rick suddenly ran into Mike, who glared at him. "Hey, what the fuck, did you just run into me? You deserve to die for that!"

Mike let out a roar and his lucrim burst up around him, so powerful that the concrete broke apart and a dozen bystanders were vaporized. Lisa shrank back with a feminine gasp of fear and Henry shouted in fear, but Rick simply stepped forward confidently.

Suddenly Rick called on the True Heart of Lucrim and his power exploded exponentially, so powerful that *two* dozen bystanders were vaporized. Mike yelled and tried to punch him, but Rick's lucrim were so dense that he just broke his hand. Rick laughed and reached out, creating a lucrim hook and stabbing it into Mike's soul, dragging him to hell.

Suddenly everything was back to normal and all the bystanders were flabbergasted. "That was amazing, man!" Henry shouted.

"Oh, Rick, that was so wonderful!" Lisa wrapped her arms around him from behind, pressing her DDD breasts into his back. Rick chuckled and pulled away from her.

"That wasn't bad, but I've seen some flaws in my technique. I should condense my lucrim down to 128x normal density next."

"You're a fucking genius man!" Henry shouted. "I bet you could even heal your sister with that much!"

"Oh, right. Guess I'd better go do that."

Rick flew back to his apartment with Lisa riding on his back, pressing her DDDD breasts against him. Henry ran along underneath, flabbergasted that Rick had mastered the power of flight so quickly.

When he arrived he found his sister sickly and pale, her illness causing her trouble again. Rick frowned and stared down at her soul, using his new powers to look deeper than before. He realized that the problem was that she didn't have enough lucrim.

It took a great sacrifice, but Rick pulled out some of his lucrim and poured it into his sister. It reduced him all the way to 126x normal lucrim density, but it managed to fix her problem. The overflow from the intensity of his power killed several hundred people in the apartment complex.

Melissa blinked in surprise, realizing that she was healed. She sat up slowly, putting a hand to her DD chest in surprise. "Wow, Rick, I feel better... and wow, you feel so much stronger! It was amazing how you healed me like that..."

At this point Lisa stepped in and kissed him, pressing her DDDDD breasts against his chest.

"That was fucking amazing, man!" Henry shouted as he ran in the door.

"Haha yeah," Rick said humbly. "Guess it just goes to show... there's no cultivation like street cultivation!"

Appendix: Lucrim Mechanics

This is my direct description of the magic system in the world of Street Cultivation, since it bends or breaks some rules of the genre. Most of the information will be duplicated in the novel, but here I present it all in straightforward form for those who requested that.

Forms of Power

Lucrim is raw power, and in the modern world, that power is often used as money. When simply held in a person's body, it provides a slight enhancement to durability and it can be used to pay for goods or services anywhere in the world. Beyond that, lucrim alone is only a resource: it's the applications of lucrim that provide greater abilities.

Lucrim is a spiritual substance, neither energy nor mass, but it can be refined in all three forms:

1) Refined spiritual lucrim becomes **Lucores**, which can have more powerful effects than simply holding lucrim. It also allows for more power to be "stored" beyond what the user can normally contain. They have a constant beneficial effect, but their true potential is only seen when "liquid" lucrim is flowed through them. Almost all fighters possess a "Foundation" that inefficiently grants some permanent power, but more importantly allows for the development of stronger lucores.

2) Lucrim used to generate energy becomes **aura**. Aura is an energy field that can flow within the body or even in a visible halo beyond it. Depending on training, this process can be very efficient, but it does burn through current lucrim reserves to enhance strength and speed. Only Lucores can provide a benefit "for free".

3) Lucrim used to generate mass becomes **ether**. Unlike aura, the process to convert ether back into lucrim is very inefficient, so it is primarily used to create permanent objects. A common example is an ether-reinforced door, which would be strong enough to withstand even blows from lucrim users.

All living beings have at least some lucrim within them. Most people (but not all) know how to convert lucrim to aura - this isn't simply for fighters, but students or businesspeople generate aura to increase their mental focus, or it can be used to commute by running/flying. The ability to convert lucrim to ether is less commonly developed, generally by professionals who build their career around it.

Lucrim is normally too ephemeral to be stolen, though certain rare techniques can drain currently held lucrim. Sufficiently large Lucores can be extracted via a complex surgical process, though the total strength is reduced. This is generally only done by parents who want to give or leave something to their children, but is occasionally seen in martial arts sects.

Generation Rate

Lucrim falls from the sky evenly all over the world. In ancient times, people would naturally gather this lucrim into themselves - this is also the reason martial artists would tend to train on mountaintops, because they can gather more lucrim when higher than the rest of the population that might draw it.

But in the modern world, nearly all of the falling lucrim is harvested by international organizations. It is then distributed by reserves as currency. The vast majority of ordinary people rarely ever gather/generate any lucrim of their own, they simply get their supply of lucrim from their job as income.

For this reason, "generation rate" is an outdated term. It does still mean the amount of lucrim that a person can carry at once, and as such is it used as a shorthand measure of power. The value is essential for developing Lucores and for those who fight. For average people, generation rate is just their budget of overall lucrim to spend on things.

Note that there are exceptions to the above. It's possible to create Lucores that generate new lucrim, and this is an essential method of building power for some. However, it requires a significant initial investment of lucrim that can't be spent or used to increase power, so many people don't take advantage of it. Institutions like banks and sects have staff dedicated to lucrim generation to increase their wealth by these methods.

The most common exception is Birthright Cores. Technically these are any cores passed down through a family, but many people leave no cores, or only cores small enough that they are just liquidated. The derogatory term "Birthrighter" refers to people who received a sizable core from their parents, one that immediately grants them either an ability or (more commonly) a steady flow from free lucrim.

Though it's beyond the reach of most people, it's entirely possible to have enough Lucores generating lucrim that you could quit your job and just live off them. This is easier said than done.

Development

Lucrim doesn't come from nothing anymore, so development is limited without income. Fighters who want to improve can train or meditate to develop Lucores or increase efficiency overall, but this won't increase their generation rate or overall capacity. However, currently held lucrim can be invested into power, the process of which will slowly but surely increase generation rate.

Faster ways to gain strength include receiving lucores from other people and purchasing raw lucrim in some form (such as philosopher's elixir) then investing the surge of new strength. There are also more complex methods, such as techniques that improve the efficiency of one's current lucrima soul.

While a lucrim is a unit of measurement, the lucrima soul refers to the collective of all a person's power. Permanent investments like the foundation or Lucores form the core of the lucrima soul, while lucrim are held around it.

Though generation rate is a good measure of the total power available to someone, it's not an exact measure of combat strength. A highly trained fighter with well-invested Lucores could defeat someone with a higher generation rate who just attempts to throw that power around haphazardly. Between two fighters of equal skill, generation rate is a good measure of power, but there are many more or less efficient ways to invest that amount.

Lucrima Portfolios

Reading someone's lucrima portfolio is effectively seeing a list of which attributes and skills they have invested time and lucrim into. Items are ranked both by raw lucrim (a measure of power) and Level or Stage (a measure of skill and efficiency). Here are common items contained within a portfolio...

Foundation: The bare minimum for a competent lucrim user, allowing the development of all other abilities.

Secondary Foundations: Highly advanced fighters may use different types of foundations or have more than one investment granting specific abilities.

Attribute Lucores: These cores grant a permanent improvement to a physical attribute, such as strength or durability.

Skill Lucores: More advanced cores that allow the use of a supernatural ability that would not be possible by any level of physical strength.

Investment Lucores: Non-combat cores that serve to keep or generate lucrim. These could either be for a bit of extra income, to save for retirement, or to leave a core to one's children.

Utility Lucores: Non-combat cores that serve a specific function. A common (but expensive) core is a Transportation Core that allows for flight at a level that isn't useful in combat, but makes it convenient to travel.

Aura Leeches: These unnatural creatures embody large lucrim debts, draining the user's strength in order to gather lucrim. They remain attached until the debt is completely paid, hindering stamina and also reducing available generation rate by the core value of the debt.

Demonic Bonds: Both debt and power, these bonds grant strength but require steady repayment. There are an exceedingly high number of variations with different requirements and restrictions.

Appendix: Rick and Melissa's Final Portfolios

[Name: Rick Hunter

Ether Tier: 15th

Ether Score: 282

Lucrim Generation: 40,000

Effective Rate: 37,891

Current Lucrim: 37,891]

[Rick Hunter's Lucrima Portfolio

Foundation: 3400 (Lv IV)

Offensive Lucore: 7125 (Lv IV)

Defensive Lucore: 16,225 (Lv VII)

Bunyan's Step: 6625 (Lv IV)

Graham's Stake: 6625 (Lv II)

Aura Leech: -2109 (Stage I)

Gross Lucrim: 40,000

Net Lucrim: 37,891]

-

[Name: Melissa Hunter

Ether Tier: N/A (minor)

Ether Score: 110 (preliminary score)

Lucrim Generation: 7752

Current Lucrim: 7752]

[Melissa Hunter's Lucrima Portfolio

Foundation: 2050 (Lv II)

Lucore Mass: 3602 (N/A)

Steel Lucore: 2100 (Lv I)

Total Lucrim: 7752]

Printed in Great Britain
by Amazon